BEYOND THE HORIZON

ANN PALMER

BEYOND THE HORIZON

Copyright © 2022 by Ann Palmer

All rights reserved. No part of this book may be used or reproduced in any manner whatsoever without written permission from the author, except in the case of brief quotations in critical articles or reviews.

This book is a work of fiction. Names, characters, businesses, organizations, places, events, and incidents either are the product of the author's imagination or are used fictitiously. Any resemblance to actual persons, living or dead, events, or locales is entirely coincidental.

Cover design by Christine Hammacott.

First Edition 2022.

Dedication

To the Special Duties Pilots who flew Lysanders to take SOE agents to France during the German Occupation, sometimes returning them by Lysander or Hudsons if they were injured. They used other planes to drop parachutists, armaments and supplies. They took extreme risks, knowing a Gestapo team could be waiting or they could be shot out of the sky.

CHAPTER ONE

LONDON IN EARLY NOVEMBER 1942

'Excusez-moi, Mademoiselle.'

Marie-Claire recognised her regular customer's voice as she was kneeling behind the counter and sorting out stock in Selfridge's store. She stood up and faced Madame Montague-Smyth, a svelte and silver-haired Parisienne.

'What a surprise, Madame. I wasn't expecting to see you today,' she replied in French. 'How can I help you?'

The customer glanced around to make sure they couldn't be overheard, then said quietly, 'My husband, Gerald, was most impressed with you yesterday when we were all talking in French about the Nazi Occupation of France.' She paused. 'In confidence, he spoke to a work colleague who is looking for somebody like you to do French translation work. As I know you are thinking of changing jobs, would you be interested? If so, Gerald would like to meet you again to discuss it further.'

It sounded intriguing, but Marie-Claire didn't really know this charming French lady and her English husband, other than as customers. She instantly recalled the Government posters, warning people to be aware of strangers. She sighed. On the other hand, she was beginning to lose patience with some of the tetchier customers, not to mention the departmental manageress. Maybe life as a shop assistant wasn't for her.

'It does sound interesting.'

'Excellent,' said Madame Montague-Smyth, sounding relieved. 'One moment, please.' She took out a card from her handbag and passed it to Marie-Claire, who glanced at it and raised her eyebrows: Gerald Montague-Smyth, Esq, followed by the War Office's address.

'Thank you,' said Marie-Claire. 'I really am curious to know more about this.'

'Then join us for dinner. Could you come tomorrow evening? There's an excellent bistro in Kensington High Street.'

'I will join you both, and I am looking forward to it, Madame' she said warily. She lowered her voice and said, 'Will you excuse me now. I can see my manageress walking towards us.'

'I understand. We'll pick you up tomorrow evening outside Selfridge's main entrance at a quarter past seven. That will give you time to change. One last thing—please keep what I told you to yourself.'

'Of course, Madame, I will be discreet,' replied Marie-Claire, beginning to feel a little apprehensive about the need for secrecy as they said goodbye.

The manageress came to the till, and said, in her usual officious manner. 'I would appreciate it if you could spend less time talking with that French customer of yours. As it is, she hasn't bought anything today. This isn't a venue for entertaining her.'

'I'm sorry. It won't happen again,' Marie-Claire said politely, curbing her tongue. It certainly won't if she could get another job and see the back of this place.

After cashing up, Marie-Claire hurried to the powder room at seven o'clock where she changed from her uniform into a velvet fitted dress that Daphne had lent her, combed her dark brown hair into a chignon and applied some make-up. Then she slipped into a smart black coat. Lastly, she grabbed her gas mask box and bag containing her dancing shoes and went down to the ground floor, where she left the building by the staff door and out onto Oxford Street. It was almost in complete darkness, apart from the stars and crescents of light emitted by partially covered car lights.

When she arrived at Lyon's Corner House, Marble Arch, she waited for Daphne. Ten minutes went by before she felt a hand on her shoulder.

'Sorry I'm late,' said Daphne. 'As I was coming off duty, we were called to take a badly injured motorcyclist to the nearest hospital. It's really scary driving an ambulance in the dark, I can tell you. Hugely satisfying, though, when you discover you've saved someone's life.'

They went inside and ordered tea and sandwiches. Daphne loosened her coat to reveal a green satin dress, complemented by an eye-catching gold necklace.

'Gosh! That dress is new, isn't it? It's fantastic. Where's it from?' asked Marie-Claire.

'One of my friends in the FANYs knows someone who used to run this posh dress shop, but she had to close it down because of family problems. I bought the dress at a bargain price and used the clothes' coupons I had been saving. You should join the

FANY. I've told you that before. You'd meet all sorts of interesting people.'

'Tell me again, Daphne, what the FANY stands for.'

'First Aid Nursing Yeomanry.'

'Do you do any actual nursing? I can't imagine you in that role,' she said, laughing.

'No. I did the training when I first joined, but I already knew how to drive, so I was drafted into chauffeuring the top brass around. Sometimes we drive lorries from one army camp to another, but now I'm driving ambulances and I like that best. But there's loads of other jobs for telephonists, secretaries, clerks, and translators.' She paused for a moment and then lowered her voice. 'So, how're you feeling about that doctor chap you went out with?'

'You mean Jack? I'd rather not talk about him.'

Marie-Claire wanted to forget Jack. She had been training for her SRN and had ended her year long relationship with him after discovering that he'd been two timing her with a surgeon's daughter. He'd been merciless in telling her that just because they had been going out together for that length of time, he hadn't envisaged marrying her. Subsequently she left the course.

After a long pause, Daphne started talking about her new boyfriend. 'My Rodney is super. The best one yet. He's an officer in the RAF.' She looked at her watch and added, 'Time to go. We'll catch the tube and meet Rodney at Leicester Square. He's a stickler for being on time. There's going to be lots of gorgeous airmen who'll sweep you off your feet. And you'll soon forget that beastly doctor. You'll see.'

Two weeks later, Marie-Claire grabbed her gas mask box and bag and left Selfridges after lunch. As she made her way towards Oxford Circus, the bombed-out John Lewis store, now a reduced fire scorched shell, was a constant reminder of the merciless German bombing. She turned right into Regent Street and eventually arrived in Trafalgar Square. She glanced at her watch. Her interview for the War Office job was at two o'clock. She'd been told that it involved translation work. *Was it sensitive work? When she'd met the couple for dinner, they hadn't revealed a lot. It had been more a question of Mr Montague-Smyth vetting her before offering an interview.*

She turned into Northumberland Avenue and located Hotel Victoria, a grand building with sandbags piled up against its walls, ready for any German air attack. She pulled out her identity card and paperwork from her handbag and gave them to the military policeman outside before she went through a revolving mahogany-and-glass door into a large entrance hall. The whole place looked drab and run down which surprised her.

She was shown up to the third floor by a civilian who knocked on a door; a deep voice boomed, 'Come in.' Marie-Claire was surprised to see it belonged to a slim man in army uniform with sharp facial features. He sat behind a table over which a single light bulb shone. Blackout curtains were drawn across the windows through which sunlight was peeping. The smell of cigarette smoke wafted in the air.

After a pause, the interviewer dismissed the civilian. He stood up, towering over Marie-Claire. 'Good to meet you, Miss Morris. Do take a seat.' She sat down on a rickety fold-up chair and glanced round the room and noticed a dirty-looking washbasin attached to the wall and a grubby gas fire that wasn't lit. She took a deep breath. Something was eerie about this place. What was going on?

'Were your employers happy about your having time off to come here?' asked the soldier.

'I asked my manager for an extended break to meet my uncle home on leave from the army.'

'Well thought out! I need people with initiative.' He broke into French. 'Tell me about your family.'

'My mother is French, and my father is English, so I have dual nationality, but I was born in France.'

'How well do you know the country?'

'We lived there until 1930, when we moved to England—I was ten years old at the time.'

'So, you're now twenty-two.'

'Yes, sir.'

'Why did your parents decide to leave?'

'Family reasons.'

'What jobs have you done?'

'I worked in the local hospital as a care assistant for a year. Then I started a nurse's course, but I left at the end of the second year for personal reasons. I have been at Selfridges on a traineeship for eight months, but I'd prefer to use my French to help the war effort.'

After a pause he asked her, 'Which country do you prefer?'

'France. It's livelier there. Before the war, we visited my mother's family every summer.'

'Where do they live?'

'In Olivet and St Jean-le-Blanc outside Orléans.'

'I know Olivet,' he said, smiling. 'That's where the windmill walk is by the river.'

'When were you last there?' she asked him.

'Three years ago.' He tapped the table several times as if to remind her that he was conducting the interview. 'What other parts of France do you know?'

'An uncle took me to many of the château towns in the Loire Valley.'

He leaned forward with a serious look in his eyes. 'How do you feel about the Nazi Occupation of France?'

Her face stiffened. He had his reasons and would have to reveal them shortly. Then she would tell him what she really felt and why. 'The Nazis are scum. They're like rats infesting our country, torturing, and killing people who stand up to them.' She swallowed hard. 'I was appalled to learn how those poor Jews, including children, were plastered with yellow stars and rounded up by French police and sent away to Germany.'

'How ever did you learn that?' he asked, clearly taken aback.

She flicked back her dark wavy hair. 'Someone we know managed to get out; he told us about the horrendous conditions there, especially in Paris.'

'What I want to know is whether you have any other reason to hate them.'

She steeled herself, gripping her hands under the table. 'Yes. There is something else. After France fell in 1940 and was occupied by the Germans, my cousin Philippe joined the Resistance. All we know is that the Gestapo arrested him in the Orléans area in January of this year and executed him.'

The interviewer lowered his voice. 'I'm sorry to hear that, but how ever did you come to learn about it?'

'Again, our friend, who escaped from France. I cannot say any more.'

'I can understand your caution.' He took his time before continuing. 'If you were in your homeland now, would you join the Resistance?'

She took in a deep breath. *So, this is what it's all about: nothing to do with translation for the government whatsoever.* The interviewer cleared his throat. 'I'd seriously consider it, but I need to know more about it,' she replied firmly.

'When you were working in the hospital, if you discovered another member of staff was stealing classified drugs for his or her own use, what would you have done?' he asked, watching her closely. 'Would you have reported this person, even if he or she was senior to you?'

Gosh, he jumps from one subject to another like a grasshopper. This question doesn't clarify anything. Think carefully. Think methodically. It's a catch question, she told herself. 'If I were forced to report anything, there would have to be sufficient evidence to prove it had happened, but yes, I would inform Matron,' she replied.

'Suppose it was someone you liked? A friend?'

'I'd still report it. The drugs are checked regularly and if something had gone missing, suspicion could fall on anybody.' He nodded in agreement. This interview had more to do with dangerous work in France. That was clear. She'd challenge him. 'Sir, if I were in the French Resistance and liked someone in my group, but found out that they had changed sides, what would you expect me to do?'

His eyes enlarged and he took his time to reply. 'Report it to your leader.'

'And what would he do?'

'That's a difficult question. Probably shoot him or her.' He looked at her intensely. 'Would you be interested in joining our organisation?'

'I'm not sure. It's a bit of a shock to realise that this job's nothing to do with translation, but something to do with the Resistance. I assume you would be sending me into France and that it would be to fight the Nazis?'

'I cannot give you any details at this point. You must leave and consider whether you'd be prepared to accept work that was risky. Of course, intensive training would be provided and finally you would be told if you had succeeded.'

'And if I hadn't?'

He hesitated for a few moments. 'We would offer you clerical work away from home. If you do succeed on the courses, I must be straight with you: your life would be in danger. I would have to decide whether I could risk your life and you would have to decide whether you would be willing to risk it.'

'I am interested to learn more. Have you recruited many women already who have gone to France?' she asked.

His lips curled. 'You aren't short of self-confidence, are you? That's one of the qualities I'm looking for. Yes, we have recruited a few women already, and I intend to recruit more. They work well on their own and can travel around more easily than men in Nazi-occupied territory. One of our female recruits is proving to be successful.' Looking more closely at her, he continued, 'The work we have in mind for you would be of great value to the war effort.' He closed her file. 'This interview must remain secret. I cannot emphasise this enough. Your questions have prompted me to tell you more than we normally do. Nonetheless, no one, not even those closest to you, must learn about this. A letter will be sent to your home address from the War Office, telling you if you have been chosen for a further interview and indicating the date and time of the second one, which would take place here again.'

She stood up and looked him in the eye as she shook his hand.

'I hope we meet again,' he said.

'I do too. What's your name?'

'I never disclose that,' he replied with a wry smile.

After she had left the darkened room and come down to the main entrance and stepped out into the daylight, the enormity of what the interviewer had disclosed overwhelmed her. Was she capable of taking on such a dangerous job if it was offered? And what exactly did it consist of?

A week later, Marie-Claire stepped out into Oxford Street. When she arrived at Hotel Victoria, she re-entered the room and was glad to receive an enthusiastic welcome by her interviewer.

'It's good to meet you again. I've given serious consideration to your application,' he said with a smile. 'I would like to offer you the chance of going on a training course for assessment. However, I must point out again that after the initial course, if you are chosen to do this work, it will be extremely risky.' He cleared his throat. 'I still need to discuss further details with you. You need a service position and that's why you'll be enlisted as an ensign in the FANY. You'll be given your uniform shortly, enabling you to explain to your family why you'll be away from home for long periods. If we offer you employment, you will receive pay from a special fund. Let me explain what the FANY do.'

'I already have a friend in that organisation, and she's already told me about the wide variety of jobs on offer,' she said, realising that this was a cover for clandestine work. 'Will I use weapons?' she asked him and noticed his eyes narrow.

'Yes,' he said. 'You'll learn how to shoot, and other methods of killing too. Are you prepared to end other people's lives?'

She swallowed. Looking someone in the eye and ending that person's life would be terrifying, but she would somehow overcome that fear. 'Yes, without hesitation. I've already handled guns in France when I used to go hunting with my uncle in the Sologne Forest.'

'Then I must now ask you to sign the Official Secrets Act.' He took out a sheet of paper from her file. 'At this point I must warn you that contravening this Act carries a sentence of up to fourteen years' imprisonment. You must tell no one about the contents of our conversations in relation to the secret work.'

'I understand,' she said and took her time in reading the document before looking up at him.

He leaned forward, his intense and direct eye contact making her feel ill at ease. 'I need to tell you now that we expect your chances of survival to be no better than fifty-fifty. Before you sign, are you still prepared to take such serious risks?'

Now he was levelling with her, but was she capable of taking on this dangerous work? Philippe's face flashed across her mind. How terrified he must have been, knowing he was going to be shot in the head. How had Aunt Marguerite been since his murder? How was the rest of the family?

Her interviewer's taps on the desk were increasing. 'Sorry, sir, I was thinking it through. Yes. I have no hesitation whatsoever in signing.'

She signed the paper and passed it back to him. He shook her hand warmly and said, 'If you pass all the training sessions, I think you could turn out to be especially useful in the field.'

On her way home by Underground, although she was thrilled that she'd been accepted for training, the interviewer's warning that she would be trained to kill and that the chances of survival were less than fifty-fifty, troubled her. If she were finally accepted into this strange organisation, would it be fair to her parents? They might never see her again if things went wrong. She would have to be convincing, tell them that she would be somewhere in the UK driving an ambulance and undertaking other duties. Dad would be sure to accept that and be proud of her for doing it, but she was not so sure about Maman.

When she came out of the Acton Underground station, she took the longer route home to avoid passing the bombed-out house where her friend Rose and her family had been killed in an air raid.

Eventually she arrived at her parents' house, a Victorian semi in a quiet road. As she searched for the key, her father opened the door and let her in. 'You look exhausted, Marie-Claire.' He bent down with difficulty to kiss her forehead. 'Go into the living room and sit down. I'll make a pot of tea for us. Your mother should be home any time now.'

Marie-Claire sank into the deep blue settee that Uncle Georges had bought for them on one of his trips to England. She rubbed her hand back and forth over the worn velour covering. She'd tell Dad about leaving the store first. He might even support her when she told Maman the news, however challenging that would be. Her thoughts were interrupted when her father came into the living room with the tea, sat down and poured them each a cup.

'Thanks, Dad. You're so kind,' she said as he looked across at her lovingly.

'How was work today?'

'Not busy again and the duty manager wasn't in a particularly good mood.' She looked at him hesitantly.

'What's the matter?' he asked.

She took a deep breath. 'I'm changing jobs.'

'Oh no. Your mother won't like this at all,' he answered, wiping his brow.

'It's too good an opportunity to miss, Dad.'

'What exactly is it, Marie-Claire?'

At that moment she heard a turn of a key in the front door lock and moments later, her mother came into the room. She was still in her nursing assistant's uniform. She gave Marie-Claire a kiss, French style, on each cheek.

Marie-Claire hesitated. How was she going to break the news to her mother who was already on edge? This wasn't going to be easy.

'What's happened?' Maman asked, looking from her daughter to her husband.

Marie-Claire took her courage in hand. It was now or never. 'I'm joining the FANY, like Daphne,' she said.

'I don't believe it. Not another change of job,' she said sitting down opposite her daughter. 'After your decision to leave your SRN course, I worked hard to set you up on a traineeship at Selfridges with the help of my friend who works there.' She paused, clearly shaken by Marie-Claire's decision. 'Where would you be working?'

'It wouldn't be in London, Maman. It would be elsewhere in England.'

She tried to sound convincing but telling lies to her parents didn't come easily to her. Her father stood listening quietly, but her mother's eyes were flickering as they normally did when she became upset. Her parents had lived through the horrors of the Great War. If they knew about the dangers she was deliberately seeking, they would be angry and desperate. They had lost their son, Olivier, in 1929 from pleurisy when they had lived in France, so they had devoted themselves to her.

Her mother wiped her eyes and looked desperately at her husband. He got up, went over to her, and put a comforting arm round her shoulders.

'Try not to upset yourself, Josette,' he said gently. 'Our little girl has grown up now and needs to make her own decisions.'

She paused, fingering her tightly permed dark brown hair, and then looked at Marie-Claire. 'What exactly will you be doing in this new job?'

'Learning first aid and being shown how to drive. You can train to become a telephone or a wireless operator and there are other jobs too—I might even get some translation work.' Her mother said nothing. 'I'll collect my uniform soon. You'll be proud of me. You wait and see.'

Josette shrugged her shoulders. 'When will you start this job?'

'In a month's time, At the beginning of January. I'll have to go away for a while to be trained.'

'You must give Selfridges one month's notice,' said Josette firmly.

'I will let them know as soon as possible,' Marie-Claire reassured her.

'And what are you going to do if this job doesn't work out?'

By now Marie-Claire's patience was waning. 'Can you *ever* be optimistic for me, Maman? You make me want to scream at times. I've had enough. Like Dad says—I'm an adult. You seem to forget that.'

Josette stood up, anger flaring in her eyes. 'I don't have to stay here and take comments like that,' she said and hurried out of the room.

Dad shook his head. 'I've told you several times that it doesn't pay to challenge your mother or be rude. I'm none too happy to think of you involved in this war effort either. Wait till she's had time to think things over.' He took her hand and continued, 'Then we can sit down and talk about things more calmly.'

After dinner, when she was doing the dishes, Marie-Claire thought about her mother's earlier life, which had been a hard one when she had given up schooling to look after her brothers and sisters while her widowed mother went to work during the Great War. Afterwards she went into the hall and looked at two photographs on the wall; one was of her maternal grandfather in his French Army uniform and the other was of Pierre, Josette's eldest brother. Both had fought in the Battle of Verdun in 1916 and died in the soaking trenches, where the stench must have been unbearable. No wonder anything to do with this new war distressed her mother.

When Josette returned from work the following evening, Marie-Claire asked her, 'Would you come to see *Sherlock Holmes and the Secret Weapon* with me this week? We both loved the previous Sherlock film.'

Josette smiled and replied, 'What a lovely idea. Yes, of course I'll come.'

A week later, Marie-Claire received a letter, asking her to go to a flat at Orchard Court, near Baker Street, to meet Miss Vera Atkins. When she arrived, she looked up at the imposing block of flats and wondered how the interviews would be conducted. A friendly civilian welcomed her into a thick-carpeted entrance hall. He didn't ask for her name but requested to see her identity card and her letter, before ushering her into a rickety lift.

On the third floor she was led into a small flat. As they passed the kitchen, Marie-Claire noticed several women in FANY, WAAF and WREN uniforms and men in army, RAF, and RN ones. They were all speaking French. The aroma of Gauloises reminded her of her Uncle Georges.

When her escort opened a door onto a black-and-white tiled bathroom and asked her to wait there with two other people, she had to stop herself from laughing. It was more like a scene in a comedy film. A tall fair-haired man, in his late twenties, dressed in army uniform, was sitting on the seat of an onyx bidet in the corner, while a plain-looking woman, in her thirties, was sitting on the side of a black bath.

'We haven't much room in this flat,' the escort told her in a friendly tone of voice. 'We have to use every available space. Wait here until I come and fetch you.'

Should she sit alongside the woman, or should she lean against the wall? Her thoughts were interrupted by the man saying, 'Would you like to sit here? It's not comfortable, but it will be better than standing.'

'Or falling into that bath,' she said, making him laugh, but the woman ignored them.

Moments later, the man asked, 'Have either of you seen the film *The Maltese Falcon*?'

The woman muttered, 'No. It doesn't interest me.'

Marie-Claire raised her eyebrows. 'I'd love to see it.'

'It's fantastic. Mary Astor is so convincing.'

'When does it finish?' she asked him.

'Very shortly. You'd better hurry because my first interviewer told me that the elementary training course begins in January.'

'The sooner the better. I can't wait to start.'

'What are you doing for Christmas?' he asked.

'We'll have a French Christmas celebration on Christmas Eve. My aunt and uncle run a farm and they always give us a chicken and other bits and pieces at Christmas. So Maman's going to cook chicken in wine with gratin dauphinois.'

'So, she's obviously French.'

'Of course, and she does a lot of French cooking.'

'You make me envious. I love those potatoes done in the oven and only French people really know how to cook them properly.'

'Where will you go for Christmas?'

He hesitated, taking his time to reply. 'Probably down to Surrey, but I'd much rather be spending it in London.' By the tone of his voice, Marie-Claire could tell he didn't want to pursue that area of the conversation.

'Have you ever lived in France?' she asked him.

'I went to college there while my father was working for a motor company.'

'So, your French is reasonably fluent?'

'I wouldn't say that, but I've been told that my accent is convincing.'

'Enough to charm the French girls?' she asked with a wry smile.

He shrugged his shoulders. 'When necessary, yes, of course. Why not? You must be the same with English men.'

She paused. 'I'd rather not answer that.'

'Hit a sore point? If so, I'm sorry.'

The more they continued talking, the more she hoped that she would meet this fascinating man again. He was the opposite of her former boyfriend. He was more relaxed. More interesting and oh, what sexy hazel eyes he had, and his voice was so soft and mellow.

Eventually the civilian came to escort the soldier for his interview. 'Hope to see you on the course,' he said and left the bathroom. When the civilian returned for Marie-Claire, he led her to a room at the end of the corridor. Would the interview be like the previous ones?

A tall, athletic and pencil-thin-looking man in army uniform and in his early forties opened the door. 'Come in, Miss Morris. I am Major Buckmaster. Do take a seat,' he told her in French and gave her a warm handshake.

She glanced round the room. At least there was new office furniture here, unlike the primitive items she'd seen in the first interviewer's room.

After some initial questions in French about her family in France and what she thought of the Nazi Occupation of France, he told her, 'You'll shortly be leaving for the elementary course where you will be assessed for three weeks, after which we'll contact you to give you the result. If you're successful, you'll then proceed to a more specialised course. If you pass that, we'll offer you employment.' The look in his eyes intensified. 'I have to warn you that the work is dangerous, and you will have to go on parachute training.' He stood up. 'I'm going to introduce you to Miss Atkins who looks after all the recruits, male and female.'

He took her to a room opposite his and knocked on the door. A woman in her mid-thirties, dressed in a pale blue tweed suit, answered it. After thanking Buckmaster, she invited Marie-Claire to sit down.

'I'm pleased to meet you at long last, Marie-Claire. I've received good reports about you.' As in Marie-Claire's first interview, the discussion switched to French. 'You've been selected to go on the elementary training course. Your interviewer was most impressed with your calm and logical way of thinking and excellent French.'

Marie-Claire felt herself blush. 'Thank you.'

After some questions about leaving her job, Miss Atkins asked her, 'How have your parents reacted to your change of employment? How do they feel that you're joining the FANY and having to be away from home for long periods?'

She had better not tell her that Maman disapproved. 'I think my mother guessed that there is more to the job than driving army personnel around and doing clerical work. She is concerned and keeps asking questions. She's still distraught because my cousin in Orléans was murdered earlier this year by the Nazis.'

Miss Atkins smoothed her mousy-coloured hair, rolled up at the nape of her neck. 'Yes, your interviewer told me about that and I'm sorry about your cousin's death. She cleared her throat. 'I need to talk to you about your uniform,' she said and passed an envelope to Marie-Claire. 'Take this letter and go to the address in the Strand, where our tailor at Lillywhite's will measure you up for your uniform. I must now talk to you about arrangements for the course,' continued Miss Atkins. 'Seven students, four men and three women, including yourself, will start training on the preliminary course during the first week in January. Security is paramount, and you must never divulge your real name, or talk about your family or your past and present life. That's why we'll give you a code name and you'll be known as Valérie. A week after the course ends, you'll be told by letter if you have been successful. Then you will go on another course.

'What kind of training is there on the first course?'

'I was coming to that. It will entail several skills. The instructors will make every effort to increase your level of fitness with cross-country running.' She then went on to reveal the skills that would be taught.'

'I can't wait for the demolition and weapons courses,' said Marie-Claire.

'I know that you already have considerable experience from hunting in the Sologne.'

Marie-Claire clenched her fingers. She wouldn't be afraid of what lay ahead after the courses were over and sat in silence until Miss Atkins said, 'I'm here to help you with any problems during your training and sometimes I come down to the training school. You'll also have more immediate support from your conducting officer, Lieutenant Maureen Brown. She'll report back your progress on the course to Major Buckmaster and to me. Every aspect of your training will be closely monitored and assessed to determine your suitability.'

'I realise the need for security, Miss Atkins. I accept that the job ahead is challenging and dangerous.'

On her way home, Marie-Claire thought about the wide variety of skills that she would learn on the preliminary course. She recalled her first interviewer telling her that apart from shooting, she would learn other ways of killing people. He had asked her if she was certain that she could take part in such dangerous activities, but by now, she knew her sense of revenge towards the Nazis ran deep, so she now had no hesitation in carrying out such operations.

If she were successful on this course and the next one, where would she be posted to in France? To see her country free again was what was uppermost in her mind, and she would face whatever dangers came.

CHAPTER TWO

WANBOROUGH IN JANUARY 1943

Before setting off to attend her preliminary course, Marie-Claire checked her appearance in her smart FANY uniform, admiring the smooth khaki skirt and jacket. She skimmed her hands down her stockings, much more comfortable to wear in contrast to the thick black ones she had worn as a student nurse. She took off her soft cap and gave its metal badge one more polish. She looked around her bedroom and eyed her favourite books and mementos. Would she ever see these again? She paused. Enough of thinking like that. She picked up her shoulder bag and case and went downstairs to say goodbye to her parents.

Josette was sitting down, looking tense and upset, while her father greeted Marie-Claire with a broad smile.

'I'll write to you as soon as I can, Maman. Don't worry about me.'

'Why do we have to write to a special PO box number? It all sounds very mysterious,' said Josette, wiping her eyes.

'Because we're moving around a lot and it's safer.'

'You look smashing in that uniform of yours,' said her father.

'You're right, Charles, but I wish I knew more about this job,' said her mother.

Marie-Claire hugged them both and left to make her way to Waterloo Station.

On arrival at Waterloo Station, at about 9 a.m., she saw the students assembled under the large station clock. She reminded herself that from now on she had to adopt the persona of Valérie. As she walked towards them, her heart leapt when she noticed the fair-haired soldier whom she'd met at Orchard Court; their eyes locked but she checked herself before approaching. Better not to look too interested, she thought.

A woman in her late twenties, dressed in FANY uniform, stepped forward. 'I'm Lieutenant Maureen Brown, your conducting officer, and these are my colleagues: Ensign Mary Cox from the FANY and Captain Farmer, conducting officer for the male students. Welcome to the group. We'll be delayed due to high winds and signal failure, but we must keep our ears open for the announcement.'

Moments later, the soldier came up to Valérie and introduced himself. 'My name's Christophe. What's yours?'

'Valérie,' she replied, remembering her code name.

'I'm so pleased you're on the course,' he said.

'Likewise,' she said, feeling herself blush.

'How was Christmas?'

'Not brilliant,' she replied and explained how her mother disapproved of her change of job and of her joining the FANY. 'How was your holiday?'

He took his time to answer, and she wondered why. 'I spent it with family most of the time, but I wanted to see more of my friends in London.'

They joined the other students and introduced themselves and chatted until the train arrived. Lieutenant Brown, accompanied by Ensign Cox, led the students to their carriage and told them that she and her colleagues would be in the adjoining one.

Once the journey had started, Valérie cast an eye round the railway carriage in the train that was taking them to an unknown destination. What a mixed bunch they seemed. How would they gel on the course? Like her, the two other women were dressed in their FANY uniforms while the men were dressed in army uniforms, except for one in civvies.

Florence, a slim English woman in her late twenties, with her fair hair in a chignon, started to chat up Didier, a dark-eyed Frenchman of a similar age.

'Pretty difficult to know what to talk about when we aren't supposed to reveal anything about ourselves,' she remarked in an upper-class English voice.

'Only if you've nothing else to talk about,' said Didier tartly.

'Steady on. I bet you know more than most of us about what's on this course.'

'I'm certainly not telling you,' he replied.

She turned to Christophe and asked, 'Can you tell me what all this cloak and dagger stuff is about?'

'I've got a good idea, but I'd prefer to say nothing,' he replied.

'I can see you're in the army,' she said, smoothing her chignon. 'Are you a mole who's been planted to report back to Lieutenant Brown?'

'Don't be so ridiculous,' said Simon and by his accent Valérie could tell he was a Parisian.

'You obviously don't appreciate my sense of humour,' Florence said, glaring at him with her fiery blue eyes.

'We'll be told about everything on arrival at our destination, I'm sure,' said Roger, a tall Englishman with receding grey hair and dressed in civvies.

Nicole, a young woman with wispy brown hair and almond-shaped eyes, who sat next to Valérie, remarked, 'My interviewer was kind of cagey.'

'Why didn't you ask him or her outright what it was about?' asked Valérie.

'It was a man and I felt ill at ease with him,' she murmured.

'Where were you interviewed?'

'Hotel Victoria, near Trafalgar Square.'

'I went to the same place,' replied Valérie. If it was the same man who'd interviewed her, he could be intimidating for a nervous type like Nicole.

'What did you do for Christmas?' Didier asked Christophe.

'Stayed with the family and had the usual Christmas lunch with them.'

'You make it sound as if you were bored by the whole thing,' said Didier. 'Surely you had a girlfriend in tow? I made bloody sure I did,' he said with a hearty laugh.

'I'm certainly not being drawn into that,' replied Christophe with a laugh.

Marie-Claire reflected for a moment. Maybe Christophe had a girlfriend and that was why he hesitated when she had asked him about it at Christmas. She'd better be careful, but she was really smitten with him though.

An hour later, Lieutenant Brown came into their compartment. 'We're nearly there,' she told them. 'We'll have about an hour's drive to reach our destination.'

When they reached the station, Didier told Valérie, 'It's Guildford in Surrey.'

'I know. I've been here lots of times, but stations are eerie places now without names,' she replied, shivering from the bitter weather.

They made their way to the station forecourt and climbed into the back of an army lorry with their suitcases and were joined by the staff before the driver secured the canvas flaps.

'Now we're hidden from the big bad outside world. No more signposts on roadways,' said Florence. Everyone laughed except Simon.

Nobody said much during the rest of the journey.

After an hour, the lorry made a sharp turn and moments later Valérie could feel it being driven up a gravel drive. The driver stopped the lorry and undid the flaps for them to climb out. While the men unloaded the suitcases, Valérie stood and looked up at the beautiful Elizabethan manor house in front of her with its pale brickwork, black wood, pointed rooflines and tall chimneys. Later she discovered it was called Wanborough Manor in Wanborough, Surrey.

Lieutenant Brown led everyone into a panelled hallway with an impressive Jacobean staircase. 'Leave your luggage in the room on the right and wait in the room opposite where you'll be introduced to the camp commandant,' she told them.

The students talked amongst themselves until the door opened. Everyone stood to attention when a tall middle-aged officer came in, accompanied by the two conducting officers, the ensign, and three soldiers.

As the officer stepped forward, Valérie admired the shine on his impeccable Sam Browne belt, reminding her how hard she used to rub the polish onto her leather school satchel to make it the shiniest in her class. He started to speak to them. 'Ladies and gentlemen, as camp commandant, I welcome you. I'm

Major de Wesselow, Coldstream Guards. The three weeks' preliminary assessment course here is challenging. At times it will seem too demanding for some of you. If you don't already have it, you'll be issued with standard battledress and boots as well as a PT kit and plimsolls.' He paused and looked around the room, surveying the students. 'Let me give you a brief outline of the course. After classes on weapons training, you'll be taken to a quarry where you'll learn how to handle and shoot pistols and sub-machine guns.'

Valérie smiled to herself. She couldn't wait to handle those.

'You will learn the basics of explosives. We have a pit quarry for hand grenade practice. Other classes include map-reading, an introduction to Morse Code, fitness training as well as fieldcraft. Unarmed combat is also included.'

Valérie's heart quickened. It couldn't be clearer: if they were finally recruited, they were going to France to fight the Nazis.

The commandant took off his cap and went on, 'I cannot emphasise enough the importance of security at all times. Powers of physical endurance, technical knowledge and patience are vital. Lieutenant Brown and Captain Farmer and the instructors will be monitoring you, as the staff at Orchard Court advised you. There is no telephone available and all letters, incoming and outgoing, are censored.'

The course was obviously top secret, Valérie concluded.

'At the end of your time here, those of you who succeed will be sent on other courses. My staff is here at all times to help you with any difficulties that may arise.' He looked at his watch. 'Any questions?'

Valérie took a deep breath and raised her hand. 'Sir, if we are accepted on the second course, how long will it last?'

'Six weeks,' he replied, looking at her closely. 'After that there are other specialist courses. Are there any more questions?'

'Is surveillance included?' Simon enquired.

The commandant frowned. 'You will find out in due course.' He checked his watch. 'Lunch is at one. Please be prompt. Remember you must speak French as much as you can, particularly with those instructors who speak the language. That is all for now.' He put on his cap and gloves, turned, and walked smartly out of the hall followed by his staff.

'What an informative speech,' remarked Christophe. 'Some army courses I've attended were not as well thought out as that one. This commandant only gave a brief outline, but we know what we're in for. I prefer that.'

'I couldn't agree more,' said Valérie.

'He clearly didn't like my question,' said Simon.

'Maybe it would have been wiser not to have asked him.' suggested Nicole.

'You've got to be assertive sometimes. I want to know everything about this course. You're too cautions. That's obvious. It's no use being like that here,' he said, making Nicole look away from him.

'Who do you think you are speaking to her like that?' asked Florence in an authoritative tone of voice.

'I agree,' said Didier.

Valérie nodded, sharing his point of view.

Ensign Mary Cox came up to the women and offered to show them to their rooms. As they climbed the steep staircase, Valérie looked at some photographs on the wall. They were probably members of the family who gave up the manor for the War Office. One photograph of a distinguished-looking man and two young children caught her eye.

'That's Sir Herbert Asquith,' said the ensign. 'He lived here before he became Prime Minister shortly before the last war broke out.'

On the first floor they were shown into a large bedroom furnished in the Victorian style except for the four beds which appeared new.

'You'll hear a bell before lunch is served downstairs in the mess,' Mary Cox told them. 'A corporal takes orders before lunch. The drinks are in the bar close by, but you will have to pay for all alcohol consumed.'

'Alcohol!' exclaimed Florence as soon as Ensign Cox had left the room. 'We'd better watch ourselves. They'll be taking note of who can take a drink and who gets blotto.' She threw herself onto a bed. 'This place is really swish,' she continued. 'They want to make us feel good before we find out what we've let ourselves in for.'

Valérie sank onto a bed by the window and said, 'Oh this is marvellous. I've never known such comfort.'

'Nor me,' said Nicole, relaxing on a bed alongside her.

'After PT and unarmed combat, we'll need these beds to recover,' said Florence with a laugh and left the room.

At half past twelve, Valérie and Nicole went downstairs to the bar before going to the mess, a large traditional dining room on the ground floor with a white-painted beamed ceiling and white distempered walls. They sat down at a long oak table, well worn.

'I wonder where the owners of the manor have gone?' Valérie asked Christophe who was sitting next to her.

'Probably to a smaller house. The government requisitions places like this for training purposes and stores most of the family's furniture,' he said.

'What's happened to the servants?'

'Some are in the forces. Others are employed in armaments factories or on the land.'

'Have you been on other courses in grand houses like this one?' she asked.

'Yes. Several military courses.'

'How long have you been in the army?'

'Can't tell you that,' he replied with a smile. 'You're young to be on this course.'

'I realise that, but I've a reason to pursue it,' she said.

'You make things sound even more mysterious.'

'Each student has his or her own reasons. You must have one, surely?' she asked him.

'It's all part of being in the army. You expect to rise to challenges.'

Towards the end of a delicious roast dinner and sweet, Valérie felt Nicole nudging her. 'Someone in the bar told me we've got a fully French trained chef. It's more like a classy hotel. There must be a reason for all this.'

'Perhaps they want us to relax with each other, let barriers come down and see who remains discreet, particularly after we've had a drink or two. Remember the conducting officers will be assessing us,' replied Valérie.

'What's this course all about? What job are they training us to do?' asked Nicole.

Valérie hesitated. The commandant's words 'a preliminary assessment course, standard battledress and pistols' regurgitated in her mind. Surely Nicole had heard these? Should she reveal the truth, or would Nicole be frightened off? 'It must have something to do with security,' she replied disingenuously.

'You mean we'll become spies?' asked Nicole, looking fearful.

Valérie shrugged her shoulders. 'I expect we'll soon be told,' she told her, noticing Christophe giving her a guarded smile.

'Valérie, I bet you were in some form of security service before coming here,' said Didier in a cheeky tone of voice.

'No. I wasn't.'

'Whereabouts did you work?' he continued.

'In the London area. That's all I'm prepared to say. We can't talk about our past. You know that.'

The following morning, Valérie felt someone tapping her on the shoulder as she lay in bed.

'Réveille-toi, Valérie! It's 6 a.m. Hurry up or you'll be in trouble,' said Nicole. 'There's a hot drink and a biscuit downstairs before the cross-country run starts in half an hour. Florence has already gone down.'

'Merde,' she replied. After Nicole had gone, Valérie sat up in bed and rubbed her hand over some of the condensation on the latticed windowpanes beside her, through which she could discern a large garden and lots of trees. This place is more like a luxury hotel, not a school for guerrillas, she thought. She forced herself to climb out of bed, wash and put on her PT running kit, and made her way downstairs to join the others who were starting to assemble on the gravel drive in front of the main entrance.

A sergeant appeared, dressed in a PT kit like his recruits. 'Right, take one of these,' he said, handing each student a top to wear with a large number on it, front and back, as if they were in a race. 'We're off. Follow me. As it's your first run, don't start worrying if you can't keep up with the front runners. In case you are asked, the locals think this is a commando course. We'll be exercising every morning like this and after breakfast, you will do PT followed by weapons training and Morse Code training.'

It was a cold but clear morning when they ran through a wooded area behind the manor. As they emerged onto a grassy area, Valérie enjoyed breathing in that crisp, permeating smell of wet grass which reminded her of mushroom-picking early in the morning with her cousins in France.

Gradually she caught up with Christophe near the front. She admired how attractive he looked in his uniform with his broad shoulders, slim hips, and muscular thighs. They followed the sergeant across the fields, climbed over two stile gates and caught up with him. As they passed a small quarry pit in the middle of one of the fields, he pointed at it and said, 'That's where we practise throwing grenades and there's a larger one elsewhere for explosives.' When they reached the top, they stood there breathless. Beneath them they saw rolling countryside, but

Valérie did not disclose that she knew this was the Hog's Back, a road running along a chalk ridge on the North Downs overlooking countryside between Guildford and Farnham. She had visited this area many times. Imagine Uncle William walking his dog and running into her group. She could almost see him standing there transfixed in astonishment. They were soon joined by the others with Florence trailing behind them.

'Don't worry, Florence,' said the sergeant. 'You'll soon increase your speed.'

As they were returning to the manor, Valérie realised that the manor was close to Guildford and that the hour's drive in the army lorry had been to confuse the students as to its proximity to the town.

After PT the students made their way to the back of the manor where they met a tall man with tight curly auburn hair and dressed in army uniform, who was waiting for them.

'I'm Sergeant Alan Banks, your weapons instructor. Today, we're dealing with pistols. Let me take you to a practice area near the quarry.' He asked two of them to carry some bags for him.

'Firing a pistol is for attack and not for self-defence. I need to point out one important operation in all this and it's called the "double tap". Always fire two shots because your victim's nerve system continues for several seconds. He might shoot back at you and kill you outright. You have been warned,' he said sternly.

Valérie swallowed hard. It was one thing to go hunting with Uncle Georges in the Sologne Forest, south of Orléans, but killing people was another matter. Imagine human heads blown apart with brain parts flying everywhere.

After Banks distributed pistols to them, he named the main parts of the pistol, and how it operated and the safety features. He then taught them how to strip it and reassemble it, though Nicole and Roger both had difficulty in completing the task.

'In future lessons, you will be introduced to different pistols. We will include foreign ones because if you remove them from victims, they'll be useful to your circuit,' Banks told the other students. 'We will start using ammunition shortly after the next lesson.'

Valérie was intrigued. Circuit? That was the first time anyone had mentioned that word. Was it to do with Resistance work in France? The friend who had fled from France had also spoken about that to her family.

In the afternoon, the students met a tall and well-built man of Mediterranean appearance at the back of the manor. He was carrying two bags and Didier offered to carry one of them. 'My name is Major Michel Guillard,' he told them in French. 'I'm your explosives instructor. Call me Michel. Now let's make for the quarry,' he said.

On arrival, he started to address them. 'You will use charges which are already made up and which will be delivered to you. All you do is select the right one for the job and attach the detonator and two more items. Some of you might be selected to go on one of the special sabotage courses where you'll be taught how to assemble different charges for difficult targets. For this elementary course, you'll just need to learn how to place a charge and how to make it go bang.'

He reached into his bag and pulled out a rectangular block wrapped in a rubberised fabric. 'Now,' he said, 'this is a powerful charge, but I'll use a less powerful one today.' He brought out a small square block from his bag and held it up to the group. 'This is a small piece taken from a larger piece,' he said. 'Inside this rubberised fabric is some plastique, British-made yellow plastic explosive, easy to manipulate, and in the centre, running through like a stick of rock, is the primer. The primer needs to be initiated to set the PE off. Now I'll insert the detonator—this small metallic tube—into the explosive. Finally, I need my best pal of all—my time pencil.'

'Time pencil?' asked a bewildered Nicole.

'Yes,' he replied and pulled out a small black metallic tube looking like a pencil. 'I'm going to insert the detonator into the time pencil's spring snout,' he said, pointing to it. 'You can see that the pencil has a black safety strap—its colour indicates a time delay of ten minutes before the explosion.' He turned to Valérie and told her to crush the tube to make the acid inside release the spring. 'I'm now going to release the safety strap. Move away all of you and stand by for the big bang in ten minutes. There are time pencils with different time delays. Plastique is soft and pliable. There are other types of explosives, of course.'

'Are the Brits going to supply us with lots of this plastique stuff when we're in France?' asked Simon in a somewhat haughty manner.

'If you pass the training and go into the field, the organiser will decide who uses it,' replied Michel sharply and then asked the students to stand well back.

After answering a few more of the students' questions, Michel told them to block their ears. A few minutes later, a huge bang resounded round the quarry, making Valérie's ears ring.

Simon said, 'This plastique stuff would be excellent for blowing up railway lines, wouldn't it?'

Michel hesitated. 'Yes, it would cut gaps into the rail, the train wheels would fall through the gap, pulling carriages off, and they'd probably turn over.'

'It would be a horrific and frightening sight with bodies strewn about among the wreckage,' said Nicole, her voice sounding unsteady.

Michel simply nodded and packed everything up into his two bags before accompanying the students back to the manor.

Michel must have been a saboteur at some point in France, but he clearly didn't really want to give too many details away to the students, thought Valérie.

Dinner was served at seven later and towards the end of it, Didier encouraged Valérie to have another drink, but she declined it.

'You're being a spoilsport,' remarked Florence. 'You can fill mine up, Didier.'

'You like your wine, don't you, Florence?' remarked Roger. 'You'll have to be careful if you're ever in a bar in Occupied Europe. One glass too many might be your downfall.'

'Give the woman a break, Roger. Don't take life so seriously,' said Didier as he reached for Florence's glass.

'For once, I totally agree with Roger,' said Simon. 'I will risk my life for France, but I wouldn't want my life put at risk by some fool of a woman blabbing secret information because she's too drunk to know what she's saying.'

'Steady on,' Didier snapped. 'There's no need to insult her. Or is that the only way you can get a woman's attention?'

'I think a breath of fresh air is called for here. Who's coming for a quick stroll?' suggested Christophe.

Most of the students declined, but Valérie volunteered to join Christophe.

By the light of a full moon, they took care not to slip on the ice that had formed across the uneven terrace at the back of the manor. Tall trees dominated the garden. They made their way along gravel paths adjacent to lawns now shrouded in thick frost.

High brick walls enclosed the gardens and a wooded area.

Valérie stopped and looked back at the house: smoke was streaming out of the tall chimneys. They loomed against the starlit sky, not even a chink of light escaped through the blackout curtains, but the moonlight showed up the silhouettes of topiary bushes, clipped into unusual shapes, as well as box hedges.

'It's a mystical garden and beautifully designed,' said Christophe in a soft voice.

They went further into the grounds until Valérie paused again. 'Roger certainly thinks we're going abroad somewhere. I think we'll be sent to France, don't you?'

'Yes. I thought that from the start. You handled Nicole's questions well,' he said.

'I noticed you smiling at me and giving me a nod of agreement as I spoke to her.' She paused. 'Do you think Simon will succeed on this course?'

'I have my doubts. He's rather volatile. "Prudence and caution are an agent's most important qualities"—our interviewer's words in Hotel Victoria.'

Valérie thought back to the questions her interviewer had posed about theft in the hospital and how she would tackle the problem. He had been testing her for those qualities.

Christophe rolled himself a cigarette and lit it. By the light of his match, she again admired his hazel eyes, warm and friendly ones. As he continued smoking, she became conscious of him looking at her like Jack had done. Further on into the garden they came to a swimming pool that nestled among some pine trees.

'Swimming there in the summer, after a taxing day's training, must be so refreshing,' he said.

She sighed. Swimming in there with him would be heaven. Although Miss Atkins had warned her not to become involved with any of the male students, she couldn't help her feelings towards Christophe. He'd captivated her with his gallantry when they'd first met in the bathroom at Orchard Court and she enjoyed his vivacious conversation, quite apart from his handsome appearance. As they walked towards a wooded area nearby, she tripped on a stone and fell onto the hard ground.

'Are you all right?' he asked as he knelt beside her.

'Yes. I've only grazed my knee. Nothing to worry about,' she replied, feeling his warm hand against hers, sending ripples of excitement through her body as he kissed her on the cheek. He took out a handkerchief from his pocket and tied it round her knee. As he helped her up from the ground, she noticed how tenderly he looked at her, but he only took her hand as they returned to the manor.

They re-joined Didier and Simon who were sitting at a table in a quiet corner of the bar. Christophe went to order some drinks.

Simon was talking to Didier, but soon things started to become heated between them, which did not escape the attention of Lieutenant Brown who was watching them.

'If you don't work with the British, there'll be mayhem. Otherwise, we'll never beat the Nazis. Do you want even more reprisals? Do you want the Gestapo dragging your family or friends away at dawn?' Didier demanded. 'We must work together and support General de Gaulle in London. His radio broadcasts to the French people must incite more people to join the Resistance. We must improve security too.'

'Our security is tight. Yours is shit. If we deliver a message, it's verbal and no other discussion takes place,' said Simon. 'No, of course I don't want to see my family or comrades dragged away like animals by the bloody Boches,' he shouted. 'The communist movement will come to power when this heinous

Occupation has ended. We don't need de Gaulle and his people.'

Valérie glared at Simon, wondering why he had come to Britain to be trained with their organisation? He'd obviously been in the Resistance in France.

'God help us if you and your communist friends do succeed!' Didier replied.

'You can't talk. You socialists made a right mess in the so-called socialist Popular Front government.'

'Rubbish! We made huge advances in education and in other areas,' said Didier.

'How on earth did you get involved with them? I've had enough of this. You and your kind are fucking idiots. You pretend to represent the working people, but you're as bad as the elite classes who support de Gaulle,' Simon yelled and stormed out of the bar.

Silence reigned for a few moments while Christophe returned with the drinks.

Turning to Valérie, Didier told her, 'If people like him and the rest of his communist cronies come into power after the war, France will not be a free country.' He took a huge swig of his red wine. 'He's right about one thing, though. The communists have the best security.'

'How would you know?' Valérie asked.

'I've got contacts in my hometown. That's all I'm saying.'

'The different political factions *are* going to make our work more difficult in the Resistance movement. If he's a communist, what's he doing here?' asked Valérie.

'I've been asking myself that for several days,' replied Didier. 'He must have kept it well hidden at his interviews.'

Lieutenant Brown, who had been sitting close by, stood up and left the bar.

'She's obviously going to confer with Captain Farmer about what she's overheard,' said Valérie. 'He could even be thrown off the course.'

'Good riddance,' replied Didier. 'He deserves whatever he gets from his conducting officer. Now if you'll excuse me, I need to go to sleep.'

After a long silence, Christophe looked closely at Valérie. 'Phew. That was not a very pleasant scene to watch. How are you feeling? You look drained.'

'That row brought home the dangers we'll face if we're sent to France. But I wasn't only thinking about that,' she replied.

'What else was troubling you?'

'My mother thinks I've joined the FANY and was none too pleased when I left my nurse training and my other job. If I'm accepted on the next course and get taken on by this organisation, I'll be sent abroad for long periods, and she'll suspect something more serious is involved.'

Christophe took his time to reply. 'You need to make her feel proud of you. Emphasise that you want to help the war effort.' She remained silent until he asked, 'Is there something else that's on your mind?'

'Yes, there is,' she replied, breathing in deeply. 'When Didier talked to you about girlfriends, you seemed annoyed. Have you actually got one?'

Christophe's eyes darkened before he answered. 'Yes, I have. I was on the point of telling you. Things aren't right between Angela and me.' He took her hand and caressed it. 'It's about you and me. I find you hugely attractive and I've started to have strong feelings for you, and I sense you feel the same way.' Valérie smiled at him. 'I must think of Angela and your feelings, of course.'

'And also, this resistance organisation isn't keen for students to become emotionally involved,' she reminded him. He nodded in agreement. 'I wouldn't want to destroy your relationship with Angela,' said

Valérie. 'Someone I loved deceived me, so I don't want to inflict that on Angela.'

He took her hand and said, 'We must try to help each other, Valérie, and avoid being alone together.' He looked at his watch. 'Goodness me, we need to retire.'

As Valérie climbed into bed and pulled the covers over her, she whispered, 'Luck doesn't appear to be on my side when falling in love, does it?'

At the end of the week, Banks took the students to a practice area not far from the quarry. Target boards and cut-out figures were positioned at either end of the area for safety factors. A soldier distributed pistols to the students and Banks then started to instruct them.

'I want to see your arm bent and levelled at your target between thigh and head. Then a quick draw from your trouser pocket or waistband.' Further instructions followed. 'Notice how I grip the pistol with both hands. Stand with legs apart and knees flexed. Raise the weapon to face level and look along the top of it, making sure it is pointed at the middle of the target's chest. And remember two shots.'

Most of the students had used ammunition before, but Nicole and Roger had to learn this skill with difficulty. Valérie started to help Nicole but felt a tap on her shoulder. It was Banks. 'She's got to try and master this. If not, of course, I'll help her.'

Sometime later, Valérie could see Banks helping Nicole. His eyes met Valérie and he smiled at her.

Valérie had been used to shooting with a rifle during her hunting expeditions with her uncle in the Sologne. The more she aimed for the target's chest, the more exhilarated she became, thinking that she was really aiming at a Nazi's chest.

At the end of the last lesson, when Banks had shown the students how to use the Sten gun, a semi-automatic, Valérie asked him, 'Once you've killed someone for the first time, you must feel awful. How do you face the next one?'

'It becomes automatic. Put emotion aside,' Banks told her. 'It's like drawing a curtain across a window at night. Block everything out. Your job is to destroy the enemy.'

Despite coping well with the courses, it was the Morse Code class which Valérie found difficult. She wandered into the garden and sat down under one of the beech trees. Soon she became aware of someone approaching and she looked up to see Christophe. He sat down beside her.

'What's troubling you, Valérie?' he asked.

'It's the Morse Code that I can't master; my fingers can't react quickly enough. It's utterly stupid. I can't understand it.'

He put his arm round her. 'Don't worry. They select students on the Morse Code course who show promise for training as wireless operators. It doesn't matter for this course.'

'Oh Christophe. Thank heavens you've told me that.'

He tightened his arm round her and kissed her gently on the cheek.

After dinner Didier suggested going to a local pub called The Good Intent.

'How did you find out about it?' asked Valérie.

'One of the instructors took us there last week. Obviously, he was checking up on our drinking habits. We'll have to ask first if we can go there and then one of the instructors will join us.'

'You kept that quiet,' remarked Valérie with a grin.

It was a moonlit night as they climbed up the hill towards Puttenham, the next village. Christophe held Valérie's hand, caressing it tenderly.

'No instructor's come yet,' remarked Valérie.

'Maybe we'll be lucky for once,' replied Didier.

They talked about the organisation and the instructors whom they had met so far.

'It's such a secret organisation that we don't even know its name,' said Florence with a giggle.

'And we're not likely to know either,' added Didier.

'And how do you know that?' asked Valérie.

'It's not what you know. It's who you know,' he replied with a chuckle.

'That's what I love about you, Didier,' said Florence, putting her arm round him. 'You're so full of mystery.' Turning to Christophe, she asked, 'If you were in charge of a circuit, what would you look for in a female courier? Remember we heard that word used by Lieutenant Brown the other night in the bar.'

Christophe thought for a moment. 'Loyalty, courage and above all else, someone with whom I could feel at ease,' he replied, looking into Valérie's eyes in the moonlight.

'He's sweet on you, Valérie. Watch out,' said Florence with a giggle.

Valérie blushed and Christophe remained silent.

After climbing a hill, they crossed the main road on the Hog's Back and made their way towards the village where they walked down a sloping road to the centuries-old pub. They lowered their heads as they went in; apart from a couple at the bar, the pub was empty. Didier led them to the back of the pub and they sat down on benches at an oak table. A roaring log fire soon warmed them up.

'I'll buy the first round,' said Didier and went to the bar to order.

Valérie looked round the pub with its previously white distempered walls now turning brown, and more so the ceiling, from tobacco tar staining. She watched the landlord serving Didier. Had he ever overheard anything about the so-called 'commando course' as the locals termed it? There were photographs of local notable places on the walls, and she recognised one showing the view across the Hog's Back, taken from the rough main road.

'It looks as though our friend won't turn up,' said Florence.

'The evening hasn't finished yet. He may turn up later,' said Didier.

They continued talking about generalities, avoiding mention of the manor's activities.

After two rounds of drinks, they started to make their way back to the manor. It was now bitterly cold. Florence started to try and skate on the frosty paths, but narrowly missed a dangerous fall thanks to the quick thinking of Didier. Christophe put his arm round Valérie, making her feel both warmer and reassured of his feelings towards her. By the time they had nearly reached the manor house, Didier and Florence had disappeared.

Christophe looked at Valérie and took her into his arms. He kissed her lips gently, then her neck, then finally he kissed her passionately on the lips and she responded, their lips entwined. He held her closer and started to undo her jacket. It was what Valérie had long yearned for, but she couldn't let him go all the way. She pushed him gently away. 'Remember Angela, please.'

'I might never see you again, darling Valérie. You know how much I feel for you. I know what we discussed, but I can't help myself.'

'Christophe, please ...'

When the training finished at the end of January, Valérie, dressed in her FANY uniform, joined the other students in a special service at the tiny twelfth-century church of St Bartholomew situated next to the manor. She was no longer a practising Catholic but came to the little church every Sunday to attend the Protestant service. The vicar reminded her of her father's brother—someone who was a good listener to whom you could turn if you were ever troubled. She'd told him, 'If I pass this course, I dread telling my mother that I will be going on another one afterwards.'

'Try to impress upon her the important role FANYs play in the war effort. Make her feel you are fulfilling a vital part in the war initiative,' had been his reassuring response. It matched Christophe's erstwhile advice.

As she looked around the church for the last time, her eyes finally rested on the beautiful chestnut rood screen that separated the nave from the sanctuary. Initially the Nazis had divided France into the Occupied Zone and the Free Zone, but they'd marched into the Free Zone during the previous November after the Allies had invaded North Africa. It had become more dangerous everywhere. She thought of Christophe and, although she hoped they'd both pass the course, nonetheless she wondered how they would be able to control their feelings if they were together on the next course? How would it all end up?

When the assessment ended, Valérie made her way to Acton and thought about the other students. If she was accepted on the next course, who would be included on it?

How were her parents going to receive her? Her answers to any of their questions had to seem plausible. When she knocked at the front door, her mother threw her arms round her. 'It's lovely to have you home again, but you look much thinner.'

'You expect to lose weight with all the training we do,' said Marie-Claire.

Soon they were joined by her father, Charles, who was delighted to see his daughter. 'You look very smart, my girl,' he told her. As they continued talking, Marie-Claire became aware that her mother was looking at her legs.

'How ever did you get these bruises?'

'I fell doing cross-country running.'

'Cross-country? What are you FANYs doing that kind of thing for?'

'It's all part of the training to keep us fit. I've got so far, Maman. Stop fussing,' she said, noticing her father look at her anxiously. 'I want to join the war effort even if it *is* only in a supporting role like driving army officers around and performing administrative duties.'

Josette sighed before telling her, 'I can see that it's no use my telling you not to continue your training. You are a very stubborn girl.'

A week later, Marie-Claire was listening to the wireless when her father came into the living room, holding a letter. 'This is for you,' he told her. She guessed that it was from the organisation and carefully opened it up and read its contents. Now she needed to improvise.

'Oh, I've passed the first stage of my training—my FANY training. I'm so thrilled.' She didn't tell him that it included the rendezvous, date, and time for the second course. She'd somehow have to tell her parents but not now. Her father remained silent. He was exhausted by worrying about her—she could see that from his bloodshot eyes. He must have realised that she was going to undertake dangerous work. She was all they had since her brother's death.

'I think there's more to it, isn't there, my dear?'

Marie-Claire faltered for a moment, hardly able to bear the pain she was causing him. She had to brace herself. 'Dad, I'm sorry. I can't say any more.' She kissed him and went upstairs to her bedroom where she reread the letter. She had passed the elementary course and was on her way to the next one. What would it entail?

CHAPTER THREE
BEAULIEU IN MID-FEBRUARY 1943

'Your reports from Wanborough are excellent, Valérie,' said Miss Atkins when they met at Orchard Court. After closing the file, she continued. 'I must tell you that the next course is about clandestine techniques and personal security; it's much tougher. You'll learn how to shadow a person and observe if you are being followed. You'll be roughly interrogated in the middle of the night. You'll also learn disguise, codes, ciphering and many other skills.'

It all sounded daunting, but Valérie was determined to succeed.

'You'll be joined by two other female students here next Friday at two o'clock, and you'll spend Friday and Saturday with them. On Sunday two male students will arrive and travel down with you to your training school.'

Valérie pursed her lips, recalling that it was Dad's birthday on Friday. She wouldn't be there to celebrate with him, Maman, Uncle William and his family. The job was risky. Would she be there to congratulate him on his next birthday?

Miss Atkins looked at her closely. 'Is there something troubling you?'

'Oh no. Not all,' she said, but Miss Atkins looked unconvinced.

'We're putting the three of you into a flat not far from here. On Sunday, you'll join the two conducting officers, Lieutenant Brown, and Captain Farmer, as well as Ensign Mary Cox, whom you've met already, and two male students. The drive to your destination will take about three hours.' She paused and looked directly at Valérie. 'Any questions?'

'No, thank you. You've made everything clear.'

After the interview, on the journey home, Valérie kept thinking about Christophe and hoped that he would be on the course.

A week later, Valérie arrived at Orchard Court, dressed in her FANY uniform, where Miss Atkins introduced her to a student called Francine, a French woman in her mid-forties with short curly grey hair and dressed in FANY uniform as well.

'I might look like a grandmother, but you'll soon see that I've got the energy of a twenty-year-old,' she told Valérie. 'I come from good country stock in France where we always eat well, unlike in this country. I'll soon show the Boches a thing or two.'

Valérie laughed whereas Miss Atkins raised her eyebrows. They continued talking while Miss Atkins looked at her watch now and again, until finally her phone rang. 'Bring her up please, Park.'

A few minutes later, a woman in her early thirties, with straight light brown hair, cut into a bob, and dressed in an upmarket camel coat, was shown into Miss Atkins's office. 'I'm awfully sorry for being late, Miss Atkins, but I had to return some vital paperwork to the actress who's replacing me.'

Valérie suppressed a gasp, thinking she wasn't bothered about disclosing personal details before the course even starts.

Miss Atkins frowned and said, 'Bernadette, I hope you will become more circumspect in what you tell people and I do expect you to wear your FANY uniform.'

'I'm really sorry, Miss Atkins. It won't happen again, I promise you.'

'Now let's get down to business,' said Miss Atkins, opening a drawer and taking out an envelope from her desk. 'This contains the key to your flat with instructions on how to get there. On Sunday morning, when you vacate it, put the key in the envelope and post it through the letter box when you leave.' She stood up and gave the envelope to Valérie. 'Now I must go and see Major Buckmaster.'

'Phew. She's a bit of an old dragon, isn't she?' remarked Francine when Miss Atkins had left.

'With an important organisation like ours, she's got to be strict,' said Valérie.

It was frosty but dry on Sunday morning when the three women arrived outside Orchard Court and met the conducting officers and Ensign Mary Cox.

'Our cars are parked around the corner. Ah, I can see the first male student coming towards us,' said Lieutenant Brown.

Valérie turned round and was thrilled to see Didier.

'I told you we'd meet again,' he said, 'but I'm disappointed that Florence isn't on the course, and I'm worried about her.'

'Why's that?' she asked him.

'I met up with her several times and we had a great time together. One day, I went to meet her at her flat in Kensington and she'd gone. Just like that, leaving no message or forwarding address in the post.'

'How strange,' replied Valérie, but she wasn't surprised at Florence's failure to get on the course because of her exuberance and strong opinions. She would never have melted into a crowd in France.

A taxi pulled up sharply in front of them. Valérie caught her breath as Christophe emerged, looking tired and harassed. 'Sorry I'm late. I had a family matter to attend to.'

Valérie guessed that it probably had something to do with Angela. While Lieutenant Brown distributed their passes, Valérie asked how he was, but he kept the conversation to a minimum. He decided to join Didier and Captain Farmer in the second car after he saw Valérie walking towards the first car with Lieutenant Brown and the other two women. Then she remembered how upset he had become when she'd pushed him away. As a result, he had obviously decided to distance himself from her.

They set off on their journey with the blinds pulled down over the windows. After about two and a half hours, the cars came to an abrupt halt, and everyone climbed out. They were in open countryside with ponies congregating under the trees. Valérie recognised it immediately as the New Forest in

Hampshire where she'd spent happy holidays with her family.

After a few minutes, a canvas-covered army truck arrived, and everyone climbed into the back of it and the flaps were pulled down. After crossing rough roads and occasional cattle grids, they arrived at their destination.

The canvas flaps were pulled aside, revealing a long drive. A soldier inspected their passes carefully before they were driven to a large modern house set in its own grounds. An army sergeant greeted them and showed them round the house before taking them to their individual rooms.

Later, Francine knocked on Valérie's door and said, 'Let's go and explore the grounds.'

A heather garden lay at the back of the house near a tennis court. It brought back memories of blue and pink heathers in the gardens of the Château of Chambord, south of Orléans, where her Uncle Georges had taken her when they visited the châteaux of the Loire. Was he still working in Paris? They hadn't heard from him since before the Occupation. Her thoughts were broken by Francine calling out to her, making Valérie laugh as she skipped ahead of her.

After crossing a well-tended lawn and a bumpy field, they came to a lake shaped almost like a horseshoe where they sat down.

'It's so peaceful here. Six weeks here will be heaven for me after living in London for so long. My daughter would love it too,' said Francine.

'Have you thought that if you go to France to fight the Nazis, you run the risk of never seeing your daughter again? I've asked myself the same question about my family.'

Francine rubbed her eyes. 'Yes. Of course, I have but I am determined to help rid France of those bloody Nazis.'

After lunch in another large house, they met the commandant who gave an introductory talk and handed each student a sheet which listed the training programme. He referred to many of the classes already outlined by Miss Atkins, then explained that there would also be physical training before breakfast, followed by classes. In the afternoon there would be practical exercises on the estate and outside it, including fieldcraft—how to survive in difficult weather and other conditions. Burglary, criminal activity, ciphering and resisting Gestapo interrogations. Also learning all about the German forces, including a multitude of army and SS uniforms and details of their different security organisations, was included.

The students were given the afternoon free, and Valérie suggested going for a walk in the grounds with Christophe.

'How have things been?' she asked him.

'Not easy. I don't want to say much about it, Valérie. It's painful for both Angela and me. I think she suspects that I may have met someone else. But I have never proposed marriage to her because I know very well that if I pass the training, I may never come back from France, and I don't want to inflict that on her. Also, since meeting you, as you know, I have deep feelings towards you. I need to sort this out after the end of this course. But for now, I'd prefer not to talk about any more of this.'

Valérie's heart sank, but she knew that he was right to follow this path.

Next morning the students returned to the large house where they had met the commandant and had breakfast. Then they made their way to a room at the back of the manor and waited for their instructor.

A short thin man came into their room, carrying a large worn canvas bag and a walking stick. He spoke to them in English.

'I'm Anthony Brooker, your instructor in disguise,' he told the students in English. His bright red jumper and his black spiky hair made Valérie grin at Francine. 'This is how *not* to look in the field,' he told them, making the group laugh. 'Now let's start with a volunteer on whom I can practise.'

Didier went up and stood beside the instructor. 'Let's transform Didier into a different person.' Looking intently at the class, he said, 'The secret of a good disguise is not to make too many changes. Don't exaggerate your efforts to change your appearance. Now watch what I do with your friend.' First, he rubbed some special whitener into Didier's brown hair, ageing him instantly. Then he stuffed sponge bags into his cheeks and discoloured his teeth with iodine. Turning to the class after a few minutes, he asked, 'How old would you say Didier is now?'

'In his late fifties, nearing retirement,' Francine called out.

'Hear, hear,' the others agreed.

'If an agent is blown, or "burnt" as they term it in France, you must resort to quicker methods. No time to use any of my powders or make-up,' continued

Brooker. 'It also involves play-acting.' He looked across at Bernadette and said, 'Let's work on you.'

Valérie saw the determination in Bernadette's eyes. As a professional actress she should be convincing.

'Bernadette, imagine the Gestapo has a rough idea already of what you look like. You've lived in a city. Now you've escaped to the countryside. Some of the things at the back of the room might help you to go unnoticed.'

After a few minutes, a hunched woman, dressed in a shabby skirt and black shawl, and her hair tied up under a scarf, shuffled along on a walking stick. Thin-framed spectacles completed the disguise.

Brooker approached her, his head held high, his gait imposing and authoritative. 'Votre carte d'identité,' he demanded.

She hesitated before pulling out her identity card and clearing her throat. 'Le voici Monsieur,' she replied in a croaky voice, and gave it to him.

'Vous habitez où?' he asked her, wanting to know where she lived.

'Dans une ferme près du village,' she replied in a country accent. She stopped, leaning heavily on her stick, and spat into a rag, almost collapsing. 'Je vais chez le docteur.'

Brooker stepped well back from her before turning to his audience. 'Very convincing, isn't she? Tell me why.'

After a long silence, Didier called out, 'She's got signs of TB, but if she'd really been stopped in France, she would have bitten her lip and produced blood. The Boches know there's a lot of TB about and steer clear of it. She's also totally changed her appearance and voice in the shortness of time.'

The students applauded her, and Bernadette bowed several times to her audience.

'The things we learn with Mr Brooker could be a real lifesaver,' Valérie whispered to Francine. 'There's more to Bernadette than I realised. She's bilingual and I reckon she can produce several regional accents. She speaks German too. And Didier knows an awful lot of details about recent life in France. He's obviously been there recently.'

'Tomorrow, each of you will change the appearance of one of the students and give them a part to play,' said Brooker. 'Remember, as you saw with Bernadette, it's not just a question of slapping make-up on. You must assume the personality of another person.'

Before dinner that evening when the students started drinking in the bar, Didier told them, almost in a hushed whisper, that he had discovered where they were staying. 'Our house is called Boarmans and it's one of several grand houses on Lord Montagu of Beaulieu's estate in Hampshire.'

'Sherlock Holmes strikes again,' said Valérie with a laugh. 'How did you discover this?'

'Secret agents don't reveal their sources. Surely you know that?' he replied, winking at her.

After dinner Valérie drew Didier aside and asked him, 'Master of Espionage, I've been wondering about where Florence and Nicole have gone.'

He smoothed his face and looked anxiously at her. 'Failed students go somewhere remote to work so they can't divulge anything to outsiders. Brooker clammed up when I suggested that this was the case, so I knew I'd hit the right note.'

'You must be worried sick about Florence. Let's hope we'll all pass this course and don't end up isolated.'

Later Valérie and Francine studied the list of training classes. 'This is overwhelming. How can we absorb so much information in such a short time?' asked Francine.

'Others have succeeded and so will we,' replied Valérie.

During the first three weeks, the students attended a variety of classes described by the commandant in his welcome speech with practical sessions in the afternoons.

One evening after dinner towards the end of the second week, the students were discussing how the Germans had taken control of the so called 'Free Zone' without much difficulty in November 1942.

'It's going to be hellishly difficult for us to recruit people locally to resist now that the Nazis are in both zones,' remarked Bernadette. 'I'm told many of the French aren't keen to join the Resistance movement and lots of people support Marshal Pétain, the French Head of State, installed by the Nazis.'

Valérie clenched her hands. What a tactless thing to say, she thought.

'Lots of my people are terrified of the Boches, you idiot!' shouted Francine. 'They invaded us only two decades ago and before that as well. We lost thousands of men. They are cruel bastards.' Shaking her fist at Bernadette, she continued, 'You English haven't been invaded for centuries. How can you possibly know what it's like? Shut your bloody mouth once and for all, do you hear? We're all tired of you airing your views on us.'

Valérie realised that Francine had never referred to those supporting Pétain. It was obviously a sore point with her and some of her compatriots. 'Francine, please. I understand why you're angry. You're right—our job will be much more dangerous because people are terrified of joining the Resistance. Listen, we must spend the next three weeks together. Scenes like this help no one.'

'All right, Valérie, but I can't talk to that woman,' said Francine and stormed out.

Towards the end of the fourth week, one evening after dinner, Valérie started to feel drowsy and fell asleep on her bed. Much later she woke up with a start. She listened intently, feeling her body stiffen, and thought she heard a key turn in the lock. It was probably Didier playing the fool. Then the door was thrown open and she started to shake. She half opened her eyes in the light of a powerful torch and saw a tall thin man standing in front of her. She gripped the bedclothes. *It's going to be one of those interrogations Miss Atkins and the commandant warned us about.*

'Heraus. Schnell. Heraus!' he screamed at her. 'Aus dem Bett!' By now she could hardly move and was frozen with terror. A woman, dressed in a grey-green

SS uniform, shone the torch in her face, blinding her, while the tall man and a shorter one started to pull her out of bed. She retaliated by kicking them. *Don't scream, don't say anything.* The woman blinded her again with the torch and one of the men stuffed a cloth in her mouth and ordered her to follow the woman out of the room. 'Kein Wort. Verstehen Sie?' She knew better than to resist. Someone half opened a door to one of the bedrooms. The woman slammed it shut, almost trapping the person's fingers. Valérie started to shake again.

They took her to the other end of the house where no students were sleeping and reached a small room which was almost empty and already lit. Having pushed her inside, the tall man ordered her to stand still.

The woman pointed to some telephone directories in a corner. 'Pick those up at once,' she ordered her in French with a strong German accent. Her arms almost gave way as she lifted the books.

'Now hold them on your head. It's in your interest not to move at all,' the woman screamed at her. Start counting, she reminded herself, remembering the advice of one of the instructors. The tall man, dressed in a black leather coat and trilby hat, moved up close to her, almost nose to nose, and spoke to her in French. 'We know you're French. What is your name?'

She said nothing.

'Your name. Don't waste my valuable time.'

Again, she did not answer.

'What is your circuit leader called and where is he?'

'I don't understand anything you are saying.'

Moving slightly towards her, he lowered his voice. 'I can make things relatively easy for you or …'

'Or we can use all our talents on you,' intervened the woman in a hateful tone of voice.

Valérie shuddered. What did she mean?

'And we have a wide variety,' added the short thin man who wore a cap. 'Give us his name,' he ordered.

By now Valérie felt the pain in her arms which was excruciating. She dared not drop the directories. Things could only worsen and become more painful.

Suddenly the woman pulled a leather strap out of her pocket. 'Bitch. We haven't much time. Now start telling us all we need to know, or I'll use this on you. The swine's name for a start. Then yours.'

Valérie's stomach knotted. She couldn't bear the thought of the woman using a strap, which she was holding, on her. Their voices became an unintelligible cacophony, louder and louder, deafening her. Someone snatched the directories. A raucous laugh erupted from the woman and within seconds Valérie was drenched in freezing water. She shook as much of the water off herself as she could. She stood there in defiance and remained silent.

'OK. Stop, everyone,' said someone in a distinguished English male voice. Spotlights were directed in her face that were so bright she could not make out their faces. Slowly, she started to identify them: the tall thin man pulled off his trilby hat and leather coat and she immediately recognised Colonel Woolrych, the Beaulieu commandant.

The short stout man removed his cap and revealed his short hair, cut sprightly like a hedgehog—it was Mr Brooker, master of disguise. But the biggest surprise of all was when Lieutenant Maureen Brown revealed her identity. How had she somehow managed to change her facial appearance, the tone of her voice, and become a hateful interrogator?

'There will be more sessions like this,' she said, 'but you responded well. We know you have it in you to become an effective agent. But future interrogations here will be much tougher than tonight's.' She pulled out a towel and handed it to Valérie to dry herself.

Once Valérie had returned to her room, she sat there for a few minutes, feeling disorientated. She then changed into some dry clothes. Despite a knock on the door, she was reluctant to open it, fearing that they might return and start another interrogation; she couldn't bear the thought of that and so she called out, 'Who is it?'

'Christophe.'

Relieved to hear his voice, she opened the door and burst into tears. He put his arm round her and kissed her gently on the cheek. 'I saw you being dragged along the corridor and guessed that the instructors were taking you somewhere for an interrogation, but I didn't recognise any of them.'

She looked up into his eyes. 'So, it was you I saw opening a door.'

'Yes. And whoever slammed the door on me nearly broke my fingers.'

'That was Lieutenant Brown.'

'You're joking. Now I can see why they made us learn our cover stories so thoroughly,' he said. 'But come to my room. I've got a drop of whisky. It will do you good to relax after that ordeal.'

She reluctantly agreed to accept his offer.

Christophe invited her to sit down while he opened a bottle of whisky, but the top fell onto the ground by her feet. She bent down to pick it up and as she gave it to him, their fingers touched. He put the bottle and top down on the table and turned towards her. Her body quivered. He kissed her gently on the lips, then took her into his arms and started to kiss her, his powerful lips on hers made her feel a wave of warmth sweep through her body, and she could feel his arousal. She ached for him, but she thought of Angela, and gently pulled herself away from him.

Christophe looked at her in despair. 'I love you totally, Valérie. We might never meet again.'

'Christophe, I love you in the same way, but we must think of Angela …'

Valérie's experiences on the surveillance training had been both challenging and rewarding in parts. At the end of the fourth week, she and Francine discussed the classes and practical sessions they had experienced.

'Which did you prefer?' asked Francine. 'Being followed or following someone?'

'Following but trying to keep tabs on Mr Brooker was a real nightmare. We were in Bournemouth. He was carrying a bag and dived into Beales, the department store, and changed his appearance, but he hadn't changed his distinctive shoes and that gave him away. I was waiting for him, hidden of course, outside the gents. He led me a right dance round the town, but I managed to keep my distance without losing him. Finally, he met Maureen Brown and I joined them. They both congratulated me.'

They had enjoyed lighter moments together: having been praised by the criminal skills instructor when they had carried out a raid on the commanding officer's house, leaving a cheeky message.

At the beginning of the fifth week, early one morning Valérie dragged herself upstairs, carrying a large paper bag. She fumbled in the bag for her key and heard a familiar voice. It was Francine.

'Wherever have you been?' she asked. 'I knocked on your door late last night to borrow something, but there was no reply. I guessed that you were fast asleep.'

'No such luck. At midnight, Lieutenant Brown, and her ensign, took Bernadette, Didier, and me at to Beaulieu Heath, telling us that we were going on a fieldcraft exercise.'

'Oh, my goodness me. No wonder you look in a state. Whose clothes are you wearing?'

'Lieutenant Brown's. I got soaked to the bone and my wet clothes are in this bag. Let's get into my room and I'll tell you more.' Once inside, she flopped onto her bed. 'They dropped us in different places on Beaulieu Heath. We were given a map, a torch and a compass. We had our own wristwatches. They told us to meet them two and a half hours later at the exact spot where we first arrived.

'How on earth did you cope?'

'After about two hours, fighting my way through thick undergrowth of bracken, gorse, and thorns, it started to pour with rain. I was relieved to find a clearing and knew that I only had about another half hour to go. Then guess what?

'I can't imagine,' said Francine.

'I fell into a bog.'

'Oh no!'

'I was almost up to my waist in it with an acrid smell of water, decaying vegetation, and peat, making me heave as I struggled to try and pull myself out. In the end guess who rescued me?'

'No idea.'

'Mr Brooker.'

During the last week, the finishing test, known as the four-day scheme, was a challenging one. The students had to devise and activate it within the time frame. Valérie had to identify a target and fulfil several other remits. She decided to stop some of the trains coming into Waterloo Station on a specific day. Her new operation evolved after having read an article in a newspaper about a prominent right-wing political leader who was going to hold an open-air meeting. The article mentioned that many of his followers were coming into London to support him. That meant travel by public transport.

Through clever planning and approaching some dubious characters, and rewarding them, Valérie succeeded in laying two packages on the railway lines between Waterloo and Clapham Junction in the early morning, before rush hour. When the police arrested and interrogated her, she never revealed anything. When she finally gave them a password, the police revealed that her organisation had previously warned them of her proposed scheme. And in fact, the organisation had followed her throughout the operation.

On the journey back to Beaulieu, Valérie shuddered at the thought of a German patrol arresting her, after planting real explosives on a railway track in France. She closed her eyes, took a deep breath, and pushed the thought aside. Better to think about the many skills she had acquired since the day she had been recruited and wonder which would prove the most useful when her real life in enemy-occupied territory began.

'It was a worthwhile scheme. Once in France, our organisers will expect us to take part in planning an operation,' she told Francine.

Valérie returned home, and a week later, she received a letter, telling her that she had passed the course at Beaulieu and that she should attend Orchard Court with the date and time indicated. When she reread it, she could feel the passion building up inside her. France, the country where she had been born, awaited her in all its misery and isolation. And she was going there to help those who resisted.

She would not see Orléans, her mother's town, nor meet her grandmother, aunts, uncles, and cousins. There would be no more hunts through the Sologne Forest with her uncle, nor would she enjoy large family festive occasions when tasty trout, and other fish from the Loire, were cooked in delicious sauces, accompanied by unforgettable local dry white wines. Her role as a courier and saboteur was of prime importance.

Two weeks later, towards the end of March 1943, Marie-Claire arrived at Orchard Court for an interview with Miss Atkins.

'Do sit down, Marie-Claire,' Miss Atkins told her. 'Congratulations on joining our organisation. It's a pity though that you couldn't go on the parachute course.'

'I would have loved the challenge,' said Marie-Claire, 'but I have a large scar from a recent appendicitis operation, and it was too risky.'

Miss Atkins pulled out some papers from a drawer and placed them onto her desk. 'I need to talk to you about some personal matters. Your salary will be paid regularly into your bank,' she said, looking at her more intently. 'In the event of your death, we will provide a pension for your family, so you will have to make a will. I have the forms already made out, with your next of kin as beneficiaries, ready for you to sign. If there are any special bequests, please write them down.'

Marie-Claire took the forms and found her hands starting to shake a little as she studied them. Of course, she didn't want to die. Nor did she want to make her parents suffer. But she had to take that risk to help France regain her freedom. The Nazis were sadistic beasts. She thought of Mamy, her beloved maternal grandmother in France. She'd leave her gold necklaces and bracelet to her and wrote her request and others onto the forms. After studying them carefully again, she signed them and gave them back to Miss Atkins.

Miss Atkins then took out some more paperwork from her desk, as well as a map of Central France. 'Here are your briefing forms which you must read and sign at the bottom,' she said and passed them to Marie-Claire. 'Study them while you are here, and I will return for them later. Each agent takes on a new identity, as you will have learned on your last course when we practised your cover story, and you underwent mock interrogations. The mission you will be sent on is dangerous. But before you fill in those forms, I have your cover story here. We'll practise it again.'

'So, if the Gestapo get hold of me, I need to remember everything in that cover story?' said Marie-Claire.

'Exactly. Now let's go over Véronique's life,' said Miss Atkins. 'What is your name and where were you born?'

'Véronique Perrin and I was born in 1921 in Authie near Caën,' replied Marie-Claire.

The further they went over the cover story, the more Marie-Claire wondered how she was ever going to remember all the salient points in Véronique's life.

'Is Véronique still alive?' she asked Miss Atkins.

'Yes, but I assure you that Véronique's birth and other records were destroyed in a bombing raid.' She took a few moments before continuing. 'As you know your field name is Valérie—to be used with your organiser, circuit members and Resistance people working with the circuit. However, the name on your identity and ration cards for food and clothes is Véronique Perrin and only to be used for officials, public places and outsiders. Before you leave for France, we will go over your cover story several times.'

Next Miss Atkins spread the map out onto her desk. 'Now I must talk about your travel to France and your duties out there. You will go into the field with another agent by Lysander aircraft and will be met by Gilbert, our air movements officer, and his assistant at St Martin-le-Beau, not far from Tours.' She pointed to the town on the map. 'Gilbert will give you a bicycle. Don't accompany him and the other agent. He has been told that you will be independent. These forms contain your instructions in detail. You will be given a compass. In France, your organiser, Marcel, will expect you to use his password when approaching him for the first time and when meeting the rest of the circuit. We have already practised this password which is contained in these forms. Ensure the circuit members give you the correct reply. You must always obey Marcel's instructions. Your circuit's name is *Fisherman*. You will be taking nine hundred thousand francs with you—two hundred thousand francs each for Marcel, Emile and yourself, and three hundred thousand francs for the Maquis, young men who have fled to the countryside to avoid compulsory work in Germany and who've recently joined the Resistance.'

Marie-Claire was finding it difficult to absorb everything. Miss Atkins pointed out that her code name for ciphering and deciphering messages, via the circuit's wireless operator in France, was *Editor*. Don't forget to find a hiding place, a *cachette*, when you've settled in and inform London of its location. You would use this as a place to go for safety while making arrangements to be helped on the escape line. Details are on the forms.'

Much to Marie-Claire's astonishment, Miss Atkins pulled out several picture postcards from her drawer. 'One last request, please, Marie-Claire. As your parents will think that you're going away somewhere in Britain, which we've already asked you to tell them, we need you to write a few postcards to them, showing different areas in the country. I realise this will be upsetting for you, but we need you to do it. Spread the dates over two or three years. Now I'll leave you and return in about an hour's time.'

Marie-Claire read and memorised all the information on the forms, realising what a huge responsibility she had taken on. Then she signed them. Writing the postcards was a painful exercise and she wondered whether her mother would suspect that they were a cover of some sort.

On Miss Atkins's return, she collected the forms and postcards and took Marie-Claire to meet Major Buckmaster, head of the organisation.

'Welcome to the organisation, Marie-Claire. How did you find the training on the second course?'

'Challenging but exciting,' she replied.

'And how do you feel about going to France, now a dangerous and intimidating place where you could be arrested at any time by the Gestapo?'

'I know how threatening it is out there, but I am determined to do everything I can to rid France of the Nazis.'

'I admire all you agents tremendously,' he replied and took out something from his drawer and gave it to her.

Marie-Claire removed the cover and gasped—it was a gold powder compact with a shiny stone set in an engraved surround. 'Thank you so much, but it's too good to take to France,' she said.

He placed his hand on her shoulder. 'If you're ever short of money and alone, this will fetch a good price in France.' He shook her hand and wished her good luck. 'Either Miss Atkins or I will accompany you with another agent to the airfield.'

CHAPTER FOUR

ARRIVAL IN FRANCE IN MID-APRIL

Valérie stood and admired her French-styled suit with its long jacket and tailored buttons and a blouse, which lay on her bed in a safe house where she was staying, before flying to France. A plain navy coat completed her outfit. To think these clothes had been made in London with French labels inside. It was just as well that they had been worn several times by other people, she thought. She changed into the clothes and looked at her watch. It was already gone three in the afternoon. She grabbed her suitcase and handbag and hurried downstairs where she joined Miss Atkins and a man in his mid-thirties with light blue steely eyes that hardly made contact. Not somebody one would challenge.

'Good. We're ready to leave,' said Miss Atkins and led them outside to a chauffeur-driven estate car. They left London and the suburbs and reached the Sussex countryside where trees and bushes were bursting forth in colour. At around about six in the evening, they arrived at an old ivy-covered cottage, opposite the main entrance to the RAF station at Tangmere in Sussex, partially hidden behind tall hedges.

They were welcomed by their pilot, a flight lieutenant. Afterwards Miss Atkins took them upstairs into a bedroom where they left their cases and coats. She led them downstairs into the operations room, known as the ops room, where the smoke from cigarettes made Valérie choke. Some pilots were smoking, laughing, and relaxing. And in the background a record of a French man singing a haunting, yet beautiful, song could be heard from the gramophone in the corner of the room. Shortly afterwards Miss Atkins and her agents joined the pilots for dinner in the lounge-cum-dining room where Valérie enjoyed a crusty shepherd's pie and an apple crumble doused in smooth and rich custard. English dishes she might not savour for some time. Or maybe never.

After the meal, they relaxed in the ops room where they could hear the same record being constantly played. Valérie looked across the room and noticed their pilot standing by the window, drawing heavily on his cigarette, and lost in thoughts as the French singer continued singing his song. Snatches of 'Venez

Donc Chez Moi'— 'Come Up to My Place'—captivated Valérie's imagination, especially the words, 'Love must soon come to me because it's too painful high up here and all alone.' The singer was living in a flat high up, overlooking Paris. What was their pilot thinking about? Would he make it back to Tangmere? She drew in a deep breath. Or would he die in the sky? She paused, feeling tears in her eyes. Would she survive her time in France?

Later the pilot prepared them for the flight to France. 'The pilots on this run are known as the "Moon Squadron" because we can fly people like you to France only when there's a full moon, or on a week either side of it. We're also known as "pick-up" pilots,' he said.

He pulled out a map showing the landing field, east of Tours, as well as a photograph of the area and he told them, 'You'll be flying in a Lysander. We call them Lizzies.' This amused Valérie in contrast to the poker-faced male agent. 'Once we cross the Channel and have crossed a large area of France, from your seats under the transparent hood, you'll be able to see the River Loire beneath you and follow its loops in the moonlight, a magnificent sight. A little later, you'll see the Cher, the Loire's tributary, which is close to your reception.' He paused and in a more serious tone of voice, he said, 'Once we land, the whole operation must take no more than three or four minutes and that includes time for the outward-bound passengers to board the plane.' He gave them instructions on how they would board the aircraft with their luggage and how they would disembark as well. 'In certain circumstances, I might turn back if the lights below are not laid out properly by the reception people, or if I'm not satisfied with the exchange of Morse signals with the people on the ground. Let's hope that's not the case tonight.'

Once their pilot had finished, Miss Atkins interviewed the agents in a bathroom on the first floor. This organisation was obsessed with bathrooms, concluded Valérie, trying not to laugh. When she emptied Valérie's pockets and bags to verify that there was nothing of English origin in them, and checked her identity card, coupons for food and clothes, as well as application forms for more coupons, Valérie shuddered at the thought that one day it could be the Gestapo searching her.

After rehearsing Valérie's cover story, Miss Atkins pulled out a sheet of paper from her bag. 'Now we need to go over the poem that you prepared with your code instructor. Remember the words exactly and never ever write them down in case they fall into enemy hands because it's your only means of communicating with us in code. When you send us a message, remember to indicate the section of the poem you have selected to work on, so that the operator in London can decipher it.' She paused for a moment. 'I'll always remember this part of the last verse because it is particularly poignant.' She read it out aloud:

> Who among you will return
> To the land of gentle green?
> While others lie scattered
> Never to be heard or seen.

'Who wrote it?' asked Miss Atkins.

'I did after my cousin was executed by the Gestapo last year.'

Miss Atkins remained silent for a few moments. 'Remember when to use your field name and your cover name as we discussed already. Also, if you're sending messages by code back to England, remember your code name is Editor.'

Valérie tried hard to concentrate on what Miss Atkins was saying, but the impending flight was uppermost in her mind.

'Remember your password and the response,' Miss Atkins reminded her and practised the procedure with her. Then she pulled out a small packet from her bag and as she did so, Valérie noticed how pale faced she had become. 'It's your cyanide pill.' Valérie's throat seized up. The risk of disclosing information to the Gestapo had haunted her, making her choose the suicide option. Other students had decided against it and were determined never to disclose anything to the Gestapo, whatever torture they were subjected to.

She nodded as she took the capsule and placed it in the secret cavity inside the heel of one of the French shoes she had been given. When she looked up, she saw that Miss Atkins's eyes had darkened. 'I will accompany you to the Lysander and say goodbye,' she said. 'You have proven to be an excellent student and you will, I'm sure, be a trusted and excellent courier.'

After the interview had finished, Valérie went to the bathroom to freshen up, pondering on everything she'd been told. Her stomach ached with apprehension. What lay ahead was daunting. She breathed in deeply several times, trying to unwind, but she could not get rid of the tension building up inside her. Soon she would be on French soil. Anything could happen. She had to stop thinking negatively and think about the jaunts up the West End that she had enjoyed with Daphne. When she returned to the ops room, she tried to make conversation with the other agent, but it was clear that he didn't want to socialise.

Shortly after ten o'clock the large chauffeur-driven estate car arrived and took Miss Atkins and the two agents to the tarmac, a journey of ten minutes. Valérie stepped out of the vehicle and could see a large shape in the distance, parked off to one side on the grass. As she came closer, she stopped in her tracks and admired the Lysander under the moonlight. It was larger than she'd imagined with its enormous wings dominating the body and tail. A metal ladder was attached to the side of the plane, and secured at a slight angle, so that it appeared curved like the body of the aircraft itself. She breathed in deeply. How would she ever climb that ladder in the dark, even though its rungs had white fluorescent paint on either side?

'This is where we say goodbye,' said Miss Atkins, putting a hand on her shoulder. 'Be on your guard at all times, Valérie,' she said. 'We will be thinking of you.'

'Thank you for all your help and care,' said Valérie, keeping her emotions in check, and walked towards the Lysander.

The male agent climbed up the ladder and hauled himself with difficulty into the plane. Valérie managed to climb up several of the steps and pass the suitcases to him and give him time to store them. Finally, she climbed the ladder carefully and, with his help, heaved herself into the aircraft. Once inside she could see how cramped they would be. The agent had placed their luggage in the space underneath their hinged wooden seat and on the shelf in front of it. When she sat down, she turned her head and banged it on a fuel tank behind her which blocked her view of the cockpit. Later she learned that it was an extra fuel tank that had been incorporated in the plane for the long journey. Their pilot climbed up the ladder and hauled himself into the plane. He spoke to the male agent, giving him some headphones and showing him where to plug them in. 'We can communicate during the long flight. Make sure you're alert all the time and scan the night sky for German night fighters that might intercept us. Warn me immediately, of course.' He then showed them how to open and close the canopy and went over the procedure to be followed once they had landed. 'I've already done several of these flights so you're in safe hands.' He pulled down the Perspex hood and left to climb into his cockpit.

As he turned the plane round towards the runway, Valérie looked through the canopy and, in the moonlight, she could see Miss Atkins waving to them. Would they meet again? She hoped so. She covered her ears when the pilot opened up the engine to full throttle and uncovered them only when the noise receded after take-off. Soon they were airborne and flying over the Channel, but once they reached the French coast, Valérie felt her stomach churn as the pilot descended to about four hundred feet to avoid the German anti-aircraft guns. She began to shiver and rubbed her legs and arms to keep warm. The male agent seemed a cold man and his steely eyes made her wary of him. What role was he going to play? If he was an organiser, God help anyone working under him, she thought.

One and a half hours later, she spotted the River Loire, snaking its way under the glistening moonlight. How were the Resistance people doing down there? she asked herself. And where was Francine? Was she already operating somewhere in France? How was Aunt Marguerite coping after the loss of Philippe? How were his two brothers? Would Maman eventually guess what kind of work she had undertaken? If so, how would Dad cope with her?

Two and a half hours later, the pilot announced, 'It's now nearly two in the morning in France. We're nearly ready to land at St Martin-le-Beau. You can see the Cher below. I need to spot the reception committee.'

By now Valérie knew that the operator below would soon flash a red light with an agreed Morse code to which the pilot would respond with a different letter. Then three torches, in a L Shaped Flare Path, would be lit ensuring a safe landing.

The descent made Valérie's stomach turn and, when they touched down, she was nearly jolted from her seat as the aircraft shook and jerked over the rough ground. The male agent climbed down the ladder and Valérie passed the cases and her bag down to him. She grabbed the outgoing passengers' two cases and stored them. Finally, she climbed down to step onto her homeland's ground. As she picked up her case and bag, a tall man stepped forward. 'I'm Gilbert, the air movements officer. Speed is of the essence,' he told them, making it clear that he oversaw the operation. His assistant helped the outward-bound passengers into the Lysander. Gilbert supervised its departure. As Valérie saw it climb into the sky, she prayed that everyone would arrive in England safely.

Gilbert and his assistant pulled out two bicycles from some bushes and handed them to the agents, telling the male agent, 'We'll take you to a nearby forest, and we'll stay there until the curfew ends. After that we'll accompany you to the railway station in Tours.' He turned to Valérie. 'I understand that *you* are making your way elsewhere. It's not the usual practice, I must say,' he told her in a supercilious tone of voice, 'and from a security point of view, it puts us all at risk. Once you've made your contact, return the bicycle to a bistro called Le Vieux Moulin in Tours near the railway station. And make sure you do.'

She strapped her suitcase onto the carrier behind the seat of the bicycle and checked the time on her watch. It was nearly two fifteen in the morning. It was time to be free of this man, so she turned her back on him and departed, glad of the moonlight to help her find somewhere to hide as soon as she could. No use going to the Amboise Forest nearby because that was where Gilbert and the two men were going to head for and there was something about Gilbert she didn't like.

She cycled on, looking everywhere, and was relieved to find a copse further on. That's ideal, she thought and started to make her way towards it when she heard a rumble in the distance that made her freeze. It sounded like several lorries. Surely the Nazis hadn't spotted the plane and were already searching. She swerved off the road, threw her bike into the undergrowth and hid behind some bushes. When three lorries came into view, preceded by a large black Citroën driving at a slow speed, she stiffened with fright and started to sweat. The

Gestapo were almost certainly in that Citroën and were probably investigating. After they had gone, she started to shake. This time luck was on her side, but it might not always be like that. She would always have to be on the alert wherever she went.

When she reached the copse, she hid her bicycle in some bushes. She sat down on a nearby log, thinking about what she had just seen. What were the Nazis looking for? Had the Resistance been betrayed? She started to shiver and pulled out a thick jumper from her suitcase and put it on, wrapping her coat round her like a blanket. Thank goodness one of the pilots at Tangmere had given her a packet of biscuits and she started to eat some avidly. The journey ahead to Larçay, a village about eleven kilometres from St Martin-le-Beau, would take her about three quarters of an hour. She would leave just after seven, when the curfew ended.

She thought of Christophe. If he had passed the second course, he would go to Scotland on a tough paramilitary one, he'd told her secretly. Would they ever see each other again? She often saw him in her thoughts. Did he think of her in a similar way? She started to feel drowsy, but she knew that somehow, she had to keep awake and be ever watchful for any danger emerging.

She looked at her watch: half past six. Soon it would be time to depart. She nibbled the rest of the biscuits, tidied her hair, and prepared herself ready for her departure.

Immediately after seven, she set off for Larçay. She cycled for about half an hour in open countryside around her, until she reached the bridge in Véretz, a village which boasted an imposing château overlooking the Cher. Then she continued on her way to Larçay. At about a quarter to eight, she arrived there and found Patricia's cottage, attached to the bakery, in a side road off the main street. It was typical of the area with its pale grey walls, dormer windows on the first floor, and a slated roof. It was now nearly eight o'clock. After three knocks on the door, it was opened by a short, dark-haired woman in her late twenties.

'Has Matthew recovered from his illness?' Valérie asked her.

The woman smiled in recognition of the circuit passwords. 'Yes. He left hospital three days ago and is much better.' Valérie sighed with relief.

'My name is Valérie,' she said.

'Thank goodness you've arrived safely and my name's Patricia. Mother is asleep, so we'll have to be quiet,' she whispered and showed her into a small living room. 'Wait here while I prepare something to eat; we're lucky because we barter the bread we make for other items of food.'

Valérie sank into a soft armchair and relaxed her aching limbs. The room brought back happy memories of her grandmother's living room in St Jean-le-Blanc, near Orléans. Pottery from Giennes was displayed on an oak dresser, an ancient grandfather clock was ticking away and a bottle holder, made from vine wood, was displayed on a nearby shelf. On a table by the window was a wedding photograph, showing Patricia in her wedding dress and her husband, a handsome man with an engaging smile. Where was he now? Valérie's thoughts were broken by Patricia coming into the room.

'Alain and I were married two years ago. We were …' She forced back tears from her large brown eyes. 'He was sent to Germany for STO last Spring—the compulsory work service introduced by Marshal Pétain, appointed as head of state by the Boches. I received two letters in the summer and autumn, but I've heard nothing since,' she whispered. 'Someone I know took me to meet Marcel and he asked me to join his circuit. We all want France to be rid of this vile occupying force. Let's go and have something to eat,' she said and took Valérie into a small kitchen where fried eggs, crusty French bread with butter and a hot bowl of coffee awaited her.

'I thought real coffee wasn't available in France now,' said Valérie.

Patricia smiled. 'Marcel gave me some—it came in the containers when the British last made a drop.'

After they had eaten, Patricia asked Valérie if she would like to sleep for a few hours. 'It's now nine o'clock. I'll wake you in time for lunch after twelve,' she said.

'A good idea. I'm exhausted,' she replied.

Patricia led her up a narrow staircase and showed her into a small bedroom with a beamed ceiling. 'I'll wake you up later.'

Valérie pulled off her clothes and got into bed, pulling the covers over her. As she ran her fingers over the feathered mattress, thoughts started to swirl in her mind about her immediate plans; make her way to the Ronsard Hotel in Tours, owned by Madame Duclos, stay there for two days, and contact Marcel, her organiser. He would introduce her to Emile, her wireless operator, who would send an encoded message to London, confirming her safe arrival. She would have to find somewhere to live, as well as a cachette, and inform London about the latter with Emile's help.

She would need to go to the chemist shop where it had been arranged for her to work a few hours each week as a cover, unless of course she was on a mission.

What sort of man was Marcel, her organiser?

They would be working together for long periods. How would it work out?

CHAPTER FIVE

AN UNFORGETTABLE WELCOME DURING MID-APRIL

Valérie was awoken by loud knocks on the front door below. Some minutes later, Patricia hurried up the stairs and came into her room, looking agitated. 'It's eleven o'clock. You need to leave straight away because the Boches are doing house-to-house searches a few kilometres from here and there are roadblocks. One of our circuit members will take you to a safer place.'

Glancing at her watch, Valérie realised that she had slept for less than two hours. She struggled into her clothes and checked the hem of her skirt, where some of the bank notes were hidden while the rest were hidden in a false bottom of her bag. She grabbed her suitcase and bag and hurried downstairs where Patricia introduced her to a short stocky man in his forties with grey hair.

'Jacques is going to take you away now. It'll be safer for you because our friends have a chateau where they can conceal you better,' said Patricia.

'We must hurry,' said Jacques anxiously. 'Give me your case and I'll strap it onto the back of your bicycle.'

They cycled through open countryside and villages, making two stops to recuperate. Towards half past twelve, before they approached Bléré, Jacques called to Valérie to leave the road immediately. 'There's a Citroën in the distance. Quick. Throw your bicycle into those bushes over there and lie down here. If the car doesn't turn left at the crossroads, where we need to turn off, we'll be all right,' he whispered. He grimaced as the car whisked past them. 'I've seen that black Citroën before. It's the Gestapo.'

Acid surged up into her throat. The thought of being arrested and interrogated by the Gestapo, after only a few hours on French soil, terrified her.

Peering out through the bushes, they saw the car travel beyond the crossroads and breathed sighs of relief, but Jacques insisted they remain hidden for a while. 'You never know if there are more cars to follow with detainees.' Putting his hand on her shoulder, he added, 'This is what your life is going to be like in future.'

He was right, of course. Her life would be continuously at risk by liaising with people, running messages, helping Marcel in sabotage raids on railway lines and in factories, carrying out whatever other operations he planned and working in tandem with local résistants, but Wanborough and Beaulieu had prepared her well for this work and had given her the confidence to face the dangers ahead.

They recovered their bicycles and cycled to the crossroads, turned left and continued their journey until they reached a long drive, with poplars on either side, leading to a small château. They hurried round to the back of the building and hid their bicycles in a shed before making their way to a kitchen door, where Jacques tugged at a bell pulley three times, with pauses in between.

'This is the circuit's method of gaining entry to places we need to visit. Remember this.' Someone moved a curtain slightly before the door was opened by a slim woman in her late thirties, with fair, shoulder-length hair, pale blue eyes and facial features that reminded Valérie of the delicate eighteenth-century figurine sculpture that took pride of place on the mantelpiece in her uncle's flat in Paris.

'Bonjour, Jacques. Bonjour, Mademoiselle. Do come in,' said the woman and took them into a large kitchen where she invited them to sit down at a long table. 'We've heard there's trouble in Tours,' she told them. 'Marcel stopped by to warn us that you would both be coming here so I delayed going to the school.' She turned to Valérie, 'Mademoiselle, you can stay here for a few days, but in the meantime, we need to find out what this Boches activity is all about. If danger appears in the neighbourhood, we'll have to move you out of the area for a while. I'll take you to the top floor, but firstly let me offer you both something to eat. You must both be famished. It has already gone one o'clock. Lise, my mother-in-law, will give you something for lunch and we'll bring your dinner this evening at about half past seven.'

After they had eaten, Jacques told Valérie that Marcel would almost certainly contact Madame Duclos at the hotel to explain her delay. 'Now I must leave, Jeanne,' said Jacques. Turning to Valérie, he said, 'Sooner or later we'll meet again, but remember what I told you about Tours. Be careful when you contact people. We can never be sure who is loyal to France or who might betray us to the Boches, especially in this city where many people support Pétain.'

Once they had reached the top floor, Jeanne took Valérie into a small living room and opened a large cupboard where a few dresses and jackets were hanging. She pulled the clothes aside, took out a key from her pocket and opened a small door that led into a bedroom without windows. 'This room has been in here since revolutionary times. We've used it only occasionally to hide people, but we must think of our family. Security is tighter than ever since the enemy invaded the Free Zone last November.'

'I'm sorry to put you to so much trouble, Madame.'

'Not at all. I'll leave you two keys: one for the bedroom and one for the living room. I'll lock both doors on my way out with my own set of keys. There's a toilet and handbasin in the corridor outside when you turn right. Now I must return to school where I teach and where my two daughters are.'

After Jeanne had gone, Valérie refreshed herself and changed into a dress. She sat down in the small living room and noticed a newspaper, la Dépêche du Centre, lying on a table and started to read it. Revulsion tore through her when she saw a photograph of Marshal Pétain shaking hands with a Nazi general. Then the sight of a poster sickened her because it showed several résistants' photographs, coupled with warnings of arrest and deportation to those who harboured or assisted them. She decided to continue reading the newspaper, to gain information about daily life in France under the Nazis. Feeling exhausted, she fell asleep in the chair. Her thoughts were broken by a knock on the door and when she opened it, a petite elderly woman stood before her, holding a tray of food and drink.

'Don't look so worried, Mademoiselle. There's no need to be afraid. I'm Lise, Jeanne's mother-in-law, and my son is called Arnaud. I've brought you something light to eat and drink. Dinner will be at about half past seven tonight when Arnaud returns from his surgery.'

'How kind of you,' replied Valérie.

Lise sat down. 'I've lived here most of my life. My husband died last year so Arnaud became Count Montillac and brought his family here. I'm glad to have their company, especially in these awful times in France. I can see you like reading, from the opened newspaper. I'll bring you up some more. Are there any books you would like to read and what sort?'

'Newspapers, please, to be getting on with,' said Valérie.

'I'll return with some more, I must go now,' said Lise. 'Arnaud may well come up to see you. It depends on whether he's had extra patients to see.'

Valérie enjoyed her apple tart. She decided to retire to the small bedroom and fell asleep but was awoken later when she heard someone enter the adjoining room and then a knock on the wardrobe door. The door opened to reveal a slim man dressed in a smart suit.

'I'm Arnaud, Jeanne's husband. I've come from Tours and it's not good news. Marcel narrowly escaped arrest this morning; thank goodness he never sleeps in one place for more than one night. That's why we use a go-between to contact him.' Looking closely at her, he remarked, 'You're much younger than the previous courier who worked for Marcel. She became ill, but we don't know much about it.'

'Never mind my age. I'm here to defeat the Nazis and take my revenge on them for murdering my cousin.'

His eyes flickered. 'You're not alone in that respect. I'll take you to Tours in a few days' time.' After picking up the tray and moving towards the door, he added, 'We will bring dinner up to you because we cannot risk our two young daughters seeing you downstairs. Children are of no account to the Nazis. If they can manage to force information out of them, that is their only concern, and they don't care how they achieve it.'

'Are you sure you want me to stay here? I would never forgive myself if any of you were arrested.'

'We're prepared to take that risk because we loathe the Nazis. Very few of our citizens are prepared to become actively involved in the Resistance. I can understand why because reprisals are extreme and brutal.'

After a pause Valérie asked him, 'How far away from Tours are we?'

'About three quarters of an hour by car.'

Two days later, Jeanne came to see Valérie one evening. 'Grandma and the girls are staying with relatives for the weekend, so come and join Arnaud and me for dinner downstairs.' She led Valérie into a dining room with walls lined in a heavy wine-coloured material. Valérie guessed that the long oak table and chairs and other furniture must be eighteenth century, remembering her uncle's talks to her about antiques when they had visited many of the Loire châteaux during her summer holidays. The room cheered her up after being enclosed in the rooms upstairs.

Arnaud came into the room. 'I have to do an urgent house call, so I'll eat later,' he said and left.

Having a doctor in the circuit is extremely useful for us, thought Valérie.

'We don't often have dinner here, but I thought it would cheer us up after recent events in Tours,' explained Jeanne.

During the meal Jeanne told Valérie that a group of men had been arrested outside Tours the previous day. Valérie in turn told her about her cousin's murder.

'Arnaud mentioned it to me,' replied Jeanne. 'You're not alone in losing someone close to you. A son, belonging to one of my closest friends, and only aged eighteen, was about to be deported to Germany on the STO programme. He tried to escape, and the Boches shot him. Now we are even more determined to work for the circuit and the Maquis, young men in the Resistance who've fled to the forests to avoid STO.'

A few days later, much to her relief, Arnaud told her that he was taking her to Tours.

'Marcel warned the hotel you would be coming later than at first expected,' he told her. As she walked towards his car with her suitcase and handbag, she looked back at the château. The grey slate roof, with its slight blue tint, sparkled under the morning sun and contrasted well with the grey brickwork. She admired the intricate stonework round the protruding garret windows, crowned with tiny slate roofs.

'We must go,' Arnaud called out to her as he sat waiting for her in his Peugeot saloon.

As she approached the car, she smelt a sweet aroma coming from the engine and asked Arnaud about it. 'Most vehicles are now run on a wood-burning system.' he replied. During the journey he gave her some words of advice. 'Avoid two cafés in particular: Chez Juliette and Au Vieux Renard are often frequented by informers. Don't forget that alcohol is served on alternate days. Use your eyes around the café or bar to see what other people are drinking. Be careful if anyone tries to engage you in conversation.'

As they drove further, the signposts, written in Gothic German, roused feelings of disgust in Valérie. In less than an hour, Arnaud pulled into a side road. 'This is where I'm dropping you off. Good luck. We'll see each other no doubt sooner or later. Remember, if you notice me in Tours, don't acknowledge me and I'll do the same to you. Leave any verbal messages for me with Madame Duclos at her hotel where you are going to stay for a short period. She receives messages for our circuit, mostly by word of mouth, and she has her own methods of relaying them. Sometimes she might use a go-between. She'll show you where Marcel and his circuit members usually leave coded messages if they can't contact her. You'll soon meet other members of our circuit.'

'Arnaud, I've left my bicycle at your place. I should already have returned it to a bistro called Le Vieux Moulin near Tours Railway Station. I'll ask Marcel to help me with that.'

'No problem. Au revoir,' he replied and drove off.

On entering the city, enormous ugly red-and-white banners, each emblazoned with a black swastika, appalled her. She was thinking carefully about the route she had memorised when moments later the unmistakable sound of hard-stepping hobnailed boots could be heard, making her shudder. She walked quickly into a side street. Soon a mass of Waffen-SS men in greenish-grey uniforms came into view. Their rifles shone under the morning sun and the thought of how many people had been killed by these SS thugs sickened her. The realisation that she could soon be engaged in armed combat with them reinforced her inner fear that she might soon lose her life. Every morning she would wake up, not knowing if there would be a tomorrow.

As people walked through the streets, she became aware of the clickety-click of the wooden-soled shoes of passers-by. She stopped in her tracks. She had seen queues in England outside food stops, but not as long as the ones in front of her. Women and children mostly formed the queues that snaked into nearby roads. Outside a bakery, Valérie noticed a young woman, a baby in her arms and four emaciated children huddled around her. The mother's pencil-thin frame, her sunken eyes, and her pale face, brought tears to Valérie's eyes. Old women and a few old men, mostly dressed in black, were also in the queue, some too weak to stand, propping themselves against doors. They almost certainly had little to eat.

She continued her way across the labyrinth of roads and squares, in the direction of the Ronsard Hotel, where she would be staying for a few days.

As she ventured further into the city, towards the rue Commerciale, she came to a halt in disbelief. Gone were most of the banks, individual shops, cafés, and restaurants. A few buildings remained here and there. Her favourite café, Chez Suzannne, stood like a tiny island amidst a cleared bomb site. It was like a ghost city. 'Tours is one of the few closed cities,' Arnaud had told her. 'That means the French army put up a tremendous fight in June 1940 to defend the city. Much of the infrastructure was destroyed as a result.'

She walked towards the old quarter, dominated by the Cathedral of St Gatiën with one of its towers damaged. How much more of it would be destroyed if the Allied bombers came to rescue France? She had loved coming here as a child with Uncle Georges. On impulse, she entered the cathedral, and sat near the front, noticing that the stained-glass panes had been taken away and the windows were boarded up.

She knelt in one of the pews and prayed for her family and those opposing the Boches in France and elsewhere, as well as for those poor people queuing for food hour after hour. Jeanne had told her that the Nazis claimed most of the food, sending some of it to Germany.

Gradually, the cathedral began to fill up. Altar boys made their way out of the sacristy, carrying their candlesticks. She wanted to stay for Mass and to reflect on what had happened during the last few days, but she had to make her way to the Ronsard Hotel. Thank goodness Arnaud or Jeanne had warned them of her delay. She picked up her suitcase and bag and left.

She took some time to find the hotel near the railway station. The outside had probably been painted shortly before the Occupation. It was a turn-of-the-century two-storey building with steps leading up to the main entrance. At reception, a short woman in her mid-fifties welcomed her.

'I'm Madame Duclos, the proprietor of the hotel. How can I help you?'

After exchanging passwords, the woman took a key off a rack behind her. 'Come with me and I'll show you to your room,' she told Valérie and led her towards the back of the hotel to a room on the ground floor. Once inside the bedroom, Madame Duclos continued almost in a whisper, 'This is the best room because you can make a quick exit by turning left when you come out of your door and the way out is at the bottom of the corridor. Now can I see your identity card, please?'

Valérie handed her the card which Madame Duclos checked. 'I'm known as Valérie within the circuit.'

'Have you found lodgings yet?'

'Not yet because I had to make a detour as you know.'

'I have a friend who may be able to help you. Of course, I would refer to you as Véronique Perrin when talking to her. I'll let you know. Always lock your door and take the key out. I must warn you of any trouble and if you're asleep, I can use my pass key. Breakfast is between half past seven and half past nine. Dinner is between six and eight. Marcel will soon let me know when and where he'll contact you. Now I must return to reception.'

Valérie thanked the woman and decided to wash and change clothes. Next, she made her way to the pharmacy where she would work part-time as a cover. It was set in a row of old shops not far from the station. On opening the door, she noticed the pharmacist, an elderly bald man, peering over his thin-framed glasses at her. She asked the young sales assistant if she could speak to Monsieur Auger. 'I've come for an interview,' she told her.

'Come here, Mademoiselle, please,' the man called out, beckoning her to the back of the shop. After exchanging passwords, the chemist called out, 'Mireille, take over the shop for a while. If there is an urgent query, call upstairs,' he told the young girl.

Valérie followed him up a twisting staircase until they reached the third floor where he showed her into a room stacked with books and paperwork. She looked out of the window and noticed a park in the distance.

'Do sit down. We have much to discuss. You're supposed to be working here only part-time because you have just recovered from tuberculosis. If the Nazis check up on us, and learn about you, they will soon leave the pharmacy,' he said with amusement. 'Mireille is my daughter and keeps a tight rein on security. Even so I think you should commence by working two afternoons every week. If you're on an operation, I can always say that you're ill. I'll confirm everything with Marcel.'

'It's a good plan,' replied Valérie.

'I'm not very active in the circuit, but I do what I can,' he said, smoothing his tie. 'I have family responsibilities.'

They continued talking about life in Tours and how much tighter security was in the group since Marcel had arrived six months previously. They were interrupted by Mireille calling for her father.

Valérie went downstairs with him, said goodbye, and made her way to a café further away from the station. She decided to sit inside so as not to attract any attention from the Boches passing by. The waiter tried to converse with her, but she feigned a sore throat.

Her thoughts turned to Marcel. She was keen to meet him as soon as possible and meet other circuit members. What kind of leader would he be?

CHAPTER SIX
MEETING MARCEL

A knock at the door and a turn of the key alerted Valérie to Madame Duclos's presence.

'Marcel will meet you at the Renoir Café, in the rue Emile Zola, at ten this morning, so we'll study this map of Tours I've brought along,' she said and started to spread it out onto a table, pointing first to the café. 'Avoid the Gestapo headquarters in the rue Georges Sand, and don't go near the primary school, Ecole Michelet, now turned into a transit camp for prisoners, before they're sent to concentration camps,' she explained, indicating both places.

Valérie caught her breath and looked up at Madame Duclos. 'Thanks for warning me.'

'Circuit members leave verbal messages with me to pass on to others. Some leave short and coded notes under a few bricks by the small statue in the garden at the back of the hotel. If I'm not available, I'll indicate when I'll return and leave it under the bricks. Everyone in the circuit needs to check regularly for messages. We use cover words for people and places, and I'll tell you these later. Lastly, Marcel told me to give you this book. Put the money inside it when you go to the toilet at the café and then give it to him. Now I must go. I'll see you shortly at breakfast. Would you like dinner this evening?'

'Yes, please.'

'Take great care in Tours and elsewhere.'

'I promise you that I will,' said Valérie.

After breakfast, Valérie returned to her room. She took the skirt of her suit from the wardrobe and sat down on the side of her bed. Using the tiny scissors from her sewing kit, she carefully unpicked the hem and took out the money she had been instructed to give to Marcel. Then she sewed the hem up again and slipped the money into the pocket of her jacket. Then she picked up the book and put it into her bag.

On her way to the café, the more German swastika flags she saw that dominated, distorted and disfigured the city, the more resolved she was to face any danger that presented itself. Halfway there, she noticed some Milice wearing dark blue uniforms, khaki shirts and black berets, who were checking identity cards and searching people. The idea of them groping her body repulsed her. She'd have to make a detour, even it if meant being late for Marcel. Eventually, on arrival in the rue Emile Zola at half past ten, she soon spotted the café, shabby on the outside with green paint flaking on the window frames, but the door was freshly painted in black in an amateurish way.

Much to her surprise the inside had been freshly painted and checked tablecloths covered the tables. No other customers were there. 'Don't appear tense,' they had told her at Beaulieu. She chose a table near the side door, an easy getaway.

A middle-aged man, with large horn-rimmed spectacles, came up and started to take her order when a woman, wearing a well-cut blue suit, entered the café.

'Bonjour, Hervé,' she called out.

The waiter finished taking Valérie's order and returned to the bar. 'What are you doing here at this hour, Marie?' he asked, as he started to prepare Valérie's drink and sandwich.

The woman looked across at Valérie and replied, 'Just a friendly call.'

'Are you going to stay for a coffee?'

'Why not, even if it is one of those awful make-believe ones,' she said and perched herself on a bar stool.

'I can do better than that. I have some ground coffee. It's the first I've received in months,' he said.

'You do spoil me.'

'Why shouldn't I treat a friend's wife?'

They continued talking quietly, but even though Valérie caught only the tail end of the conversation, she gleaned some useful information. After a few minutes, the waiter brought Valérie's order over to her when a stocky man in his mid-thirties, with sandy coloured hair, came into the café and joined them.

'It's good to see you, Gaston. Long time, no see. How's life?' asked the waiter.

'Busy. Hervé, is it all right to leave a bicycle in the yard for my friend here?'

'No problem,' he replied. 'What will you have to drink?'

'The usual.'

The man sat down and murmured the password to which Valérie replied. 'Sorry I'm late but I had to do some business on the way,' he told her in French. He lowered his voice. 'I'm known to outsiders as Gaston.' After a pause, he asked her, 'What have you done with the bicycle that Gilbert gave you?'

'I haven't yet returned it to the bistro, Le Vieux Moulin, near Tours railway station.'

'Where is it now?

'Arnaud's place.'

'I'll fix that.' He leaned forward and whispered, 'You're going to have to prove yourself. I need one hundred per cent co-operation. My last courier was useless and became ill. This time I asked for a male courier, but the organisation hasn't listened to me again. They've sent you instead.'

Valérie remained silent. He had no idea how to talk normally to people. How had London ever chosen him to be an organiser? she asked herself.

Hervé served Marcel's coffee. 'Call me if you want anything else. I'll be in the kitchen with my friend,' he said and walked away.

'The Boches arrested a train driver from Tours last night,' whispered Valérie.

'How the hell do you know that?' asked Marcel.

'I overheard Hervé tell his friend.'

'Lots of railway employees work for the Resistance and they take huge risks. We don't have any drivers in our circuit yet, but we're trying to recruit some,' he said and pulled his chair closer to her and whispered, 'Have you brought the money?'

'Yes. Two hundred thousand francs for yourself and three hundred thousand francs for the Maquis,' she said. 'I have the same amount as you and so has Emile.'

'Good. Now to business,' he continued in a quiet voice. 'Tomorrow morning, at around ten o'clock, cycle to Azay-sur-Cher, about ten kilometres from here to the east of Tours. Meet Emile at eleven o'clock down by the river near the end of the village. Sit down on the bench there and he'll join you. Exchange passwords. He'll take you to a safe house to conduct business. When you arrive there, hand over the crystals and money, as well as a newspaper that I'll give you. Now go to the toilet and put the money in the book.'

Marcel was drumming his fingers on the table when she returned to their table and placed the book onto the table.

'If Emile doesn't show up, what shall I do?'

'Return to Tours and leave me preferably a verbal message with Madame Duclos. If she's not there, leave a message in code under one of the bricks in the back garden.' He passed the regional newspaper to her. 'Give Emile this. It's important. Now I must be off. If all goes well today, I'll have another job lined up for you, but much further afield.' As an afterthought, he said, 'Try working at the chemist shop on Monday afternoons, unless of course, I send you on an operation.' He picked up the book and said, 'Now I'll sort my own bill out at the bar. If I hear nothing from you, I'll contact you through Madame Duclos.'

After Marcel had paid his bill, Hervé came up to Valérie with hers and she settled it. 'Your friend's put the bicycle behind the bins in the courtyard,' said Hervé.

'Thanks,' she replied.

'I'm sure we'll see you again. Gaston calls in here quite frequently.'

The next day she set off for the village called Azay-sur-Cher. She avoided the rue Georges Sand and made a detour which took her much longer to leave the city. She followed the River Cher as she rode further into the countryside until she came to wooded areas. After a while she stopped and wiped her brow from the heat. Eventually she approached the village of Véretz, bordered by a loop in the river. The Château of Véretz, with its slate roofline and pointed slate towers, dominated the village. She continued along the main country road until she reached Azay-sur-Cher, passing old terraced and single-storey houses constructed in the Touraine light grey stone with slate roofs, as well as houses with turreted windows under the roofline.

She cycled through the village and towards the river where a tall, slim young man with curly auburn hair framing a thin face, stood by a bench. After exchanging passwords, he said, 'I'm so relieved to meet you. I'm Emile.'

'And I'm Valérie.'

'Have you brought the crystals?' he asked her.

'Yes. Of course.'

'I've been waiting for them. Marcel's other source didn't materialise.' He climbed onto his bicycle and said, 'I'll take you to the safe house now where Raymond will welcome us.'

They cycled out of the village, passing countryside with few houses until they reached a traditional Tourangelle house set in its own grounds. Carrots, cabbages and other vegetables were growing in neat rows to the side of the house. Emile rang the doorbell three times, leaving a long pause in between. An old man with a long bushy grey beard welcomed them. 'Come in,' he said, recognising Emile, and showed them into a room that was comfortably furnished where Emile introduced Valérie to Raymond.

'I'll be outside gardening, but if I see anything suspicious, I'll tap the window. You can escape through the back entrance and dash to the woods at the bottom of the property.'

'Let's hope we won't have any trouble, Raymond,' replied Emile.

Once inside the house, Valérie unstitched an inner pocket in her jacket and pulled out a muslin bag containing two sugar-cube-sized quartz crystals which she gave to him.

'These are fine. The exact type I need,' he said, putting them into a cigarette case. 'Clever things they're making back home to conceal things, aren't they?' he said, grinning.

'Yes. I've got two items like that,' she replied, thinking of the cavity inside the heel of one of her shoes. 'Oh, I forgot to bring in a newspaper for you. Marcel's sent it and said it was important, but I left it in the basket on the back of my bicycle,' she said.

'I'll fetch it,' he said.

While he was gone, she looked round the room and noticed the titles of some of the books on the shelves. Most were historical and when she selected one, she noticed the Tours university stamp inside it. Had Raymond lectured in history at the local university? Her thoughts turned to Emile. Whereabouts did he send his wireless messages to London? How much time did he spend on the air? Many of these wireless operators were traced within six weeks, according to a Beaulieu instructor.

Emile returned with the newspaper and opened it up, looking for a specific page. Once he'd found it, he pulled out a pencil and a piece of paper from his pocket and wrote something down and put it into his cigarette case. Then he tore the newspaper page up into pieces and went into the kitchen to burn them.

On his return to the living room, Valérie told him 'Now I have some money to give you,'.

'I'm in desperate need of it.'

She pulled out the money from the inside pocket of her jacket and gave it to him. 'How can I contact you if I'm in the area?'

'We need to discuss that now. I've already had a word with Father Dominique Lemars, the local parish priest of Véretz and Azay-sur-Cher,' he said. 'He's agreed to let us leave messages at the presbytery in Azay under a slab by a pile of logs in his garden.' He took off his boot and stuffed the money inside his socks. Then he looked at his watch. 'We must leave together now. I'll leave you outside Azay and let you get back to Tours.' He unlocked the door and took Valérie out into the garden. 'We're off now, Raymond. Thanks for everything.'

Valérie was the only guest in the hotel restaurant that evening, but halfway through her meal a German army officer walked into the dining room, accompanied by an attractive young woman. As they passed by her table, Valérie's heart quickened. When Madame Duclos came out of the kitchen, Valérie could see she wasn't pleased to see the German officer.

'Ah, good. We'll start with a whisky and a small light rosé,' the officer told her in his guttural German accent. Madame Duclos gave him the two menus and went to fetch the aperitifs. As soon as Valérie heard the woman making her choices for dinner, she could tell that she was French. Valérie wanted to hurry her meal and leave as soon as she could, but she had to appear unconcerned, despite the woman looking across at her several times. Eventually she stood up and had to pass the couple's table near the exit and as she did so, she heard the woman whispering something to the officer and caught a snatch of the conversation. 'It's too warm for clothes like that.'

The woman, dressed in a summer dress, had obviously noticed Valérie's suit. She would buy more suitable clothes the following day. It was unusually warm for the month of April.

Towards seven o'clock Valérie made her way to the teacher's house in the rue du Cygne. It was on the end of a long row of old three-storey houses that had survived a recent bomb attack. Much to Valérie's amusement, the metal door knocker was in the shape of a fearsome gargoyle.

A short, stout woman in her fifties answered the door. 'Bonsoir. Qui êtes-vous?' she asked.

'Véronique. Madame Duclos gave me your name.'

'Do come in. You're very welcome,' she said, relaxing a little as she showed Valérie into a sitting room, elegantly furnished. 'Madame Duclos told me that you are going to start work at a chemist's shop.'

'Yes. I'll begin next week,' replied Valérie. 'It's part-time so I can help my aunt to care for my grandmother. She lives outside the city, so I'll be here only some of the time.'

'I have a comfortable room for you on the first floor,' said Madame Lelong. 'There's only my work colleague from school who rents the other room. It'll be four hundred francs a month with one month's notice if you need to leave.'

'Yes. That's fine,' she replied and pulled out enough cash from the inside of her jacket pocket and gave it to Madame Lelong.

'Thank you. I've only lived here for a short while,' said Madame Lelong. 'After my husband's death, I came back home to Tours. Now I wish that I hadn't because the atmosphere in this town in untenable. You feel as if you're living in a fortress.'

'That's what everyone keeps telling me.'

'With good reason. One of my sons-in-law, who lived in Tours, was sent to work in Germany a few weeks ago, and we've heard nothing from him since. The family is going through hell now and my daughter is a nervous wreck.'

Valérie stood there, recalling Patricia's husband having been sent to Germany too.

'When will you be moving in?' asked Madame Lelong.

'Is tomorrow evening about eight o'clock convenient?'

'Of course, my dear. Now I must do some work for tomorrow. I've books for two classes to mark this evening.'

Valérie left the rue du Cygne, relieved that she'd found a place to live, and that Madame Lelong had not asked her any questions about her personal life.

The following morning, Madame Duclos came to see Valérie. 'How did your meeting with Madame Lelong go?'

'Fine, thanks to you. I will be moving in tonight.'

'That's good news. I've come to tell you that Marcel is pleased you arrived back safely. Tomorrow morning, he will meet you in the Mirabeau Parc near the Tours railway station at ten.

Was this about the job further afield to which he had already referred? How far away from Tours was it? What kind of operation had he in mind?

CHAPTER SEVEN

A DANGEROUS MISSION IN LATE APRIL

'Valérie, I'm sending you on a mission to Paris,' said Marcel when they met in the Mirabeau Parc near Tours Station. 'Prosper's wireless operator needs crystals to give to another circuit and he will be updating you on an operation that we have to carry out.'

'Who's Prosper?' she whispered.

'He's the organiser of the largest British Resistance circuit in France. We're one of his subcircuits, but I have my own methods of running ours. You'll soon meet his wireless operator, Archambaud, in Paris.'

'How will I make contact?'

'That has yet to be decided,' he replied in a pompous and official tone of voice. 'I'll brief you fully in the next few days.'

A week later Valérie prepared for her journey to the capital. She felt the crystals sewn into her inner jacket pockets. Her rendezvous in the capital, where she would meet Archambaud, was fixed in her mind: Madame Lemercier's flat at sixteen bis Place Dauphine, a square at the far end of the Ile de la Cité where she would hand over the crystals.

As she made her way to the station in Tours, Miss Atkins's warning was uppermost in her mind: 'Be extra vigilant at railway stations in France.' On entering the station, she noticed the Milice, recently introduced, were patrolling everywhere, like wolves seeking their prey. To realise that these thugs were French citizens, ready to arrest those opposed to Marshal Pétain, the so-called head of state, overwhelmed her.

After buying a return ticket to Paris, she joined the queue for identity checks at the barrier guarded by German military. A tall, middle-aged official with protruding dark eyes and dressed in a dark suit, stood alongside the Milice who were inspecting passengers' identity cards. The official looked closely at a woman in front of Valérie and stepped forward to examine her identity card and to ask her questions. The tremor in the woman's voice made Valérie grip her hands to stop them from shaking. Protruding Eyes asked the Milice to take the woman aside and he then took his time to examine Valérie's identity card. Her stomach started to churn, and she prayed he wouldn't question her. To her relief, he returned her card and waved her on.

By now she could feel her legs almost give way, but she forced herself to remember Arnaud's advice about avoiding the first-class carriages because that was where the German military sat. The thought of being confined with the enemy in such a small compartment on a long journey alarmed her. That had been Jeanne's dreadful experience after a German officer had invited her to join him and his colleagues on a journey to Paris.

She climbed up into a second-class carriage, walked along the corridor and managed to find a compartment with a few seats left. A middle-aged couple, accompanying a frail old man, were seated next to an elderly woman. Opposite sat a young man in his late twenties, dressed in a crumpled suit, his hair dishevelled. He was gazing out of the window. A young woman, dressed in shabby clothes, sat further away from him, looking miserable. Marie-Claire decided to sit next to the elderly woman.

Once the train had left Tours, nobody spoke much for the first half hour, but eventually the silence was broken by the arrival of a ticket inspector and the official whom Valérie had noticed at Tours. She'd never seen anyone with such evil-looking eyes.

'Your ticket identity card and ticket please, Mademoiselle,' asked the ticket inspector.

Rummaging inside her handbag and trying to control her shaky hands, Valérie thought her mind was coming to a standstill. If he asked questions, she must remember the drill. The ticket inspector gave her a nervous smile as she handed him her ticket.

'Merci, Mademoiselle. Pas de problèmes,' he said.

However, when it came to the turn of the young man and young woman sitting opposite her, it was another matter. Protruding Eyes stepped forward. 'Your ticket and identity card, Monsieur,' he said in a stern French voice. While he perused them, Valérie saw the ticket inspector's eyes twitching. Looking closely at the man's identity card, the official asked the young man, 'Monsieur Tournier, why are you travelling to Paris?'

'To visit relatives.'

'And where do they live?'

The young man hesitated. 'Near Montparnasse Station.'

'At what address?'

He hesitated before answering, 'Eight rue du Château.'

Protruding Eyes requested more paperwork and stared at the man. 'So, you're a motor mechanic. Who do you work for and where?'

'I run my own motor car repair business in Montrichard outside Tours.'

There was a long silence before Protruding Eyes returned the items to him. Turning his attention to the young woman, he asked for her ticket and identity card. She pulled them out of her inside jacket and handed them over to him.

'Are you accompanying Monsieur?'

'No,' she replied.

'What is the purpose of your visit to Paris, Mademoiselle Botton?'

'To look for a job.'

'Where did you last work?'

'At the hospital in Tours.'

'And do you know Monsieur Tournier?'

Valérie could see the anger increasing in Mademoiselle Botton's grey eyes which were narrowing. 'I've already told you that I don't.'

'And I don't appreciate your insolent tone of voice, Mademoiselle. Be careful.'

Next, he went up to the old woman. 'Your identity card and ticket, please,' he asked her in an exasperated tone of voice.

The woman's hands were trembling as she tried to open her bag, so the middle-aged woman sitting near Valérie got up and undid the stiff zip.

'Thank you, thank you so much, Madame,' said the old lady in a high-pitched voice. She pulled out her identity card and ticket and gave them to Protruding Eyes.

'Why are you travelling to Paris?'

'To meet my brother.'

'His name and address.'

'I've done nothing to warrant this interrogation, Monsieur,' she replied, having regained her composure. 'I've never been treated in this way before by a Frenchman.'

'How dare you address me in that manner? In fact, now I'm going to make a note of your details. I want your brother's as well.' The passengers looked away from the confrontation.

She reluctantly gave Protruding Eyes the details and when he returned her ticket and identity card, she almost snatched them out of his hands. Defiant to the end, isn't she? was Valérie's immediate thought.

'Next carriage,' said the official to the ticket inspector who followed him like a lapdog.

'Phew,' said the old woman. 'To think that bastard's a Frenchman. He's not in uniform but I reckon he's a senior milicien.

'They can be more dangerous than the Gestapo,' said the old man.

'Hush, Papa,' his daughter whispered.

'I still can't believe that in the space of just over two decades, the Boches are hounding us again in our daily lives,' commented the old woman. 'And as for Marshal Pétain, our so-called head of state, he should be dealt with by someone in the Resistance.'

A long silence ensued. Valérie noticed Monsieur Tournier's eyes darken and a look of hate that swept across his face at the mention of the marshal's name.

'I can understand how you feel, Madame,' said the middle-aged woman, 'but it would be wise to watch what you say in public.' Turning to Valérie she asked, 'Don't you agree with me, Mademoiselle?'

Should she give a point of view in public? Never do so, one of Beaulieu's instructors had told her. 'It sounds like practical advice,' she replied, noting the disappointment on the woman's face at her response.

Clearing her throat, the old woman asked Valérie, 'Where do you come from?'

'Tours.'

'I'm Madame Guérin. What's your name?'

Valérie paused before giving the woman her cover name on her identity card. 'Véronique.'

'Where do you work?'

'In a chemist shop in Tours. Where do you live in Tours?'

'Not far from the station. We should meet up some time. I've lived in Tours nearly all my life so I'm a true Tourangelle,' she said with a smile, fingering her mop of white curly hair. 'I used to work at the town hall as the deputy mayor's secretary.' She gave a huge sigh. 'It's now a divided and horrible place: those for Pétain and those against. Most adore him. Thank the good Lord that I'm now retired.'

The old man stood up with difficulty. 'I fought in the Battle of Verdun. I'd like to say much more, but I don't want to upset my daughter and her husband. Now I must attend to nature's needs,' he said, unsteady on his feet as he stood up.

'Do you want any help, Papa?' asked his son-in-law.

'Non. Merci,' he replied and stood up to leave the compartment.

Valérie pushed the door aside for the old man.

'Merci, Mademoiselle,' he replied.

Valérie was glad when she noticed Madame Guérin had fallen asleep. Now everyone could enjoy some peace and quiet. She presumed that the young man and young woman, sitting opposite her, knew each other by the occasional glances they exchanged.

Shortly before the train approached the outskirts of Paris, Valérie caught a fleeting glimpse through the corridor window of the unsavoury interrogator striding towards the front of the train. Moments later Mademoiselle Botton stood up, grabbed her bag off the luggage rack and left the compartment, but Monsieur Tournier did not look at her. When the train was approaching Montparnasse, Valérie stood up and started to lift Madame Guérin's case down, but the middle-aged man insisted on doing it. At that moment, Madame Guérin woke up with a start. 'Oh merci. Vous êtes très aimable,' she said, half yawning.

'I'll help you off the train,' said Valérie, 'but let's wait a little until the others leave first.' It was better to melt in with the crowd. Once the carriage had cleared, they waited a few minutes before Valérie helped Madame Guérin climb down onto the platform and then bring their luggage down before joining the queue.

Where had Mademoiselle Botton disappeared to? The queue suddenly came to a halt near the barrier. Armed German soldiers were guarding it, but it was a tall man, dressed in a black leather jacket and dark trousers, who caught Valérie's attention. He had taken Monsieur Tournier aside and was inspecting his identity card and ticket. Voices began to rise, and Protruding Eyes appeared.

'My identity card is in order. You're mistaken,' shouted Monsieur Tournier.

'You think so,' said the tall man. 'Your forger didn't make a particularly good job with the paper he used.'

Monsieur Tournier remained silent. The official pulled something out of his pocket: menottes. Valérie wasn't surprised to see these. In no time at all he handcuffed the young man and marched him away, leaving Protruding Eyes on duty. During this time the Milice continued inspecting identity cards, but with smug expressions on their faces. Had Mademoiselle Botton gone through already? If so, had she had probably changed her appearance in the toilet.

Once the women had passed the barrier, Madame Guérin whispered, 'That young man must be in the Resistance. You could tell that the milicien on the train already knew something about him by the type of questions he was asking.' She looked at her watch and took the suitcase from Valérie. 'Well, my dear, I must go and wait for my brother in a café outside the station. He's a doctor and cannot always be on time. Would you join me for a drink and allow my brother to give you a lift to where you are going?'

Valérie apologised. 'I have to meet someone,' she said. How would she cope with the woman if she met her again in Tours? She was friendly, but far too talkative, not taking care about what she was saying in public and laying herself open to trouble with the enemy.

Outside the station, Valérie walked down one side of the main street, pausing to look in shop windows and noting reflections of other pedestrians walking past. She crossed the road and walked back to the Metro station but checked her shoes and slightly turned to see if anyone was watching her. She was glad that her meeting with Archambaud, Prosper's wireless operator, had been arranged for three o'clock in the afternoon because it gave her time to visit the Tuileries—the spectacular gardens near the Louvre.

Down inside the Metro, Valérie sensed people were on edge and as the train came into the station, a group of German officers quickly entered the first-class red coaches in the middle of the train, while Valérie joined the other passengers in one of four packed green second-class coaches, with remaining coaches set aside for Jewish people. Two stations later, two German soldiers entered the carriage and stood by a mother with her little fair-haired daughter. One of the soldiers looked down at the child and started to talk to her in basic French. Nearby passengers frowned, and the young mother put her arm round her daughter and drew her closer.

'I'm sorry, Madame, you seem offended. Your little girl reminds me of Greta, my daughter back in Germany.' He wiped his eyes. 'It's hard, isn't it, for such young children to live during wartime, but at least you have your little girl with you. Entschuldigung. Excusez-moi, Madame,' he said and moved further down the carriage with the other soldier accompanying him, looking rather glum.

Valérie sighed. Seeing a scene like this makes war even more futile, she thought. And when she got out at the next station, she noticed three passengers emerging from the last coach, each wearing a yellow star. A sense of shame, witnessing Jewish people being segregated like this, swept through her.

When she emerged from the Metro at the Place de la Concorde, a different Paris awaited her from the one she remembered. There were no motorists sounding their horns or racing along. The stillness unnerved her. White signposts with black Gothic German script disorientated her. Streetlights, now covered in a blue fabric, puzzled her. She continued walking along the streets. A rickshaw, being driven by a cyclist, slowed down and parked in front of a restaurant. A young pretty woman, wearing a well-cut floral dress and a tiny haute couture hat, stepped out onto the pavement, accompanied by a German officer who put his arm round her. By the few words spoken, Valérie could tell that the woman was French. Probably satisfied the officer in bed. She continued her way. The quietness of the city made it all seem surreal, but eventually it was broken by a Mercedes and a large Citroën dashing past at high speed, carrying uniformed German officers. Were they in pursuit of any of her organisation?

A busy eating place, reasonably priced, was what she sought. Somewhere where she could melt into the background, somewhere devoid of German officers entertaining their French women. Finally, she decided upon a small brasserie down a side street and chose one of the few seats left in a corner near a side exit. Useful if she needed to leave the restaurant quickly. It was a jour sans. No alcohol was being served as was the custom now on certain days since the German Occupation. The fixed menu of vegetable soup, black sausage, apples, and green beans, followed by a fruit tart, was inviting, but made her feel guilty, remembering how little food many people, apart from the rich, were able to purchase.

After lunch, she set off for the Tuileries, passing the Carousel Archway. She turned and looked straight ahead down the Champs Elysées and the Arc de Triomphe in the distance, a magnificent sight in spring with all the blossom out. She recalled her last visit here to celebrate the fourteenth of July, Bastille Day, in 1939. She and Uncle Georges had watched the armed forces march from the Arc de Triomphe down to the Place de la Concorde. President Lebrun had taken the salute, surrounded by mounted Republican Guards, their metal helmets glinting under the strong sunlight. Now a vile dictator had eliminated this annual patriotic event, even though the French still commemorated the 1789 revolution and the creation of a republic. France was now classed as a state, no longer a republic.

She passed the grandiose Louvre and was amazed to see the transformation in the Tuileries. During her last visit, the gardens, with their structures and orderly paths, the flower beds ablaze with different coloured flowers and plants, arranged carefully in patterns, had basked under a hot July sun. Now everything had been dug up: carrots, potatoes, broccoli and other vegetables were laid out in neat rows. She paused, feeling unnerved. Would she be alive to see the gardens restored once the war was ended?

She remembered the man who had fled from France, telling her family about Jews being made to wear yellow stars on their clothes and who were later rounded up in vast numbers by French police and sent to Germany. There was no sign of them now.

As she crossed the Pont Neuf, scene of bloody battles across many centuries, she recalled the enjoyable boat trips on the Seine with her parents and Uncle Georges. Now there was little activity on the river. She stopped and looked across at the Conciergerie, Queen Marie-Antoinette's prison before the revolutionaries guillotined her. It was a timely reminder of résistants incarcerated in the Gestapo headquarters in Paris, at rue de Saussaies or at the HQ of the Sicherheitsdienst, the Gestapo counter-intelligence service, at eighty-four Avenue Foch.

Marcel had spoken about them because one of his best friends had told him before being arrested in Paris.

Now she was close to the Place Dauphine where she was going to meet Archambaud. What would he be like? She prayed that neither of them would be followed. The square was accessible from halfway across the Pont Neuf, at the western end of the island called Ile de la Cité. She checked her shoulder bag and looked casually behind her. When she entered the square, she was amused to find it triangular in shape. Tall houses with rectangular windows and steep slate roofs containing dormers occupied much of the square. A young boy was tugging a small dog along on a lead, followed by a girl in her teens. A few other people were going in and out of a restaurant and a bar on the other side of the square. Valérie noticed where number sixteen bis was situated. She sat down on a bench and took out a newspaper from her bag which she pulled up to hide her face.

Moments later the silence was broken by a squeal of tyres. Valérie looked above the edge of her newspaper and saw a black Citroën Traction Avant, a Gestapo car, as it tore into the square and stopped abruptly, with a screech of brakes, in front of the restaurant. Everyone froze; the young couple clung to each other, the young boy grabbed his dog and other passers-by stood motionless. It was as if they had all been caught in a film still. Two men in dark suits, armed with revolvers, rushed out of the car, and made their way into the restaurant. It wasn't long until they re-emerged. A young woman, handcuffed to one of the men, was being dragged towards the car. Her piercing screams resonated round the square and made Valérie shudder. Her captors forced her into the back of the car and the driver sped off at high speed. Suddenly the Citroën swerved to avoid a young child and one of the Gestapo pulled down a window and screamed at the child, 'Next time we might not stop.' The cruelty in his voice was something Valérie would never forget, nor the petrified looks on people's faces.

Soon after the commotion, a tall man, wearing a cap pulled down over his forehead, arrived at Madame Lemercier's flat and was shown in. That must be Archambaud.

After a while, Valérie crossed the square to the building and rang the doorbell three times and waited for a few moments. An elderly woman opened the door and asked Valérie what she wanted. Relieved after the exchange of passwords, the woman led Valérie up a winding staircase and into her comfortably furnished flat on the first floor where Valérie instantly recognised the tall man who had entered the building shortly before her. He looked as if he was in his early forties. His penetrating eyes, beneath bushy eyebrows, made Valérie feel ill at ease. 'It's good to meet you,' he said in a mellow voice.

'I need to do some shopping now,' said Madame Lemercier and departed.

'How are you getting on in Tours?' Archambaud asked Valérie.

How could she possibly answer truthfully? She took her time to consider her reply. 'I'm trying hard to do the best I can for Marcel.'

'You don't seem to be very enthusiastic.'

'We just need time to get to know one another,' she replied.

'I do know that Marcel can be difficult at times, but he is one of the best circuit leaders in terms of security. It's his inability to socialise that's the problem.'

'I heard that his previous courier had been ill. What was wrong with her?'

'The pressure was too much for her, but to be fair it wasn't only due to Marcel.' He paused. 'She wasn't suited to the work, but London hadn't spotted it.' He looked down at her closely. 'Have you brought the crystals with you?'

'Yes. I need to undo an inner pocket of my jacket.' She took a pair of scissors from her handbag and noticed Archambaud cross the room and stand to the side of the window, checking outside. He stroked his dark moustache back and forth. What was troubling him?

She cleared her throat to gain his attention. 'Here are the crystals,' she said.

He moved towards her. 'Thank you. I need them desperately.' He sat down on the sofa while Valérie sat opposite him. 'Now I want to talk to you about a joint operation between your circuit and one in Meung-sur-Loire that we have in mind.' He pulled out a pencil and a piece of paper and leaned on a nearby coffee table to draw a map.

'I want you to memorise several things. The Meung team will destroy a train en route for Tours, travelling from Paris. Meanwhile, your circuit is going to sabotage the rail track, signal box, and two of the telegraph poles, between Tours and Amboise. This is to destroy an important ammunitions train going to Paris,' he said, pointing to the places on the map. 'Equally, both teams will have sabotaged all trains going to and from Paris. Marcel will organise his own two teams. The train will pass through at 12.15. You must let a passenger train, en route for Paris, go through safely at 11.45. Then Marcel must lay his charges under the track. The signal box, as well as the telegraph poles, will need to be destroyed so that there will be no communication between Tours and the signalman at Amboise.'

What an introduction to her sabotage work! Valérie could imagine the armaments train zigzagging off the rails and hear the screams and shouts from the German soldiers within the carriages.

'When will the operation be?' she asked him.

'May the fifth.'

'What about the group in Meung? Have you already told them?'

'Yes. They will contact Marcel. They will blow up the line at a village called Mer, which lies between Beaugency and Blois, at 12.20 so that the line is blocked both ways. We don't usually use two circuits, but on this occasion we must.'

'Phew! That's a lot to retain.'

'London will contact Emile, with the date of a weapons drop and a coded message. When you hear the message on the BBC French service, it confirms the drop.'

Valérie picked up the map and smelt the rice paper. 'Revolting stuff.'

He smiled at her. 'Study the map and then dispose of the paper in the usual way.'

'You mean down the hatch,' she said with a laugh.

'I must leave you now. It's been a pleasure meeting you.' Looking at her more seriously, he added, 'Remember to be careful at all times. Never allow yourself to be distracted when you're on an operation.

Leave one train and wait for the next one and see if anyone gets off at the same time and hangs around. If you spot someone, change trains, and go in the opposite direction. Then restart your journey, again checking.' He put on his jacket and left.

Madame Lemercier returned and during their conversation, Valérie mentioned the arrest that had taken place in the square. 'Things are becoming more dangerous for people like you and other résistants every day.'

That evening her hostess cooked a special meal of chicken in wine. 'It's not often I get a chicken, but my niece's husband is a farmer and occasionally comes to Paris on business and brings me poultry and vegetables as well as a bottle of wine from Burgundy.'

Later Valérie retired to her bedroom, beautifully wallpapered, and furnished. She put the light out and took care to look out from the edge of the window. Never had she seen a Parisian square shrouded in a blue, mystical light, and remembered having noticed the streetlamps, hooded for the blackout, with pieces of blue material. Paris, the city of bright lights, existed no more, just as the country she loved had changed into a dangerous and fearful one. Was the Gestapo lurking out there in the shadows? Had they succeeded in making the woman on the train divulge important information and were they looking for accomplices?

The following morning when Valérie made her way to Austerlitz Station, security was tighter than ever with more Gestapo and German soldiers guarding the barrier. The Milice were checking identity cards, but she passed through the barrier without incident. During the journey back to Tours, she thought about her time in Paris. Although the sight of large Nazi flags and German military everywhere desecrated the city in the centre of the capital, little had changed for the well-off French inhabitants. In the deprived areas in the north of Paris, where poorer people lived, food was rationed, as well as coal and other necessities because many of these basic human needs were being sent to Germany.

When the train arrived in Tours, three hours later, Valérie heaved a sigh of relief and was glad the gendarmes were checking identity cards with only a few Milice in attendance.

As she made her way back to her lodgings, her thoughts turned to the forthcoming operation. It was a daring and dangerous one. Would they succeed?

CHAPTER EIGHT
SHADOWS OF DOUBT

Early one morning at the beginning of May, Marcel met Valérie in a wooded area outside Tours where she updated him on the mission outlined by Archambaud.

'I don't usually work in tandem with another circuit, but I can see that this operation needs two teams,' said Marcel. 'We'll be dealing with that once we've received some containers. Yesterday, Emile received a message from London, warning us of a container drop this coming Monday, outside Montrichard. Most of the reception committee has been there before. We'll meet tonight to listen to the personal messages, broadcasted by the French in London, on the BBC service. "Lucille will be celebrating her birthday" is the message that we'll be listening for each evening and when we hear it, it means confirmation of the container drop.

'Where will we meet tonight?' asked Valérie.

'Father Antoine will meet you, Arnaud, and me tonight at the presbytery of St Martin's Basilica in Tours at a quarter to seven. I contacted the others earlier. I need you to contact Arnaud as soon as possible. I will show you how to locate him in a minute, as well as the priest.'

'How will the other circuit members listen in?'

'Patricia will listen into her radio tonight. When she does hear the message, she will contact the other members of the circuit, and confirm the venue, date and time of the drop. When the reception committee meets at Montrichard, the Maquis deputy leader and another maquisard will join us to guard the field.' He pulled out a piece of paper and a pen and started to draw the two diagrams. When he'd finished, he told her, 'Take a look at these. They show you how to get to the presbytery and Arnaud's surgery. Study them for a few minutes and then I'll destroy them.' After a few minutes, he continued. 'I want you to observe very carefully the procedure we use for showing lights to the pilot who is dropping containers. As you know from your training, the system is different to pilots landing agents and other personnel.'

'Yes, of course I have learned both systems.'

'If ever I am captured, you will be taking charge, temporarily, so you need to learn everything I show you or explain to you in the meantime.'

'I understand that.'

'Are you afraid at all of what is expected of you? My last courier was and that's one of the reasons why she had to be replaced.'

'I was trained in sabotage work, explosives and other skills; I am here to carry out your orders.'

'Well said and I've already seen that demonstrated when you went to Paris.'

'Thank you for your encouragement.'

He smiled at her and then said, 'Now let's get rid of these drawings.' He lit a match and destroyed the paper. 'I must be off,' he said, giving her a smile.

Valérie cycled back to Tours, feeling more confident now that Marcel was showing her respect and trust. When she made her way to Arnaud's surgery, she noticed an unusual amount of Milice activity outside a nearby café. Several miliciens had gone into the café, leaving three sentries outside.

She returned to the surgery later, making sure the Milice were no longer patrolling. At first the receptionist was reluctant for her to see Arnaud because no appointment had been made.

After a delay, the receptionist showed Valérie into Arnaud's consulting room. To her surprise, Arnaud looked up at her with disapproval. 'I presume your visit is of importance.'

'Yes. There's a meeting tonight at St Martin's presbytery at a quarter to seven. We're due for a container drop next Monday and we'll be listening for the coded personal message on the BBC Free French service. "Lucille will be celebrating her birthday" is the message.

'That is usual before a drop,' he replied briskly.

'It will be my first one.'

He paused then said decisively, 'I can't take part in any future operations.'

She looked at him in disbelief. 'I can't believe what you're telling me. It will endanger the operation without your help to store the containers. What shall I tell Marcel?'

'I'll come to give my reasons to him. That's all I am prepared to do.'

She remained silent and turned away. Something must have happened. Something awful to make him do this. And how would Marcel react when she told him? With absolute fury if she wasn't mistaken.

Before a quarter to seven that evening Valérie arrived at the presbytery, an old beamed house behind a high wall, not far from the basilica. She knocked three times on the door before it was opened by Father Antoine, a short thin priest in his late thirties. After exchanging passwords and introducing herself, he invited her inside and they went into his study where Marcel and Arnaud were waiting.

'We need to keep this meeting short,' said Marcel. 'Since this new kommandant's arrival, meetings like this have become riskier. We're due for a container drop next Monday that will lead to an important operation. The BBC programme is due shortly.'

Father Antoine unlocked a cupboard and took out a small radio. He switched it on to the BBC and they huddled round it. After introducing the programme at 7.15 p.m., the announcer started to read the *messages personnels*. Marcel and Valérie laughed when they heard the words 'Hickory Dickory Dock, a fat mouse ran up the slow clock' but Arnaud remained silent.

'Can Valérie listen in with you, please, Father, so that she can warn the others of when the drop is going to take place?'

'Yes, of course.'

'Now I need to talk to you about arrangements for the drop,' said Marcel. 'It will be at Montrichard, in the same field that we used last time. and we will use the same methods of transport.' He turned to Valérie and said, 'Father, Luc, the vet, as well as Arnaud and Jacques all have late-night passes. Jacques owns his own garage business but he's also an electrical engineer and has a late-night pass for emergencies like car breakdowns for doctors, farmers and people like that.'

Arnaud hesitated. 'I've something to tell you. I can't take part in the drop. I'm sorry. You also need to find someone else for transportation and storage of the containers. I can't support the circuit for the moment.'

Deep furrows formed on Marcel's forehead. 'I can't believe you would do this to all of us just before a drop,' he told him in a restrained voice, but Valérie could detect anger simmering underneath. 'Why won't you help us? I insist you explain everything.'

Valérie caught Marcel's eye. *Oh Marcel, don't speak in that pompous manner. That riles people*, she thought.

'It concerns something that's happened within my family. That's all I can say. It's serious.'

Father Antoine cleared his throat. 'I know a farmer who lives in a parish outside Tours and who is already involved in another circuit. He lives not far from the drop zone.' Looking anxiously at Marcel, he added, 'I realise you rarely contact other circuits, but this is an emergency. I think this farmer could hide the containers for a limited period.'

'Please ask him if he can help us?' Marcel said in a more reasonable tone of voice. After reflecting for a moment or two, he looked again at Arnaud and asked, 'I accept with reluctance that you cannot take part in the drop, but could you hide the containers later for a limited time, if this farmer can't store them?'

By the shrug of Arnaud's shoulders and his general demeanour, Valérie could see his unease in agreeing to Marcel's request. 'I've no option, have I?' he said, glaring at Marcel.

Three days later, outside Montrichard, in a moon-drenched field, the reception committee, consisting of circuit members and maquisards, waited for the drop.

Valérie joined Martin, the deputy Maquis leader, and another maquisard patrolling the perimeter of the field with Stens and grenades at the ready in case of any trouble. She looked up into the sky, straining her neck to see if she could spot the aircraft. Hoots from owls and animals scurrying through the undergrowth close by unnerved her. Moments later, she detected a slight humming noise in the distance. A huge dark shape, like a giant bird, came into view. The plane was bigger than she'd imagined. Four members of the reception committee had formed a straight line, parallel to the wind, at hundred-metre intervals, longer than required for a Lysander to land. Marcel flashed the Morse letter *V* with his white lamp. The pilot responded by indicating a letter *T*. Then the four lights were lit, enabling the drop of armaments to take place. The Halifax passed over them at about a thousand feet, its engine noise vibrating through Valérie. Then it turned and circled, banking against the stars and, for a moment, almost wiping out the moon. Subsequently it returned, making her pray it wouldn't alert the Boches. As the parachutes opened, the containers drifted down and landed beyond the lights. Valérie watched the shadows of the men in the cold moonlight as they dragged the containers towards the bushes on the edge of the field. She could hear the rustle of the parachutes being torn away from the containers before the men buried them.

The roar of the plane's engines, as it climbed and turned ready for a second delivery, deafened Valérie's ears. As the plane returned, dropping more containers, Valérie gripped her Sten, ready to attack any Boches who might be hiding while the men retrieved the second drop. Valérie's shoulders tightened as she looked up at the sky. How brave the pilot was, taking risks with the danger of being shot down at any moment. How was he feeling now? Was he relieved that he'd succeeded in dropping the containers and was he now praying for a safe return to England? She looked at the shadows of the men busy burying the second lot of parachutes. She contemplated what risks these men on the ground were taking too in ensuring the safe delivery in receiving the containers and delivering them to secure places. Thank goodness Arnaud had at least agreed to store half the containers on a temporary basis.

When she had returned to Tours with Father Antoine and had reached the rue du Cygne, she immediately retired to bed and started to reflect on the night's activities and on Arnaud's reluctant decision to store half the containers on a temporary basis. What lay behind Arnaud's decision to withdraw from the circuit for a while? Was he being followed? If so, why hadn't he told Marcel if he suspected he was? If that were the case, their subcircuit, Fisherman, might soon be broken up and they would all have to disappear. Or worse still, they could all suddenly be arrested. She'd have to try and find the answers as soon as possible.

Two days later, Valérie met Marcel in the Mirabeau Park in Tours and she noticed him ill at ease.

'I need Arnaud back in the circuit,' he told her in an agitated manner. 'He's invaluable. Have you any idea why he's deserted us?'

'I've no idea, but we need to find out.' She moved closer to him and whispered, 'Does he suspect that someone has him under surveillance? That thought has been bothering me.'

'It's possible. Could you talk to Jeanne?'

'I don't know her well enough yet, but I could ask Patricia to sound her out.'

Marcel remained silent for a while. 'We must find out as soon as possible. I can't afford to take any risks whatsoever at this time. If Patricia fails, you'll have to insist he tells you.'

'I'll go and see Patricia after she leaves work tomorrow,' she said.

'Now we need to talk about our next operation. As you must know, the organisation doesn't favour joint operations but for our next one, we are working in tandem with the group based near Meung. It was imperative to ensure timings were right and I needed to check some other details with the Meung circuit, so I met two of them yesterday. I met the leader and his courier. The woman, middle-aged, was highly intelligent and completely bilingual. I was most impressed with her.'

Bilingual and middle-aged like Francine? Could it possibly be her? 'What did the woman look like, Marcel?' Valérie asked herself.

He looked at her curiously. 'Why do you want to know?'

'It would be someone I met on one of the courses in England.'

'She was small, short curly greyish hair and she has a vivacious personality.'

'I'm sure it's Francine. We became close friends when training.'

'You're unlikely to meet her and you must not. And that's an order. Now I must go.'

CHAPTER NINE

RAILWAY SABOTAGE

It was now the second week in May. Valérie tossed and turned throughout the night; her only thoughts were of the forthcoming rail sabotage between Tours and Amboise. Marcel's instructions were engraved in her mind like the detail in a wooden carving.

In the late afternoon, Valérie cycled to a farm near Noizay, a small town between Tours and Amboise. She passed through a village called Vouvray and admired the flower buds on the vines, already sprouting in the vineyards.

Towards half past six in the evening, she arrived at a grey-walled farmhouse where a large sheepdog came bounding towards her. Someone from the doorway shouted at it. Moments later a plump middle-aged woman came out and hurried towards her. 'Good evening,' she said, shaking Valérie's hand. 'Marcel told me you would be coming. I'm Cathérine.'

She led her into a large, whitewashed kitchen. Onion soup, simmering on a black range, whetted her appetite and Valérie gasped when she saw country sausage, ham, terrine, crusty bread and a huge apple tart displayed on a long well-scrubbed table.

'Your friends are out in the barn. Benoît used to work for us, but then went into forestry,' Cathérine told her. Soon Valérie recognised Marcel's mellow voice in the distance. Moments later he came into the kitchen, accompanied by a tall and muscular man in his early thirties. With his dark hair and lively dark eyes, he was an attractive man, thought Valérie. But there was something about him that told her that he was not a man to be crossed.

'Good to see you. This is Benoît, our Maquis leader,' said Marcel.

'Enchanté, Mademoiselle. I've heard nothing but the highest compliments about you,' he said.

'Merci, Monsieur,' she replied.

'No formalities, please,' he replied.

'Do sit down, everyone,' said Cathérine. 'My husband will join us later.'

Benoît waited until Valérie had taken her seat and sat down opposite her. Marcel sat alongside him. Cathérine brought a large saucepan of soup over to the table.

'Help yourselves,' she told them.

Halfway through the meal a short and stocky man joined them. 'Bonsoir, les copains,' he said in a country accent. 'Now you're going to tell me how excellent my pigs are,' he said, laughing and pointing to the remains of the ham set out on the table.

Everyone complimented their hosts on the food. Benoît asked Valérie about her journey to the farm and wanted to know if she had seen any Boches.

'No, thank goodness,' she replied. 'It was what I had been dreading.'

He poured out a second glass of wine for himself and asked if she wanted more herself which she politely declined. 'You are obviously French. Have you been a courier elsewhere in France?'

Valérie looked at him uneasily, noticing Marcel looking equally perturbed. 'Monsieur, you should know better than to ask me that. Surely security means something to you?'

'She's right,' Marcel told him. 'Watch your drinking. We are on high alert. Too many glasses of wine can make for slack observation. Save those extra glasses for the liberation.'

'Do you have to sound so formal? You make it sound as if we're going into a bloody medieval battle,' replied Benoît with a sour expression on his face.

'It could end up like that if we're not careful,' replied Marcel sternly.

'I know how to hold my drink,' said Benoît, thumping the table.

Her instincts were right. He was definitely not someone to challenge, thought Valérie and turned to Cathérine who had sat down beside her to join them, looking equally ill at ease.

About eight o'clock Marcel, Benoît and Valérie made their way to the barn at the back of the farm. Valérie had already changed into trousers. Marcel gave Valérie some plastique, primer and two detonators, as well as two pencil timers which she put into her rucksack. They discussed the evening's arrangements and Marcel asked Benoît, 'Is one of Eric's friends in the signal box tonight, as agreed?'

'In theory. Yes.' he replied.

'Let's go,' Marcel told them. 'It's already half past eight.

They left the farm and cycled to a village further on from Noizay, frequently checking to see if anyone was following them. On arrival in the village, Marcel gave them instructions how to reach his friend's shed.

'I'll go first and open up the shed and you follow next,' he told Valérie. 'Benoît, you follow fairly soon after, keeping her in your sight in case of trouble. We'll leave our bicycles there. The owner doesn't want any contact whatsoever.'

After they arrived there, as they blackened their faces and pulled their caps well down, Valérie thought of the secrecy and danger that lay ahead of them. Her mouth felt dry, and she took a deep breath, telling herself to control herself. This was her first operation and although she admitted that she was terrified of being caught by the Gestapo, she was determined not to let the team down. They made their way to the back of a church in the village and waited for six of Benoît's men.

After about ten minutes, Benoît became agitated. 'They're always on time. I drill them about that regularly,' he told Marcel and Valérie.

He was clearly a tough and determined leader, thought Valérie, and he trained his men well. The two maquisards we used on our previous operation did a thoroughly good job.

At last, six maquisards appeared, one of whom was Martin who had been so supportive to Valérie during their previous operation.

'Why are you so late?' asked Benoît in a stern voice.

'Soon after we left our camp, we could see two Boches lorries parked in the distance, so we had to take an alternative route to get here,' explained Martin who looked across at Valérie and acknowledged her.

Benoît nodded. 'Now my instructions for tonight. You are to cover Marcel and his courier during the entire operation and afterwards until they retrieve their bicycles. If we are attacked any time, we will, of course retaliate, allowing Marcel and his courier to escape.' His determination and hatred towards the enemy were evident in his tone of voice. He peered at his watch in the dark. 'It's now almost ten o'clock. We need to reach our destination at the track just outside Amboise, which you've already been shown on our map. Marcel and his courier will be the first to leave, followed by my men in pairs, leaving intermittently.'

Marcel then took over the instructions. 'It will be just after half past ten when we arrive in a small copse, near the track, so that we are in position well before curfew at eleven. Remember the passenger train will come through at a quarter to midnight. Once it has gone, we need to act quickly. I will lay charges on the railway track to derail the goods train of arms and explosives. It is due to arrive at approximately fifteen minutes past midnight. You have been given instructions by Benoît on how to shield me while I am laying charges on the track and my courier while she carries out her work on two telegraph poles.'

Leaving the church, they skirted fields and used the hedgerows for cover. Finally, they arrived at the copse where the trees and foliage gave better cover near the railway track. The train was due to arrive at approximately fifteen minutes past midnight.

Valérie felt the excitement building up inside her, knowing that she was about to embark on her first sabotage operation. She started to shiver with fear in case the Boches got hold of them, knowing the potential of being tortured or even shot. She must now concentrate on her work to destroy two nearby telegraph poles, so that no communication could take place between the Boches in Tours with the authorities in Amboise. This train, carrying arms and explosives, must be blown up and not reach Paris.

'Benoît, we'll hide in those bushes nearer the track, as already agreed,' Marcel reminded him. 'Get one of your men to check for Boches further down the track, ten minutes before the passenger train comes through at a quarter to midnight.' Turning to Valérie, he said, 'Then begin your work once it has gone through.'

When the time came, the maquisard who had been checking for Boches came and gave the all-clear. The maquisards cocked their guns on the alert in case of any signs of trouble. By now it was nearly midnight and there was still no sign of the passenger train. It was a quarter of an hour late. Had someone denounced the Meung circuit to the Gestapo? She thought of the middle-aged woman whom Marcel had told her about. Was it Francine? If it was, she prayed that she would come to no harm.

Were the Boches watching her and the others from some vantage point ready to arrest them? She strained her ears and at long last heard the train chugging in the distance. 'Thank goodness it's coming,' she whispered to Marcel, 'but it leaves us little time for our work.'

As the passenger train came into view, she wondered if any of the organisation's agents might be on board. Marcel had told her that they often chose to travel at night. She spotted the fire box glowing in the dark and saw steam coming over the top of the locomotive and caught a glimpse of the train driver leaning forward over his controls.

After the train was well out of sight, Marcel hurried towards the track to place his block charges, covered by maquisards, while Valérie ran to the telegraph poles, followed by Martin and another maquisard.

She added the primer to the plastique and wrapped it round the bottom of each telegraph pole, attaching detonators and time pencils and setting a short time lapse.

As she made her way to rejoin Marcel and the other maquisards, she fell heavily on a large flint which dug into her leg. Blood trickled through her trouser leg. She groaned in pain as Martin and another maquisard helped her back towards the bushes on the embankment and then carried her some distance away from the track. Martin split her trouser leg open, pulled out a handkerchief from his pocket and put pressure on the wound while the others kept watch. After a few minutes, he bandaged her leg with his scarf.

'Thank you, Martin, you were so gentle with the wound.'

'It was the least I could do, but we now need to get out of here as soon as possible.'

'Oh, my God,' said Marcel when he returned from the track. 'How ever did you do that?' he asked Valérie.

'I guess the passenger train being late made me nervous. I did the job, but I fell when I was running for cover. I'll be all right once we can get someone to look at it later,' she said, trying to reassure him.

Jacques and four other maquisards had also been waiting for the passenger train to pass through before attacking the signal box. After it had gone through, Jacques said, 'Now we must move fast. The signalman at Montlouis Station will ring through at 12.10 a.m. to say that the freight train is on its way. That leaves us five minutes in which to leave before the box goes sky high.'

Jacques and two maquisards burst into the signal box while the other two remained outside. As fear swept the signalman's face, Jacques realised that it wasn't Eric's friend who was on duty. Pointing the Sten at the signalman, he said, 'We have little time. We need your full co-operation.'

'You'll get no trouble from me,' he told them.

Jacques began to lay the charges, attached to detonators, to the signal levers and set the timer. His concentration was interrupted by raised voices and scuffling outside. Moments later there was an eerie silence before the door was thrown open by a maquisard. 'We had a bloody intruder, a German sentry, and had a hell of a fight with him, but we've dealt with him like Benoît told us to and we've hidden the body.'

Jacques froze, knowing what the maquisard meant: they had slit the soldier's throat, putting them all in peril. He completed his installation and prayed it would work. The telephone bleeped at 12.10 a.m. A maquisard moved the signalman forward to answer it while the other one raised his Sten. 'Yes. Everything's all right. No problems here,' said the signalman. Turning to Jacques, he whispered, 'The goods train is on its way.'

'We're going to have to tie you up,' Jacques told the signalman. 'And we'll have to leave you on the roadside. We need to convince the Boches that you're not involved with us.'

'I hate them as much as you do, so you can count on me not to give anything away,' he told the men.

As they hurried away on their bicycles, they heard a loud explosion and saw huge flames leaping out from where the signal box had once stood.

'We must leave immediately,' said Marcel. 'Benoît, when we return to the shed, I may ask you for some help with my courier.

Moments later there was a tremendous crashing sound, confirming that the telegraph poles had collapsed. Oh, thank goodness Valerie had succeeded in her first sabotage job. She felt elated. Shortly afterwards several explosions erupted. Chaos now reigned on the track. The locomotive was overturned, causing the wagons to scatter and smash about. Valérie stopped, turned round and so did the others. The armaments had been set on fire; she could see the flashes in the sky and the glow of the fires lighting up the clouds. An acrid odour spread everywhere, making some of them cough. They looked at each other, overwhelmed by the chaos they had created, but thrilled in that they had succeeded in their operation.

On arrival at the shed, Marcel asked Benoît if he could stay and he agreed, dismissing his men. Valérie wheeled her bicycle outside and tried to ride it. 'How far is it to the next farm. Marcel? You told me that you had asked a farmer if we could come to his farm in an emergency.'

'About two kilometres.'

'If we stop several times, I can just about cycle there,' she told him, even though she knew it would be agonising.

Valérie did her best to keep up with them but the wound in her leg was throbbing. She gritted her teeth.

For the first few minutes Valérie struggled to keep moving on her bicycle until she noticed that blood was beginning to ooze out of the makeshift bandage.

Marcel stopped and tore off his scarf and wrapped it round her leg. Somehow, she had to continue. Halfway to the farm, Marcel and Benoît slowed down.

'You're in terrific pain. I can see that,' Marcel told her gently. Turning to Benoît, he asked, 'If we hide our bicycles, could you help me get her to the farm? There's a barn where the farmer said Valérie can spend the night.'

'Of course,' replied Benoît.

On arrival near the barn, Marcel turned to Benoît and thanked him. 'I'll contact you in a few days.'

When Marcel and Valérie reached the barn, they found rusty machinery, an old cart and a few bales of hay were spread about. Valérie lay down on one of the bales, glad at long last to rest her leg.

Marcel fetched a bucket of water and some soap from the farmer's wife to wash away the blood that was caking on Valérie's leg. He then ripped one of the sleeves of his shirt to cover it. 'The farmer is going to bring you some food and drink,' he said.

She looked at him and said, 'That's better. At least you've got the dirt out.'

He put his arm round her shoulder and said, 'You'll be safe here, but you mustn't have any contact with the farmer or his family—I promised him that. When you finally leave here at dawn, you'll find that I will have brought your bicycle here. It will be outside. I want you to go to the Dubier family who live in les Closeaux, a little village further on. I'll arrange for Luc to collect you and your bicycle later.' He pulled a pencil and a piece of paper out of his pocket and drew a map. 'Take a close look at this for directions to les Closeaux when I leave and destroy it immediately.' He put his hand on her shoulder and patted her and said, 'You've done well on your first sabotage job. That should give you confidence to take part in our next operation which will be even more demanding.'

From the way he had looked after her, Valérie realised that Marcel really cared for her. But why had he been so aggressive when they'd first met? He was a good organiser and the maquisards respected him. Benoît was a determined man, but Marcel knew how to handle him.

'Take care,' he told her and left.

Towards dawn Valérie heard movement at the barn door. Her leg was throbbing, but she managed to pull herself up and hide behind a stack of hay. It had to be the farmer. She heard someone walking about the barn.

'Valérie, where are you?'

She felt tears of relief running down her face when she recognised Marcel's voice. 'I'm here behind this stack of hay,' she said. As he came up to her, his dishevelled hair, his grubby face, and damp clothes made her realise that he'd been up all night.

'Why have you come back?'

'I've had to come back because there are roadblocks everywhere. I couldn't return to my hiding place, so I had to stay in the woods all night.'

'How are we going to get out of this mess?' she asked.

'I've spoken to the farmer. I've hidden your bike—the farmer knows where it is. He's not happy but says that we can hide in the back of one of the cowsheds.' Pulling something out of his pocket he said, 'It's some ointment that the farmer's wife has given me for you and some bandages. Let me quickly see to your leg,' he told her and removed the makeshift bandages and started to clean the wound and dress it as he continued speaking to her. 'One of the maquisards, who was guarding the signal box, attacked a German sentry and cut his throat.'

A wave of fear swept through her body. 'Oh no! she cried. 'There will be reprisals; men and women will be beaten and taken away, with their children screaming and left alone. And later those people will be shot. Already, many people blame the Resistance, making our work to recruit even more difficult.' She started to sob.

Marcel put his arm round her. 'I realise all this, Valérie. But even so, we must continue the fight. But we must concentrate now. The farmer's coming over to lead us to the cowshed.'

'What are our chances of not being arrested?'

'It depends on how thoroughly the Boches search if they come here,' he said with a grimace.

'I wonder how our friends at Meung are?'

Marcel shrugged his shoulders and said, 'We can only hope they haven't been arrested. And I hope that the courier isn't your friend.'

CHAPTER TEN

HIDING IN A CATTLE SHED

'It's seven in the morning now,' Marcel whispered to Valérie as she stirred from her sleep. She snuggled up to him as they lay in a storage cupboard at the back of one of the farmer's cattle sheds. Bales of hay hid the door though there was a small gap at the bottom of it. Valérie wiped the sweat off her brow, and she rubbed her leg, which was throbbing intensely.

'Sip this water,' said Marcel. Moments later she heard a distant rumble of wheels. She looked at him in horror. 'It can't be them. Please God don't let it be them.' He put his arm round her. The noise increased until there was a screech of brakes. Doors slammed. The sound of jackboots resounded. Dogs barked and an officer started shouting orders to his men. Then silence.

Valérie shivered and clung closer to Marcel.

'The officer must have gone into the farmhouse and left his men on standby,' whispered Marcel.

Valérie groaned as she felt blood oozing from the bandages. Marcel wrapped a rag, given to him by the farmer's wife, over the blood-sodden bandages.

Later the silence was broken by the officer's harsh voice outside. Valérie shuddered at the heavy tread of soldiers' boots coming closer to the cattle shed. Dogs were barking. She gripped Marcel's hand. Bang! Bang! The shed doors were flung back. She started to tremble. They were for it now, that was for certain.

'Suchen die Terroristen,' shouted the officer. Soon she could hear soldiers were turning over bales of hay and urging their dogs to find the résistants, but a ferocious snarl from one of the dogs made a cow moo and struggle to free itself. The noise vibrated through Valérie's head.

'Scheisse,' swore one of the soldiers.

'Um Gottes will!' screamed another.

An officer shouted at the soldiers above the din, ordering them to remove the dogs.

'Der Bauer muss sofort hereinkommen,' commanded the officer and shortly afterwards the farmer's voice could be heard. Soon the cow calmed down and the soldiers stopped searching. 'Nous retournerons bientôt,' the officer told the farmer. 'C'est sûr.'

They would return. There was no doubt about that. If they were found, could she really withhold information under torture or would she take the cyanide pill? The soldiers were slamming the shed doors behind them. Soon vehicle engines were being started up. They were leaving. Thank God.

Marcel said, 'Well done for keeping a cool head.'

He valued her more than ever, thought Valérie.

It seemed almost like an hour before the farmer returned to the shed and pulled the bundles of hay away from the cupboard. 'We have to think quickly,' he said, rubbing his cheeks back and forth. 'We must find somewhere else on the farm to hide you. You can't stay here. The Boches are coming back later.'

Valérie swallowed hard.

'Do you have a phone?' Marcel asked the farmer.

'Yes. I'm a local councillor. Why do you ask?'

'Could you make a call to a doctor friend?'

'You Resistance people are very insistent. What do you want me to say?'

'Could you tell him that one of your farm hands has gashed his leg. It doesn't look at all good. You need his help,' replied Marcel. 'Emphasise that.'

'I'm loath to do this. This is the last favour. Understood? Afterwards I want no more contact.'

'I promise you.'

The fear in the farmer's eyes pierced through her like an arrow.

It was now half past eight in the morning. Arnaud was sorting out paperwork while waiting for his first patient at the surgery when the telephone rang. He lifted the receiver.

His heart sank as he listened to the farmer's request.

'I'll come as soon as I can,' he said and replaced the receiver. It had to be Marcel or one of his circuit. They were almost certainly behind this morning's derailment announced earlier on the wireless and needed help. He dialled a number and looked at a photograph of his two daughters while waiting for Frédérick, a retired colleague, to answer.

'Bonjour, Frédérick. Sorry to trouble you. Can you take over from me at the surgery? I've received an urgent call-out.' He paused. 'Thanks a lot.'

After half past nine, Arnaud made his way to the Vouvray area to the west of Tours. Should he have agreed to visit this farm? The Boches were arresting more and more people in the Resistance and sending them to concentration camps in Germany.

Arnaud groaned at the roadblock ahead because it meant being questioned. Moments later when a milicien walked towards his car, he tightened his hands on the driving wheel.

'Votre carte d'identité, Monsieur,' the paramilitary demanded, and Arnaud handed it over.

'Why are you in this district?' asked the milicien.

'I have a patient to see who is extremely ill.'

'His name and address?'

He'd give him a farmer's address and tell him later. He would understand, thought Arnaud.

The milicien noted the details and gave him back his identity card.

Somewhat agitated, Arnaud continued to drive through the town and out towards the farm. Half an hour later, he arrived and introduced himself to the farmer.

'The Nazis came here today at seven this morning. It's not one of my men who is injured, but a woman in the Resistance who had my permission to stay overnight here. Then her leader turned up unannounced at six this morning. Later when the Nazis had gone, he asked me to phone you. Earlier I had to move them to a cattle shed. It's a wonder the Nazis didn't find them when they searched it.'

'I can understand your dilemma.'

'You're taking a risk yourself coming here. The Nazis warned me they would soon be returning.' He looked at his watch. 'Your friends will have to leave straight away, so you'd better come to see them.'

By now the farmer had transferred Marcel and Valérie to a barn further away from the main house. Valérie vaguely heard the barn door open. She looked at the man who came in. Was it Arnaud? Was she dreaming? 'Is it you, Arnaud?

'Don't worry, Valérie. I've come to help you,' said Arnaud.

'She fell heavily on a flint,' explained Marcel.

'I prayed that you would risk coming to help me,' said Valérie.

Arnaud undid the bandage and examined the leg carefully. 'This needs suturing. Let me give you some pain relief, first of all,' he told her, searching in his bag.

'Just give her the pain relief. See to her elsewhere. You must all leave immediately,' the farmer told them.

'I'm sorry to have caused you so much trouble,' said Valérie.

'There's been a massive train derailment near here a few hours ago. Being a local councillor, I was one of the first to hear about it. A German soldier has been killed. And we all know what that means. There will be reprisals And I don't doubt that you two are in some way involved.'

'Reprisals? Ah non. Non,' cried Valérie.

'And that's why more and more people are against the Resistance,' said the farmer.

As they drove away, Valérie lay sprawled on the back seat of Arnaud's saloon car. She looked at the wound, thinking of the planning and preparations needed for Marcel's next operation. She'd have to find a good excuse to explain to Madame Lelong how she had injured herself.

On arrival at the château, Marcel and Arnaud helped her into the kitchen where Lise was reading a newspaper. 'How ever did you injure yourself, my dear?' she asked.

'She fell off her bicycle, Maman. That's all it is,' said Arnaud.

Lise looked at Valérie and shrugged her shoulders in obvious disbelief.

'Sit down and rest yourself while I fetch my bag from the car. Maman, can you fetch a pillow, blanket and sheet and lay them out on the chaise longue in the lounge?'

'This is like being treated as royalty,' said Valérie.

'Reserved for circuit members in distress,' he replied with a smile.

As soon as he came back, Arnaud started to treat Valérie's wound, cleaning and suturing it. 'It will soon heal.' He turned to Marcel. 'Jeanne will be bringing the children home from school at about half past three, so I think it would be a good idea if you left before then. Then I'll tell the girls that Valérie is one of my nurses who has had a bad fall.'

Towards half past three, children's voices could be heard coming from the hall with one child crying. Jeanne came into the sitting room, holding her younger daughter's hand, and stopped in her tracks when she saw Valérie. 'Whatever's happened?'

Arnaud winked and said, 'My nurse fell off her bicycle and needs to spend the night here.'

'Of course. I understand,' she said and sat down while Stéphanie ran into her father's open arms, sobbing. He caressed her and pulled back her fair hair. Moments later, Stéphanie's elder sister,

Angéline, who had her father's dark hair and complexion, entered the room subdued and red-eyed.

'Sarah and Rebecca have left the school. They've gone away with their family. That's all the teachers are telling us, but I know it has something to do with two nasty men, Daddy, who came to the school two days ago.' Arnaud nodded. 'I was coming out of the toilets, and I saw Monsieur Cordier, our headmaster, walking to his office with these men who were talking in German. I knew there would be trouble—they were the Boches visiting our school.' She stopped and looked up at her mother, wiping her eyes. 'Today when I asked our teacher where Sarah and Rebecca were, she became upset. She told me that Sarah and her sister wouldn't be returning to the school. Neither would some children in other classes. She couldn't say anything else.' She slumped into one of the armchairs. 'One of the boys in our class said that he'd gone to the home of Sarah and Rebecca last evening to borrow a book, but no one was in and the curtains were drawn.'

Valérie somehow supressed her tears. Even Jewish children would be sent to the concentration camps that she'd heard about, and she'd never forgotten the terrified Jewish faces in that cattle train going towards Vierzon and then on to Germany. She'd seen all this on her way back from Paris.

After a long pause, Arnaud answered in a sombre tone, 'I'm afraid we live in dangerous times, Angéline. We can only hope for a better future.'

'Who's this lady, Papa?'

'She's one of my nurses who's just had an accident. Now why don't you and Stéphanie go and have afternoon tea with Mamy?'

'What a good idea,' said Lise and took her granddaughters out into the kitchen.

Jeanne turned to Valérie. 'The Gestapo came to the school, demanding to see all the attendance registers. When the Headmaster didn't want to co-operate, they threatened to take him away and make his family suffer too. He had no alternative but to hand the registers to the swines who extracted all the Jewish children's names and addresses.' She wiped the perspiration from her brow. 'By yesterday morning, the Gestapo had raided the families' homes and taken them to the Michelet Primary School which they are using as a holding place for prisoners.' She buried her face in her hands for a few moments then looked up at Arnaud. 'Our girls must not be told the truth. They're far too young. Thank God, Arnaud, you were able to rescue your brother's wife and help her escape to England.' She put her hand to her mouth. 'Oh, I'm so sorry.'

'Don't worry, Valérie's a circuit member. She's hardly going to repeat that to anyone,' he replied.

'I promise you that I won't,' intervened Valérie. 'Not even to Marcel.' So that was the reason for Arnaud's reluctance to help the circuit with the recent operations, she realised.

While Jeanne was preparing a meal of chicken and carrots, Arnaud and Valérie talked about recent events in Tours and how a résistant had escaped from the local prison and that the authorities were looking for him everywhere.

'My commitment to the Resistance will never wane now,' he told her. 'Never. No matter what it costs.'

Valérie thought back to when Arnaud had declared that he could no longer help the circuit at that meeting at Father Antoine's presbytery. Now things made sense after what Jeanne had let slip.

Chapter Eleven

A NIGHT OF HORROR TOWARDS THE END OF MAY

Marcel rubbed his bloodshot eyes as he came into the sitting room at Arnaud's home where Valérie was resting.

'There's bad news,' he said tersely.

'Whatever's happened?'

'A reprisal. The Boches shot ten people at random in a village close to Amboise, in retaliation for the sentry who was killed by one of the maquisards, and also for the train sabotage.'

'Oh no!' she cried. 'How brutal.'

He shrugged. 'This is war, Valérie. We have to accept that what we do brings retaliation from the Boches. Anyway, they're making more roadblocks and house-to-house searches. So, we've got to be very much more on our guard when we go on the next operation. How's that leg of yours?'

'It has almost healed,' she replied.

'Good, because I need you with me on our next operation. We're going to plant explosives on some machines at Comitéls, which is on the edge of the factory area at St Pierre des Corps near Tours. They produce vital component parts for telephones and electronic equipment for the tracer vans that the Nazis use to search for our wireless operators,' said Marcel. 'It's a risky mission. Their security is tight.'

'How are we going to break in?' she asked.

'I've met one of Benoît's friends, who used to work in the factory, but who still has an inside contact. He has given me a key to a side door of the building and drawn me a layout of the machines. Benoît has recruited a trained telephone engineer. Immediately before we go in, the engineer and Jacques will let themselves in to disconnect the telephone and inside and outside alarms.'

The more he continued with the details of the operation, the more Valérie realised just how challenging it would be.

A week later, at ten in the evening, Marcel and Valérie were hiding in bushes along the front of a woodyard, facing the side entrance to the factory. They were waiting for two sentries to pass by. One maquisard was hidden opposite the main entrance, keeping an eye on the sentry box. Neither Marcel nor Valérie was armed, but Marcel wore a haversack with his equipment inside. Soon the sentries came into view; Valérie's legs shook, and she gripped her hands. Once they had passed out of sight, Marcel and Valérie dashed across the road to the high fence. Marcel looked at his watch in the moonlight. 'Ten thirty. We're spot on,' he whispered and called out a password which prompted someone to throw a rope over for them to climb the high fence. Martin and another maquisard were waiting for them on the other side. Valérie felt reassured to see Martin, a dependable maquisard.

'Stay here and be vigilant. If there's any trouble, one of you must come and warn us immediately.'

After unlocking the side door, Marcel and Valérie quickly made their way to the area where the machines were. They used their torches sparingly, so as not to draw attention to outsiders. They wrapped plastique, with the primer running through it, round the central point of several machines and attached detonators and time pencils to them, but Marcel had difficulty with the last time pencil. Valérie searched his rucksack for another one and passed it to him. She looked at her watch. Time was not on their side. This new time pencil had to work, otherwise the entire operation would be jeopardized.

On hearing footsteps, they were relieved to see it was Martin. 'Hurry up because the maquisard guarding the main entrance has just warned us that the two sentries from the sentry box are already waiting outside to take over from the other two.'

After finally fixing the time pencil, Marcel said, 'Right, let's get the hell out of here.'

Valérie's head started to throb as the four of them hurried out of the building, climbed the fence and ran towards the woodyard. They continued to run like whippets until they reached the other side of the woodyard and climbed over a fence onto a road which ran alongside the main road outside the factory area.

Marcel told the three maquisards, 'You cover us, but keep right back in the distance because there may be other sentries about. Shoot only as a last resort. This road leads to where Benoît is waiting for us in his van, hidden in a yard behind an office block on the right.'

It was a long road, where smaller company buildings stood, and as they were halfway down it, they spotted two sentries in the distance. Valérie's heart quickened, and her throat became dry. The three maquisards quickly fell back out of sight and Marcel grabbed Valérie's hand and told her, 'Remember our cover story.'

The two sentries hurried towards them. One of them flashed a torch into their eyes, blinding them. 'You're breaking the curfew. Your identity cards,' the senior sentry ordered them.

Marcel pulled out his identity card from his jacket pocket and handed it to the sentry.

'What are you doing here after curfew? Don't waste my time by giving stupid answers.'

'We're more intelligent than that, Monsieur,' said Valérie.

'Be careful, Mademoiselle,' he replied and turned to Marcel and repeated his question.

'I work in the nearby chemical firm,' said Marcel. 'Mademoiselle and I are going out together—you know what I mean.' He stifled a laugh. 'The work premises are the only place where we can meet. We were on our way home.'

The sentry then examined Valérie's identity card. 'Where do you work?'

'In a pharmacy.'

'Where exactly?'

'In Tours, near the railway station.'

'And yet you choose your little love nest so far from your own workplace,' he remarked in a sarcastic tone of voice. After consulting his colleague in German, he told them, 'I'm detaining both of you because I'm not satisfied with your stupid stories.'

He was about to handcuff them when there was a deafening sound of shots being fired from behind them. Both sentries fell to the ground. Marcel grabbed the identity cards and pulled Valérie away. 'Run for it. Don't stop. Keep running.' As he was turning to flee, one of the sentries dragged himself up and fired at Marcel, causing him to slump on the ground.

'That bastard's got me in one of my legs,' he shouted.

The maquisards returned fire and put the soldier out of action. Almost at once, a van hurtled towards them, out of the darkness, and reversed. One of the maquisards flashed a torch where Marcel lay. Valérie ran to open the doors while Martin and another maquisard lifted Marcel and heaved him into the van and stayed with him. Valérie jumped in alongside them. The third maquisard slammed the van door and joined Benoît, who drove the van quickly off the factory site as fast as he could towards the open countryside.

By the light of the maquisard's torch, Valérie could see Marcel's eyes were half open. He was writhing in agony and gripping his leg. Blood was seeping between his knee and ankle and was dripping onto the van's floor.

'Quick! I need your shirtsleeves,' Valérie told Martin. Seconds later, he had pulled off his shirt, torn off the sleeves and given them to her. Arrest the flow of blood from above the wound, she thought, her nurse's training coming back to her as she quickly tied the sleeves together and twisted them round and round to make a tourniquet, instructing the other two to hold Marcel's leg up to stop the flow of blood. The van started to zigzag, causing her to fall almost on top of Marcel, but she recovered her balance and tied the tourniquet round Marcel's thigh, pulling hard to increase the pressure as she secured it. Some blood still seemed to seep through his trouser leg, though much less than at first, but by now Marcel was barely conscious. Tears came to Valérie's eyes as she pulled off her jacket, rolled it up and put it under his head, then held his hand and rubbed it, wondering what on earth she was going to do if he died.

Martin put his arm on her shoulder and said, 'He's a lucky man to have you care for him.'

'And I'm lucky that you're both here to help us, Martin. Let's hope Benoît can get safely back to Véretz.'

Once out of town, Benoît increased his speed, driving along bumpy country roads, causing Marcel to moan. About half an hour later, he slowed down and went up a roughly made track and finally stopped. He opened the doors at the back of the van and told Valérie, 'I've parked in the woods behind Raymond's house. Go and warn him and ring Arnaud from his phone to get here as soon as possible. And remember the operator will be listening, so just say there's been an accident. Meanwhile we'll carry Marcel into the house.'

Valérie knocked on Raymond's front door three times. Eventually he opened it, still in his nightshirt. 'Whatever's happened, Valérie? You look terrified.'

'I've some bad news, Raymond. Marcel's been shot and is severely injured.'

Raymond closed his eyes. 'Ah non. C'est pas possible. C'est pas possible,' he cried and put his arm round her.

'We're sorry to burst in on you but this is a real emergency. Can I phone Arnaud?'

'Oui, oui. Bien sûr!'

A few minutes later, Benoît and Martin carried Marcel into the house and laid him on a bed in the adjoining room. Valérie sat down beside him, held his hand and willed him not to die as he slipped in and out of consciousness, racked by terrible pain and increasingly delirious when he was awake.

When Arnaud eventually finally arrived, he gave Marcel an initial shot of morphine. Valérie sighed, reassured that Marcel's pain would soon be relieved. Next, she saw him slowly release the tourniquet and cut away the trouser leg. Much to her relief she saw the blood was hardly seeping now, but the wound itself looked ghastly. Arnaud cleaned it and applied a dressing over it and bandaged it firmly into place. Finally, he immobilised the leg with an improvised splint to stop further damage.

'He'll need a skilled surgeon to operate on this leg because the bullet's lodged right inside and will undoubtedly spread infection. Also, the bone is shattered in places.'

'Do you know of anyone in Tours prepared to operate on him?' asked Valérie.

Arnaud shook his head. 'Non. Absolument pas.' It's too risky. You must send him to England by plane. I'll take him to my place, but I'll need one of the maquisards to help lift him both here and on arrival at the château. Let me know when you've arranged for a plane to pick him up and arrange for someone in the circuit to come and collect him.'

'I'll get the message sent as soon as I can,' she said.

Benoît and Martin carried Marcel out to Arnaud's car and laid him out on the back seat while Martin sat alongside Arnaud. Then Benoît immediately left with the two other maquisards, leaving Valérie to spend the rest of the early hours of the morning with Raymond. She tried to sleep, but thoughts of the challenges before her, as well as the dreadful events of the night, kept her awake. Somehow only the memory of Martin's kind words, as they crouched in the van beside poor Marcel, comforted her. Kind words and a look in his eyes that said more than the words themselves.

Valérie was ready to leave as soon as the curfew had lifted. She needed to leave a message for Emile under the pile of logs outside the presbytery in Azay, but there was no guarantee that he would pick it up later in the day. She had to send a coded message to London, asking for a plane to pick up Marcel as soon as possible, explaining the circumstances briefly. She borrowed a bicycle from Raymond and cycled to the presbytery at Azay. To her immense relief, she saw Emile's bicycle outside. She knocked three times on the side door. There was no response, but she could see a movement from behind one of the curtains on the first-floor window. A few minutes later Emile opened the door and ushered her inside.

'Father Dominique is out for a few hours. What's happened? You look shaken.'

'Marcel has been shot in the leg. I need you to send a message to London to request a plane to come and collect him.'

'Oh my God! How the hell did it happen?'

'Last night on a sabotage operation.' She pulled out a scrap of rice paper and added, 'I need to write a coded message to London now and give it to you. It won't take long.' After having completed the message, she told Emile, 'Marcel needs urgent surgery that can't be done here. A new organiser needs to be sent to replace him.' She passed him the message.

'I can't call them before six,' he replied, taking the paper. 'Now I must be off. Take care of yourself.'

As she cycled back to Raymond's house, Valérie slowed her pace, almost giving way to exhaustion. The loving look that Marcel had given her, before he had been carried into Arnaud's car, was imprinted on her mind. He was a brave organiser and true friend, but she would have to move forward, be ready to face challenges; the fight for freedom had to continue. She would somehow lead the circuit until London sent a new organiser and prayed for a moonlit night to send Marcel back to England. But again, during one of their operations, German soldiers had been killed. There would again be more reprisals.

A few days later, arrangements were in hand for Marcel's flight to England. Gilbert and his assistant would be guiding a Hudson in on a field south of Tours. Marcel's leg was now in a metal splint, and he was feverish and in great pain. Valérie was determined to see him onto the plane and decided that she and Luc would place him on a stretcher and take him in his van to the landing strip.

As Valérie sat beside Marcel in the van, he took her hand. 'Come closer. I want to tell you something.' She bent over his stretcher to hear him. 'I'm sorry that I was so rotten to you when you first arrived,' he said in a soft voice.

'Marcel, forget it,' she urged him gently. 'You made up for it later.'

He smiled. 'Yes, but I want you to know this. You reminded me of my wife—you look remarkably similar to her. I adored her, but she started an affair with one of my best friends in the regiment and finally left me.' Valérie caressed his hand. 'At first you reminded me so much of her, but as I grew to know you, I realised you were different. My feelings for you grew and grew until I knew that I had fallen in love with you.'

It was as if a pair of cymbals had been clashed, making Valérie feel helpless. How was she going to respond? She had grown to feel close to him as a true friend, but she had never guessed how he felt. She kissed him gently on both cheeks and whispered, 'Marcel, I'm very fond of you. I want you to know that and I'll be thinking of you a lot in the coming days, especially.'

After Luc had parked the van in a copse, where it was well hidden, he and Valérie carried Marcel on a stretcher to the landing strip, about a ten minutes' walk. They stopped from time to time because it was difficult to carry him over rough ground.

Finally, they arrived at the field where Valérie noticed four pickets with unlit torches attached, set out at specific distances. She heard the aircraft approaching. Gilbert, using a white lamp, flashed the letter U in Morse code and in turn the pilot flashed a letter in reply. The torches were then lit. The Hudson, a twin-engine plane, circled and prepared to land. It touched down on Gilbert's right. The pilot applied his brakes and went past the stakes. He faced the wind and completed a long oval shape, finishing where he would take off a few minutes later.

Valérie saw someone climbing down the steps of the aircraft. That must be Pablo, the new organiser that London had informed her about via Emile. She bent down to kiss Marcel who clung to her. She could hear his faint voice. 'We'll meet again. Things can change, can't they, Valérie?' Not knowing how to answer him, she squeezed his hand and bent down to kiss him on his cheek before Luc and Gilbert's assistant carried him towards the aircraft. A tall man was approaching her. She wasn't sure whether she was imagining things, but as he came up to her, she gasped. It was Christophe ...

CHAPTER TWELVE

A COMPLICATED ARRIVAL IN EARLY JUNE

Neither Valérie nor Christophe spoke while Gilbert and his assistant carried Marcel onto the plane and then Gilbert supervised its departure. In the moonlight, Christophe's warm hazel eyes locked on to Valérie's. A surge of warmth swept through her. It was no use denying it. His presence magnetised her again. How would they ever be able to work together? she wondered.

'I was expecting an organiser called Pablo,' she said.

'Well, you've got me instead. Aren't you lucky?'

There was an awkward silence until Gilbert walked over to them.

'I understand that you're making your own way to your destination,' he said tersely. 'Usually, we provide bicycles to agents and accompany them to the nearest railway station. We had the same problem with your lady friend when she arrived,' Gilbert told Christophe. Neither of them replied.

Once they were alone, Valérie said, 'A vet called Luc and I brought Marcel and me here in his van, but we parked it in a copse, and carried Marcel here ourselves. We didn't want that air movements officer to see the van.'

'A wise move. There's something about him I don't trust.'

'Why did London send you instead of Pablo?'

'I can't tell you.' Then as an afterthought, he said, 'London called me back for personal reasons and it was decided at the last moment to send me here.'

Was his recall connected to his girlfriend? If so, what had happened? It must have been something serious. These were the thoughts flooding Valérie's mind.

As they made their way to the van, Luc told Christophe, 'We've got urgent work to do before we set off.'

'What the hell do you mean?' asked Christophe.

'I've got some boxes containing manure covered with straw, hidden under some tarpaulin nearby. We need to bring these boxes to the van. You and Valérie will climb into the boxes, and I will cover you both with the straw. It's the best way that I can conceal you.'

'I can't believe it,' said Christophe.

Once they had climbed into the boxes, Valerie started to retch, and Luc handed her a rag to try to help mask the stench engulfing her. 'If we're stopped, here's my cover story: a cow was having a difficult labour and the farmer needed my urgent help. I have a special pass for driving after the curfew.'

'That's a clever plan you have there,' said Christophe.

Grabbing bundles of straw, Luc covered both boxes until they could not be detected. Once in the driver's seat, he turned the engine over several times. Valérie took in deep breaths. The engine must start, she kept saying to herself. Finally, Luc succeeded and drove off quickly but carefully, unlike Benoît who had driven like a maniac when they'd fled from their attack on the factory. After a while, the straw began to make Valérie's legs smart; she tried to rub them, but it was difficult being confined in a box. Suddenly Luc applied his brakes. 'Merde! Merde!' he shouted. 'It's a bloody roadblock!'

By now Valérie was hyperventilating. If the Boches decided to search the van thoroughly, they would be arrested and thrown into a Gestapo cell. Questioning and torture would follow. She prayed the gendarmes were on duty. They'd stand a better chance if they were.

Her hopes were soon dispelled by a German guttural voice interrogating Luc. They moved to the back of the van and the doors were thrown open. They would soon be discovered; she was certain of that. From where she was curled up in her box, she could make out some of the conversation between Luc and the soldier.

'What is that disgusting smell?' the soldier asked.

'Manure given to me by farmers for use on my garden,' replied Luc.

'It's appalling,' replied the soldier, coughing. 'Lift the straw out of these boxes,' he ordered. Luc started to remove the straw slowly during which time Valérie could hear the soldier cursing in German. 'Hurry up,' he shouted. 'I want to see inside them.' After several minutes he started to choke and when he had recovered, he shouted, 'Stop. I've had enough.' He paused. 'I will give you a piece of advice, Monsieur. Don't let me come across you again after curfew with this disgusting stuff in your van. Even so, I want to see your identity card.'

'I understand,' Luc replied and closed the van doors. After checking his identity card, the soldier allowed Luke through the barrier.

Moments later Valérie heard Christophe mutter, 'Phew! What a smelly and hair-raising welcome back to France!'

She gave a nervous laugh and added, 'I never thought London would send you.'

'Is that a compliment or a criticism?'

'That's for you to fathom out,' she said, laughing.

After about three quarters of an hour, they arrived at Luc's place. He drove quickly into the garage, secured the doors, and opened the back of the van, removing the straw from the boxes and helping them climb out. By now Valérie's legs felt solid so she rubbed them several times to restore the blood circulation.

'I took you in the back way because Mrs Nosy Parker opposite watches everything. I'm almost certain she's a Pétainiste, and I wouldn't put it past her to inform on me given the chance. That's why I rarely receive Resistance people in my home. Anyway, let's feed you both.'

As they entered the house, loud barks could be heard.

'That's Didi. He's a guard dog. It pays to be careful,' said Luc, leading them into another room. 'Wait here, while I put on a lead.' He called them into the kitchen where a large Alsatian growled at them. It took some time until the dog had accepted Valérie and Christophe before Luc released him. He came and sniffed them for some time and then sprawled on the floor.

'He obviously likes the manure smell,' Valérie said, making them both laugh.

'Now let's have some food,' said Luc. 'You must be starving hungry. My wife left some onion soup. Fancy that with some fresh bread? There's some chicken left over from yesterday as well.'

'You're well stocked,' said Valérie.

'I'm lucky. Lots of people aren't. Local farmers are good to us and sometimes give us food in lieu of payment for vet fees.'

While he was preparing the food, both Valérie and Christophe were relieved to wash and rid themselves of the dreadful manure smell. As Valérie was dressing, she wondered where Christophe had been posted to in France previously and why he had been called back to England. Had something happened to Angela or someone in his family? And why had he been sent to a new circuit? How would they be able to work together, knowing that they couldn't form a relationship? It would be almost impossible because she still felt passionate about him and she sensed he felt the same.

After having enjoyed Luc's meal and having heard some of his escapades with farm animals, they followed him up the stairs to the bedrooms.

'You seem to know each other very well,' he said, winking at them. 'If you want to share one room, be my guests. Vive l'amour!'

Valérie told him, 'Sorry to disappoint you, but we're simply good friends.'

'You could have fooled me,' he replied with a chuckle. 'Eh bien, bonne nuit. Ah non, it's early morning. Till we meet later,' he said and turned to go downstairs.

Christophe's face was flushed, but that didn't stop Valérie from remarking, 'Maybe it's the way you look at me, Christophe, that made Luc think we aren't just good friends.'

He remained quiet for a few moments, looking into her eyes. 'Those sea-blue eyes of yours are enough to rouse passion in any man.'

'If you were free, you could show me,' she said, trying not to show any reaction, 'but you're not.'

She turned to go into her room when she felt his arm on her shoulder. 'I must tell you that Angela and I are no longer together. She was killed in an air raid.' A sob caught in his throat, but he continued, 'I'm swimming in a sea of devastation, guilt and anger.'

Valérie stared at him, finding it difficult to absorb his words and respond. 'I'm so sorry. I really am. Give yourself some space, Christophe, before moving on emotionally.'

'For someone so young, you understand human nature very well.'

'I'm used to coping with people's emotions, especially with my mother's,' she said, putting her arm round his shoulder and whispering, 'There will be another time for us.'

'Yes,' he whispered. 'Another time, another place.'

Later that morning at about half past eleven, Luc knocked at Valérie's door. 'May I come in?' he asked.

'Bien sûr,' she replied.

'It'll soon be time for lunch. Omelettes with some fried potatoes, OK?'

'Formidable. Do plenty of them. My mother makes fantastic ones.'

At lunch Luc's mood had changed. 'The days and nights in Tours and the surrounding area are becoming more daunting and dangerous.'

'Do you have any contact with the Boches in your work?' Valérie asked him.

'Indirectly, yes. Unfortunately. I hate treating dogs belonging to some of those French tarts who sleep with the Boches. The other day I had to put down a dog belonging to one of those women. Of course, I felt sorry for the animal, but I wished it had been its mistress or her Hun lover on my operating table. I would have given him or her a slow and painful death. That's how much I hate those bastards. They've tightened security everywhere.' The phone interrupted their conversation and when he returned, he told them, 'I must leave you. There's an emergency in the practice.'

After Luc had left the room, Christophe started to talk about previous sabotage work undertaken by Marcel and Valérie, having been briefed about it in London beforehand.

'We must now concentrate on our future plans. We need to build up our network, especially with the Maquis. I'm surprised Marcel hasn't encouraged Benoît to enlarge his group.'

'Marcel considered small circuits were more effective as well as small Maquis groups,' answered Valérie in a sharp tone of voice.

'You were obviously a most loyal and devoted courier to your organiser,' he replied abruptly.

'Yes. Marcel was considerate and brilliant in his job. He commanded respect from Benoît and all the maquisards.'

She heard Christophe breathe in deeply, taking his time to continue the conversation. He started to outline his future plans for the circuit. 'Soon London will arrange for more and more air drops of weapons and explosives. More raids on railway lines, roads, bridges and factories are vital to stop German supplies reaching the North of France where their troop numbers are increasing.'

'Is this in preparation for the invasion?' asked Valérie.

'It's possible, but I heard no mention of it in London. But we must always be on the alert. That's why I want you to train as many young men as you can—more and more are flooding into Maquis camps.'

Valérie reflected. The idea of suddenly increasing numbers wouldn't cut any ice with Benoît, who wanted to limit his number of men. Marcel had been patient with him. Flattery and compromise had been his weapons of dealing with the Maquis leader and it had often worked which had made her role easier.

Luc returned to the room. 'I can only keep you both here until the early evening when I will have to ask you to leave.'

'I wasn't planning on staying, Luc,' Christophe replied. 'I must make my way to my temporary place. Leave me near Tours railway station later today.'

'It will be after surgery hours at about six o'clock. Now I must prepare for my afternoon clinic,' he replied and left the room.

Christophe continued with his plans. 'I need to meet Benoît as soon as possible. How do you contact him?'

'We leave messages, preferably coded, under some bricks by the small statue in the garden at the back of the Ronsard Hotel. I will give you a map before we leave here.'

'Go ahead and fix a meeting. Also, we must have more support for our future operations, which as I told you are going to increase considerably.' He lit a cigarette and inhaled deeply. 'Have you started training any of Benoît's recruits?'

'No. I was on the point of arranging that. He lost one maquisard during our last operation.' She paused, trying to find the right words. 'He doesn't want to enlarge his group for the time being. He is cautious and well aware that moles are often planted inside Maquis groups by the Gestapo. It's easier to keep tabs on a small group.'

'I will have to persuade him otherwise,' said Christophe. 'Our job is to harass the enemy and to do that effectively, we need more men.'

'The two of you will have to sort out numbers by yourselves. Now I need to ask you about finances. Have you brought money for us and Benoît?'

'Yes. I have it with me,' he replied, retrieving his money belt and pulling out two wads of franc notes. 'Here are three hundred thousand francs for you, five hundred thousand for Benoît and his men and three hundred thousand for Emile.'

'London's been far more generous this time with the money,' said Valérie.

Towards six o'clock Luc returned to drop them near Tours railway station. During the journey Christophe hardly said a word to Valérie.

After a drive from a suburb in the south of Tours. Luc said, 'I'll drop you both here. It's about ten minutes to the station.'

They thanked him and started to walk into the city. Valérie told Christophe where the dead letter box was in Azay. As the station came into view, he put his arm round her and said, 'Take care at all times, Valérie,' and kissed her gently on the cheek.

'I always do,' she replied.

He smiled and walked away.

'Those sea-blue eyes of yours are enough to rouse passion in any man,' he'd told her. It was obvious that he loved her, but she recognised that he needed space to recover from the shock of Angela's death.

Her love for him would be for ever.

CHAPTER THIRTEEN

A SURPRISE RECRUIT

Valérie's alarm awoke her from a disturbed sleep. She'd been thinking of Marcel in England. Had they managed to ease his pain and operate successfully? Christophe's idea about increasing the number of maquisards also troubled her because she knew Benoît wanted to keep his group small.

It would be her first weapons training at Benoît's camp in a dense forest near Amboise. She would be training some of his recent younger recruits, who were on the run from compulsory work in Germany or Pétain's work camps for young people, as well as those who had responded to underground Resistance pamphlets. Some of these young men would be very tough, but discipline and humour would win them round. She was sure of that.

She left the rue du Cygne before seven thirty, just after the curfew, and made her way to Tours Station to catch a train to Amboise. On Christophe's advice, she had bought an annual season ticket for travel within the centre region, and it had proved a good investment. Queueing at ticket offices always carried a risk.

On arrival in Amboise, she made her way to a small cottage in a village on the other side of the town and hid in a garden shed belonging to people who were sympathetic to the Resistance. She waited patiently there for one of Benoît's men to lead her through the forest to the camp. After more than a quarter of an hour, she heard someone's footsteps outside. After three taps on the shed door and the exchange of the passwords, she opened it.

'Salut, Valérie,' said Martin.

'It's good to see you again, Martin.'

'We already have another name for you—la Capitaine.'

Valérie laughed. 'I've heard it before. So, it's taken my arrival in Vichy France to gain instant promotion.'

'French promotion is superior,' he replied with a grin. 'Now let's make our way to the Amboise Forest.'

Bright sunlight tore through the gaps in the wide variety of willow, ash, poplar and chestnut trees and the fresh smell of the night's rain permeated the forest. Movement among the ferns made Martin pull out his gun, but it was only a fox, its wet auburn-and-black coat gleaming in the morning sun. It paused, looking in their direction, before disappearing into the undergrowth. Rabbits scurried here and there.

'You'd need your gun at night-time for the boars,' she said.

'Yes, as well as for anyone hiding in those ferns and bushes.' After a pause he asked, 'Have you heard how Marcel is?'

'No, and I don't expect to because our organisation takes security seriously.'

'You must miss him.' She nodded in agreement. 'I could see how close you were together after the shoot-out when you were tending to him in that van.'

She caught the intense look in his light blue eyes. 'Marcel and I enjoyed a deep friendship and a professional respect for each other, but that's as far as it went.'

They walked on in silence for a while until Martin started to tell her about some of their chronic shortages. 'The lads could do with better clothing and we're running short on money for food and clothing coupons. Soon we're planning to carry out a raid on one of Vichy's compulsory youth service camps for food and money.'

'You won't have to because London has increased funding and I have money to give Benoît when I meet him.'

'That'll put him in a better frame of mind. He's been quite irritable lately.'

They continued walking together through the forest. From time to time, Martin pulled back some of the branches that invaded their pathway. Half an hour later, shots rang out, followed by the ferocious barking of a dog in the distance. Martin grabbed Valérie and led her behind a tree. 'Never run away from a dog, however ferocious it appears,' he said, taking her hand.

Suddenly a big brown hunting dog bounded towards them, growling and showing its teeth.

'Ici, Roco. Au pied. Tout de suite. Ici, je te dis,' shouted someone in a gravelly voice, silencing and controlling the dog. A short and sturdy man, dressed in expensive hunting clothes, approached them, carrying a large rifle. 'You're both taking chances walking through here,' he told them. 'I'm the Comte de Montignon and this part of the forest is my land. I've been trying to shoot some pheasants.'

'We're strangers here,' said Martin. 'We've been staying with a family in Amboise, but we wanted time on our own.'

The hunter winked at Valérie. 'I was young myself once,' he said. He looked at his watch and said, 'I must be off. Good luck. Viens, Roco. Viens.' Roco obeyed his master, and both departed.

Valérie released her hand from Martin's, though he seemed reluctant to let it go. They continued walking for a further kilometre when they became conscious of someone's presence behind them. A familiar voice called out, 'Not bad timing, Martin.'

Valérie turned and saw Benoît coming out from behind some bushes. Dressed in a black leather jacket and wearing German field boots, he looked impressive.

'Come and meet the team. They're all waiting for la Capitaine,' he said with a grin. 'We'll start the training after lunch which my chefs are preparing right now for you.'

As they came into the camp, a voice yelled out, 'Bienvenue, la Capitaine,' followed by a guffaw of laughter from the other men and young boys. She smiled at them as several of them walked towards her. 'We've been waiting patiently for you,' said one of them.

'I'm pleased to meet you all,' said Valérie. 'I'm here to help you fight the Boches.'

Several men shouted, 'Bravo, la Capitaine. Bravo.'

'La bouffe est prête,' said a chef who was bending over a cauldron while another one held up a chicken leg.

'We prevent the smoke from going up in the air by using this tarpaulin,' Benoît told her, pointing to a thick cover which was tied overhead to branches near the fire. 'We don't want to advertise our presence here. Security is crucial in everything we do. It'll be tough on anyone who doesn't adhere to my rules. Now let's get in the queue for lunch.'

In contrast to their leader, most of his men wore blue overall trousers, drab-coloured shirts and they walked in clogs or tattered boots. A few, like Martin, were dressed in scraps of British and French battledress. Some wore caps or large black berets.

Valérie held out her plate for the chef to serve her.

'Voici un bon poulet de campagne,' he told her, 'made with local chickens and veg.'

Winking at her, he added, 'Of course I've made a wine sauce, courtesy of my old dad who owns a vineyard.'

'There's nothing like using good local wine,' she replied with a smile. 'The chicken smells absolutely delicious.'

'And it tastes just as good,' added the other chef.

About fifteen maquisards sat down on the grass in a large circle, drinking red wine in tin mugs with their lunch. Valérie started talking to a young man and later in the conversation, he lowered his voice and said, 'I want to fight the Boches. I came some distance to avoid any repercussions for my family. I have a false identity card and it's as good as a genuine one. Even so there's always a risk they could break me down with torture and find out where my parents, brothers and sisters live.'

Another young man, heavy eyed, explained sadly, 'My brother was attacked and dragged away from our home in April in front of the family, including my eighty-year-old grandmother, who collapsed on the ground outside when she saw it happen. When one of the soldiers started to beat my brother even harder, I felt like pulling out my pen knife and stabbing him in the heart.' Valérie stopped eating. The young man continued, 'So when I turned eighteen last month, I was determined that no one was going to arrest me like that. I'm never going to be dragged from my home and shoved into a cattle train to be sent to Germany to work for those bastards. So that's why I'm here. My family have known Benoît for several years.'

Halfway through lunch, Valérie could see a young man emerging from the dense forest. She strained her eyes. Was she imagining things? No. It can't be. She stood up as he ran towards her and flung his arms round her. 'I can't believe it's you. Are you la Capitaine?'

Valérie did not call him by his name—Beaulieu had trained her well. She was aghast at his presence in the Maquis.

'Who is it?' shouted one voice.

'Tell us, la Capitaine!' cried another person.

What should she say now?

Benoît intervened, much to her relief. Facing his men, he said, 'I don't know how these two know each other, but in the interest of security, we want no further questions. Follow me,' he told them gruffly, and led Valérie and the man to a group of tents made from parachute material. He took them into the largest one and asked them to sit down. 'Explain what this is all about.'

'He's my cousin André,' Valérie replied, 'and I had no idea he was a maquisard and that he was in your group.'

Benoît took his time to answer. 'For reasons of security no one must know you are cousins, so find a reason to explain how you know each other.'

'We went to the same school, which is true, but he was in a higher class. That should be good enough,' suggested Valérie.

Benoît replied, 'Il n'y a pas d'autre solution.' He was right, there was no other answer.

Valérie rubbed her face. She loved her cousin, but she remembered seeing him drunk on several occasions in front of his family in the summer of 1939. He would have been about twenty years old then. If he still drank like that, he would be a security risk.

Towards five o'clock in the afternoon Valérie met six new recruits. More experienced maquisards were assisting her, including Martin. She started to tell the recruits that apart from weaponry, they would be shown how to defend themselves and would have lessons in unarmed combat.

'We'll now deal with the Sten, this time,' she said, picking one up from the crate. 'Before I show you how to strip it and load it, remember this: if ever you're found with a gun and ammunition, you will be tortured and then shot. Bury it if in danger. Remember you are going to fight a vicious enemy.' By the fear in their eyes, she realised that her words had taken effect.

After dinner that evening, when they were on their own, Valérie asked Benoît if she could organise a competition for the young men and whether he would be willing to judge it.

'We'll need to organise another training session for pistols and grenades. Also, we need more recruits to join your Maquis,' she told him. 'Christophe is keen for you to increase your number of men. We've more operations on the agenda that will require larger numbers.' She noticed a deep frown spread across his forehead. He did not respond to her comment which was unusual. She would soon wipe that frown away. 'I have something to give you, Benoît,' she said and took out a bundle of notes from her jacket pocket and handed them to him. 'Here's five hundred thousand francs from London.'

He smiled broadly at her and came up to her and kissed her on both cheeks. 'This increase is most welcome. We are desperate for money. I'm so relieved because I'll be able to pay a local farmer for two weeks' supply of food. He'll be happy too.'

After three days of instruction, Martin helped Valérie organise competitions in the use of Stens, as well as armed combat. A sixteen-year-old won first prize in the rifle stripping and assembling competition and was applauded as he went up to Benoît to receive a smart black beret as his prize.

When it came to the unarmed combat competitions, Valérie and Benoît tackled their recruits. A tall muscular young man managed to throw Valérie over his shoulder, much to the amusement of Benoît, but she surprised them all by falling without injuring herself.

It was time to leave the camp. Benoît escorted her to the edge of the forest where he took her aside and said, 'Christophe needs to realise that this is my Maquis. I decide the numbers. I've heard it all go wrong further south when large numbers were involved. It's not unknown for the Gestapo to plant moles in Maquis groups. When the invasion comes, that will be a different matter. Then we will unite in larger groups and support the Allies. But for now, as far as my Maquis is concerned, we will do it my way. Marcel understood that.'

After Benoît had gone, Valérie started to make her way to Amboise railway station. Would André resist the temptation to drink? It was vital to warn both Christophe and Benoît for the safety of everyone involved. Then there was every likelihood that there would be confrontation between Christophe and Benoît regarding the number of recruits needed for future operations. She wasn't going to take sides.

CHAPTER FOURTEEN

CONFRONTATION AND LOVE IN JUNE

Two days later, Valérie set off in the early morning on her bicycle to meet Christophe outside Larçay. On the outskirts of the village, she saw children, dressed in traditional blue cotton overalls over their clothes, walking to school. Valérie heard the rumble of lorry wheels coming from behind them. A boy started to run away from the group and dash towards some bushes. 'They took my granddad away. I'm not letting them find me,' he shouted. A young girl screamed at the girl in charge of the group, 'Bernadette, don't let them see us. Please don't.'

Valérie dismounted and wheeled her bike over towards the children. 'Don't be afraid. I'll stay with you. There's no need to hide.' Within a short time two German open staff cars approached, followed by several lorries full of troops, but they sped by. 'You see, there was nothing to worry about,' she told the children and said goodbye to them and continued on her way.

Her thoughts turned to André. When she told Christophe about André's presence in the Maquis, how would he react? As for Benoît not wanting to enlarge his Maquis group, that would only make Christophe angry. No. She didn't feel like being wedged between him and Benoît when they met.

On arrival at a small farmhouse on the outskirts of the village, she rang the doorbell three times and waited for several moments before it was opened by a middle-aged woman. After exchanging passwords, the woman said, 'Your friend is waiting for you in there,' and pointed to a barn some distance from the house. 'Don't stay there for too long, I beg you.'

'Another man is going to join us shortly. Don't worry. We'll soon be gone,' Valérie assured her.

'God be with you,' the woman replied and closed the door.

Valérie entered the barn with her bicycle and noticed Christophe's there too. He was sitting on a bale of hay, absorbed in reading something, when Valérie closed the barn door, startling him. 'It's good to see you. How did the training go?'

'Fine,' she replied, sitting down beside him. 'I even ran a competition, but I was surprised and somewhat concerned to find that my cousin from Orléans had joined Benoît's group.'

'Why are you worried?'

'He may not be suited to doing Resistance work because his brother was executed by the Gestapo in the Orléans area where he belonged to a local Resistance group. That could pose a problem because the Boches will almost certainly have his family on file.'

Christophe took his time to answer her. 'Did you tell Benoît?'

'No. I wanted to consult you first. We've promised him not to divulge that we are cousins to any of his men. There's also another risk: before the war, the last time I saw him, he was drinking heavily. I haven't seen him since 1939 so I don't know whether he's managed to curb it and, of course, we have no direct contact with his family.'

'Does Benoît know?'

'No. Again, I felt I should consult you.'

Christophe looked at her closely. 'We'll have to discuss everything with Benoît when he arrives.' He ran his hand through his hair. 'Let's talk about our first operation together. If we're to cause as much disruption as possible for the Boches, better-trained men are crucial for our future operations. And more of them. Our next sabotage job involves blowing up the reformers in the electric power station in Tours.'

Valérie raised her eyebrows. 'That's the most daring project yet. And potentially extremely dangerous.'

'There are German sentries outside the depot who patrol regularly as well as security staff inside the building all the time. We will need highly trained maquisards on this operation. In the first instance, I'll be asking you to carry out a recce on the venue.'

'How many people will be involved?'

'We need ten well-trained and experienced men. You told me Benoît has fifteen maquisards and that these include six young men that you're in the middle of training. So that leaves us nine trained men.'

'Benoît won't go beyond twenty men for the moment,' she replied. Before he could respond, the barn door was slowly opened. Benoît would have marched straight in like he normally did. Only the birds chirping outside could be heard, which added to the tension. Christophe pulled out a pistol, cocking and aiming it at the doorway. Valérie wiped her brow. The adrenalin inside her was pumping away to such an extent that she was beginning to feel dizzy until a familiar voice called out, 'Don't worry. It's me, Benoît.' Valérie cursed under her breath. The Maquis leader placed his bicycle near theirs and then walked up to her and kissed her. 'Bonjour, la Capitaine.' Turning to Christophe, he said, 'That's our pet name for your courier.' Looking into Valérie's eyes, he added, 'I hope you've got the new leader in good spirits,' and laughed as he sat down on a bale of hay opposite them.

Valérie made the introductions, but the glare in Christophe's eyes troubled her.

After a long pause Christophe said, 'Marcel, Valérie and the maquisards succeeded in putting the Comitéls factory out of service for some considerable time.'

'I led my men,' he added sharply.

Christophe cleared his throat. 'However, future operations we are planning will intensify and become riskier. And for these reasons, I want you to consider enlarging your group.'

Benoît frowned. 'I won't increase the number of men in my Maquis at the moment because I've heard how other groups have taken on lots of people, without having time to check their papers properly, and to supervise the men closely. It has led to trouble, denunciations and reprisals. Gestapo moles are often hidden inside Maquis groups. Like all of us, I want to destroy the enemy, but if you want to use my men, it's on my terms.'

Christophe grimaced. 'If that's the case, we may have to look for support elsewhere.'

Benoît glared at Christophe, his dark brown eyes burning like a jungle cat. 'You can say what you think, but don't talk down to me. Marcel never did.'

'I don't need you to compare me with my predecessor, thanks,' Christophe replied tersely.

'You're not French,' Benoît shouted and turned to Valérie. 'Your courier *is*. We have our French pride. She understands how the French mind works. Clearly you bloody well don't.'

Valérie bit her lip. This row had to stop right now, she decided. Benoît was a good Maquis leader and was respected by his men. Finding another reliable Maquis group would take up valuable time. Christophe shouldn't have dived straight into talking about numbers straight away with Benoît.

'Benoît, we have a complicated and dangerous operation in mind, and we need experienced men to succeed in it,' Valérie explained in a soft voice. 'We know you're a dedicated leader and we trust you. Think carefully. Remember Christophe wants to increase the number of sabotage operations before the invasion, and we need to train more men now.'

She looked at him directly. 'I'll think of a compromise.'

Benoît smiled at her and put his hand on her shoulder. 'I'll be back in a few minutes. I need a cigarette. It's too risky in here with all this hay lying about.'

During his absence Valérie sat for a while, trying to work out a plan. 'How about this?' she asked Christophe. 'Maybe we could persuade Benoît to appoint two groups: Benoît could nominate Martin as the leader of the second group. And each group could have a deputy leader. That way they could keep control of the maquisards in small groups and increase them gradually with new recruits. Also, they could verify the men's paperwork.'

'That's a brilliant idea. Could you explain it to him? It will work better if you do.'

She nodded in agreement.

Benoît returned to the barn in a more relaxed manner and sat down opposite them. Firstly, Valérie reiterated that their next operation would undoubtedly be the most dangerous one they had planned so far in the circuit. Secondly, they needed his help if they were to succeed. As she outlined her idea of running two groups and how that could be achieved, Benoît started to warm to the idea.

After she had finished, he replied, 'Of course we need time to recruit and once we've increased a few more men, I'm prepared to try your idea. If it doesn't work, we'll abandon it.' He cleared his throat several times. 'I've been thinking about André, your cousin. He's older than the other recruits and they like him. He's also got a vast knowledge of firearms and could become an instructor.' There was an awkward pause. 'What's the problem?'

Christophe intervened. 'Benoît, are you aware that André comes with a history? I've only just found about it all from Valérie.'

'Yes. I know they're cousins.'

'There's more to it than that,' Christophe replied. As he explained about the execution of André's brother and André's drinking problems, Benoît became uneasy.

'Maybe it would be wise to ask my cousin to leave your Maquis and move out of the area,' Valérie suggested.

Benoît reflected for a moment. 'I've seen no evidence of it in the camp. Quite the contrary. He usually only drinks a mug of wine. Never more. Give him a chance. His van is useful to us and he's the best shot out of everyone. He's also a qualified telephone engineer and all those skills will be very useful to us all. I think you're exaggerating things, la Capitaine. After all, you told me that you last saw him four years ago. He was younger then. Leave it with me.'

'We need your help and once I've made all the necessary plans, we'll contact you,' said Christophe.

'We will support you like we did on the last mission. I'll talk to André as soon as we get back to the camp. He's picking me up in the next village where he's collecting some meat from a farmer.'

After he had gone, Christophe told Valérie, 'You saved the day.'

'The next operation is highly risky. We are going to destroy the transformers in the electricity power station in Tours,' Christophe told her.

'My goodness,' replied Valérie. 'That will require a lot of research.'

'Yes. I will be asking you to conduct a recce in the area surrounding the electricity power station. The reason for cutting the electricity supply is to cause havoc inside Tours and the surrounding areas and slowing the work down in the Liotard factory near Tours, where the Nazis produce parts for their fighter planes.'

'Mon Dieu. This is the most dangerous operation yet,' she exclaimed.

'I do not intend to tell the maquisards the ultimate aim,' replied Christophe.

'And if they ask?'

'We will tell them that they will find out later,' said Christophe.

Christophe and Valérie cycled through the woods, but after a while Valérie felt weary due to the initial fiery exchange between Christophe and Benoît and sat down on a large log. Christophe joined her, and they started talking about their time in Wanborough and Beaulieu.

'I was supposed to go on a commando course in Scotland after Wanborough; I remember telling you, but because I was army trained, they sent me straight out to France.' He paused and took her hand. 'Valérie, we need to talk about us. I told you at Wanborough how deeply I felt for you, and I took you into my arms at Beaulieu and showed you how I felt. Neither of us have a commitment now with anybody else.'

She swallowed hard and looked into his eyes alight with desire, his hair bleached by the sun, almost golden. She caressed his face and said, 'I've longed for you to say these words.'

'I love you in a way I've never felt about a girl before.' She felt his strong warm arms wrap round her, drawing her close to his chest, as he nuzzled his face into her hair. She didn't resist as his lips sought hers and their kiss was long, searching and passionate, making her body tingle.

'My darling, I've waited so long for this moment,' he murmured huskily, echoing her own thoughts because this was what she had been aching for ever since that moonlight walk in the mystical garden at Wanborough.

He undid her blouse, cupped her small, firm breasts in his hands and kissed them with a growing intensity that left her breathless.

'Oh, Christophe, I feel so happy,' she said as she felt him start to remove her clothes and felt the air on her skin and the warmth of the sun seeping through the trees. She helped him remove his trousers and they lay down on their clothes. His kisses increased in intensity, his hands caressing her breasts gently then more passionately. She caressed his chest and lower down, feeling the passion within her increase. She felt him hard below and they fulfilled their love for each other.

Afterwards Valérie slept only briefly and woke feeling as if all the cares and tensions of her time in France had been swept away. Moments later

Christophe awoke and ran his hands over her face. 'I will always love you, my darling.'

'And I feel the same,' she replied, running her hand through his soft silky hair. 'I shouldn't ask this, but what is your real name?'

He hesitated. 'You know it's against the firm's rules,' he said, looking straight into her eyes, then whispered, 'Paul. And yours?'

'Marie-Claire.'

At midday, they heard children's distressed voices in the distance, and they quickly dressed.

'They're going home—it's half day for them on Wednesdays,' said Valérie.

When the children came into view, Valérie recognised Bernadette, who ran up to her and fell into her open arms, sobbing uncontrollably. Once she had recovered, she explained.

'The Boches came to our school and took away one of our teachers—Madame Charrier.'

Valérie swallowed hard. Charrier? She knew that name from somewhere. She remembered now. Jeanne, Arnaud's wife, had talked to her about a friend called Yvonne Charrier. If that was the same woman, how would Jeanne cope?

Christophe comforted the other children. Once they had stopped crying, Christophe whispered to Valérie, 'We'll have to explain to them that we have to go somewhere urgently. We can't afford to become involved with them and their families. We can't.'

Valérie sighed deeply. In wartime everything was disrupted. Every strand of human life was affected. No time to comfort children distressed by the cruelty of evil men.

They said goodbye to the children and started to cycle through the woods. Christophe paused. 'I must leave you here, Valérie. I have to meet Emile soon.'

'When will we meet again? And where?'

'In a few days' time, preferably in this area. I suggest meeting at Raymond's house if he agrees.'

'Of course, he will,' said Valérie and gave him details of how to find Raymond's address.

'I will leave you a message under the dead letter box in Tours,' he replied.

CHAPTER FIFTEEN

ARRESTS AND WARNING

A few days later Valérie was walking towards Hervé's café when a familiar voice from behind her called out, 'Quelle surprise, Marie-Claire.'

She turned and came face to face with André, anger mounting inside her. 'Don't you ever dare call me by that name again! And don't call out at me. It draws unwelcome attention.'

'I'm sorry,' he murmured. 'Really sorry.'

'If you want to talk, let's go down that side road opposite,' she told him.

'I wanted to see you before now, but Benoît only allows us out of the camp if we are doing jobs for him,' he told her.

'A good Maquis leader is vigilant. I wanted to see you as well about an important matter,' she replied, noticing a concerned look sweep his face. 'Has Benoît talked to you about drinking too much?'

His face reddened. 'No. Why should he?'

'Because the last time I saw you in 1939 in Orléans, when you were about twenty-two years old, you were drunk on more occasions than I like to remember.'

He looked away from her.

'Do you still drink?'

He took his time to reply. 'Occasionally, but I know how to control it. After the Gestapo executed Philippe, I began drinking heavily again to block it all out. Mum pleaded with me to go and see our local priest. Thanks to his counselling I managed to reduce it.'

'If we see you can't control it, Benoît will throw you out of the Maquis and we'll support him.'

He looked into her eyes. 'Would you really do that to your cousin?'

'No hesitation at all.' He gave no response as they continued walking along together in silence until she suggested, 'Let's go to a café I know,' and noticed his relief.

On arrival at Hervé's café, they went into the courtyard and began to talk quietly. Hervé came to their table and took their order, but as he walked away Valérie noticed how troubled he seemed.

In a low voice André said, 'Benoît told us yesterday that Louis will lead a second Maquis group. That means he's looking for more recruits and a deputy. As I'm older than some of the boys and young men, he might choose me. Only yesterday, he told me how pleased he was with my work.'

'Steady on. You've only been with him for a few weeks.'

'You'll see—next time we meet, we'll be about equal in rank.'

Valérie laughed nervously. 'Not quite, André. I've been professionally trained.' She bit her lip as she said the last word and cursed her indiscretion under her breath.

'Oh, tell me more.'

'That's for me to know and you not to find out,' she replied, 'and keep your voice down.'

Hervé brought the drinks to the table and gave the bill directly to Valérie. There was a message inside, that was for sure. Something serious had happened.

'How's Aunt Josette? I couldn't talk to you properly at the camp to ask,' he asked her.

'My mother never changes,' she replied with a sigh.

'What about Uncle Charlie?'

'Cheerful and relaxed as usual. I miss him terribly. How's your mother?'

'She's started helping out at the local junior school after our priest suggested it and enjoys working with the children. But she still hasn't fully recovered. That's why I wanted to join the Maquis and when a friend of mine in Orléans told me about Benoît, I got in touch with him.'

Valérie put her hand on his shoulder and whispered, 'Don't be under any illusions. Not everyone shares our way of thinking about the Nazis, especially in Tours. And remember lots of families lost relatives in the Great War. I can't say much here. Just be wary and use your eyes and ears all the time. Trust no one you meet.'

He looked at his watch and picked up the bill. 'I must go now, but I'll pay the bill.'

She felt a spurt of alarm. 'No. Leave that with me,' she replied, grabbing it.

After André had left, she opened it and inside was a note asking her to stay and wait for Hervé in the courtyard. He arrived and sat down opposite her. 'There have been several arrests in Paris and in the area south of Orléans. Don't travel by train or car to those areas now,' he told her in a low voice.

'Do you have any names?'

'No definite confirmation. Added to that, someone called by just now and told me that a couple have been arrested not far from Meung. I have friends there so you can imagine how worried I am.' Valérie's heart quickened. 'I can see you are concerned. I'll keep you and your male friend informed.'

'Thank you, Hervé,' she said.

She checked the dead letter box in the garden at the Ronsard Hotel, and found a note from Christophe, asking her to meet him the following day at eleven o'clock at Raymond's house.

The next day, Valérie cycled to Raymond's house outside Véretz. Halfway there she stopped to rest by the riverbank. Throughout the first weeks in June, the weather had been glorious, but today it was cloudy, and a strong wind had whipped up the Cher, now darker in colour than on previous days. Finally, she arrived at Raymond's home and left her bicycle round the back of the house before giving the customary three taps on the front door.

'Come in, my dear,' said Raymond. 'You seem upset. Whatever has happened?'

'Arrests have been made in Paris and to the south of Orléans and a couple have been arrested near Meung. Christophe left me a note and asked me to meet him here. I hope that's all right.'

'Of course. You know I'll help you both in any way I can in the same way as I did for Marcel and you.

What's this new chap like? Did you know him before coming to France?'

'Yes,' she replied coyly.

They spent the next hour talking about the general state of the country and how more young men were flocking to join the Maquis; Raymond started to tell her about a local lad working in the Resistance.

'He's only in his teens and he ferried people to safety across the demarcation line until last November when the Boches took over the Free Zone. Parts of Véretz were in the Free Zone. Even his family know nothing about it, and I only know because I helped him out one night when he and a young couple wanted a place to hide. I've known him since he was a toddler. And I'm proud to know him.' His eyes misted over before he continued. 'But one of my friends is in turmoil. His son denounced his brother for harbouring a Jewish man and he's been arrested.' He lowered his head. 'The more I hear of these denunciations, the more outraged I feel when people like you, Christophe and the others are risking your lives.'

They continued talking about other events in Tours until there were three knocks on the front door. 'That's probably Christophe.'

'I'll let him in,' said Raymond. Christophe came into the room and kissed Valérie.

'You must both be hungry, so I'll prepare you something to eat,' said Raymond.

'I haven't eaten for two days so that's most welcome. I had to leave the place where I was sleeping last night because the Boches were approaching the village,' replied Christophe.

Valérie told Christophe about the arrests in the capital and near Meung that Hervé had told her about. 'We need to find out more details about a couple from Meung who worked with Marcel.' She looked at him anxiously. 'From Marcel's description of the middle-aged woman and his remark about how vivacious she was, I'm sure it was Francine.'

'Francine? Bloody hell. She was one of the best students on our course. And she was immensely popular. Yes. You're right. We must try to find out more details, but we will have to tread carefully.'

Halfway through the meal, there was another knock on the front door. They looked at each other in trepidation. Raymond told them to go down into the cellar while he went to see who it was. As they started to go down the stairs, Valérie heard a young male voice speaking to Raymond in a distressed manner.

After about ten minutes, Raymond closed the front door and called them to join him.

'I've bad news for you both. Valérie, the young man who used to pass people over the demarcation line called in and told me that there have been arrests in a village near Chambord. A couple have been shot badly by the Boches. One of his aunts has just come back from that area and she heard it from someone who works at Blois Hospital and who has important contacts. A woman in her forties was taken there seriously ill. The man was detained in a military infirmary.'

Valérie looked at Christophe in horror.

CHAPTER SIXTEEN

THE ENEMY ADVANCES

Two days later, Valérie received an urgent message in the dead letter box in Tours from Christophe telling her to meet Emile down by the River Cher outside Larçay. As she approached the riverbank, she could see Emile drawing heavily on his cigarette.

'I'm so relieved to see you. I haven't been able to send London any messages or receive any from them because both my transceiver and my spare one won't work either. Both need valves. London will be anxious, thinking I've been arrested. We'll have to contact another circuit.'

Valérie stroked her lips. 'I know another wireless operator who might be able to help us, but it will mean a long journey for me and there are even more risks in that town than in Tours. I'll contact him as soon as I can. I went to see him in Angers on behalf of Marcel. In the meantime, I'll make a false bottom in my shopping bag and put any valves in there.'

'Thanks a lot. Leave me a note at the presbytery in Azay if you make contact. Now I must be on my way.'

After contacting Madame Duclos, who acted as a go-between, a meeting was arranged between Valérie and a circuit in Angers. She boarded a train for Angers early in the morning, during the third week in June, having dyed her hair lighter and cut it shorter. Light-rimmed spectacles, a thick cardigan, and one light summer skirt worn over another completed the disguise. She'd placed several vegetables inside her shopping bag over the false bottom.

She squeezed into the last seat in a compartment and placed her shopping bag up onto the rack above her. After the train had left the station, she took out a detective novel from her handbag and started to read it.

From time to time, she looked out of the window to admire the vineyards with their vines covered in white flowers. Herons and other birds pecked away on islets in the wide River Loire. Now and then she spotted châteaux dominating the landscape.

On approaching Saumur, halfway between Tours and Angers, Valérie decided to stretch her legs and went to stand in the corridor, but she hadn't counted on several German soldiers boarding the train at the next station. She pressed her face against the window, not wanting to make eye contact with them as they passed her down the corridor, but one officer stopped and stood beside her. 'On your way to meet your boyfriend?' he asked her with a snigger.

She swung round. 'No. I'm going to visit my aunt who is dying,' she replied, seeing the smile disappear from his face.

'Entshuldigung, Mademoiselle. My profuse apologies,' he said, clicking his heels and leaving her alone.

She returned to her carriage and sat down, burying herself in her detective story, and was relieved when tickets were asked for by a friendly ticket inspector. On arrival in Angers, she hurried through the barrier without any trouble. So far so good she thought, but she mustn't put a foot wrong in this city because it was the Gestapo's nerve centre for controlling the west of France.

Apart from a few bombing raids, Angers had not suffered anything like the destruction in Tours. She made her way to the Place du Ralliement, where a beautiful nineteenth-century theatre took pride of place, and caught a bus to Trélazé, a small slate-mining town outside the city. Her destination was a bicycle repair business where she was going to meet

Bertrand, the local head of the Angers circuit. She'd memorised the instructions of how to find the house several times. She alighted from the bus and made her way to his house, set in a row of eighteenth-century one-storey houses with slate roofs. On entering the courtyard, she noticed him bent over a bicycle he was repairing.

'C'est Bertrand?' she asked him.

He swung round, giving her a broad smile, and replied, 'Oui, oui.' Then they exchanged passes. 'It's good to meet you. You've come at the right time because we're about to have lunch. Rabbit casserole is being cooked today and it's always delicious. Let me introduce you to my wife, Louise,' he told her and led her into a large kitchen with beige painted walls and old furniture.

'Thanks for having me at such short notice,' said Valérie. Later in the conversation she asked Louise, 'Is Yves here?'

'Well, you might ask. He's always late for meals,' explained Louise.

It wasn't until halfway through lunch that Yves, a studious-looking man, with thin mousy hair, appeared. He excused himself for his late arrival, acknowledged everyone and sat down beside Valérie.

'How was your journey? he asked her. 'Uneventful, I trust?'

'Fortunately, yes.'

He leaned forward. 'Be even more on your guard in this city. It's far more dangerous here than in other towns in the west.'

'I sensed that straight away,' she replied, bemused by his formal way of talking which reminded her of Marcel when they had first met.

After lunch, he took her upstairs to his bedroom. 'You're lucky that we have three spare sets of valves, and you can have two of them. I'm expecting more from our next drop.' While he located the valves under a floorboard, Valérie removed the vegetables from her shopping bag.

He passed her the valves, contained in a small cardboard box, and she hid them in the secret compartment of her shopping bag, placing the vegetables on top.

'How is the situation in your circuit?' she asked him.

'Not at all good. For security's sake, I can't say much, but I can tell you that a local Maquis leader executed one of his men who was an informer.'

'Mon Dieu!' she replied as a cold wave swept through her. Would Benoît ever resort to that?

'You need to make your way back. Travel with the workers going home. There's safety in numbers as they say.'

Valérie smiled and thanked him before going downstairs to show her gratitude to her hosts for their hospitality.

Sometime after leaving the bus in Angers, she noticed a fat man, who looked more like a tramp, following her. How would she lose him? Thank goodness she knew Angers well, having stayed in the city with her aunt when she was younger. She decided to walk towards the castle because she was familiar with the alleys and side roads around it, but he continued to follow her. She turned suddenly into a nearby alley where she saw a car parked nearby and noticed he'd continued walking on. Maybe it was unlocked, she thought. She opened the door and couldn't believe her luck. She dived into the back of it and lay on the floor. After about ten minutes, she could see no sign of the man. The cathedral was nearby. She'd go in there. It was dark inside. She crept out of the car and continued walking along the alley which came out by the cathedral. She stopped to tie up her shoelaces and checked to see if a second person was following her and was relieved to see that there wasn't.

She walked quickly to the cathedral, hoping that no one was pursing her. As she entered, a confessional box on the left-hand side caught her attention. That's where she would hide. She quickly walked over to it and pulled the curtains aside, slipping into the box and leaving a slight gap in the curtains as she drew them across and leaving the door slightly ajar. Her hand shook as she wiped the sweat off her brow. A few minutes later, she heard the entrance door being opened. Footsteps could be heard coming down the aisle. Through the narrow gap in the curtains, she could see the shape of a tall thin man looking everywhere for someone and she was certain it was her. She gently closed the door. When he approached the confessional box, she clung to her seat; her face stiffened, her head began to throb, and her heart started to race. She pressed her hand over her mouth. Not long afterwards the man walked away and, much to her relief, she heard a loud clang of the main entrance door.

After a while she removed her spectacles and pulled out a jar from her bag and rubbed some black powder into her hair and pulled off one of her skirts which she left in the confessional box. She crept cautiously out of a side entrance. Nobody was about, much to her relief. She took the longest route to the station, keeping to the side roads and alleys again.

On arrival at the station, she found a seat in a third-class compartment at the back of the train for Tours. She placed her bag again on the rack above her, then sat down and opened her detective novel. A middle-aged couple with their grandson came in and sat next to her. Soon the compartment filled up.

Once the train set off, she started to read her detective novel but had trouble in concentrating and kept thinking about the radio valves that were hidden in her bag. She prayed there would be no trouble on the train, but halfway through the journey a middle-aged man in a grey suit, followed by a ticket inspector, burst into their carriage.

After examining the other passengers' identity cards, he moved to Valérie. 'Your identity card,' he asked her in a heavy German accent. He perused it for a long time, making the other passengers stare at her, which only made her feel more awkward. She started to sweat but avoided wiping her face. Had the tramp been an agent in disguise? Had they been watching Bertrand's house and arrested him immediately after she had left and followed her?

'Why are you travelling back to Tours at this hour?'

'I've been to visit a sick friend.'

'And who is this friend and where does he or she live?' he snapped.

He suspected her. Heaven help her if he started to examine her bag. She mustn't be afraid. She mustn't give in. She looked up at him; his dark grey eyes were fixed on her, eyes devoid of emotion. She gave him a fictitious name and the name of a bombed street that she had seen earlier.

He cleared his throat, looked around at the other passengers who tried to avoid eye contact with him. 'Your card appears to be in order,' he said, staring at Valérie, 'but one can never be sure. The Resistance scum fighting against us are ruining any chances of Germany and France working together for the good of Europe.' Looking up at the luggage rack, he asked, 'Is that your bag above?'

'Yes,' she replied.

'I want to look at it.'

Valérie's heart thumped. This could be her burnt, as Wanborough termed it. She stood up and lifted the bag off the rack and gave it to him.

'Where did you get these vegetables from?' he asked her. 'Rather strange after visiting a sick friend,' he commented in a menacing tone of voice.

'Her mother gave them to me. She'd just come back from visiting a relative in the countryside who has a smallholding.'

When he started to remove a few of the carrots and green beans, she started to breathe heavily. He mustn't notice that she'd become agitated. She had to control herself.

'Mm,' he murmured. He moved closer to her. 'I trust you are not involved in any way with the terrorists, Mademoiselle, but I shall remember you,' he told her and to her relief, he replaced the vegetables and returned the bag to her. 'There is something about you that I cannot identify. Let's hope we do not meet again under serious circumstances.' He left the carriage with the ticket collector who looked ill at ease.

She sat down on her weakened legs.

After the door had closed, a woman, who was sitting opposite Valérie, took out a flask from her bag and poured some ersatz coffee into a mug for Valérie. 'You are truly a brave French citizen. God bless you, my dear.'

The other passengers looked at her with sympathy and one man said, 'You stood up to his questioning very well.'

On her return to Tours, Valérie felt the need to go somewhere quiet to recover from her ordeal. There was no question of returning to her lodgings, putting Madame Lelong immediately at risk, so she made her way to the basilica and sat in one of the pews at the back.

Moments later, Father Antoine came out of the sacristy and on noticing her, he walked over to her. 'What a surprise, Valérie. Come with me,' he whispered and led her into the sacristy and shut the door. 'You look frightened.'

'I have every cause to be.' As she related what had happened to her, the priest became more agitated and distressed.

'You're a brave courier and Christophe is lucky to have you.' He leaned back in his chair and sighed. 'The situation is worse than ever. The Gestapo have been rounding up lots of people in Tours. It may be in connection with the arrests in Paris and Chambord two days ago.'

'Have you any details about arrests in Chambord?' asked Valérie.

'I heard that there was trouble there, but as yet I haven't any details.'

'I daren't return to my lodgings, Father.'

'Arnaud's home is the only safe place. I'll phone him with the password for emergencies.'

Father Antoine returned in a hurry. 'Arnaud can shelter you for one night only.' By the tone of his voice, she could detect something serious had happened. The priest looked at his watch. 'We must leave now. If my car is stopped, I will use the excuse that I am visiting someone who is terribly ill and needs the last rites and that you have accompanied me as their friend. Of course, I'll have to risk giving them a false name and address and hope they won't check.'

During their journey to Arnaud's place, Valérie thought about Arnaud's children and their friends. When would families be able to meet at weekends and enjoy scrumptious summer picnics by the river? Or hear their children laughing and playing tag in the woods? But some families would have a father, a brother or a son missing from the family outing, wouldn't they, after the Occupation ended? Or even a mother or a sister?

They finally arrived outside Bléré. As Father Antoine drove down the long drive to the château, Valéric could see some children playing in the distance. When they parked, Arnaud's eldest daughter, Angéline, ran towards Valérie and threw her arms round her, followed by Stéphanie who joined in the big hug.

Straggling behind were a boy and a girl of a similar age to Arnaud's children. Angéline introduced them to Valérie and Father Antoine. Dark circles round the girl's eyes emphasised the fear within them whereas the boy avoided eye contact. They entered the château by the kitchen entrance with Stéphanie calling out to her mother, 'Maman, Maman, Valérie's here with Father.'

Jeanne came into the kitchen and spoke to her eldest daughter in a whisper, 'Angéline, please take the children to the playroom and look after them.' After they had gone, she led Father Antoine and Valérie into the sitting room.

'Do sit down, please,' she told them. 'I've dreadful news to tell you. The Gestapo have arrested my close friend, Yvonne Charrier, the mother of the young boy and girl you've just seen. They took her to their headquarters in the rue Georges Sand. Thank God her children weren't at school that day and were taken away to a safe house, before coming here.'

Valérie gasped, remembering her encounter with Yvonne's pupils, and told Jeanne.

'So now you have seen what effect it has had on the children. This is a dreadful time for all of us. Her daughter screamed several times in her sleep last night and I spent most of it cuddling her.' There was a long silence before she asked the priest, 'Father Antoine, you'll stay for dinner, won't you?'

The priest shook his head. 'I'd love to, but unfortunately I must leave for Tours shortly because we have an urgent meeting tonight regarding security in the basilica.'

'Has there been trouble?'

'Yes. The Boches have increased patrols nearby. As you know, some of the circuit members meet occasionally inside the basilica if they have messages to pass. That will have to stop, unfortunately. They will have to find somewhere else to meet.'

Jeanne continued telling Valérie about her friend. 'Yvonne is loved by all the children. Thank goodness our Angéline and Stéphanie don't attend that school, but her arrest has nonetheless had a devastating effect on them and all the children. Yvonne's husband fled to avoid arrest.' She sat down and took her time to continue, 'I've had to contact the grandmother myself because the rest of the family don't live anywhere near Tours. She is coming down to collect the children and take them back to her home in Paris. Arnaud will keep his ear to the ground and try to find out as much as he can with a contact he has in Tours.'

Later they were joined by Lise who looked exhausted, although pleased to see Valérie and the priest. A car swept up the drive. Lise reassured them, 'It's Arnaud. Not the Boches.'

'I hope they never come here,' said Valérie.

'They've already been, wanting Arnaud's help with an injured soldier who'd been involved in an accident nearby. Fortunately, he was in the German army and they're generally better behaved than the SS.'

Ashen-faced and tired, Arnaud came into the room and slumped into a chair in front of Valérie. He looked across at Jeanne and said, 'Just give me a bowl of soup if you have any and some bread. Nothing else, please.' She walked across to him and kissed him before leaving the room.

'Christophe is coming here for the night,' Arnaud told them. 'He came to the surgery urgently to update me with some terrible news. When he found out that you were coming here, Valérie, he asked if he could join you.' Valérie looked at his taut face. 'With what Christophe told me, I must tell you that we are all at risk more than ever. I could have picked him up, but he had to see someone urgently and will arrive later.'

Valérie explained that she thought she had been followed on her last journey, prompting Arnaud to reply, 'You can see that I'm right. We don't know how far down the line these arrests in Paris have led to others outside Paris. The enemy is closing in.'

Father Antoine excused himself and said that he had to leave promptly. 'Valérie, if you need to make urgent contact, come to the presbytery and if I'm out leave this prayer card in my postbox and make sure you add your initials. Then I'll leave you a note in the dead letter box indicating a date and time when we can meet at the presbytery.'

Jeanne returned to the sitting room and announced that dinner was ready, but Lise went to eat with the children. Much later when Christophe arrived, Valérie felt greatly relieved. He sat beside her and whispered, 'I'm so glad you're safe.' He was ravenous and ate his meal as if he hadn't eaten for days.

Later when they were alone, Valérie gave him the valves and told him about her time in Angers. 'As soon as I knew that I was being followed, I kept repeating the same words: "Don't be afraid, don't give in." The train journey was even more harrowing. The carriage was full of other passengers and when this Gestapo officer entered and started questioning me, their faces were full of fear. His last words to me are ones I can never forget. He hoped that we wouldn't meet again in more serious circumstances and warned me that he wouldn't ever forget me. That was daunting, I can tell you. He referred to us as terrorists.'

'That indicates their hate for the Resistance,' he replied and put his arm round her. 'You were very brave, and you handled it very well.' He kissed her and caressed her. 'You will have to change your appearance right away,' he said. 'Now I must tell you the up-to-date plans. I'm meeting Emile early tomorrow morning. Let's hope he can repair his transceiver and send the messages I've given him for London. When we receive a reply, we'll have to prepare ourselves for a large drop of arms and explosives for the next operation. We will need to use your cousin André, who is a trained telephone engineer, but Jacques has guaranteed to supervise him.'

Valérie shook her head. 'We can't possibly use André. He's too much of a risk.'

'We'll discuss this another time, Valérie. Now's not a suitable time or place.' She looked away from him and remained silent as he continued. 'We must have Benoît on our side and ensure that his men are well trained. I'm meeting Emile tomorrow. As soon as we hear from London regarding the drop, we'll have to put the others in the circuit on the alert and arrange a reception committee. We need these armaments and explosives for the next operation.'

He tapped her on the shoulder and said, 'Valérie, please don't sulk. We need to be united in our work. We'll discuss André another time.'

At that moment, Jeanne came into the room. 'I've put you both in the room behind the cupboard, Valérie. You'll have to get up early and leave separately.' Turning to Christophe, she said, 'I know you came by bicycle. We'll lend Valérie one that she can leave in the courtyard behind Arnaud's office in Tours.'

The next day Valérie left the château at half past seven, half an hour after Christophe. On arrival in Tours, she put the bicycle in the courtyard as instructed and returned to her room in the rue du Cygne. Then she went to the chemist where she worked and bought a hair dye and returned to her lodgings to colour her hair auburn.

In the afternoon, as she was walking along the rue Commerciale, she felt a tap on her shoulder—it was Martin whom she hadn't seen since training Benoît's new recruits.

'I nearly didn't recognise you.'

'I had to change my hair colour after being questioned by a milicien on my last train journey. It was a horrible experience.' she replied. She then continued to describe her experience in more detail.

'Train journeys are always risky. Try to avoid them if you can,' he said, clearly concerned. 'I've come to town to see a relative, but how about a quick drink together?'

'Fine by me.'

They decided to go to a bar in a side street off the Boulevard Béranger. Even though he was friendly and keen to talk about training his recent recruits, Valérie sensed he was perturbed. He looked at her intensely and whispered, 'Valérie, I don't like to raise something, but I must.' She began to tap the table. Whatever was he going to reveal to her?

'Look, I know you said that you knew André from school, but my guess is that he is family.' She nodded. 'Last week I saw him with a woman in a bar on the Boulevard Béranger and he'd obviously had too much to drink; he should have been collecting meat from a farm outside Tours.'

Valérie squeezed the edge of the table and remained silent, disappointed, but not surprised, by her cousin's behaviour.

'I'm sorry but I'll have to tell Benoît.' Then drawing closer to her, he whispered, 'Likewise, you will have to tell Christophe.'

She tightened her fingers. 'Of course. Of course,' she replied with difficulty.

It was not going to be easy but now that she had evidence that André was drinking and disobeying orders, surely Christophe would take notice of her and warn Benoît?

CHAPTER SEVENTEEN

ATTACK ON THE ELECTRICITY POWER STATION

Two days later in early July during the morning, Valérie met Christophe outside Tours and told him about Martin's warning.

'Surely this is enough proof, Christophe, that we need to insist that Benoît dismisses André? We can't possibly take any risks with my cousin. It's shameful what he's done, and he is putting everyone, maquisards and the circuit, at a serious risk.'

'The problems we have are these, Valérie: we must put that electricity power station out of action as soon as possible. We need someone qualified not only to put telephones out of action but also quite a complicated alarm system. There is no one else available other than André with the help of Jacques, who is a trained electrical engineer. We will have to insist that Benoît keeps a much tighter rein on him.

Once he has done his work, I will persuade Benoît to find someone else.'

'As your courier, I have to follow your orders, but you are wrong on this occasion, Christophe. It would be better to delay the operation until you find that person,' she told him, glaring into his angry eyes.

She walked away from him. Despite her deep feelings for Christophe, she wished Marcel was still her organiser. He would never have accepted André right from the start if she'd told him about her cousin's drinking problem. There was now no alternative but to put pressure on Benoît herself and she'd have to do it quickly.

Two days later, following a message from Emile, Valérie cycled to Azay. Mist hovered over the Cher and fields, but soon it would lift, and the gentle landscape of the Cher Valley would emerge with its picturesque villages, some bordering the river. Her thoughts returned to what Father Antoine and Arnaud had talked about. The Nazi menace hung over the nation. Gestapo agents were infiltrating Resistance circuits and Maquis camps more successfully than they had ever done, notably after they'd moved into the Free Zone.

She was glad to find Emile waiting for her in a wooded area outside Azay. 'This venue is much safer,' she told him.

'Thanks for making that dangerous journey to obtain those valves for me. I'm now in communication with London and I've just received a message from them,' he replied. 'Ten containers will be dropped next Wednesday, and they've specified a new drop zone.' He pulled out a piece of paper from a cigarette container with a false bottom and handed it to her.

Valérie studied it. 'It's outside Bléré-la-Croix, not far from Arnaud's place,' she told him. 'He's agreed to receive some of the containers and Gérard, a farmer he knows, will take the rest. What message must we listen for on the BBC service?'

'The badgers have come out of their sets.'

'The person who's sending these messages must be an animal fanatic,' said Valérie with a laugh but there was no reaction from Emile.

'I need to talk about security. The priest in Azay thinks he might be under surveillance,' he said. 'So, I've decided to move our dead letter drop there. The Bardin family, whom I know, is willing to help us. They have a white marble family tomb at the end of the cemetery. Place any messages inside the empty pink flowerpot. Let other circuit members know. Now I must be off. We'll meet here again soon. I'll leave a note in the usual place in Tours.'

'Look after yourself. Keep on the move like Marcel and Christophe, even if it means living in barns or sheds. It's much safer,' she told him.

'That's easier said than done. It's hard to find people even prepared to let me use such places,' he replied as he climbed onto his bike and left.

As Valérie made her way back to Tours, she remembered a Beaulieu instructor telling her that the life expectancy of a wireless operator was only six weeks.

A week later, after midnight, the reception committee collected the containers from the drop and loaded half of them onto a horse-drawn cart which the local farmer took to his farm while they put the rest into Jacques's van. He then drove to Arnaud's château, accompanied by Valérie.

On their way there, Jacques started talking about the forthcoming raid. 'I've thought about Christophe, you and me. Two of my friends work in an abattoir not far from the electric powerhouse. They may be prepared to hide the three of us in there.'

Valérie shuddered. 'You can't be serious, Jacques.'

'I am. It's a perfect hideout. They could conceal us in cold rooms for a short period of time if there's trouble. The Boches will be searching everywhere, and you can imagine how enraged they will be with the blackout.'

'I don't relish your idea one bit,' she told him. 'It makes me feel quite sick.'

'Desperate times call for desperate measures,' he said. As they approached the château, he remarked, 'Arnaud is taking more risks than he was willing to do earlier.'

'He must have his reasons,' she replied, remembering what Arnaud had told her when he'd dropped her off in Tours a few weeks previously. His commitment would never wane in the future, whatever the circumstances. Not after what he and his family had recently experienced. She recalled how distraught his daughters had been after the disappearance of their Jewish school friends. Added to that, Angéline's words were embedded in her mind: 'I know where my friends have gone. They were thrown into cattle trains and sent to concentration camps where they'll die. A boy at our school said he'd heard his parents talking about it. When I told Mamy, she started to cry.'

Valérie could visualise how difficult that must have been for the grandmother. The child's awareness of these heinous things, occurring around her, must have horrified the poor old lady.

Jacques drove to the back of the château and Arnaud came out to help them, looking haggard. 'I've cleared more space in our wine cellar for these containers,' he told them, 'but this is the last time that I'm prepared to accept future containers back here. The farmer's going to try and find an alternative place for the ones you've just delivered. I cannot take any more risks. Jeanne and I could be shot for doing this and there's no knowing what the Boches would do with my mother and the children.'

Valérie could see the distress in his face. Undoubtedly Yvonne Charrier's arrest and the dreadful impact it had had on her children, had led to Arnaud's change of mind again.

They started to unload the containers and take them down to the wine cellar.

As they started to unload them, Valérie found a box. 'Look what London's included,' said Valérie. 'Here's a box that says *Enjoy* so we can guess there are goodies for us inside there.'

'Maybe they've included some fresh coffee,' said Jacques with a chuckle, but Arnaud gave no reaction.

Once they were welcomed by Jeanne, Valérie produced the box. 'This was included in the drop,' she told Jeanne. They gasped when she started to pull out fresh coffee, tea, sugar, chocolate, and precious items of food, as well as French cigarettes.

'London has done us proud,' said Jeanne who was thrilled to receive these gifts from London. 'I'll make us some real coffee.'

Valérie felt comforted by the rich aroma of coffee being prepared, recalling how Maman used to make her some. How were she and Dad coping? Her father's words came to mind: 'I think there's more to it, isn't there, my dear?' He'd guessed she was being sent to France and that the work would be dangerous. But had he managed to keep his thoughts to himself? Or had Maman pestered him so much that by now she knew her daughter was in France engaged in risky work?

Valérie noticed Arnaud sink into his comfortable chair. Although the others continued to talk about how well the drop had gone, she could see that Arnaud was preoccupied with his own thoughts.

Jacques and Valérie left the following morning.

Two days later Christophe had arranged to meet Valérie, Jacques and Benoît at Patricia's house.

'Here's a detailed plan that I've drawn for our attack on the electricity power station in Tours,' he told them, laying out a diagram onto the table. 'We're going to destroy the transformers to cut the electricity in Tours and to the Liotard factory where the Nazis make components for their fighter planes.'

'That's the most challenging operation we've had so far,' remarked Benoît.

'As you can all see from my diagram, the electricity power station is not far from the St Sauveur Bridge and the Cher. Good for a quick getaway. At a quarter to eight in the evening, this coming Friday, about four night-shift workers will arrive at the electric power station, but they like to have coffee in the kitchen beforehand. Benoît and another maquisard will guard the main entrance. Someone will have already hidden Louis and two maquisards inside the building and they will lock the kitchen door and guard the room. One of them will let in André and Jacques, who will deactivate the telephone and alarm systems, leave and go to André's van which will be well hidden in the area. After the operation, André will drive the maquisards to the nearby forest area. I have a key to a side entrance and once inside, Valérie and I will lay our charges while Martin and another maquisard will be on guard outside. Jacques will join Valérie and me and we will hide elsewhere.

'And if there's trouble?' asked Louis.

'Deal with it as best you can, but don't kill anyone or cause them serious injury,' replied Christophe.

On Friday everything seemed to have worked according to the plan but while Christophe and Valérie were still laying their charges, detonators and time pencils, one of Louis's men rushed up to them. 'Get the hell out of here now. One of the night workers arrived late and started to attack Louis viciously when he forced the man into the kitchen. Louis had no choice but to defend himself and he's hurt the man quite badly. and locked him in with the others. We'll all have to get out of here now, even if you haven't finished all your work.'

'Oh hell!' whispered Christophe. 'I didn't want any casualties, but at least he's not killed him. We've laid most of our charges,' he said and packed his tools into a rucksack, helped by Valérie. They hurried to the entrance, locked the door and climbed over the wall, protected by Martin and the other maquisard who then joined the other maquisards as planned.

Christophe, Valérie and Jacques made their way to the abattoir where they were met by Lucien, Jacques's friend. He led them to the cold area down in the basement. 'If the Boches do come, we'll put you in one of the cold rooms,' he told them. 'We've already taken the handle off one of the doors for safety's sake, and we've brought a cupboard down to place in front of it.'

'I can't thank you enough, Lucien,' said Christophe.

'We'll do anything that helps to fight the Boches.'

'Can your other men be trusted?' asked Valérie.

'It's a Friday night so there are only three of us on duty and I can vouch for them.'

While Jacques was talking about the wounded employee at the power station, the electric lights went out while loud explosions could be heard from the power station.

Valérie and Christophe nodded at each other.

'Well done,' said Lucien.

They continued talking until one of Lucien's men interrupted them. 'There are fire engines and police at the power station, Lucien. The Boches will soon be making their way to the abattoir.'

'When the Boches arrive, take your time opening up to them while I hide these three elsewhere,' Lucien told his colleague. He then took Valérie, Christophe and Jacques into one of the cold rooms, which had a gauze window on the outside wall, and closed the door. Valérie could hear Lucien and someone else pushing a cupboard against the door.

Later, Valérie heard a commotion and people coming into the cold area. She started to shake all over and buried her face inside Christophe's jacket. A man started to scream in heavily accented French. Valérie's hands became numb. It had to be a German officer. Now they would all be in trouble. They stood close to the cold room door and the shouting continued. Doors were being opened and things moved about. After a while it became quiet. By now she was shaking more and more from the cold night air seeping through the mesh window as well as from the icy room itself. She felt comforted as Christophe started to rub her back and arms and began to feel warmer after he had slipped his jacket over her. Then he cuddled her while Jacques kept rubbing himself, trying to keep warm.

Later, Valérie heard the cupboard being moved aside. She recognised Lucien in the darkness as he opened the door. 'It's serious and that's why that Nazi bastard was screaming his head off. Most of Tours is without power. He was also ranting about one of the power station's employees having been rushed to hospital with a serious head injury.'

'Oh my God!' cried Valérie. 'That was what we wanted to avoid. It will lead to more searches, arrests and reprisals.'

'You've all taken huge risks,' said Lucien.

He took them out of the storage area and down into a cellar. 'Now I must go. I'll wake you up in the morning,' he said and left them.

'I've known him for years,' said Jacques. 'He's always been a true friend.'

'There are few like him, but I can understand why people don't join the Resistance. Remember this is the third German invasion since 1871.'

Jacques raised a smile. 'Here's someone who knows her French history.'

Early next morning, before the curfew had ended, Lucien woke them up. 'You must leave as soon as possible. As you can see, Jacques has already gone. Go separately in different directions.'

After Lucien had left, Christophe told Valérie, 'We'd better go to ground for several days. Then I'll contact you, but now I must leave, my darling.' He kissed her and left through a side door.

After a few minutes, Valérie left. Outside she could see soldiers and Milice in the distance. She shivered and walked quickly in the opposite direction towards a park she had sometimes frequented.

The Boches would pursue them with more hatred than ever because of the disruption caused by the lack of electricity. She'd hide in some bushes until the curfew lifted at seven in the morning and take the longer route back to the rue du Cygne, avoiding the rue de Commerce.

CHAPTER EIGHTEEN
TROUBLED WATERS

After a week, towards the middle of July, some electricity had been restored to Tours. The Nazis were enraged by the attack on the power station and had carried out numerous house-to-house searches, as well as installing roadblocks in the city and surrounding area. Circuit members had to continue in their normal day-to-day jobs while Christophe, Valérie and the Maquis had to keep out of sight.

After a few more days, Valérie went to the Mirabeau Park, not far from the station in Tours, where she was expecting Christophe. She sat down on a bench near where a group of mothers were sitting and chatting. Children were enjoying themselves and were shrieking with delight as they whizzed round on a carousel or climbed up a steep slide and screamed as they slid down. Valérie checked the time on her watch; a quarter past eleven and there was still no sign of Christophe. A German soldier walked past and stopped to watch the children at play. After a while, he pulled something from his pocket and offered some sweets to the children. One of the mothers shouted, 'Don't accept anything from men like him who shoot mummies and daddies.'

The children ran away from the soldier, who stood motionless, looking down on the ground. The mothers' hateful glares troubled Valérie. The silence was menacing, but it was broken by the soldier's unexpected response. 'I hate this war. I don't want to harm your people. If it wasn't for my wife and daughters, I wouldn't want to live.'

The mothers said nothing, stunned by his words, but eventually one mother with golden blonde hair stood up and walked towards him. 'God be with you,' she told him. He smiled and handed her the packet of sweets which she accepted. 'Merci,' he replied. Tears welled up in Valérie's eyes. All this epitomised the futility and savagery of this long and terrible Occupation.

Another woman's angry voice diverted her attention. 'You shouldn't have accepted those sweets. You're nothing but a turncoat.'

'Not everyone feels the same. For God's sake show some humanity.' The other women remained silent.

Valérie stood up and walked away from the playground and saw Christophe hurrying towards her. She felt comforted by his warm embrace, and they started to walk hand in hand towards a wooded area at the other end of the park.

'Why are you so quiet?' he asked her.

After she had described what she'd witnessed, he said, 'There must be many like that soldier on both sides. Now we must talk about our next operation.'

'What have you planned?' Valérie asked.

'The next train carrying food supplies for Germany and the Russian front will be passing between Tours and Vierzon in six days' time. We must ensure it never reaches Vierzon from where it goes on to Germany.'

'You're well informed.'

'Our train driver friend told me. I want you to contact Benoît this afternoon because we need him and some of his men for our next operation. The railway line is patrolled frequently, but less so between St Aignan and Selles-sur-Cher, I'm told by our friend. We need to move those weapons at Arnaud's place. He isn't prepared to keep them anymore. As you know already, a farmer has the first half of the weapons from our last drop and has agreed to take a few more and we'll make arrangements to collect the rest.'

'Do you know why Arnaud has refused to keep his half?' Valérie asked.

'One of his friends has recently been arrested and thrown into the holding place at the primary school and his wife and family are being constantly watched. Unfortunately, his friend wasn't one of the two prisoners who escaped from there last week thanks to our activities.'

Now Valérie understood Arnaud's change of mind.

'We need to remove the remaining weapons at Arnaud's place. I want you to go and see Benoît and arrange for him to collect them within the next four days and take them back to his camp. I will meet him at Arnaud's to outline our next operation once I know when he plans to go to Arnaud's.'

'Christophe, I need to talk to you about my cousin. I know that he did an excellent job on the electric power station, but I don't want him included in the next operation. Remember I'll talk to Benoît about it and find out if André is drinking in the camp. Remember I told you Martin found him drinking heavily with a woman in Tours when he was supposed to be at the farm.'

Christophe sighed. 'We don't need him for the railway sabotage, but we want him for the one after if Benoît can't find a replacement. Having him watched by Jacques and taken back to the camp by the other maquisards, after the power station operation, worked well.'

'We must sort this problem out now. For Heaven's sake, think of everyone's safety. You're going back on your promise to me.'

'Valérie, who leads this circuit?'

'It's certainly not someone who's thinking rationally. You could easily force the issue with Benoît by withdrawing London's financial support. He would soon agree to it then.'

'I don't need a confrontation before preparing a complicated operation.'

'If things go wrong, I'll leave this circuit,' she told him.

He took his time to respond but ignored her comment. 'Please leave a note in the usual place about when I need to go to Arnaud's place to talk to Benoît.'

Two days later, Valérie went to Tours railway station and boarded a train for Amboise. She began to think about her relationship with Christophe. She loved him, but his stubborn nature could cause arrests within the circuit and Maquis. Most of all she was furious with him for breaking his agreement with her. She would have a firm word with Benoît.

On arrival in Amboise, she noticed an increased Nazi presence in contrast to her last visit. The soldiers had apprehended two men, and this enabled her to slip past them and walk out of the town in the direction of the forest. Benoît had moved his camp elsewhere in the forest, but he'd given her instructions on how to find it. She pulled out her compass and set it to north-west. It was an unusually dull day for the month of July, making the forest sombre. She battled with some of the thick ferns and bushes. A rustle in the undergrowth put her on her guard. She stepped back. Moments later a V-patterned snake started slithering towards her. From experience she knew other adders could be close by, so she chose a less dense area in which to continue her journey. She made for a north-westerly direction until she heard movement and was startled to see Benoît.

'You've done well finding your way here,' he told her.

'Thanks to this,' she replied, indicating her compass, 'and of course your excellent instructions.' A broad smile spread across his face. As they walked towards the camp, she outlined the next sabotage operation and Christophe's plan for Benoît to collect the weapons from Arnaud's place and meet Christophe there to discuss the next operation.'

'When could you collect them after dark in André's van?'

'The day after tomorrow, at nine in the evening.'

'I'll warn Arnaud and Christophe tomorrow,' she replied.

'I've made a decision about André. He will be excluded from the next mission,' said Benoît.

'Fortunately, we don't need him for this train sabotage, but Christophe says that he needs him for the following operation. I'm furious with him because he promised me to persuade you to dismiss André and find someone else.'

'Drink is a problem for him. You're right. He kept it hidden for a while. We've started to notice it in the camp and elsewhere.' He stopped and turned to her. 'He was with Martin the other day, collecting chickens and rabbits from a farmer whom I've known for a long time. The farmer offered them some wine. Martin settled for one glass, but André was into his third glass in no time and was flirting with the farmer's daughter who seemed a little too curious about him. The girl was joking and said, "You must have a huge family to feed." Fortunately, her father intervened. He was annoyed and told her to mind her own business and that in fact the men were collecting produce for the hospital in Tours. He only helps me out occasionally and doesn't want to get too involved with the Resistance.'

'But surely, Benoît, this has gone far enough? Wouldn't it be best to ask André to leave now?'

'It's too risky to throw him out immediately. He knows too much. I need him where I can see him. That's one of the reasons why we're thinking of moving to the Sologne. Also, the forest is denser and more difficult for the Boches to penetrate. If we can't find anyone else to replace him for the next operation after this one, we'll have Jacques accompany him like he did on the electric power station operation. Rest assured when we move to the Sologne, he will be made to leave with a strong warning of saying nothing to anyone. He will be sent to a town where I know someone who will keep an eye on him. He will have to agree to this. Otherwise, we will deal with him in no uncertain terms.'

'But why didn't you get rid of him right from the beginning as I suggested?'

'Because his van and his electrical experience were useful to us and at that point he was never drunk—merry yes—like a lot of us in the evenings, provided there was no operation the following day.

Incidentally, apart from Martin, Louis and his deputy, none of the men know that we're planning to leave this area. Maybe you and Christophe will join us.'

'That's up to him to decide,' she said. 'Benoît, I beg you again, to get rid of André now. Otherwise, something will go wrong. I sense it, even though he's not needed for the next operation.'

'Valérie, we've always been good friends. Don't push me too hard. I know what I'm doing.'

When they arrived at the camp, the men gave Valérie a warm welcome and she was soon joined by André. Dark shadows under his eyes and his inability to concentrate on what she was saying, made her realise something was troubling him deeply. If she could find a way of talking to him privately, she would.

Immediately after lunch, Benoît took Valérie to one of the tents and discussed the next operation. 'I'll leave Martin here with André and the maquisards not needed for the next operation. As usual my men won't be told the location until a few hours beforehand.'

During the afternoon Benoît asked Valérie to instruct his men on the technique of short-range shooting and grenade throwing, but without ammunition. She wasn't the least surprised when her cousin outshone the other men.

After she'd said goodbye to the men, André came up to her and embraced her. He clung to her and kissed her several times. 'Goodbye, ma Capitaine,' he whispered. 'I often remember our times together with Philippe and Daniel in the forest outside Orléans where we had so much fun there making camps and picnicking.'

Valérie put her arms round him and replied, 'That shouldn't make you sad. What's troubling you?'

'Nothing. It's nothing,' he replied with tears in his eyes. As she left the camp with Benoît, she looked back at her cousin, a solitary figure leaning against one of the chestnut trees.

Five days later, towards the end of July, at 11 p.m., their faces blackened, and caps pulled down over their foreheads, Christophe and Valérie made their way towards the track between St-Aignan-Noyers and Selles-sur-Cher, sixty-four miles from Tours. Christophe had assessed the sentries' patrol movements and had allowed time in which to lay charges under the rail. They waited in some bushes until the passenger train had gone by before Christophe made his way onto the track area. Close by were Benoît and several of his men, armed with Stens and grenades. Christophe laid the charges under the rails, having attached detonators and time pencils, and returned to the railway bank. 'Now let's get out of here,' he said, pulling out his pistol, and Valérie did too.

'We'll cover you,' Benoît told them.

They started to run like whippets, but they were stopped by a maquisard who had been acting as a lookout further down the track. 'The sentries are already approaching. Make for the woods and then split up and go in different directions.'

'How on earth have the Boches spotted us?' whispered Valérie. She gasped as she saw two sentries with torches examining the track.

'Mein Gott! Sabotage,' shouted one of the sentries while the other ran in the opposite direction along the track.

'He's going for reinforcements,' said Christophe grimly.

Christophe, Valérie and the maquisards left the track area as quickly as they could. Soon they were being pursued by the Boches. Shots were fired: two German soldiers were badly hit as well as a maquisard. Christophe grabbed the maquisard's Sten while Valérie continued running. The shooting continued. Suddenly a German voice yelled 'Haut les Mains!' Valérie swung round, horrified when she saw a German officer with his handgun trained on Christophe. She pulled out her pistol and aimed at the officer's head. Pieces of bone and blood erupted from his skull. Bile swept up into her mouth, the bitterness of it making her retch and choke. She started shaking all over. They'd all be at greater risk now than ever.

Christophe grabbed her by the shoulder, shook her and picked up the Sten and the officer's pistol. 'We must get the hell out of here. Run as fast as you can,' he shouted as bullets and grenades exploded around them.

The maquisards, now eleven of them, were taking part in a bloody battle, to keep the Boches from reaching Valérie and Christophe. Agonising screams could be heard, making Valérie start to shake. Once they had reached the wooded area, Christophe cried, 'Bury the Sten.'

Movement from behind made them throw themselves to the ground. Valérie froze, but it was one of Benoît's men who emerged. 'We've lost three of our men already,' he told them. 'Benoît and the others are still defending themselves. My name's Christian. I'm coming with you on Benoît's orders.

We need to make for the River Cher. It's our only chance of escape.'

It was now midnight. Valérie kept looking behind her, fearful of soldiers following them. She wished there was a full moon with a Lysander about to land and whisk them back to England.

When they reached the River Cher, the three of them waded into the water and started to swim across to the other bank. Soon Valérie struggled to keep going. She became more and more traumatised. Pictures of the officer's head exploding flooded her mind; somewhere soon a German father and mother would grieve the loss of their son. The cold water almost solidified her entire body. She had no more strength left. Christophe grabbed her and pulled her along against the current with the help of Christian. When they struggled onto the riverbank, she collapsed onto the ground; Christophe told her to rest for a few minutes while he squeezed some of the water out of her jacket and trouser legs.

'We must leave now,' he told her, taking her hand, and pulling her up to her feet. Soon they came to a small copse. Frantic barks hit the night air. Valérie cursed. A light came on and a young man ran towards them and said, 'We heard the shooting from our house. I can't take you in as I have young children to consider. Go over there to the right and continue down the track for about half a kilometre and you'll find a woodyard and a small house that have been abandoned. The woodcutter and his family fled last week.'

The thought of a resting place gave Valérie inner strength to join the others down the bumpy track until they arrived at the woodcutter's home.

'I reckon the family who ran this business were in the Resistance. Look at those saws flung down in haste when they fled or were arrested,' remarked Christophe. 'I'm going to investigate.' On his return he told them, 'The house must have been raided by the Boches. Every room has been ransacked, but it's still habitable, so let's go inside.'

By now Valérie wanted to vomit, and she started to shake again. Christophe took her hand and led her up some steep stairs, broken in places, into a bedroom where covers had been tossed about the floor. Christophe opened a wardrobe. 'Look at all these clothes—enough for the three of us and some spare sheets and blankets as well. I'll take some down for Christian, as well as clothes.'

'I can't forget the officer's face. I can't. I can't,' she cried.

'Remember, my darling, what one of our instructors kept telling us, "It's him or me in warfare." You had no other option but to shoot him,' he said and went downstairs.

Valérie pulled the sheets onto the bed and roughly tucked them in and threw blankets on top. She pulled off her damp clothes and hung them over a chair. Then she opened the wardrobe and grabbed two men's shirts and pulled one over her head and staggered into bed.

As she lay there waiting for Christophe to return, she buried herself under the covers. They'd all be in greater danger because she'd killed the Nazi officer. There would be reprisals. She would have to change her appearance again and move out of Tours as quickly as possible.

Christophe returned shortly afterwards, took off his wet clothes and joined her in bed.

'Let's treasure this time we have alone together.' He took her into his arms and caressed her, kissing her gently, and together they kissed deeply before they made love more passionately than ever. If only we weren't living under the Nazi Occupation, she thought as she lay in his arms.

Towards dawn Valérie heard tapping at the door. She climbed out of the bed quickly, put on her clothes and opened it.

'We need to move now,' said Christian. 'We must go into the woods further north as quickly as possible and stay there for a couple of days. I know a wine grower not too far from here and he has a hidden cellar running underneath his farmhouse where we can hide.'

Four days later Christophe sent Valérie to the Maquis camp to learn how Benoît and his men had fled from the battle. She was more alert than ever, conscious that the Boches were after whoever had killed their officer. Fortunately, no other Nazi had seen her shoot him or seen her fleeing, so they were not looking specifically for a woman.

On arrival at the camp, she sensed an air of sadness among the men and feared the worst. Some were sitting in small groups, looking despondent and exhausted. Others were busy, taking their Stens apart and cleaning them. Benoît was absent so she spoke to Martin, who looked equally haggard and desperate as he told her what had happened during their battle with the Boches.

'The rail exploded but the train was intercepted by the Boches,' he told her. 'Then an all-out battle took place. Several Nazi soldiers and three of our men were killed. The injuries were awful—one maquisard has a leg blown off.' Valérie closed her eyes and remained silent. After a long pause, Martin continued, 'Benoît took a great risk in going to see the families of the dead. They were holding on while you, Christophe and Christian escaped. Fortunately, the three dead maquisards had no identity cards on them. Also, another maquisard, Gérard, who was shot in the shoulder, is in agony. It was extremely difficult crossing that river with the two injured men, I can tell you.'

'Did you manage to get medical help for him?' Valérie asked him.

'Yes. Arnaud came to see Gérard here in the camp, but he couldn't do much for his shoulder injury. It needs a complicated operation inside a hospital which is out of the question. After giving it considerable thought, Arnaud offered to approach one of his colleagues, a surgeon, to see if he would agree to perform it at the château. We've just heard that his colleague, a doctor from another city, is prepared to operate. In fact, he's going to do the operation the day after tomorrow. Arnaud's coming back to collect Gérard and take him to his château. I'll leave a note in the usual place in Tours to tell you when I'll meet you next.'

'It's not a good idea for Arnaud to revisit the camp for security purposes. I'll arrange for Jacques to collect Gérard and take him to Arnaud's place,' Valérie told him.

'That would be much safer, I agree.' He paused before asking her, 'Has Christophe decided to join us in the Sologne Forest? I hope you both will,' he said wistfully.

Valérie didn't share Martin's enthusiasm because she had misgivings about Benoît's security after learning that Arnaud had visited the camp.

CHAPTER NINETEEN

EARLY AUGUST. THE NET CLOSES IN

Valérie kept thinking about Arnaud as she left the pharmacy in the mid-afternoon, a few days later, and started walking into the centre of Tours. Thank goodness Jacques had collected the maquisard from the camp. Her thoughts were broken by a familiar voice from behind her.

'Véronique, how lovely to see you.'

'Oh hello, Madame Guérin.'

'How's your work in the chemist shop?'

'Very well, thank you,' replied Valérie.

'I wasn't sure if it was you because you're much thinner and you've cut your hair shorter. I'm glad to have caught up with you,' said Madame Guérin in a quiet and serious tone of voice. 'I've a feeling it might help someone of importance you might know who works in Tours.'

Why was she so secretive? From her previous conversation with Valérie on the train to Paris, it had been obvious that the old lady disapproved of Pétain which could make her sympathetic towards the Resistance.

'Remember, I told you that I used to work for the deputy mayor of Tours for several years.' Valérie nodded. 'The kommandant, whose offices are in the Palais de Justice, close to the town hall, sometimes visits the mayor. Someone I know, who still works there, told me that the Boches are about to arrest a well-respected family doctor in Tours following the murder of one of their officers.'

Valérie stared at Madame Guérin in disbelief and swallowed hard, trying to retain her composure.

The old woman moved closer to Valérie. 'The doctor, whoever he is, must be involved in the Resistance.' Valérie felt comforted by Madame Guérin's warm hand caressing her shoulder. 'You look as if you need to sit down somewhere. You've become very pale. Come back to my house which is in the next road: number five rue Balzac. I'll make you a warm drink and something to eat.'

'I can't, Madame Guérin. It's most kind of you, but I have an urgent appointment.'

'Don't upset yourself, my dear. Be careful, please. These are vicious times in which we are living.' She stepped forward and embraced Valérie who then knew that Madame Guérin had suspected that she was in the Resistance and that was why she had given her a warning.

'Merci, Madame,' she whispered and hurried away in the direction of the presbytery. Finding that Antoine was out, she slipped his St Anthony prayer card into his postbox on the wall outside. Now she would have to warn Arnaud in case it was he who was involved, so she hurried to his surgery and was surprised to see no patients waiting.

'The doctor left to do home visits,' said the receptionist. 'Is there anything I can do because you look very worried?'

'No thanks. I must go now,' replied Valérie and hurried to collect her bicycle from her lodgings to make the long journey to Bléré as fast as she could.

By half past eight in the evening, Valérie's legs ached from cycling so far. She was about to turn into the drive leading to the château when she heard a familiar rumble in the distance. Oh Arnaud, it must be you they're coming for! A terrifying thought pierced her mind like a bayonet. Was Madame Guérin an informer? Had she led Valérie into a trap?

She must concentrate on hiding herself. There would be a lot of Boches arriving. The Gestapo often brought dogs with them, and if that were the case, there would be no escape. They would find her and arrest her as well. She left the drive, flung the bicycle into some undergrowth and ran through ferns, thrusting brambles aside as best she could, aware of blood trickling down where the thorns had torn her skin. She crouched behind some thick bushes and prayed that she would not be discovered.

From where she was hidden, Valérie heard a rumble of several vehicles which suddenly came to a halt. Doors were slammed. Gestapo officers were shouting orders. A silence descended on the scene. She waited for what seemed like hours. Pictures of Arnaud being beaten, with his family watching, kept flashing across her mind. By now the Gestapo would be tearing the place apart. Would they arrest Jeanne and the rest of the family? Would they requisition the château as they had done with so many others in the Loire Valley? Or would they torch it?

A light came on at the main entrance. Screams hit the night air, tearing Valérie apart.

'Papa! Papa!' cried one of the children.

Shouts from the Gestapo almost drowned the child's pleas. Engines started. Vehicles turned round and made their way down the long drive. While they were leaving, Valérie heard more screams coming from the girls. Then silence.

Valérie's heart began to pound and the faster it raced, the more her head began to spin. The bestial Gestapo would work on Arnaud straight away at their headquarters. Had they arrested Jeanne and left the grandmother with the children? If so, would Jeanne and Arnaud manage to hold out for forty-eight hours to allow others to escape, as they'd been advised? Somehow, she would have to alert all the members of their circuit and the Maquis, but it was too late to return to Tours. Raymond's place was an hour's bicycle ride from the château, so she'd cycle there, spend the night with him and go to Tours the following morning after the curfew lifted.

It was pitch dark when Valérie arrived at Raymond's house. She tapped three times on the window and waited. Moments later there was a slight movement behind the curtain before it was pulled back slightly to reveal Raymond. He switched on a torch and waved his hand towards the back entrance where he opened the door and said, 'Christophe's been here for about an hour. Come down to the cellar,' he told her and led her down some narrow steps.

By candlelight she saw Christophe and fell into his arms and started to sob uncontrollably.

'Whatever has happened?' he asked her.

She tried to answer him, but it was as if her tongue had solidified.

'Valérie, take your time.'

'She's in deep shock. I'll fetch her some brandy,' said Raymond.

'The Gestapo—they've—they've arrested Arnaud,' she told them.

'My God!' cried Christophe, holding her more closely.

When Raymond returned, Valérie grabbed the glass and took a large swig.

'They took him away from the château after eight this evening, but I don't know whether they arrested Jeanne as well.' She finished her drink. 'I heard the children screaming and calling out, "Papa, Papa." I will hear those pleas forever.'

'It's what I've been afraid of for a long time. Arnaud was taking too many risks, responding to night calls from the circuit,' said Raymond.

'Whoever could have betrayed him?' asked Valérie.

'We'll have to warn all the circuit members tomorrow, as well as Benoît,' said Christophe. 'Can

Valérie come back here tomorrow and spend the night while I make arrangements for us both to leave the area?'

'Yes, but for one night only,' said Raymond. 'I'm going to leave as soon as possible too. That's for sure.' He paused. He stood up and said, 'It's time we all got some sleep. Come to one of the bedrooms on the ground floor. If there's trouble, you'll have the chance of fleeing into the woods at the back of the house.'

Who had betrayed Arnaud and why? These thoughts somersaulted in Valérie's mind as she lay in Christophe's arms. Visions of each circuit member appeared in her mind, but she dismissed each of them in turn. Benoît, Martin, Louis and his deputy were the only maquisards who knew the circuit members well and who had met them several times. They'd always seemed fanatical about security with their own men, but following her conversation with Martin, she was beginning to have a few misgivings. She remembered Arnaud's visit to the Maquis camp when he'd gone to treat the injured Gérard. Some of the men may well have seen him. Who would have denounced him? But that person would have to know his name and where he lived.

Christophe held her tighter and whispered, 'You're torturing yourself. I can sense that. Come closer, my darling Valérie …'

CHAPTER TWENTY

DAYS OF RECKONING

Valérie wasn't surprised by Christophe's response to Benoît's suggestion that they should both move to the Sologne.

'No. Not after what has happened,' he told her early the following morning. 'I'll contact Emile urgently because I need to send a message to London to tell them what has happened and that the circuit has broken up. Once the curfew has ended, you'll have to go and see Father Antoine and warn him. Ask him to contact all the circuit members except the Maquis. I'll ask Jacques to go to the Maquis camp as soon as possible, to warn Benoît about what has happened and tell him that I'll meet him on the edge of the forest, where we last met, this evening at seven.' His eyes became more intense and troubled. 'Leave your lodgings tomorrow and go to Raymond's where I'll join you in the late afternoon. We need to leave the area. I know of a contact outside Vierzon, so we will be making our way there once we've left Raymond.'

Valérie started to cycle back to Tours after the curfew lifted, knowing what a huge risk she was taking because of Arnaud's arrest. In principle, no one knew where she lived but she could never be sure. She thought about Christophe's decision to make their way to Vierzon and wondered who the contact was. An informer was responsible for Arnaud's agony and for the destruction of the circuit. Who could it possibly be?

On arrival in Tours, she went straight to the presbytery where Father Antoine welcomed her. 'Bring your bicycle inside.'

'Father, an elderly lady, called Madame Guérin, warned me that the Boches were about to arrest a well-respected family doctor in Tours.'

'That doesn't surprise me because she must have suspected you were in the Resistance and wanted to help you. She's one of my most trusted parishioners, but when did you first meet her?'

'During a train journey to Paris and in town afterwards,' she replied. While giving her account of what had happened, she noticed Antoine's face become more troubled and his hands quiver. 'We're all in extreme danger. Christophe is going to ask Jacques to contact Benoît, but he wants you to alert all the circuit members. Speed is of the essence because Arnaud might not be able to hold out for forty-eight hours, and then we would be even more at risk.'

He put his arm on her shoulder. 'None of us knows whether we could refrain from giving anything away during those first two crucial days. I'll contact Luc, Patricia, Raymond and the chemist and I'll ask Raymond to leave a note for Emile at the presbytery to contact me.'

After leaving the presbytery, Valérie retrieved a note from Martin in the dead letter box, asking her to meet him in a church not far from Tours Station in the late afternoon.

She was relieved to find the church empty and sat down in one of the pews at the back and waited. The events of the past two weeks kept spinning round in her head. How would Arnaud's family cope in the coming months? His daughters would need a lot of support from their mother and grandmother. And that was assuming Jeanne hadn't been arrested. Otherwise, Lise would have to care for the children.

A warm hand on her shoulder made her surface and she found Martin sitting beside her. 'Jacques broke the news to us earlier about Arnaud. It's terrible. Benoît's now decided to move immediately to the Sologne.' He looked at her intently. 'I know that

I've already asked you this. Will you and Christophe be joining us?'

'I'm sorry, but Christophe is adamant about leaving this area and we definitely won't be coming to the Sologne.'

'Does he suspect someone in the Maquis?'

'He hasn't gone into detail, but I certainly think it's possible.'

'If anyone is guilty of informing, Benoît will find out, I can promise you. Now I must concentrate on our move. I'm in town to see if Luc can help us with his van. Jacques has promised to use his.'

'What's happened about André?'

'He's grounded for the moment, but we'll soon be dismissing him from our Maquis. In fact, Benoît is sending him to an area far away from both Tours and the Sologne and Louis's deputy is going to accompany him there and someone in that area will be keeping a close eye on him.'

'I've been asking Christophe and Benoît to do that for ages.'

He frowned. 'They should have listened to you long ago.'

They left the church together and walked into the centre of town when suddenly Martin pushed her into a shop doorway and embraced her. 'Stay still,' he told her. 'Pretend you're my girlfriend.' He held her close to him. After several minutes, he released her and looked back down the street. 'You must go now,' he told her in an agitated tone of voice. 'After I've seen Luc, I need to return to the camp as quickly as possible.'

Who had he just seen? The fear on his face troubled her. It had to be someone who posed a danger to all of them.

'Who was that you saw passing by? What's this all about?' she cried.

He pulled her closer and put his arms round her. 'Valérie, I care for your safety. I care for you in every way. Sometimes it's hard being Benoît's deputy of the first group. I'm sworn to secrecy as you must be with Christophe. Remember that, please. Now I must go. Leave Tours as soon as you can.' He kissed her and by the sad look in his eyes, she knew that they both realised that they would not meet again.

The following morning, Valérie packed her clothes and other possessions into her suitcase. She wrote a letter to Madame Lelong, explaining her grandmother's health had deteriorated and that she needed to look after her. She also included a month's rent. Then she set off on her bicycle with her suitcase strapped to the back, arriving at Raymond's near Véretz later that morning to find him subdued.

'Christophe came here early this morning, but he seemed to be anxious and had planned to join you here, but decided it was too risky. He has arranged for you to go and stay the night with him at a farm in Montrichard which is some distance from Arnaud's home. He knows a farmer there called Thomas and has drawn a map for you to memorise and then destroy. You need to leave here as soon as possible.' He paused to gain his breath. 'After you both left yesterday morning, the Boches carried out a house-to-house search in the neighbourhood and arrested Father Dominique, the priest in Azay, after the morning Mass. Thank goodness, Emile had already fled.'

Valérie felt her legs giving way and sat down, torn apart by Raymond's revelations. Oh, if only the priest had left the area when he'd first suspected that he was being watched. His arrest was despicable. Who had denounced him?

By the late afternoon, Valérie arrived at the farm outside Montrichard. Thomas and his wife, Rosine, welcomed her and offered her an evening meal. 'I've left you and Christophe some bread and ham for breakfast as well as some milk in the barn,' she told Valérie. 'I've also put water and bowls for you to wash in and some towels too—everything is hidden behind one of the bales of straw. We daren't invite you in for breakfast because people call in here early. We'll come for you when it's safer to leave. Sorry, but we can only manage one night because it's so risky now, especially with people denouncing neighbours.'

After a tasty meal, Thomas led Valérie to a barn and showed her where food and other items were hidden. After he'd gone, she sat down on a haystack and looked around the barn by torchlight. It was used mainly for storing animals' feed and some farming tools. How kind, she thought, the farmer and his wife had been, knowing how risky it was to support the Resistance. Much later, the barn door slowly opened. It was Christophe.

'Thank goodness you've finally arrived,' she said, and stood up and walked towards him.

'I had a lot to discuss with Benoît who kept trying to persuade me for us to join him. Luc brought me here. I was unable to see Emile.'

'Raymond told me he had already fled.'

'Luc told me that too.'

He placed his suitcase and a small bag onto the floor and walked towards her and took her into his arms and kissed her, but his kisses lacked their usual passion.

'Something's not right. What is it?' she asked him.

He nodded, staring at her in a strange manner.

'I met Martin yesterday in Tours. Someone passed by us, and he suddenly became afraid and told me to take great care of myself and leave Tours as soon as possible.' She moved closer to him. 'What you're going to tell me is connected to that, isn't it?'

'Yes,' he replied.

'Tell me! Tell me!' she cried. She clung to him. 'Tell me. Do you hear?'

'Why are you so distressed?'

'Because of what happened in Tours when I met Martin. When someone passed us, he became afraid and pushed me into a doorway to avoid the person. So, it must relate to that.'

'I met Benoît as agreed at seven this evening and he told me some devastating news.' He took in a deep breath. 'Your cousin André is the person who betrayed Arnaud.'

She felt herself go limp like the rag doll she used to carry everywhere with her as a young child.

'André and Martin sometimes pick up meat and vegetables from a farmer, Benoît's friend, who lives in a village outside Montrichard.'

'I know about that already,' said Valérie impatiently. 'Benoît told me how my cousin drank too much and how the farmer's daughter flirted with him.'

'André made a bad choice in sleeping with that girl.'

'Sleeping with her? I can't believe that. How could he? Benoît confines his men to the camp except for outside duties and in any case, André has been grounded.'

'He lied to Benoît, saying he wanted several days' leave so that he could visit his mother in Orléans because it was the anniversary of his brother's execution. Instead, he spent two nights with that farmer's daughter who, it appears, also sleeps with a milicien. Afterwards he hid for two nights in the forest, afraid to return to the camp.'

Valérie looked at him aghast. 'No! No! It can't be true,' she screamed.

'When André returned to the camp this afternoon, almost in a state of collapse, Benoît became suspicious and questioned him. André broke down. He admitted telling this girl he was in a Maquis group and how Doctor Arnaud came to the camp to examine a wounded man. Presumably the one who sustained a serious shoulder injury.'

'Yes, but how would my cousin know Arnaud's name or where he lived?'

'He told Benoît that he'd seen him in the camp and had recognised him going into his surgery when he was in town and looked on the doctor's nameplate.'

Christophe tried to put his arm around her, but she pushed him away. Gradually, when she had gained some self-control, she said, 'Right from the beginning, I told you and Benoît several times to get rid of André because of his drink problem. His brother had been in the Resistance and shot by the Gestapo. The family was known to them because of that. What more did you need to know about my cousin before deciding whether you would challenge Benoît?'

Christophe grabbed her hand. 'Listen to me, please! I've more to tell you!'

'Tell me and be quick about it!'

'The girl told her milicien. Of course, he immediately told the Gestapo who arrested André when he came to see her again. "Become a mole in your Maquis. Feed us with information and we won't kill you or your mother," they told him.'

'His mother? My own Aunt Marguerite? My God! It becomes worse every minute.'

Christophe tried to take her into his arms, but she pulled herself away from him.

'Listen. Please!' he cried. 'Please prepare yourself for some shocking news.' He faltered for his words before he finally revealed everything. 'Benoît shot André late this afternoon. As you know I met him at seven. There's nothing I could have done. The deed was already done.'

Valérie looked at him in horror and started to cry hysterically. She slapped his face several times and hammered her fists into his chest. 'I told you to throw my cousin out. Martin did too.' She stared into his eyes. 'You and Benoît are nothing but swines and you're the worst one. You're not professional. You're useless. You had the upper hand with Benoît. You could have refused to give him London's money. I've told you several times to threaten him with that and insist he throw my cousin out of his Maquis.'

'Valérie, you know—

She cut him dead. 'Marcel was a true pro, brave and wise. It's a real pity he injured his leg. And more's the pity too that you took his place.' She stopped shouting at him because there was someone banging on the door. Christophe opened it slowly. It was Thomas who came into the barn.

'I heard raised voices when I was walking the dog. What in heaven's name is going on between you two? I can't have this! It's too risky.'

Valérie put on her jacket and grabbed her suitcase. 'Thomas, I'm sorry. I really am, but I'm leaving now.'

'It's curfew. If you're picked up, you'll put us all at risk.'

'Valérie, please listen to Thomas,' Christophe pleaded.

Turning to him, she screamed, 'I never want to see you again!' She hurried to the barn door and vanished into the night.

CHAPTER TWENTY-ONE
A DILEMMA

Thank goodness it was a dry night. Somewhere to hide during curfew was Valérie's priority. At daylight, she'd take a risk and return to Tours to seek help from Father Antoine. There was no one else to whom she could turn. Raymond was about to leave Véretz. She had little money and she'd have to sell the compact given to her by Major Buckmaster. As she cycled along the side roads, she thought of Christophe. His pleas for her to stay with him reverberated in her mind and the thought of his distraught face sliced through her. If André had been thrown out of the Maquis long ago and had been forced to leave the area, he would still be alive. Her thoughts returned to the long journey by bicycle to Tours. She'd have to avoid Azay and Véretz because of the German presence.

After a few kilometres, she felt her legs giving way and her head started to spin. As she approached St Georges, a village by the Cher, she decided to make for the church which she'd once found open late at night when delivering a message for Marcel. Relieved to find it open, she walked towards the confessional box and went inside and sat down. Eventually, she fell asleep for a while.

Towards dawn she pulled back the curtain to let in some air. As daylight seeped in through the windows, she half opened her eyes and closed them again. If only she had been able to sleep through the night, but she had merely dozed from time to time. She rubbed her legs to alleviate sharp cramping pains from being confined in such a small space. She started to consider her two options. Would she stay in France and try to contact Father Antoine? Or would she flee to her cachette outside Tours and follow London's instructions to write a simple coded message on a postcard to an address in Lisbon? Then she would wait for someone to contact her and arrange for her to cross the border into Spain and make contact with the British Embassy in Madrid.

Her thoughts were interrupted by a noise in the church. She peered out and saw a priest approaching the altar. Maybe he could help her. She stepped out of the box and coughed, making him walk towards her.

'I can see you are very troubled, ma petite,' he said in a whisper.

She hesitated and took in a deep breath. She couldn't divulge too much to a stranger. 'I need to speak to Father Antoine who is at St Martin's Basilica in Tours,' she whispered.

'What a coincidence. I know him well because we go back as far as lycée days. My name is Father Yves.' Then looking more closely at her he said, 'What is troubling you, my dear? You look exhausted. Let's go into the sacristy where we can talk more privately.'

Once she had sat down, he said, 'I am Father Yves. What is your name?'

'Véronique.'

'You look very distressed. What is the matter?'

As he was Antoine's friend, she'd risk telling him. 'I lost my cousin yesterday. He was betrayed.'

'By whom?' asked Father Yves.

'I can't tell you, Father.'

He nodded in an understanding manner and checked his watch. 'The curfew has just lifted. I came here to prepare for Mass at half past eight, as we've a special request from a farmer's wife whose husband has been taken away by the Gestapo. He was betrayed by a family member.'

Valérie put her hand to her face. 'Where does the family live?' she asked him.

'Outside Chissay.'

Valérie swallowed hard. Chissay? Wasn't that where Martin and André went to collect meat and vegetables from one of Benoît's friends? Was there a connection? Oh, how awful if that was the case.

'My presbytery is only a few minutes from here. I'd like to take you back there and ask Mathilde, my housekeeper, to give you some breakfast and look after you until I return. Later, after Mass, I'll phone Antoine, but of course I won't speak directly about you. I'll ask if I can go and see him tomorrow about an important matter.'

'He knows me as Valérie, but to outsiders I'm known as Véronique. Please remember that. It's important, Father. You may call me Valérie when we are alone.'

'I can guess what your circumstances are.'

Valérie arrived at the presbytery, a small Tourangelle house that boasted a large garden with lots of fruit and vegetables. Father introduced her to Mathilde, a large woman in her late fifties who gave her a warm welcome. Soon the aroma of real coffee filled the kitchen. 'You've come at the right time because Father's just been given this coffee as a present.' She toasted some French bread and spread it with butter and home-made strawberry jam.

'Father grows strawberries in his garden and some of the local children help him.'

After breakfast Mathilde said, 'Well, my dear, you look as though you could do with a good bath and tidy up. Come upstairs and we'll sort you out.'

Towards lunchtime Father Yves joined Valérie in his study. 'I took the farmer's wife and family back home. It was the least I could do. On my way here, I stopped off at the convent to see Sister Agnès.' He looked closely at her. 'Don't worry. I didn't divulge any details but mentioned your name as Véronique. She knows that you're traumatised but not the reasons why and she is happy for you to stay at the convent for a few days. I've also phoned Father Antoine and when I go to see him in Tours tomorrow, I'll tell him that I've helped you and that you'd like to see him as soon as soon as possible.'

'Thank you, Father, for your kindness. When you see Father, remember to refer to me as Valérie.'

He smiled. 'I remember. Of course I will.'

As an afterthought she asked him, 'Did you see much Boches activity while you were out?'

'Someone did tell me after arresting the farmer, the Gestapo swept into Azay and arrested Father Dominique. They were also searching for a young man who visited Father.'

She stared at him. She already knew about Father Dominique's arrest. If it was Emile they were after, he might not hold out for forty-eight hours without revealing vital information. She started to shake all over.

'Valérie, tell me what's troubling you.'

'I cannot go into details, but if you learn anything about the young man, please tell me at once.'

She spent the night at the presbytery and then Father took her to the convent the following day where he introduced her to Sister Agnès.

It was now the middle of August. Valérie had settled into her life at the convent when Father Yves collected her several days later and drove her to his presbytery in the early afternoon. When he opened his study door, Valérie gasped. 'Father Antoine, it's marvellous to see you.'

'It's a real pleasure to see you again, my dear.'

'I'll leave you two alone for a while,' said Father Yves and left the room.

'I was expecting you to contact me because Christophe came to see me in a dreadful state and explained why you had become angry with him and fled. He also explained he'd somehow have to let

London know what had happened to the circuit, and also about your departure from him,' he told her, as they sat down.

'I couldn't accept his refusal to consider my previous warnings to him and Benoît about my cousin. As a result, my cousin has been executed, Arnaud has been arrested and probably tortured and the priest at Azay has been arrested too. And now Emile is on the run.'

'I can understand your reaction but maybe in time, you will learn to forgive him,' replied Antoine. Valérie pursed her lips and remained silent and there was an awkward pause.

'Most of the others have gone into hiding, aware they could be traced if Arnaud breaks down,' he continued. 'Christophe is thinking of joining Benoît.'

'That is awful after what has happened. How could he support the man who has killed my cousin?'

The priest replied, 'I can understand your reaction.' After taking their seats, he asked her, 'Have you thought where you want to go?'

'I'm reluctant to ask for help from my family in France. I'll probably go to my hiding place. There's a plan I can follow to escape from France.'

'That might prove risky right now and you might not succeed. I have another suggestion to make,' he replied.' Someone you know has been to see me and is concerned about your welfare.'

'Whoever can that be?'

'Martin Sautereau.'

Valérie looked at him in surprise. 'Martin?'

'Yes. Martin disagreed more and more with Benoît about André. Martin kept telling him that he should have listened to your concerns earlier. He was not at the camp when your cousin was executed and knew nothing about Benoît's plans.'

'Thank goodness for that,' she replied.

'Martin is concerned for your safety and has suggested meeting you near here. As you know already, the Maquis has moved to another area. Martin's family in the north of Orléans may be able to help you.'

Valérie sat back in her chair. Martin had always been a good friend to her. In fact, she knew he more than liked her. The solution he was offering was safer for her and her family. Fortunately, her family lived in the south of Orléans. It was safer too, for the moment, than risking making her way to Barcelona. 'When would I meet him and where?'

'Martin is passing through near here next week and will contact Father Yves.'

'Have you any more news about Arnaud, Father?'

The priest's face became taut and his eyes downcast. 'Prisoners like Arnaud are often transferred to the Michelet Primary School. It's heavily guarded, although there have been two escapes in the last few months.' He paused and wiped his brow. 'We know that Arnaud is being held there. One of the recent escapees told a Resistance leader in Tours whom I know. Arnaud is imprisoned with Resistance people, robbers, black street marketeers and others. Soon they'll travel in a cattle train and be sent to a concentration camp in Germany or elsewhere.'

Valérie closed her eyes and lowered her head. Pictures of Arnaud's children clinging to their mother and grandmother swept into her mind. She looked up into Father Antoine's eyes which were damp and raw.

'I'm afraid I have other distressing news,' he said. 'A young man was arrested by the Gestapo not far from Chenonceaux. He had connections with Father Dominique at Azay.'

'Oh no!' cried Valérie.' 'Father Yves already warned me about this, and I guessed it could be our wireless operator and it is.' She put her head in her hands and stayed silent for a while.

'Brace yourself for the third piece of distressing news. Madame Guérin was arrested last night. She is one of my most loyal parishioners. A neighbour of hers came to the presbytery yesterday in a dreadful state to inform me.'

'Madame Guérin? It cannot be true, Father. She wasn't in the Resistance.'

'I know that, but she spoke her mind too freely. She knew people at the town hall. The wrong person might have heard her criticisms and reported her to the Gestapo. Remember our conversation when we talked about the way she warned you about Arnaud.'

Valérie bowed her head as tears ran down her face and onto her clothes. Four appalling denunciations. How could French citizens denounce others? They would pay for this once France regained her freedom. She was sure of this.

The priest moved over to her and placed his hand on her shoulder. 'Try to calm yourself. We live in evil times. Let us pray that the Allies will soon land and free our country. Now I must return to Tours. I have, of course, informed the other circuit members and Jacques has told the Maquis.'

Life at the convent was busy in the morning for the nuns. Valérie never attended Mass with them at half past five each morning, but she joined them for breakfast at seven o'clock and for their prayers afterwards. Housework and gardening followed.

One morning, while Valérie was polishing the wooden floor at the entrance, she fainted. She gradually came to with Sister Agnès and two other nuns in attendance.

'Whatever is the matter?' asked Sister Geneviève. 'You need to stay in bed and rest. You look very pale, but you've not lost weight since you've been here.'

Quite the contrary, thought Valérie. She was in more serious trouble than ever: she was two months pregnant with Christophe's child. She dared not even mention it to Sister Agnès. She would have to admit it to Martin and could not possibly work for his sister. No. There was only one place she could go to in this condition: her grandmother in St Jean-le-Blanc, a small town to the south of Orléans, even though she knew that she would be putting her at risk and had previously promised herself never to go there.

Towards the end of the third week in August, Father Yves drove Valérie to a café outside the town. 'Martin will drop you back into the town,' he told her. 'Ring me, and I will take you back to the convent.' Martin was already there; his face lit up as she joined him.

'Do you want something to drink, or shall we go for a walk where we can talk more freely?'

'Let us go straight away and find somewhere quiet to talk,' she replied.

After settling his bill, they walked into the countryside.

'How have things been wherever you've been staying?' he asked her.

'The people have been really kind to me.'

'That's good to hear. Father Antoine told me that you already know about the young man caught at Azay who belonged to your circuit, but several members have gone into hiding. Jacques, Raymond, and others. Father Antoine is being sent some distance from Tours to another parish.'

'Thank goodness. I need to leave the area as soon as I can. That is obvious. Father told me that you have a plan.'

'That's why I'm here today. I have come to offer you a way out of the mess you're in. My sister runs a grocery and greengrocer's shop in Fleury-les-Aubrais to the north of Orléans. She is a war widow, which is why my brother gave up his job to help her run the shop. He escaped forced labour because of a serious leg injury. My sister's son, Xavier, is becoming a bit of a handful. She'll be glad of some help with him and round the house and will take you in.'

Valérie looked at him anxiously. 'But Martin, there is something I must tell you. I don't know where to begin.'

'Whatever is the matter, Valérie?'

'I—I'm pregnant with Christophe's child.'

He was speechless for a few moments. 'I can't believe it.'

'Well, it's true.'

'Christophe is a bloody swine to land you in such trouble.' He touched her cheek and caressed it. 'You must know by now that I've always loved you. I fell in love with you when we were in that van taking Marcel to Raymond's after the raid on the factory. You were so kind and devoted to him.' After a long silence, he looked at her tenderly and said, 'Maybe in time you might find it possible to love me.'

She smiled. 'I'm overwhelmed by what you've just told me. I've long suspected that you had fallen in love with me.' She moved closer to him and put her arm round him. 'In time, I'm sure that I could return your love.'

He took her into his arms and kissed her gently, then passionately, making her feel that she could learn to respond to him if only things were different.

'But I could not possibly go to your sister's house in my condition, Martin,' she told him a little later. 'Be realistic.'

'Say nothing to her. I will accept the baby as mine.'

She looked up at him with tears in her eyes. 'Those are kind and wonderful words, Martin. Not many men would make that offer under the circumstances.'

'You mean everything to me, Valérie, and the baby can't help who the blood father is. Become my wife. We'll marry when I return to Orléans, towards the end of September, when I leave the Maquis. I will look for any work. Nicholas has lots of contacts, so we'll find a place to rent more easily.'

She shook her head. 'We can't. We'll have to wait until the war has ended.'

'Why ever not?'

'All my paperwork to do with my real identity is in England, so I can't marry you until France has been liberated. If that ever happens.'

He ran his fingers over her lips and kissed her again. 'Then I will wait patiently, but we now need to talk about practical things. I have asked my sister and brother and they are happy to take you in.'

'Goodness me. But are you sure that could work?' she asked.

'Yes. I am sure. Now to return to arrangements. You will take a train from St Pierre-des-Corps the day after tomorrow at half past eight in the morning and arrive at Les Aubrais interchange station, north of Orléans at around a quarter past eleven. Father Antoine is going to collect you from Father Yves's presbytery at a quarter to eight. When you arrive at Les Aubrais, go, and sit in a nearby café, called Le Chêne, where my brother, Nicholas, will meet you. He's taller than me but has the same auburn hair as me, but he has brown eyes. He has been given a description of you.'

'I hope it was a flattering one,' she replied, much to his amusement.

He told her more about his family until Valérie broached the subject of Christophe.

'Martin, if you come across Christophe, I don't want him to know anything about the baby or us.' She looked at him earnestly. 'Promise me that.'

He took her hand and caressed it. 'Of course.'

'After the war, I'll tell you my true name. Valérie is my field name.' She paused. 'To outsiders, I'm known as Véronique and that's the name on my identity card.'

He smiled. 'You're the first woman I've met with three names. You're unique,' he said with a chuckle.

'I don't want to leave you,' she told him. 'When will we meet again?'

'At the end of September in Orléans,' he replied. 'Now we must hurry back to town where I'll leave you.' Later, at the convent, she thought more and more about the baby, Christophe and Martin. A feeling of guilt about not telling Christophe about the baby was beginning to build up inside her. And pretending that Martin was the baby's father would be difficult and painful, wouldn't it? What would happen if Martin were killed in action? How could she continue to stay with his family and continue with the pretence?

After a while she decided that somehow, she would have to continue as planned, for Martin's sake. She couldn't let him down now after all the trouble he'd already gone to. Going to live with his sister in Orléans would also make it less likely that Christophe would find her.

She knew that Christophe had given Emile details to send to London about Arnaud's arrest and the break-up of the circuit. She wished she could have contacted London herself shortly afterwards. Ultimately, she'd be disciplined by the organisation for not contacting them once the Occupation was over. This troubled her. But the baby's safety and future were now her priority.

CHAPTER TWENTY-TWO
ARRIVAL IN ORLÉANS

It was now towards the fourth week in August. Valérie looked at her identity card where she was named as Véronique Perrin. She revised Véronique's story in her mind as the train steamed past fields and woods on the journey to Les Aubrais, in the north of Orléans. From now on, she had to become that young woman for outsiders. On arrival at the interchange station, she climbed down onto the platform and joined a long queue. It was now eleven o'clock.

'It's the Milice at the barrier,' said a voice from behind her. A voice that was weary and dejected. Valérie turned to see an elderly woman, dressed in black, clutching the hand of a young boy who was carrying a small suitcase. Soon they reached the barrier and made their way to some trestle tables.

'First of all, give me your identity card,' a milicien told Valérie and spent some time studying it before returning it. 'Now empty your suitcase and put your things onto the table.' After having examined everything minutely, he told her to repack her items.

Now she'd soon be through the barrier, but her hopes were dashed when a woman in the SS, dressed in a grey-green uniform, stepped forward, blocking her exit. As the woman started to body-search her, all her muscles tensed up and she had the urge to be sick.

'What is the purpose of your visit to this town?' the woman barked at her.

'I've come to do a domestic job.'

'Name of employer and his or her address.'

She hesitated before giving false details. After a long pause, the woman told her briskly, 'You may go now.'

As she turned to leave, she heard a child sobbing and saw the old woman and child being led away by another SS woman who looked across at her colleague with glee. Véronique wished she could wipe the smirk off the woman's face. What did the SS woman find in the suitcase or what information did she extract from the poor woman or the little boy? Were they Jews who would be sent to a concentration camp?

She fled out of the station as fast as she could and made her way to Le Chêne café, where she sat in the courtyard as instructed, and ordered an ersatz coffee. Half an hour later, she became aware of someone hovering over her, and looked up at a tall man with auburn hair who resembled Martin. He held out his hand to her. 'Sorry I'm late. I've come to collect my brother's friend.'

'I'm Valérie.'

'Enchanté, Mademoiselle. I'm Nicholas. Before you meet my sister, Sylvie, I think it would be easier if she called you Valérie. Is that all right?'

She hesitated. 'Yes, since Martin has already referred me to you as Valérie.'

After paying the bill, he led her to a van parked nearby and set off for the family home situated in Fleury-les-Aubrais, not far from the interchange station. During the journey Valérie was overwhelmed by the destruction around her: many of the district's houses had been bombed. Others had been partially destroyed and displayed interiors, open to the elements: snapshots of family life gone for ever. 'When were these areas raided?' she asked Nicholas.

'The Nazis destroyed large parts of Fleury in the beginning of June 1940. I was staying with my sister, Sylvie, and she was lucky that her house and shop stayed intact. But surely you read about all this in the newspapers or heard it on the wireless?' he asked her, somewhat bewildered.

Quick, reassure him. 'I was a sales rep, travelling all over the place, so I wasn't always able to catch up with the news.'

'But everyone knows about the exodus in June 1940 when thousands of people, from Belgium, the North of France, Paris and other areas, came in cars, vans, horse-drawn carts or simply traipsed on foot, towards Orléans, to escape the advancing Nazis. You must have heard how the German planes flew low over them killing hundreds of people and animals. And when the Boches entered Fleury and came into Orléans, they destroyed lots of buildings. Many local people fled from the city, including most of the firefighters, so Orléans burnt for several days,' he told her, looking at her still puzzled by her response.

They finally arrived at Sylvie's home, a two-storey house, built in the nineteenth century, and attached to the grocer's and greengrocery shop. A woman with fair hair and in her late thirties came to the door with her arm round a young boy with an impish smile.

'I'm Sylvie and this is my son, Xavier. You're most welcome here, Valérie' she said, embracing her, and took her through a kitchen into a cosy living room. Its beamed ceiling and pretty pink floral wallpaper reminded her of a similar room in her Aunt Marguerite's house at St Jean-le-Blanc, to the south of Orléans on the south bank.

'I'll unload the van while you two continue talking,' said Nicholas.

'Xavier comes home from school for lunch every day and so we shut the shop for an hour and a half,' Sylvie told her. 'Do sit down, Valérie, and we'll have an aperitif together, which we rarely do now.' She walked over to a cupboard and took out two bottles. 'Which would you prefer? A glass of red or a Pineau des Charentes?'

'I'll go for the red, please.'

During their conversation about conditions in Orléans, Martin was mentioned. 'He used to teach here, but then moved to Tours. That lasted about two years, but he suddenly left the lycée due to personal circumstances,' said Sylvie.

What were those? Maybe she'll tell me another time, thought Valérie.

'Do you know my Uncle Martin?' the young boy asked her.

'Yes, I do, Xavier,' she replied and then bit her lip.

Sylvie's grey eyes met Valérie's eyes. 'You're far too inquisitive,' she said to her son. 'Go and play with Filou in the garden until we call you in for lunch.'

'Oh Maman, must I?' he moaned. 'I'm tired of playing with the dog.'

'Xavier, I won't repeat myself,' she told him firmly and he hurried outside.

Nicholas joined them and poured himself a drink while Sylvie started to talk about her customers. 'I have to be discreet,' she told Valérie. 'Gone are the days when you could have a good chat with everyone. You must become more wary.' She fingered her glass nervously. 'The other day, early in the morning, there was a disturbance opposite our house when the Milice arrived and took away a customer, Monsieur Bordier, whom I've known for years. He's a married man, approaching retirement age, who has had an ongoing dispute with his neighbour about boundaries. The neighbour, a woman whom I don't like serving, kept telling Monsieur Bordier, "I'm going to the kommandant about this matter. You'll soon see, and I mean it."' She put her glass down. 'And last week, she did just that. It was horrible seeing Monsieur Bordier being led away forcibly into a van. His wife stood there in tears, pleading with the Milice, but in vain. I'm disgusted how more and more people are denouncing others for petty offences.'

'When an army occupies your country, even those whom you think you can trust sometimes let you down,' Valérie told her.

Sylvie looked across at her in sympathy. 'You seem to be speaking from experience.'

Valérie pressed her lips together. 'Yes. I've been let down by someone, but your brother rescued me from that situation. I will always remember his kindness.'

'Martin told me that you were in deep shock after losing someone in your family.'

Valérie nodded and finished her wine quickly.

Sylvie said, 'Let's take your luggage upstairs, and I'll show you your room. Then I'll serve lunch.' She took Valérie into a comfortably furnished bedroom with an oak wardrobe and chest of drawers, overlooking the garden. 'There's a washbasin in the alcove, as you can see. The toilet is on the right when you come out of your room. I've also left you a few books to read.'

'Thank you for going to so much trouble,' replied Valérie.

'Now, let's go downstairs for some lunch,' said Sylvie.

Xavier joined them for a meal of grated carrots done in an oil-and-vinegar dressing, followed by a beef stew and apple tart. What appetising food this was, but Sylvie probably bartered for meat and other commodities like Patricia did, thought Valérie.

During lunch Nicholas and Sylvie talked about business and orders that had to be prepared and delivered. After they had cleared the table, Sylvie asked Valérie to take Xavier back to school. On the way there he asked her, 'When did you last see my Uncle Martin?'

'Recently,' she put her arm round his shoulder and replied. 'He's keeping well.'

The boy looked up into her eyes then squeezed her hand. 'Uncle Martin's my favourite uncle. He's fun to be with and always has time for me. Uncle Nicholas is all right one day, and on another day, he doesn't want to know me.'

'He has a lot of work to do with the shop. Maybe he has to deliver food in the evening.'

'He often does that and sometimes he stays away for several days. I don't understand it. Maman tells me that I mustn't tell anyone about it, but I trust you, Valérie.'

'You need to get to know me first before telling me something important like that. Some people do bad things and report others to the Boches,' she told him, looking into his soft brown eyes.

'Maman and Uncle Nicholas keep telling me that.'

'Well, I must be right then,' she replied, laughing.

They continued chatting along the way to school and when it was time to say goodbye, he kissed her on both cheeks and ran into the playground. Before he went in through the main entrance, he turned and waved to her.

Valérie thought about Nicholas on the way to Sylvie's. Was he possibly in the Resistance too? Surely not? Martin wouldn't have wanted to put her at risk. If Nicholas wasn't engaged in Resistance work, maybe he had a lover. It was more likely to be the latter.

Once inside the house, she went upstairs to her room to unpack, thinking about Martin's intentions for the future. He planned to leave the Maquis, find another job and rent a flat for them both. Telling Sylvie and Nicholas about the baby would be difficult enough but explaining why they couldn't marry straight away would raise awkward questions. She could hardly tell them that her paperwork was back in England. Martin was kind, honest and romantic. In time she knew she'd grow to love him.

Inevitably her thoughts turned to Christophe. Her bitterness towards him for her cousin's death remained, but she still couldn't forget their moments of happiness and passion together and pondered on them. Had he informed London of her sudden departure? Or was he still in France? If so, where? If they were aware of the capture of Emile and of her disappearance, he would most likely be recalled. Had he made contact with his friend outside Vierzon? Would his contact know someone who had radio contact with London? She began to feel drowsy and lay down on the bed, falling into a deep sleep until she was woken up by someone knocking on the door. She half opened her eyes and saw Sylvie standing by her bed.

'Sorry to disturb you, but I forgot to tell you something important. If you meet anyone who comes to this house, or anywhere else, say you've come from another town but never Tours!'

'What's the reason?'

'News has filtered through that there's been a big round-up of the Resistance in the Touraine area and some people have managed to escape. Never tell Xavier any of this. Do you know any other town well?'

'Blois,' she replied.

'A smaller town?'

'Saumur?'

'Use that.'

Valérie nodded and Sylvie left the room. She sat up in bed, wide awake now. Some agents had managed to escape, Sylvie said. Who had escaped and who had been captured?

She thought of Martin and tears started to roll down her face. He was her future. She prayed nothing would take him from her.

CHAPTER TWENTY-THREE
SECURITY AT ALL COSTS

When Sylvie was busy serving in the shop, Valérie took Xavier to and from school each day. Halfway through September she was waiting outside Xavier's primary school when a tall woman in her early thirties with dark, deep-set eyes came up to her and said, 'I've only seen you here this term. Are you a newcomer to the district, if you can call it that with half of it burnt down?'

Mrs Busybody. Tread carefully, Valérie warned herself. 'I'm helping out a family,' the told the woman.

'Who's that? I know most of the people round here.'

'Sylvie Duvier,' she replied, then bit her lip.

The woman didn't answer straight away. 'Oh, the grocery woman,' she replied in an offhand manner. 'Xavier's a handful. Always has been.' Her face hardened. 'No consistent discipline at home. Since his father died in 1940, his mother has spoiled him, and as for Nicholas, he's hardly ever at home to discipline him. I can hazard a guess why—he's one for the ladies.' She moved closer to Valérie. 'Anyway, what's your name? Mine's Christine.'

'Véronique.'

Before she could answer any more questions, a teacher stepped into the playground and rang the half past three bell. Valérie was relieved to see that Xavier was one of the first to appear in the playground and he rushed up to her.

'Now if you'll excuse me, we must be off,' she said to the woman.

'As you wish, Mademoiselle,' she replied with a huff.

They hurried away before Xavier pulled out a drawing from his bag. 'Monsieur Lebrun told me off today,' he said, showing Valérie a drawing of a large dog attacking a German soldier with the caption *Bravo Filou*. Valérie looked down at Xavier and whispered, 'It's beautifully drawn, but let's put it back in the bag.' She put her hand on his shoulder and said, 'I can understand how you feel, but don't show this drawing to anyone outside your family. We're not supposed to write or draw anything that shows we don't like the Boches.'

Xavier nodded and replied, 'I won't let you down, Valérie. That's a promise.'

On arrival at the house, Valérie prepared Xavier's afternoon drink and snack. Outside in the garden, Nicholas was engrossed in conversation with a young man and both men looked deeply concerned about something.

At dinner that night, Nicholas was unusually silent, but when he joined his sister in the kitchen, Valérie heard him say, 'There were arrests last week in Tours, including two of Jean Meunier's men.' She recognised the name because Marcel had maintained regular contact with this Resistance leader in Tours who produced false identity cards and other documents in his printing premises. Was Nicholas in the Resistance? And if this were the case, did he hold a key position? Was it Martin who had told him about the arrests, using a liaison person? Had more members of her own circuit been arrested? These thoughts troubled Valérie.

Nicholas came into the room, interrupting her thoughts. 'I must leave urgently Valérie. Can you help Xavier with his homework, please?'

When she was alone with Sylvie, Valérie steered the conversation towards Martin. 'I know he was a lycée teacher in Tours, but what made him leave so suddenly?'

Sylvie sighed. 'It was a difficult decision. He was going out with a teacher colleague, and they were about to become engaged. Once the Germans invaded our country, it became obvious to Martin that Laure was pro-Vichy like the rest of her family. He couldn't tolerate their arguments and so he left the lycée and decided to do something different.' She took her time to continue. 'Tomorrow Nicholas would like you to help him with collecting vegetables and other items in town. You need to be up early and leave just after seven when the curfew ends.'

Nicholas almost certainly had Resistance plans on his agenda, and having a woman accompany him made things easier, Valérie reasoned. Someone at Beaulieu had also explained that a man accompanied by a woman helped with security.

The following morning, they set off in Nicholas's van for the centre of Orléans. During the journey Valérie stared at the destruction around her; her mind stood still, and she closed her eyes. After a while she opened them and told Nicholas, 'They've torn our beautiful city apart.'

'I'll shortly go past what remains of St Paul's Church. It's a shocking sight,' he replied and drove into a small square.

'What dreadful destruction!' she cried. All that remained of the church were some of its outside walls and its altar. She somehow refrained from crying. Maman sometimes had taken her inside to light a candle in memory of her father who was killed in the First World War, but she mustn't mention it to Nicholas. She didn't want him to know that she used to live in this area.

'Let's hope it will be restored one day when France is liberated,' replied Nicholas. He pulled into the kerbside and parked the van. 'It's quiet here and out of the way. I must visit some people. You can wander down to the river and see the changes there. I'll see you back here at a quarter past eight. Don't be late. We'll pick up the boxes of vegetables from the market afterwards.'

Valérie walked past the German soldiers on duty on the Chatelet quayside by the River Loire. As she looked down the river, she could hardly believe what she saw: the George V Bridge, which she and her mother used to cross to come into Orléans, was now severely damaged. It used to span the river, its twelve arches creating a majestic and breathtaking view. Three of these had been destroyed and a metal monstrosity, supported by concrete blocks, stood in their place.

Valérie passed the bridge and walked further along the quayside. Across the river, on the south side, was where her grandmother and Aunt Marguerite lived. It would only take her half an hour or so to reach their homes. If only she could visit them, but she knew that the Nazis might have Marguerite's house under surveillance. Safety was paramount for Martin's family, her family, as well as for herself and her unborn baby. She felt a tap on her shoulder and jumped.

'Sorry. I didn't mean to frighten you. I only saw one person because the others didn't turn up and that's worrying. Let's leave here,' he told her. They walked back to the van and drove away in a hurry. On arrival at the market, Valérie turned to him and said, 'If you want any other kind of help, you only have to ask.'

He turned and smiled. After picking up supplies of vegetables, they set off to Fleury. During the journey back to the north of Orléans, Nicholas told Valérie, 'I have some disappointing news for you: Martin won't be visiting us until towards the end of October. It's too risky for him to travel here.'

Valérie felt her stomach churn. Sylvie and Nicholas would soon become aware that she was pregnant, but how would she cope with this? The situation in France was becoming more fraught with danger. Would they ever become free of this merciless enemy, and would the Allies ever come and succeed in overthrowing the Nazis? How did Martin and Nicholas keep in touch with each other? Was Martin still in the Sologne with Benoît and his Maquis? Or had he joined another group?

CHAPTER TWENTY-FOUR

ANOTHER DILEMMA

Without Martin there, it was going to be difficult for Valérie to tell his family that she was expecting a baby. Lying about the identity of the baby's father troubled her considerably. One evening when they were alone, she summoned up the courage to tell Sylvie.

'I have something important to tell you and I was hoping Martin would be here tonight.'

Sylvie nodded. 'I know what you're going to tell me, and I can understand why you wanted Martin here.'

'I'm expecting a baby.'

Sylvie gave her a big hug. 'That's marvellous news. I'm so happy for you both and Xavier will be thrilled. We'll have to wait patiently for Martin, but as soon as we know he is coming, we'll prepare for the wedding. Of course, it'll have to be a quiet affair and we'll only invite a few people from both families.'

Valérie smoothed her hair back in place. 'I'm sorry, but that won't be possible.'

Sylvie stared at her in disbelief. 'Not possible? Why ever not?'

'I haven't got access to the necessary paperwork. I can't explain more than that.'

'I suspect you've been active in the Resistance with Martin. I've thought this now and then.'

'I can't answer that.'

Sylvie looked intensely at Valérie. 'Are you a British agent?'

Valérie remained silent.

'If you are, then we're all in a dangerous situation. Martin never disclosed any of this to Nicholas when they met before your arrival. He shouldn't have suggested you coming here if you are in British intelligence.'

'By the same token Martin should have told me that Nicholas was in the Resistance.'

'Who ever told you that?'

'It's obvious from things Nicholas himself has told me and from what I've overheard when he was speaking to you. Martin is a good man, but he seems to tell those closest to him the minimum of details. I would never have agreed to come here had I known of

Nicholas's involvement in the cause, for both your sakes, Xavier's and mine.'

Sylvie looked across the room at photographs of Xavier on the dresser. 'The most important person in all this is my son; he is only seven years old but old enough for the Boches to interrogate him and find out what they want.' She stood up and looked down on Valérie, who was sitting on the settee. 'I will have to talk to Nicholas about all this. We are all at risk now with your staying here. Please believe me, Valérie, I don't want to seem unkind towards you, but surely you can see my point of view?'

The screams of Arnaud's children, which had pierced the night air when their father had been taken away by the Gestapo, rang in Valérie's ears. To put this family at risk was out of the question. And where she thought of going was equally risky, but she had no alternative.

'What about the baby? How are you going to register his or her birth?' asked Sylvie.

'I'll have to declare him or her under my present name.'

'You do realise that being an unmarried mother will carry an enormous stigma for our family?'

'Again, I'm sorry, but what else can I do under the circumstances?'

Silence reigned at dinner that evening until Xavier asked, 'Maman, why is everyone so quiet? I don't like it.'

Sylvie looked across at Nicholas, indicating that she wanted him to answer the question.

'Everyone's tired. It's been a long and difficult day,' he explained.

'Why, Ton-Ton?'

'You always ask too many questions, Xavier. Now please be quiet,' replied Nicholas.

The meal continued in silence for a while until the little boy took Valérie's hand. 'Have you all had a big row?'

Valérie swallowed hard, trying to control herself, fighting back her tears. 'There's a problem we need to sort out, Xavier, that's all.' She stood up and hurried out of the room, climbing the steep stairs as fast as she could. Once she reached her bedroom, she collapsed onto the bed and sobbed. The little boy's distress had brought out her own pent-up fears, her anxiety about Martin and the baby, the potential dangers they were all in, as well as concerns for her grandmother and aunts. She must have fallen into a deep sleep because she awoke suddenly and could vaguely hear someone knocking on the door.

'Come in,' she called out and was surprised to see Nicholas.

'We didn't like seeing you in this state. Sylvie told me about the baby. We recognise it is wartime, but your involvement in the Resistance is what we are most concerned about. The truth is that Martin should have never put us all at risk and he has put you in danger by sending you here. You can stay until we sort out another place for you, but it's becoming riskier here in this neighbourhood day by day. I'll be leaving here soon, and I'll be away for some time.' He sat down on a chair by the side of her bed. 'There's one question that I must ask you. Has anyone approached you since you've been here and questioned you?'

Valérie steeled herself. 'Yes. There was one person,' she replied, noticing fear invade his eyes. 'A woman in her early thirties, smartly dressed, came up to me outside the school soon after I arrived.'

'What did she ask you and did she tell you her name?'

'Yes. Christine, but I only gave her my cover name which is on my identity card.' A look of horror swept his face. 'She persisted in asking me where I lived, and I eventually told her.'

'What exactly did she say?'

'That Xavier was spoilt and that you were ...' She stopped in her tracks, blushing more and more.

'Tell me.'

'That you were hardly ever at home in the evenings and that you were almost certainly a ladies' man.'

'Try to give me a fuller description of this bitch.'

Valérie started to give him a good description, including mention of the woman's expensive shoes, but Nicholas interrupted her. 'I know who it is. She is the wife of one of the most influential miliciens in this area. You'll have to move out as soon as possible.' Valérie stared at him in horror. 'The fact that the woman knows I go out frequently confirms to me that I am being watched. I'll try to find somewhere else for you to go, but do you know of anyone who could help you?'

Valérie thought quickly. She would have to go to Mamy for help. She didn't want to go to a safe house where she knew no one, especially in her condition. 'I do know someone who could help me temporarily, but it's some distance from here.'

'Whereabouts?'

'St Jean-le-Blanc, to the south of Orléans, on the other side of the river.'

'I know a man, let's call him Pierre, who could take you there. He has a night pass for his job. He'd transport all your belongings to the new address as well.' He looked concerned for her and said, 'I'm thinking of your own security as well as ours. I'll go and see him tomorrow morning when he comes off duty from his job. I'll discuss it with you tomorrow evening.'

'How will I contact you in future so that I know when Martin returns to Orléans?' she asked him.'

After reflection, he said, 'When you're ready, phone the shop and order a kilo of green beans for Mademoiselle Lenoir and say where you would like them delivered. Name a public place in the town and when you would like them delivered. Then ring again and see if this has been accepted. I'll give you the shop number before you leave. It could be either Sylvie or me who meets you.'

After he left the room, Valérie thought about her grandmother. It was going to be a shock for her, she realised that, but she had nowhere else to go. Mamy would take her in for a short period, but where would she go after that? And how would she cope with hardly any money?

CHAPTER TWENTY-FIVE

HIDEAWAY IN MID-SEPTEMBER

Pierre collected Marie-Claire the following evening, well before curfew, and drove her through the city of Orléans. The sight of official buildings and shops sliced in half, family homes destroyed, swastika flags flapping in a strong wind and hearing a German military band playing in the distance, tormented Marie-Claire. And when they reached the banks of the River Loire, she exclaimed, 'Pierre, it's monstrous that the Nazis have renamed our repaired George V bridge after Hitler.'

'We can only hope that in the end the Allies will come to our rescue,' said Pierre. 'The days of reckoning for the Nazis will come, Marie-Claire. Rest assured. The Allies will bomb the hell out of Germany.'

After crossing the bridge, they motored along by the river with its sandy banks and in the distance on the opposite riverbank, Marie-Claire admired Orléans cathedral, a source of comfort to its citizens in times of war and other troubles. They passed a few remaining one-storey houses and tall terraced ones as they approached the little town of St Jean-le-Blanc. On the right-hand side, she saw the little primary school that she had attended with Philippe and his brothers. School days had been happy ones, but for André they'd often been troubled ones, including a suspension. Finally, there had been serious trouble and she had been partly blamed because she had covered for him. This was one of several reasons for her own family's departure to England in 1930.

A little later she asked Pierre to stop in a road that ran parallel to Mamy's house. 'Thanks for bringing me here,' she told him.

'My pleasure. Keep a sharp lookout everywhere you go here. There has been trouble recently in this town.'

She walked briskly into the next road, which was lined on either side mostly with terraced houses with slate roofs, built in the late 1800s. Mamy's house was on the left at the end of a terrace. A dim light shone inside. Marie-Claire looked over her shoulder to check that no one was following her. Then she knocked on the front door but there was no answer. She turned to see if anyone was passing by. Reassured there wasn't, she knocked a little louder. Almost at once the door opened a crack and Mamy's face appeared. Her eyes immediately became transfixed and her face taut. Fighting for her words, she whispered, 'Marie-Claire? I—I must be dreaming? It can't be you.'

'No, it *is* me, Mamy,' she replied. 'Come in quickly and let me shut this front door,' said Mamy and took Marie-Claire into her arms, cuddling and kissing her.

'Oh Mamy. It's lovely to be cuddled again by you. It's been such a long time.'

'Whatever are you doing here in France, Marie-Claire?' she asked, her face pale with shock.

'I'll explain in a moment.'

'Give me your coat and let's go into the living room.' They sat down and her grandmother continued, 'How ever did you get here?' A look of fear swept over her face. 'You're not in the Resistance like Philippe was, I hope?'

How could she answer her? She had signed the Official Secrets Act. She wasn't even allowed to tell Maman and Dad, but she would tell Mamy something to satisfy her.

'I can say little. I was sent to France by the British. And I shouldn't even be telling you that.' After a pause, she said, 'I had to leave the family who was sheltering me in Orléans urgently because of security. Can you help me? Can I stay here for a while?'

She seemed lost for words and after a few moments, she said 'You can only stay here for a few days, and I'll explain why. You remember Madame Lefèvre, the wife of the right-wing local councillor.' Marie-Claire nodded. 'She lives in the next road. She's a nosy woman and her husband supports the Nazis. She knows your family went to live in England. You dare not be seen in the neighbourhood whatsoever. You will have to stay inside all the time until we can find somewhere else for you to live.'

'I need to tell you something important,' said Marie-Claire. Her heart quickened as she fought to find the right words.

'Whatever is it, Marie-Claire?'

'I'm— I'm three months pregnant.'

'Oh no! I can't believe it!' she cried and remained speechless. Marie-Claire stood up and sat beside Mamy on the couch and cuddled her. 'How ever are we going to cope?' asked Mamy.

'My boyfriend is supporting me. We'll marry after France becomes free because my paperwork is in England. He's unable to be with me in Orléans, at the moment.'

Mamy wiped her eyes. 'You mean he's in the Resistance like you?'

'I can't say anything. Sorry, Mamy,' said Marie-Claire.

'I have an idea. Your Uncle Maurice might help you. It's risky but last year one of his friends was arrested and sent to do forced labour in Germany and now he hates the Boches even more.' She looked deeply into Marie-Claire's eyes and rubbed her hands gently. 'I may be able to persuade him to take you in, but Aunt Gisèle is incredibly nervous as far as the Nazis are concerned.' She paused. 'She will need to be persuaded, but they've always been extremely fond of you, especially never having had any children of their own. They always enjoyed having you and your mum to stay with them each summer.'

'How will I explain why I'm in France? And who sent me?'

After a few moments, Mamy said, 'That's going to be difficult. We will have to tell them about the baby, but they will soon guess that you have been working in the Resistance. In the meantime, I'll ring Maurice tomorrow and ask him to repair something. It's our kind of password to indicate trouble. We started using it after Philippe's death. You never know whether operators listen in and report what they hear.' She laughed and added, 'You could say we're doing our own little bit of resistance. When Maurice comes, we'll ask him whether they would be willing to take you in, but we'll have to think about an explanation.'

'I realise that' replied Marie-Claire. 'It would be a huge relief for me, even if it was only on a temporary basis until we can find somewhere else. And where they live in Olivet is more remote than round here.' She bit her lip. 'But if they don't agree, what am I to do?'

'I will keep you here until we find someone else to help us. But there is just one thing I must insist upon,' she said.

'I can't imagine what that is,' said Marie-Claire, noticing her grandmother's eyes mist over.

'I must buy you a wedding ring. None of the family must know you're not married. Gisèle would be appalled if she knew the truth. More especially as you're expecting a baby and you will have to tell them both about that.'

Marie-Claire bit her lip. More deception, but what Mamy was proposing made sense, didn't it? What a pity she had to deceive her own family whereas Martin's had understood her dilemma. But they too would have been relieved to see a wedding ring on her finger, wouldn't they?

'There is one other matter. Why haven't you mentioned André?' asked Mamy. 'You and he were always so close to each other.'

Lying to Mamy was out of the question. And in any case, she would soon detect that she wasn't telling the truth. Marie-Claire realised that.

'I've thought long and hard about this, Mamy. But what I must tell you must remain between ourselves for the moment. Prepare yourself for a dreadful shock.'

'It sounds serious.'

'It is.' She put her arms round her grandmother. 'André became drunk and betrayed one of the circuit members and ...'

'What happened?'

'The Maquis leader shot him dead.'

'Oh no! No!' she cried and dissolved into tears, shaking all over. Marie-Claire comforted her as best she could. 'You will have to tell Maurice and Gisèle as well as Aunt Marguerite.'

'I can't. You must not tell them, nor Aunt Marguerite. She might not be able to restrain herself from telling people. It would put all of us at risk. Can't you see that?'

Mamy eventually responded to Marie-Claire. 'I will say nothing for the moment to anyone, but if you leave the area, I will have to tell the family.'

'Once the Occupation is over, I will tell the family myself.'

'I can see we have no other choice.'

Marie-Claire hadn't seen Maurice for four years and when he arrived at Mamy's, she was shaken at how much older he appeared; his once-thick black hair was now turning grey and thinning all over and he'd lost a lot of weight.

He embraced her warmly. 'It's lovely to see you again even if it's in a France we no longer recognise. But I am staggered to find you here. What's it all about?'

While Mamy prepared some hot drinks, Maurice listened to Marie-Claire's dilemma, though she kept details about her Resistance work to a minimum.

'I'll talk to Gisèle and let you know how she feels.'

'I realise it's a lot to ask and risky too, but I don't know where else to go.'

Mamy served the drinks and added, 'Don't worry, Marie-Claire, you can stay until we've found an alternative.'

After having talked about the family, Maurice had to leave, promising to do what he could.

After his departure, Marie-Claire asked Mamy, 'May I ask if my boyfriend's brother could leave messages under the bricks outside your house? It would only be a temporary arrangement.'

'It's taking a risk but if you have no other choice, he can leave them for only a short while.'

'Thank you, Mamy. That means a lot to me.'

A few days later after having made a phone call to Sylvie's shop and requested the green beans, as she had been instructed, she met Nicholas outside the primary school in the middle of town.

'You look well,' he told her. 'We've heard nothing from Martin. Let's go for a walk and sort out how we're going to exchange messages. It could be Sylvie who meets you if I have to go away,' he warned her.

Marie-Claire explained the arrangement she had made with Mamy to receive his messages. If any emergency arose, she would phone the shop again.

A week later, although Marie-Claire was greatly relieved to learn that Maurice and Gisèle would take her in, she could tell by his manner that it hadn't been an easy task for him to persuade Gisèle to agree. A few days later he collected Mamy and Marie-Claire and took them back to Olivet to spend the weekend with them. As he drove them towards Olivet, passing through countryside, Marie-Claire wondered how her aunt and uncle had coped so far during the Occupation. Maurice's job as a fireman, which also involved tending medically to the injured, often brought him into contact with the police. And Mamy had told her that some of the police were sympathetic towards the Vichy regime and the Nazis. Hiding his hatred towards the Nazis must be extremely difficult for him. In addition, Gisèle's clerical job, at the local mayor's office, obliged her to watch what she said to colleagues; Marie-Claire recalled the arrest of Madame Guérin, who had previously worked at the town hall in Tours and who had been an avid critic of the Nazi regime.

They arrived in Olivet where Marie-Claire had spent many enjoyable holidays with her aunt and uncle. She admired the old house with its slate roof gleaming under the autumn sun. The blue rectangular window frames contrasted well with the newly painted white shutters. Most of all she had loved the large garden, with its fruit trees and numerous bushes, where as a child she had played hide-and-seek and other games with her brother and cousins. Her aunt and uncle had enjoyed looking after them and spoiling them. Gisèle opened the front door and embraced her warmly. 'Welcome, Marie-Claire. I couldn't believe that you were in France when Maurice told me.' She led them into a living room furnished in beautiful oak furniture, complemented by walls decorated in a burgundy wallpaper. 'Give me your coat and case. Sit down and relax while Maurice prepares some aperitifs.'

'I can offer you both a Pineau and a port.'

'I'll go for the Pineau,' replied Marie-Claire.

'The same for me,' said Mamy.

'How long have you been in France?' Gisèle asked her.

'A few months, but I can't tell you any more than that.'

'Tell me about your husband.'

'He's called Martin and he is working far away from Orléans.'

Gisèle looked up at a photograph on the wall of Josette, Marguerite and their brother Georges. 'Knowing your mum as I do, she must be out of her mind worrying about you. She must know you're in France and she must guess, like we do, that you've been involved in the Resistance.'

'Like I said, Gisèle, I can't say anything.' said Marie-Claire. 'It's not that I don't trust you or Maurice, but I'm bound by the rule book.'

Maurice handed them their drinks and said, 'We've decided that it would be better if Marguerite isn't told about you being in France. She has deteriorated since André left Orléans about five months ago. We know he wanted to join a Maquis, but we've heard nothing from him. His poor mother is in a dreadful state again. We sent his younger brother Pierrot to live with Uncle Georges in Paris.'

'I'm not surprised,' replied Marie-Claire.

'We have no idea if André is still alive or if he's been killed,' said Gisèle.

Marie-Claire blushed, distraught by not telling them the truth.

Gisèle looked at her in a quizzical manner before resuming the conversation. 'You'll have to stay in as much as possible, and also change your appearance.'

'I've dyed my hair on at least two occasions since I've been in France,' said Marie-Claire, then bit her lip.

'Now that tells me how much you were embedded in the Resistance. And your husband, Martin, too, I don't doubt.'

Marie-Claire looked away from her aunt.

During a delicious lunch, Gisèle asked Marie-Claire when her baby was due.

'In March. And I need to make arrangements to find a doctor and where to give birth.'

'I can help you there. Our own doctor is superb, and he will help you all he can, I can assure you. If he considers there are any complications, there is a hospital outside Orléans where he knows a gynaecologist.'

'Oh, I am so grateful to you, Gisèle, for your help. I've been worrying about it for some time. My husband will pay for all the expenses. Don't worry about that.'

'We live in horrendous times, and we all want to help you,' said Maurice.

CHAPTER TWENTY-SIX

MARTIN'S RETURN IN LATE OCTOBER

At long last Martin was returning to Orléans. Valérie was waiting for him in Olivet at the gateway for the Windmill Walk along the Loiret, a tributary of the River Loire. Since a child, this had always been her favourite walk with differently styled windmills turned into homes. She heard heavy footsteps on the gravel path and soon Martin came into view, his auburn hair glistening under the autumn sun. She rushed into his open arms, and at first, he kissed her tenderly. Then he pulled her close to him; he kissed her passionately until Marie-Claire felt carried away into a state of sheer ecstasy.

'My darling Valérie, I can't believe we're together at long last.

'Oh Martin, I've lived for this moment. It's been a long while. I've thought about you so much.'

They started to walk along by the Loiret, his strong fingers laced through hers as they walked hand in hand, stopping from time to time to admire the windmill homes. Valérie sniffed the sweet-scented smoke of a log fire escaping through the chimney of her favourite windmill, a four-storey dwelling with a pink façade and a slate roof, in line with most of the houses in the region. There was hardly a ripple in the water and the only sounds were from the ducks. She was transfixed by the mill's reflection, but gradually she felt Martin squeezing her hand.

'What are you thinking about?' he asked her.

'When I was about four years old, Papa used to tease me when we came to this spot, saying that there was once an underwater mill in which a wicked witch was imprisoned. A handsome prince had caught her and punished her for taking his princess away, but in the end the witch told him where she had locked up the princess, and so there was a happy outcome,' said Valérie.

'What an intriguing story. You must have been close to your father. How long did you live in France?'

'Ten years. We returned to England because my English grandmother was poorly. And my mother wanted to leave because of trouble with André at primary school when I had supported him. It led to quite an unpleasant business within the family. Now tell me about your parents.'

'Papa died about three years ago. He was killed in the fighting when the Boches invaded France so Maman moved away from Orléans, but I can't tell you where she is now.'

'I understand,' she replied.

They came to a bench and sat down to rest. 'How long will you be here for?' she asked him.

'Only a few days, I'm afraid.'

'You've obviously seen Nicholas,' she said.

'Yes. Things are dangerous. Three leaders of the Libé-Nord circuit were arrested earlier this month and seventeen communists were shot at the Groues shooting range outside Orléans on the eighth of October, along with a Nazi soldier who refused to fire on them. It was an awful and distressing time for the families. Even the prefect pleaded their case with the Boches, but it made no difference.'

Valérie gasped and took his hand. 'Both you and Nicholas must be even more cautious.'

'We realise that.' He pointed to her wedding ring. 'Who bought you that?'

'My grandmother. She thought it was the correct thing to do.'

'That was good of her. Did you tell her about me and the baby and that it's my child?'

'Yes. Of course I did. And I explained why we couldn't marry, and she wanted to buy the ring to avoid embarrassment within the family. My aunt in Olivet would have strongly objected,' she said.

'As soon as this Occupation is over, I will buy you the most beautiful wedding ring that I can find, ma chérie,' he replied, kissing her.

'Oh Martin! How I long for that day.'

'Have you told your family about André?'

'Only my grandmother who has been sworn to secrecy. Unfortunately, my Aunt Gisèle and Uncle Maurice guessed that I was involved in the Resistance and that you were too, but I told them nothing. And I didn't meet Aunt Marguerite, André's mother, because she is in a bad mental state which is not surprising.'

'That must have been painful for you to learn. But it was kinder at this time to avoid distressing her further.'

'It was. And difficult not being able to confirm that we were involved in the Resistance with my aunt and uncle.'

They continued to walk along the riverbank, admiring the reflections in the water. Flutters of brittle and curled leaves descended onto those leaves already mashed by rain and walkers. Squirrels, intent on increasing their winter stocks, whisked through branches, whipped up and down tree trunks, and disappeared into the undergrowth. Occasionally they saw young boys and old men casting their fishing lines into the Loiret and sitting on the riverbank, in deep concentration as they bent forward to see if there was a pull. Where were the young men who used to enjoy peace and quiet here as they fished? Were they now forced to work in German factories? How many of them would ever come home? Christophe had told her that he loved fishing. Where was he now? Had he contacted the organiser in Angers and sent a message to London via the wireless operator? Had he been recalled to London? Or had he been arrested by the Gestapo?

'You look as if you have something on your mind, Valérie.'

'Yes. It concerns the organisation in London that sent me to France as a courier. I need to find some way of contacting them through the Resistance. I must give them my side of the story when circuit members were betrayed and arrested, and the rest had to disappear. I must also tell them why I fled, after my cousin's execution by the Maquis leader and following a serious disagreement about it with Christophe. I would have to disclose that I had found myself pregnant. If I don't make contact, I could be in serious trouble when the Occupation ends.' She stopped walking and turned to Martin. 'Do you know of anyone in the Resistance who has contact with a circuit led by a British trained leader?'

'Not at the moment, but I am thinking of leaving Benoît's Maquis. A friend of mine leads a larger Maquis and has already approached me to join. In fact, he wants to try and get ammunition and arms drops like your circuit did. I know he has already made contact with someone who has a connection with a British-led circuit.'

'This could be a godsend to me,' she replied.

'I can't promise anything, but if anything comes of it. I'll let you know through Nicholas.'

'If you do make contact, can you remember this piece of information?

'I'll do my best.'

'This British-trained leader will have a wireless operator. He would need to send the following message: "Courier with Fisherman alive in France. Arrests. Circuit betrayed. Dispute between organiser and courier. In confidence courier expecting baby." Can you remember this, Martin?'

'Easily. Already I have to carry complicated Resistance verbal messages between people.'

They continued walking, but after a long period of silence, Martin tugged at her sleeve. 'You're thinking about Christophe, aren't you?'

'Yes,' she admitted to him, 'but it's you whom I love now, Martin.'

Despite her assurance, Martin looked troubled. 'It's about Christophe. He came to us in the camp.'

'Father Antoine told me he had gone there.'

'At first, he never mentioned you, but I remember one evening, when we were all sitting in our circle, like we normally do, enjoying dinner. Halfway through the meal, he returned to the tent area. When I joined him later, he was sitting with his head in his hands. He looked up at me and said, "Every night since Valérie left the circuit, I've not been able to sleep. I worry about her all the time. Is she alive? Have the Gestapo arrested her? Has she been tortured? Has she been put on one of those cattle trains and sent to a concentration camp? I still can't understand why she refused to see that André's death was not my responsibility." The following morning, he packed his things and disappeared.'

Martin turned to Valérie and said, 'After the occupation has ended will you ever contact Christophe in England and tell him about the baby?'

'No, Martin. I have no intention whatsoever of contacting Christophe. It wouldn't serve any purpose. My life is with you now. Even if I tried to find him, I wouldn't know his full name. I only know his first real name and that he came from somewhere in Surrey in the south of England. Christophe was his field name.' She paused for a few moments. 'Remember Martin, always call me Veronique in front of strangers. That's the name on my identity card.'

'I promise, though I am dying to discover your real first name after the Occupation is over.'

They kissed each other and continued their walk until they came to a small windmill home situated on a bend in the river, which was not as well-maintained as the others.

'Let's explore it,' suggested Martin.

'Although it looks unkempt, someone might still be there,' warned Valérie.

'Let's be adventurous,' he replied and hurried towards the house. Curtains were drawn across some of the windows, but they were able to peer into the kitchen and living room. Thick dust lay on the windowsills.

'There are some priceless eighteenth-century pieces of furniture in the living room,' said Valérie.

'When did you study furniture?'

'Never, but my Uncle Georges used to take me on tours of the Loire châteaux. He brought them to life. He had a hoard of exciting stories about the people who used to live in them, like the scheming Queen Catherine of Medici and her son, the Duke of Guise, who was murdered in the castle at Blois,' she explained to Martin. 'He compared the different styles of furniture. That's how history should have been taught at school.'

'I wonder how this German Occupation will be taught in schools in the future?' His eyes were fixed on her and his expression serious.

'As long as the truth is told about how those who supported the Nazis often denounced résistants, friends, neighbours and those close to them.'

As they wandered into the garden, the sky had become overcast, and rain began to fall heavily. Martin seized her hand, and they ran, laughing, to shelter beneath the porch of a wooden summer house. He tried the door, found it unlocked and Valérie followed him into a room furnished with a few comfortable chairs. Martin sat down onto a chaise longue and reached out his hand to her.

Suddenly aware of an intimacy growing between them, afraid it was too soon, she said nervously,

'Martin, we shouldn't really be in here. We shouldn't even have come into the garden.'

'But chérie, in time of war we break the rules all the time.' His face was serious now. 'I should not have fallen in love with another man's girl. But I did. The moment you walked into the Amboise Forest, my heartbeat increased rapidly, but I knew you were spoken for already.'

'Martin, let me explain how I feel.' She sat down beside him, took his strong hand in hers, aware of his light blue eyes fixed on her. 'I've had time to reflect. Of course, I was passionately in love with Christophe, but after the trouble with André, it was destroyed. It was if a huge block had descended upon us, separating us. There was no turning back, despite my expecting his child.'

He leaned his cheek against hers and she felt the merest hint of a kiss on her ear, and he whispered, 'Even though you lived in England for some of your life, you were born in France, and you are a French girl through and through in the way you think and act, and only a French man can make you happy.' His lips slid down her neck in a trail of soft kisses. Suddenly a little breathless, she felt herself succumbing as he gently caressed her. Could she love Martin? Suddenly, in spite of all that had happened, all that was still happening to her beloved France, she felt secure in his strong arms. Wanting to deny him nothing, knowing they might not see each other again, they sealed their love. As she lay in his arms, she asked, 'When will I see you again, Martin?'

'I was going to talk to you about this. As I told you earlier, I am thinking of leaving Benoît's Maquis soon. Firstly because of what happened with André and secondly, as I told you already, a friend of mine has asked me to join his Maquis that he set up a few months ago. I can't tell you where it is, for security, but I will keep in touch with Nicholas and let you know when I can see you. And if I find someone who can help you contact London, I'll let you know through Nicholas.'

Valérie understood why he couldn't give her any details; she was relieved that he was leaving Benoît himself but remembered how much she had grown to like his fellow maquisards and hoped that the new Maquis that he wanted to join posed no problems.

After making their way back to the gateway to the Windmill Walk, saying goodbye to each other was painful and uncertain in the dangerous situation in which France found herself.

When she returned to Aunt Gisèle's home, Marie-Claire went upstairs into her room and sat on her bed. Martin had been caring, sensuous and passionate, but after she had felt her baby move for the first time, she felt a degree of guilt, knowing that the child she would bring into this world would never know the identity of his or her true father. However, she knew that her love for Martin would ensure a secure future for her child.

CHAPTER TWENTY-SEVEN
DECEMBER

'Marie-Claire, let's go for a walk along the Loiret where the windmill houses are,' suggested Mamy when she was staying with Gisèle and Maurice during one weekend in the beginning of December.

It was bitterly cold as they both set out, and when they arrived by the river, it was frozen in places, creating mini platforms for the ducks and other waterfowl to rest on. But at least it was a dry day. Apart from evergreens, other trees sporting dead branches against a cold grey sky, and those bearing a few brittle leaves, added to the winter scene. Marie-Claire enjoyed again the sweet-scented smoke of log fires escaping through chimneys of the windmill houses.

'Thank goodness Gisèle took Marguerite to visit her doctor because she could see that she was beginning to deteriorate as a result of pining more and more for André, not knowing why he hadn't contacted her for months,' said Mamy. 'I was relieved when Gisèle told us yesterday that Marguerite is now in a convent which has facilities for people in her position.'

'Yes. It is a relief, but at the same time, I feel guilty in not telling her what I know. When I arrived in Olivet in late August, Gisèle soon guessed that I had been in the Resistance. I remember telling you that she had challenged me about it, but I told her that I could say nothing. She thought it would be better if I didn't meet Marguerite. Otherwise, she might tell other people that she had seen me and put everyone at risk. So, it was obvious that she realised I was in the Resistance,' replied Marie-Claire. 'So, by ensuring Marguerite is somewhere safe but secure, that in turn ensures everyone's safety.'

'Yes. You're right. Have you heard any more from Martin's brother?' asked Mamy.

'No, but I hope he'll contact me with news about Martin before Christmas.'

After she had retired to bed, Marie-Claire thought again about the arrival of the baby in March and of Martin's safety. When would she see him again? The more she thought about him, the more she realised how much she loved him and how she owed her safety to him. Christophe and the organisation came to her mind again. It did this from time to time.

Before she had known about being pregnant, she had seriously considered going to her cachette and following the emergency procedure to return to England. Had Christophe contacted London and updated them about everything? Had he returned there? A slice of guilt cut through her about Christophe. Had she been cruel and obstinate in deserting him? But even if she had decided to return to him, she had no way of knowing where he would have gone in the Vierzon area. Finally, when she'd discovered her pregnancy, Martin had come back into her life and had offered her love, safety and acceptance of the baby as his.

She closed her eyes, seeing the stricken faces of her parents who still didn't know what had become of her. She had agonised about accepting the courier's job, but the reasons for her decision to come to France outweighed them. Had Miss Atkins stopped sending her postcards to her parents? If so, they would be frantic with worry? She was powerless and helpless regarding her parents. She prayed that somehow Martin and Nicholas would be able to help her contact a British-led circuit and that Miss Atkins would contact her parents.

Shortly before Christmas Eve, Nicholas contacted Valérie by leaving a note under a vase in her aunt's garden. He arranged to collect her from the centre of Olivet.

'I'm glad you could meet me. How is Martin?' she asked him when they met.

'I've only been able to see him once—last week as it happens. Things are becoming more dangerous where he operates in his new Maquis, so he can't come to see you for some considerable time, but he sends his love and has given me more money for you to pay for the confinement.' He pulled out a wad of notes from his jacket and gave them to her.

Valérie held back her tears. 'Please thank him and send him all my love. And thank him for the money.'

'It's normal for him to pay for his baby's safe arrival.'

Valérie felt a clench in her stomach as if a belt were squeezing her. With difficulty she replied, 'Of course,' hating herself for keeping up the pretence. 'How are Sylvie and Xavier?'

'Sylvie is finding things difficult with me not being there, but she understands that's how it has to be. Of course, we meet outside Orléans, once we realised I was being watched. He sighed and said, 'Xavier keeps on asking why you left and where you've gone. We're thinking of sending him to live with his grandmother.'

Valérie wondered whether she lived in Tours and was the person whom Martin used to visit.

'Nicholas, has Martin told you that I desperately need to contact my London organisation? Has he talked to you about this?'

'Yes. I was about to tell you some news. His Maquis leader does know of someone who might be able to help you. This person is in a British-led circuit that works with a Maquis. They receive ammunition drops and arms from London. They do have someone with a radio. Martin will let me know if he has any news. I gather you've given him the details of what you want to send to the organisation.' She nodded and thanked him. 'Now I must go. I'll make contact again soon in the usual way.'

Towards the end of February 1944, when they were preparing the evening meal, Gisèle asked Marie-Claire, 'Do you think Martin will be able to come and see you after the baby has been born?'

'I doubt it very much. I don't even know where he is,' she replied.

As Marie-Claire carried the plates into the dining room, she felt something trickle down her legs and called out to Gisèle.

'He or she is obviously keen to arrive early,' replied Gisèle, putting her arms round her. 'Don't worry. You're in good hands with Dr Dubier—I'll call him straight away and I'll get the room upstairs ready as we planned together.'

The pains intensified. Normally, Martin would be holding her hand and comforting her, but she was blessed with a loving family who had helped her throughout the pregnancy.

Soon, Dr Dubier arrived and by now Marie-Claire was lying down upstairs in the room prepared by Gisèle for the birth.

'Good afternoon, Madame, now just relax while I examine you,' he said gently.

After the examination, he told her, 'Everything looks fine. I think it will be a straightforward and fairly quick birth.'

The doctor's prediction came true and three hours later, Marie-Claire heard the baby's cries and learned that her daughter had been safely delivered.

'What are you going to call her?' he asked.

'Lucie,' she replied and asked for Gisèle.

She was overwhelmed with sheer happiness when Gisèle passed the baby to her. She kissed her gently on the forehead and cuddled her closely, loving every moment. She sighed a little as she looked at Lucie's thick fair hair—it was shiny and silky to touch like Christophe's and her skin was so soft and warm. If Martin returned safely, he would take Lucie into his arms and love her. She paused, dreading the thought if anything ever happened to him.

Later, when caressing Lucie, she recalled the time that she and Christophe had made love in the tatty bedroom of the woodcutter's cottage. That was almost certainly the night Lucie had been conceived. Then the harrowing moments, when she had shot the German officer in the head, revisited her. She swallowed hard and after some time, she tried hard not to think of it.

She again thought of both men who had entered her life. Would she be able to reconcile her most intimate thoughts? Divided loyalties that would trouble her as Lucie grew up: divided love, one daughter.

One evening in April, when it was almost time for bed, Maurice finally returned late from work while Gisèle and Marie-Claire were still up.

'What's kept you?' Gisèle asked him.

'I got a call from Mamy today, asking me to pick up post for Marie-Claire,' he replied. 'I was told it was important, so here it is, Marie-Claire.'

'Thanks so much, Maurice. I really do appreciate it.' She opened it and started to read a small scrap of paper on which Nicholas had written a few words. 'Valérie, we've managed to send your good wishes to your friends, as you had asked—N.'

Marie-Claire sat back and heaved a huge sigh of relief.

'Someone's made you happy.'

'They have, but I can't explain because it's to do with my previous work.'

'We understand,' said Gisèle. 'It's good news, and that's good enough.'

CHAPTER TWENTY-EIGHT
SPRING 1944

After the Nazi air raids during June 1940, Orléans had experienced no aerial attacks, but Allied bombing had started in the surrounding areas in April 1944. Now the city was to suffer destruction again. Two bombings occurred in the first half of May, causing considerable damage to the interchange station and surrounding houses at Les Aubrais, in the north of the city, as well as many deaths. Massive destruction and casualties occurred in the centre of Orléans.

Mamy had become terrified by the night attacks and in spite of security concerns for herself and the baby, Marie-Claire went to stay with her for a few days.

'Look at this headline in *Le Républicain*,' said Mamy.

Marie-Claire was not in the least surprised to read the title *Terrorist Bombings* about the Allies' aerial attacks. She picked up the newspaper and read the beginning of a long article entitled *Liberators Continue to Massacre the Population.*

'These Vichy newspaper proprietors and journalists will pay for their connivance when the Boches are destroyed, you'll see, Mamy,' Marie-Claire replied.

Shortly after midnight, on the twenty-third of May, Marie-Claire woke up and heard the distinct sound of bombing emanating from the city. Mamy rushed into her bedroom to comfort Lucie who had started to scream. Marie-Claire grabbed her daughter from Mamy. 'Quick, Mamy, let's get under the bedstead.' They huddled together with Marie-Claire holding the baby and comforting her. After the bombing had stopped, Marie-Claire crawled out from underneath the bed frame and put Lucie into her cot. Then she helped Mamy come out from under the bedstead.

'Why do the Allies have to cause so much death and destruction?' asked Mamy.

'They have no other option. They must target German headquarters, trains carrying their armaments and soldiers, industries who support them, transport and other places used by the Nazis. I'm sure they'll soon invade to give us our freedom.'

'Where do you think they'll strike first?'

'One of the ports in the north probably.'

'Your parents must have given up hope of ever seeing you. Do you now regret having become an agent?' asked Mamy.

'I thought deeply about my parents before accepting the challenge, but in the end, I had to come and help get rid of these evil aggressors and train the Maquis,' said Marie-Claire. She looked at the clock and added, 'We'd better get to bed and get some sleep, Mamy,'

At about seven o'clock in the morning, Marie-Claire was awoken by a frenzied knocking on the front door. 'I'll answer it, Mamy,' she called out. On opening it, she was astounded to find a grey-haired man, dressed like a tramp, standing in front of her. It was Nicholas. From the fearful look in his eyes, she realised something dreadful had happened. 'Come in,' she told him. 'Whatever has happened?' He remained silent. She led him into the living room where he collapsed into the nearest armchair. His eyes resembled marbles, devoid of expression. She knelt by his side, holding his limp hand. By now Mamy had come downstairs, shaking and ashen-faced. 'Who is this?' she asked.

'Nicholas. Martin's brother,' replied Marie-Claire. This is Mamy.'

Nicholas looked up at Marie-Claire and said in a low voice, 'Sylvie's suffered terrible injuries because of the bombing by the Allies. She's been taken to hospital. Our home and shop have been destroyed.'

'Oh, mon Dieu,' cried Marie-Claire, 'but what's happened to Xavier?'

'He's in a distressed state. I've had to leave him with a close friend.' he told her and breathed in deeply before continuing. 'He ran out of our house to look at the planes. Sylvie wanted to pursue him, but I stopped her and shouted, "Go down into the cellar. I'll bring him back." I left the house to run after him, and I could see three formations of planes approaching. I ran after Xavier. Then the planes were above us and they started to drop flares. I managed to catch up with Xavier and grab him and he clung to me and shook, asking whether we should go back to his mum. We lay flat on the side of the road, and I lay over him. Moments later, the pilots released their bombs. We shook and shook as they exploded around us. Columns of flames rose, lighting up the sky. People started to choke from the smoke. I turned round. My heart sank. In the distance I could no longer see our home and shop, left to us by our parents; it had burst into flames.' He closed his eyes momentarily. 'Other houses and buildings were burning too. Somehow, we managed to go back to where our home had stood. It was burning like an inferno and there was no sign of Filou, our dog. Xavier started to scream—an ear-splitting scream I will never forget. I felt as if I had been cut open. A group of people were carrying Sylvie towards a nearby van. Xavier rushed towards them, shaking uncontrollably. "Maman, Maman, wake up! I love you. I love you," he cried and grabbed her hand, kissing it. A woman came up to me and took me aside. "Nicholas, we're taking Sylvie to the main hospital. Xavier needs to go somewhere for comfort. He can't come with his mother to the hospital."' Nicholas slumped forward, saying, 'I did what the woman advised and took Xavier to a friend whose house had not been hit. There were dozens of homes burning and I heard someone saying that the interchange station had been attacked yet again, but this time even more damage had been done. There were trains tossed about in all directions.'

'But why are you here? Surely you should have gone to the hospital to be with Sylvie?'

'After leaving Xavier with my friend, of course I went to the hospital and stayed with Sylvie for a short while. She is unconscious and is severely burnt.' He held her hand tightly. 'I came here to tell you but also because of Xavier. He's asking for you all the time. He doesn't want to stay in Orléans. I'm planning to take him to his grandmother in Tours after the funeral.' He looked at her imploringly. 'Could I bring him to see you for a short while? I couldn't bring him here today and describe everything that happened in front of him, Valérie.'

'But why do you call her Valérie?' asked Mamy in a bewildered manner.

'It's a slip of the tongue, Mamy,' she said, although she could see her grandmother wasn't convinced. She needed to talk to Nicholas about other important things on her mind, so she turned to her grandmother and asked, 'Could you go and fetch Nicholas some brandy?'

'Yes, of course,' she said and hurried out of the room.

'Nicholas, can you manage to contact Martin as soon as possible?' asked Marie-Claire.

'Yes, through someone we know, but it would be highly dangerous for him to return here.'

'What do you mean?'

'The Maquis to which he belongs has been infiltrated. There have been arrests so he's on the run.'

Marie-Claire found herself shaking. Yet another terrible blow. *Without Martin, the future for Lucie and me is bleak. God, please protect Martin*, she prayed.

Mamy returned to the room with the brandy which Nicholas took into his shaky hands. She patted his hand and said, 'Bring Xavier here for a few hours tomorrow morning. Stay for lunch. Marie-Claire lives elsewhere for security. She's only come for a short while because I am afraid of the bombing. I haven't had time to tell her, but yesterday I met a woman whom Marie-Claire already knows about—Madame Lefèvre. She's married to a Vichy councillor and once taught Marie-Claire and André, her cousin. She came up to me and said, "I saw your granddaughter, Marie-Claire, in Orléans a few weeks ago. I thought she lived in England? What's she doing in France?" I thought quickly and told her that Marie-Claire had returned to France and married a Frenchman just before the Occupation and that he'd been sent to work in Germany. I don't know whether she believed me, but either way Marie-Claire will have to leave here after lunch tomorrow, much as I love her.'

Mamy's revelations about Madame Lefèvre reminded Marie-Claire that there were always repercussions and potential dangers around her. Denunciations were increasing. When would they ever stop? Would the Allies ever come and set them free? Or was it a dream?

The thought of Sylvie and the possibility that she might not pull through her ordeal made her ask Nicholas if she could go and see her in hospital. She asked Mamy if she would look after Lucie while she went to see Sylvie.

After feeding her baby, Marie-Claire climbed into Nicholas's van, and they set off for the hospital in the centre of Orléans. As they approached the city centre, water was gushing out of the drains everywhere and streets were littered with rubble. Buildings that appeared intact were sometimes attached to skeleton ones, but as they approached the rue de la République, they looked at each other in glee: the Kommandantur, nerve centre for the German army, now lay in ruins. No longer would people have to pass this loathed site with its huge swastika flags, emblems of a vile and cruel enemy.

On arrival at the hospital, they found that Sylvie's condition had deteriorated. 'Her head injury is serious. Even if she ever recovers, she could have brain damage,' the consultant told them. 'That's quite apart from her serious burns. Our resources are stretched, and we are overwhelmed by the number of casualties.'

Nicholas took Marie-Claire by the hand and followed the doctor into a side room where Sylvie lay in bed, her head and upper body heavily covered in dressings.

'She's in a coma, as you can see. I'll leave you alone with her for a while,' the doctor told them and left the room.

Nicholas bent forward and kissed a part of his sister's hand that had not been burnt. Tears dripped down onto the sheets; Marie-Claire put her arm round his shoulders. Before they left Sylvie, Marie-Claire kissed her gently, knowing she would probably never see her again. Nicholas took her back to St Jean-le-Blanc and told her that he would bring Xavier the following morning early so that he could see Marie-Claire, as Nicholas referred to her now, before she left for Olivet.

When she returned to Mamy's house, Marie-Claire told her everything that had happened.

'If Martin is anything like his brother, you're going to marry into a good and caring family,' Mamy commented. If only her grandmother knew that in marrying Martin, he was taking on another man's child and that he was exceptional in doing this.

After breakfast the following day, Marie-Claire heard a knock on the front door. She looked from behind the curtain and saw that it was Nicholas and Xavier, who was clinging to his uncle. When she opened the door, the little boy burst into tears and fell into her arms.

'Maman has died. I won't see her ever again. We've got no home and Filou is nowhere to be found.' Marie-Claire gulped and held him closer. Her mind jarred as if she'd been shot. Sylvie, the lovely Sylvie who had welcomed her into her home and had cared for her and protected her, had gone for ever.

'Come and sit down,' she told Xavier and led the shaken child to a settee and helped him sit down before she joined him and cuddled him.

Marie-Claire noticed how distressed Nicholas was. With difficulty he said, 'Sylvie died yesterday. Her funeral will take place in a week's time, to which of course you're invited. Meanwhile there is a service for three hundred people who were killed in the raids, in three days' time, at the Church of Saint Marceau. We can't use the cathedral because one of the towers is severely damaged and debris is lying inside and outside on the square in front.'

Marie-Claire ran her hand through Xavier's soft hair while listening to Nicholas.

'I promised Xavier that he could see you before going to Tours, where his grandmother will look after him. He has insisted on coming with me to the service even though I feel it is too much for him.'

So, it was the grandmother whom Martin used to visit in Tours, Marie-Claire realised. She must be the brothers' go-between. She was obviously doing her bit of Resistance work.

'Let me make you both warm drinks while Marie-Claire goes upstairs to show Xavier baby Lucie. It might take his mind off things,' suggested Mamy.

'Why do you call her Marie-Claire?' asked Xavier in a bewildered tone of voice.

'It's a pet name used by Mamy and the rest of the family, but you can call me that now as well,' replied Marie-Claire and led him upstairs and into her bedroom where Lucie had just woken up in her cot. When Marie-Claire released the side of the cot, Xavier asked her if he could hold the baby.

'Of course, as long as you're gentle with her,' she replied, handing Lucie to Xavier.

He ran his fingers through the baby's thick fair hair and then stroked her cheek. 'She's lovely. How old is she now?'

'Just over a year,' she replied.

After a pause Xavier asked, 'Marie-Claire, will you come and live in Tours when Uncle Martin returns and then I can see all three of you?'

'I don't really know,' she replied. 'In fact, I've not given it any thought until now.'

As Xavier stroked the baby's hair, she pondered on what he had asked her.

Orléans was her hometown, and it was Martin's too, but Martin's mother lived in Tours. Christophe might come looking for her in the Tours area after the war, so Orléans would have to be where they would set up home.

Thank goodness she had never told Christophe where her family lived. She looked down at Xavier and squeezed his hand. 'I think we'll have to stay in Orléans where my own family live, but you can come and stay with us.'

He looked up at her, his hazel eyes now lit up. 'I've always wanted a sister,' he told her. 'Maman wanted one for me.' He looked straight into her eyes and asked, 'I suppose a cousin is almost as good as a sister?'

'Yes. She certainly is,' she replied, hating herself for agreeing with him. She had an urge to break down and cry, but somehow, she mastered her feelings for the boy's sake.

Life with Martin, however happy it might be, would be built on a huge lie and she didn't know how she was going to manage deceiving young Xavier and others about the baby's identity.

CHAPTER TWENTY-NINE
ORLÉANS IN MAY-AUGUST 1944

'It's taken me ages to bring Julien back home to safety here in Olivet,' Maurice told Marie-Claire as she helped his elderly friend out of the van. 'There were hundreds of people fleeing Orléans, making for villages and small towns outside the city.' He slammed the van door and locked it. 'How much more Allied bombing can we take? Whenever are they going to land?'

'Soon. I'm sure they'll come.'

'There's rumours they might land in the Pas-de-Calais,' he said.

'Yes, that might be the plan,' she replied.

While Maurice carried Julien's case upstairs, Marie-Claire led the old man into the living room and pointed to a comfortable chair. He looked exhausted but managed to smile. 'I used to teach Maurice at the lycée,' he told her. 'He's been a marvellous friend to me and my family. My wife, God bless her soul, thought the world of him.'

'Yes. Both he and Gisèle are wonderful and have been so kind to me,' replied Marie-Claire.

Gisèle came into the room and said, 'You can join us in the cellar, Julien, tonight when we go to sleep. Now I'm going to prepare dinner for us all.'

'I'll come and cut up the vegetables, if you like,' said Marie-Claire and followed her into the kitchen.

'I heard you complimenting us, but I felt it important to cut the conversation, in case Julien started to ask you awkward questions. We've told him that your husband is in Germany doing forced labour and that you came to us for help with the birth of your baby.'

Maurice came into the room wearing his fireman's uniform. 'I've got to leave you all now,' he announced. 'Julien, Gisèle and Marie-Claire will look after you.'

A week later, on the sixth of June, Marie-Claire woke with a start, hearing Maurice's excited voice from the kitchen. Was she dreaming? Could it be true?

'They're here. I've just heard it on the radio. The Allies have landed in Normandy!' cried Maurice as he charged down the cellar stairs.

It was as if a huge electric current had swept through Marie-Claire's body. 'Bravo! Bravo! We're coming,' she cried and threw her arms round her grandmother who was beside herself with joy. Marie-Claire peeped into Lucie's cot, glad to see her still asleep after her early morning feed.

'At long last, ma chérie,' said Mamy. 'Who would have thought they would land in Normandy?'

Marie-Claire looked across at Maurice and Gisèle, who were locked in a passionate embrace. Would Martin soon be here? she wondered. She longed to be locked in his strong and warm arms and yearned for his deep and passionate kisses.

Later Gisèle came and put her arm round Julien. 'Your grandson was one of the true heroes who died for France.'

'He was the last of my line,' he whispered, wiping tears from his face.

'Let's drink to him and others like him,' said Maurice. 'I'll go and fetch some wine while Gisèle fetches the glasses.' By the time he returned with two bottles, Denis, a gendarme friend, had arrived. 'You've come in time for a glass of my best wine.'

'My goodness,' said Denis, 'it's early for celebrating, but we all need a boost I can tell you. The Boches have already increased patrols in the city and there was an alert at six this morning. I've just finished my night duty and I'm glad to be out of it. Things are only going to worsen until we are all free again. The SS and Gestapo may well start taking hostages.'

Marie-Claire's lips tightened. Although her papers were good ones, it only needed some observant milicien or SS soldier to spot that they were false and arrest her.

Denis joined her as Maurice gave the toast. 'May freedom for our country come quickly. Let's not forget Julien's grandson and others who gave up their lives in the fight for our liberation.' He raised his glass. 'Vive de Gaulle! Vive la France! Vive la liberté.'

Everyone cheered, but once the furore had died down Denis told Marie-Claire, 'Orléans might soon be free, but there are other areas that will be much harder to liberate and that will take some considerable time in some cases. Particularly with people who still support Pétain and the Boches.'

'What do you mean?' she asked.

'My brother lives in Saint-Nazaire where the Nazi U-boat fleet is. It's more like a fortress there.' He hesitated for a few moments, then added, 'Let's just say he has to be careful.'

She nodded and smiled at him and sensed that he realised where her sympathy lay with his brother and why.

During the second week in June, the family decided to celebrate Gisèle's birthday. She and Mamy had started to prepare lunch when Maurice suggested going for a walk with Marie-Claire and Lucie in the pram. They crossed the Olivet Bridge and started to walk along the Loiret. Lucie was nearly four months old now and was sitting up, enjoying the sunshine and playing with her small teddy bear.

'Remember how Maman and I used to walk along here with you and Gisèle, and having picnics on the riverbank?' Maurice nodded with a smile. 'I wonder how soon we will be able to enjoy ourselves like that again?'

'It could take longer than you think. Of course, we're all relieved that the Allies have landed in Normandy, but it will take several weeks before they reach us here. And remember some areas, which support the Nazis, will take much longer to liberate.'

Denis's warning about the situation in St Nazaire, which resembled a fortress, flashed across Marie-Claire's mind.

'You must think a lot about Josette and Charles. How on earth do they cope, not knowing anything about you?'

'Don't worry about that. People in London keep them up to date,' she replied, 'but of course I can't say any more.'

'I understand.'

They continued talking about how they were going to enjoy celebrating Gisèle's birthday and about Maurice's job and that at times, it was difficult for him to conceal his utter disgust with those who supported Pétain and the Nazis.

Marie-Claire told him about betrayals that she had encountered. Then Maurice looked at his watch and suggested they return home. They crossed the Olivet Bridge and started to walk home when Marie-Claire stopped in mid-sentence as she heard the familiar drone of planes approaching from the north.

'The Allies are going to destroy the Olivet Bridge. That's for certain,' said Maurice. Marie-Claire looked over at the bridge and started to scream as she noticed a cyclist who was halfway across. 'Quick. Get off there now,' she shouted at him.

'Let's get over there,' cried Maurice, pointing to some hard, open ground on the right. Marie-Claire grabbed Lucie from the pram, wrapped her in a blanket and joined Maurice, who was already lying on the ground. She curled herself up to protect Lucie who had started to cry. 'Oh God, please spare us. Please.'

The noise of the planes increased. Marie-Claire could hear the whistle of the bombs falling before the explosions started, destroying buildings around them. Their vibrations swept through her, making her feel that her body was going to disintegrate. Her ears began to ring, and she started to have difficulty in breathing. She clung to Lucie, trying to pacify the baby's screams. Clouds of dust clogged her throat and Maurice's, making them choke.

'Keep still. Don't move. We must stay here for a while,' Maurice told her as the planes departed. She drew back the blanket and caressed Lucie who had now stopped crying.

Eventually, they stood up and looked across at the bridge and gasped; it had started to collapse in the middle, with smoke billowing everywhere.

'Thank God that cyclist got off there in time,' said Marie-Claire.

'St Christopher was watching over him,' said Maurice, rubbing brick dust and splinters off the pram.'

On arrival at the house, Gisèle ran up to Maurice and fell into his arms. 'Thank goodness you're safe,' she cried, 'but what's taken you so long to return?'

While he explained what had happened, Mamy comforted Marie-Claire and Lucie.

'You're safe. Thank the Lord the three of you are safe,' said Mamy. A few minutes later, she continued, 'We rushed outside and saw the bombs dropping and exploding near the bridge. "That's where Maurice goes for a walk," Gisèle kept screaming.'

Marie-Claire gave her grandmother a hug. 'Where would we all be without you, Mamy?'

Josette had often talked about her grandmother's resilience during the Great War when she had struggled to provide for her children after her husband's death in the Battle of Verdun. Now she was showing the same courage and concern for three generations of her family.

As the aerial attacks continued, mostly over Orléans, but also sporadically in the surrounding countryside, the family continued to sleep at night in the cellar.

'It's the Brits that bomb at night and the Americans in the day, according to the Nazi press,' said Marie-Claire.

The Americans advanced eastwards towards Paris during the following weeks and by mid-August were approaching Orléans. The Nazis reconsolidated their positions and security everywhere was tightened. Anyone caught in the streets after curfew could be taken as hostage and shot in reprisal for Allied attacks. The Resistance had moved in, wearing armbands with the Cross of Lorraine on their sleeves, making valiant attacks against the highly trained German army.

In the middle of one night, sirens woke everyone up in the cellar. Marie-Claire was the first to hear the drone of the British planes approaching and lit her torch, noticing that Gisèle was clinging to Mamy and Julien was cowering under his blankets. She picked up Lucie who had started to scream and tried to console her.

Bombs started to drop in the distance. Then suddenly another dropped nearby, causing the walls to shake.

'Oh, if only Maurice wasn't on duty,' cried Gisèle.

'You're safe with us,' replied Marie-Claire, trying to calm her.

Later, Marie-Claire said, 'I'm going to heat up some milk for us all, and I'll add a little brandy. That will all do us some good.'

After reaching the kitchen, Marie-Claire could hear some commotion in the distance. Through the window she saw that a house further down the road had been partially bombed and saw the arrival of police cars and an ambulance.

She returned to the cellar to tell the others what she had seen.

'I know one of Maurice's friends lives down there. He'll be mortified if anything has happened to any of them. He'll soon be off duty.'

One morning, when Marie-Claire volunteered to go shopping, she passed a burnt-out German tank, still smouldering. Further along the road she was waved down by two men in civilian clothes, wearing Resistance armbands and holding Sten guns. 'Get down at once.' one of them screamed at her. 'The Boches are on the opposite side of the Loiret.' She threw herself to the ground and lay there trembling. During a break in the shooting one of the men shouted, 'You shouldn't be out here at a time like this. Go back home.' Deeply shaken, she stood up and returned to her aunt and uncle's house.

At around one o'clock in the afternoon on the sixteenth of August 1944 the family returned to the cellar. A huge storm was raging. It was as if the elements were trying to block the thuds of artillery in the distance. Marie-Claire could feel Julien's nails digging into her. Maurice passed the remains of a bottle of red to her.

'Here, Julien, take a sip of this,' she told the old man who by now was shaking all over. Mamy was comforting Lucie, who was crying intermittently. Gisèle lay against Maurice, blocking her ears. Eventually the artillery died down and everyone fell asleep, only to be woken after curfew by hammering on the front door. Maurice climbed up the cellar stairs, two at a time, and let in Gwenolé, a gendarme friend of Denis. As Marie-Claire followed the others up the stairs to the living room, she heard Gwenolé's flustered voice, 'The Americans are approaching the city, but it will be a bloodbath.'

'Tell us more,' said Maurice.

'I saw the American troops in the distance when I was on night duty. There were tanks, personnel carriers and other vehicles, but the Boches were well prepared with machine guns already mounted, as well as cannons and grenades. They even lit fires and set light to the telephone exchange. We saw firemen being shot down and screaming.'

'Thank goodness, your next shift is tomorrow,' Gisèle reminded Maurice.

With an almost hysterical laugh, Gwenolé continued. 'And amidst all this, we saw the Gestapo fleeing, grabbing cars, bakers' vans, bicycles and even horse-drawn carts.' The others shouted, 'Bravo! Bravo! They're leaving.'

Towards two o'clock, Denis arrived in a state of shock and red eyes. 'Am I glad to be here,' he told everyone and slumped into a chair. 'It's total carnage in Orléans with explosions and more fires. The Americans and Resistance fighters are putting up a huge fight to defeat the Boches. I saw American army officers holding small portable radios and directing their troops with them and I've never seen that before.' He wiped his eyes. 'Bullets were flying everywhere. Bodies were littering pavements and streets. The Americans fired at a machine-gun manned by two young German soldiers. It burst into flames, engulfing the men.' He slumped forward, choking and shaking. 'I'll never forget what happened to a young boy. He couldn't have been more than six years old. I was working with one of your ambulance crew, Maurice, with street-to-street fighting around us. It was those screams coming from a woman that cut right through me; I'll never forget them. "Dédé, stay where you are for God's sake," she cried. "No.

No. Let go of me," she screamed. "I need to go to my son."'

'We entered the square and took cover in a doorway. A group of people were restraining the woman from running into the crossfire to reach her child. When the firing subsided, we saw Resistance fighters dashing to the nearby park, being fired at and pursued by the Boches. Once there was no more shooting, we went into the square, a few yards to our right, and there we saw him—a young boy lying on his side.' Denis lowered his head for some moments before looking up at them. 'As we came up to the boy, we saw his body twitch and then there was no more movement. The mother, supported by the group, came over and collapsed by her son's body.' He sat back in the chair and closed his eyes.

Marie-Claire stood up and went over to comfort him. 'Say no more. We'll get you something strong to drink.'

Towards three o'clock in the afternoon there was another visitor. This time it was Antoinette, one of Gisèle's colleagues. She was bubbling with excitement. 'They've gone! The Boches have finally gone! The Americans forced them out of town. Everybody's gone mad, hanging out their Tricoleurs from their windows. Just as I was leaving, French, British, American, and Russian flags were flying in front of the town hall and a huge crowd was singing the 'Marseillaise' in the Martroi Square round the statue of St Joan. Tomorrow there will be a huge celebration.'

'This calls for a toast with my last bottles of champagne,' said Maurice and went to the cellar while Marie-Claire went to fetch Lucie, who was crying.

Gisèle set out the glasses and when Maurice returned, he filled them and handed them to everyone. 'We are free at long last in this region but at a huge cost. As I said in an earlier toast, let us not forget Julien's son and others like him who gave their lives to rid France of the Hun.' He raised his glass, saying, 'Vive de Gaulle! Vive la liberté! Vive la France!'

Everyone clinked their glasses, saying, 'A la tienne,' acknowledging each other.

Marie-Claire looked across at Mamy enjoying the celebrations. *We have our freedom in Orléans and le Loiret, but it will take months, like Denis said, before France is completely free*, she thought.

How would people learn to live together again after all those denunciations and killings?

She paused and wiped her eyes. Where was Martin? She and Lucie needed him more now than ever.

She pulled Lucie closer to her and rubbed her face against the baby's satiny fair hair, so like Christophe's. Where was he? Where had the circuit members fled to?

CHAPTER THIRTY

CELEBRATIONS IN ORLÉANS ON 18ᵀᴴ AUGUST 1944

Marie-Claire admired the dress she'd borrowed from Gisèle; it was an eye-catching blue summer dress with white buttons down the entire front which was tailored in true French style. A fluffy woollen jacket, in a similar colour, completed the outfit. Both accentuated her blue eyes.

On the previous day, she'd found a message from Nicholas in their dead letter box: *I'll collect you tomorrow at ten in the morning. There will be official celebrations in the Martroi Square and Martin will be there.*

She'd almost jumped with joy on learning that she and Martin would soon be united and when she had returned to the family, they had been thrilled for her.

'I'll look after Lucie for you,' Mamy had suggested.

'And I'll be in the Square too, on duty. I know that there's an important person coming,' Maurice had told her and when she had asked whether it was General de Gaulle, he'd more or less confirmed it.

She said goodbye to the family and made her way to the entrance of the Windmill Walk and could see Nicholas in the distance. She hurried along and joined him. He wore a smart navy-blue suit with the armband of the Cross of Lorraine.

'I can't wait to see Martin,' she told him.

'And he'll be thinking the same. I reckon he's counting the minutes, not the hours,' added Nicholas, laughing. 'We'll go back to my flat and have something to eat. Then I will have to leave you because I've got to meet up with some Resistance people. Martin must go to the official celebrations at the Prefecture after de Gaulle's speech. Later, he'll join you here. I'll be staying with a friend for the night,' he said with a chuckle.

Towards half past one, Marie-Claire made her way to the Martroi Square where the statue of St Joan of Arc on her horse stood, somewhat damaged. There were already several people there and by the time soldiers and dignitaries arrived, there were thousands of citizens in the crowd. After a while, she almost leapt with joy when she spotted Martin among a large group of maquisards as they arrived and positioned themselves not far from the Chamber of Commerce and Industry. They wore their typically ragged clothes and black berets, as well as their Cross of Lorraine armbands. Nicholas had told her that their colonel was in the interior army and had been directed by General de Gaulle to command the regional Maquis.

She looked across at them proudly and was greatly moved. She thought back to her time with the circuit and maquisards and how they had faced many dangers and challenges in destroying some of the infrastructure and transport systems in Tours and surrounding areas.

The general chatter of the crowd died down when a tall figure, in army uniform, appeared on the balcony of the Chamber of Commerce and Industry, dwarfing the mayor and Prefect of the Department. Marie-Claire recognised General de Gaulle immediately and joined in everyone starting to cheer and clap the general. Pent-up hatred and terror experienced under the Nazi occupying forces had given way to relief and sheer joy. The applause lasted for several minutes. After the mayor and prefect had withdrawn from the balcony, the general began his speech. Hardly a sound could be heard as the people listened intently to his eloquent words.

'Where else could liberty adopt greater significance than in Orléans, here in front of the statue of St Joan of Arc, the Liberator?' he asked the people.

He spoke about how the city of Orléans had, at long last, been set free, but that there were still other cities and areas which had yet to be liberated. He also emphasized that once France had gained all her freedom, the country would have to be totally reconstructed.

After other points he made in his speech, he ended it with the memorable words: 'Long live Orléans! Long live the Republic! Long Live France!'

After the official party had left and most of the crowds had gradually moved away, Marie-Claire approached the statue of Joan of Arc. She recalled how once a year, in the month of May, Maman, Mamy and she would attend the ceremony of St Joan. A young teenager would be chosen to arrive in Orléans, dressed as St Joan in armour, and riding a horse. The procession would proceed through the city and finally end up at the cathedral where a service would be held.

She remembered too, the shopping expeditions with both her mother and grandmother and how she would be treated to some special chocolates in one of the famous chocolate shops. Once the Occupation was over, she and Martin could treat Lucie to the delicious chocolate, as well to the chocolate bunnies and chocolate eggs at Easter. And she looked forward to that.

She looked at her watch. It was already nearly half past three. She decided to walk along the Loire, admiring the bird life on little islands in the river. Then she made her way to Nicholas's flat and made something to eat.

Later she heard the door open then click. 'I'm here,' cried Martin.

Marie-Claire rushed to the door and fell into his arms. They kissed each other gently then deeply, sealing their love after months of separation.

'My darling Valérie. My dearest, I've spent night after night, thinking of this moment,' he told her, caressing her face.

'And when I tried to sleep at night, I gradually saw your face appear in my mind,' she said. 'Only then could I fall asleep. Let's open a bottle of champagne that Nicholas has left for us,' said Valérie. 'And he has left us some food as well.'

After they had celebrated, Valérie pulled out some photos of Lucie from her bag and showed them to Martin.

'What a beautiful little girl,' he said. 'Just like her mother. I can't wait to hold her in my arms, and I really do mean that.'

'You'll meet her tomorrow when I take you to Olivet where my relatives live,' she replied. 'Whereabouts have you been all this time?'

'Initially I was in my friend's Maquis outside Blois and then I joined the Maquis of Lorris in the Forest of Orléans, commanded by one of de Gaulle's colonels. Despite betrayal of many of our men, on the fifteenth and sixteenth of August, the Maquis of Lorris took part in the liberation of Chateauneuf and Orléans alongside an American infantry regiment. We were under orders never to disclose where we were. That's why I could never divulge anything to you.'

A deep sadness spread over his face as he continued. 'I met Jeanne in Tours after I had left the Sologne. She told me that Luc and Jacques had been arrested but she knew no further details.'

'How did she come to know?' asked Marie-Claire.

'She wouldn't disclose that.'

He put his arms round her and fondled her breasts. She stared at him and could see the burning desire that matched her ache for him. He took her hand and led her into the bedroom. She undid the buttons that ran down the front of her dress and let it fall onto the floor. And took off her brassiere and knickers, standing naked in front of Martin.

'You are so beautiful, Valérie, I have been longing to show you how much I love you,' he said, and started to remove his clothes too.

What followed swept them to the heights of ecstasy and then a peaceful period of happiness and then sheer bliss.

CHAPTER THIRTY-ONE

SEPTEMBER 1945

Marie-Claire, Martin and Lucie were now living in a house near her grandmother in St Jean-le-Blanc. Martin had returned to teaching in the local lycée while Marie-Claire stayed at home and looked after Lucie.

One morning she received an official-looking letter from London. Her heart sank. Wary of its contents, she dreaded opening it. She ripped the envelope open and pulled out the letter. Major Dobson requested her presence at the Hotel Cécil in Paris, to explain her message to the organisation in 1943 about why she had left the circuit and her organiser. It gave a date and a time for the interview.

She put the letter down onto the table; her heart quickened, and she began to feel shaky. Would she be accused of desertion? That had always haunted her. But she would explain everything that had led to it.

She arrived in Paris in early September and made her way to the Hotel Cécil on the Left Bank of Paris, in a mediocre district.

She showed her identity card, which had been updated, to a woman at the entrance of the hotel, and produced her letter from the War Office. She was immediately accompanied to a room on the first floor. Her hands began to shake, so she gripped them as tightly as she could. She must not appear nervous in front of this interviewer, she told herself.

A stern-looking, middle-aged British army officer awaited her. He introduced himself as Major Dobson, the officer who had written to her. After making polite conversation, he started to ask her questions.

'We received your radio message in December 1943, alerting us to the break-up of the circuit and your circumstances, but we would like to hear your explanations for deciding to leave your organiser and stay in France.'

'Christophe, my organiser, would not listen to reason about my urging him to put pressure immediately on the Maquis leader to dismiss my cousin who was in the Maquis and who had a serious drinking problem and was putting people at risk.'

She continued to explain the full circumstances of how her cousin had betrayed Arnaud, resulting in arrests of other circuit members. She paused, overwhelmed by her disclosures. She also spoke about the confrontation that she had had with Christophe and when she referred to the execution of her cousin by the Maquis leader, she noticed the officer's lips tighten.

There was a pause as if he was considering what she had said. 'We have questioned your organiser and he informed me that he had told you that he planned to contact someone in Vierzon who would put him in touch with us. His plan was to request permission for both of you to return to London. He was both shaken and disappointed when you disappeared. The organisation, to put it bluntly, became extremely concerned. Had you not contacted us, you would have been charged with desertion. It was the organiser's intention to attempt repatriation through a contact in Vierzon, so why did you decline this?'

Marie-Claire took a deep breath, relieved that there was no question of desertion, but she would have to choose her words carefully when answering his questions. 'Christophe, my organiser, never spelt this out to me. I can truthfully say this. We had to flee the Tours area quickly and agreed to meet outside Montrichard. He had explained briefly beforehand that we would make our way to Vierzon where he knew someone who might help us. He never told me that the purpose of going there was for possible repatriation. I assumed he was thinking of forming another circuit. You can appreciate that I was in a dreadful emotional state following my cousin's execution by the Maquis leader. I still stand by my decision to leave Christophe for the reasons I have already explained to you.'

After reflection the officer said, 'I will accept your explanation, in view of the circumstances you have told me. You explained that you were expecting a baby and in accordance with your wishes, we did not disclose that to the organiser. May I ask whose baby he or she is?'

She felt a stab in her chest before replying. 'A French résistant, whom I met in the course of Resistance work, is the father, but again I am telling you this in confidence.'

He looked at her in a dubious manner and she guessed that he knew she was not telling the truth, but he went no further.

After further questioning, the officer said, 'When I interviewed your organiser, we told him that you had contacted us through a third party. He asked if he could pass a letter to you, and I promised him that I would ask you. What is your wish?'

'Under the circumstances that I have described, I prefer to decline his request.'

The officer asked her more questions about the circuit and about the operations they had conducted.

'Do you have any news about Marcel, my previous organiser?' asked Marie-Claire.

'He sadly lost his life in the Normandy Landings.'

Tears filled her eyes, and the interviewer asked if she'd like some refreshment. She thanked him and declined. He discharged her from the organisation and wished her a happy future.

On the train, returning to Orléans, Marie-Claire thought about Christophe and how he would receive her rejection. She hadn't liked lying, but to safeguard Martin, Lucie and herself, she had had no alternative but to conceal the truth. She had been disappointed that Christophe had not explained the full circumstances to Major Dobson about her warnings. That made her determined to have no contact with Christophe in the future.

She knew that Arnaud and Emile had been arrested and almost certainly sent to concentration camps, and Martin had told her that Luc and Jacques had been arrested when he had seen Jeanne in Tours, after leaving Benoît's Maquis in the autumn of 1943. She would return to Tours and go and see Jeanne.

She had already made up her mind to do this, but she was conscious that Christophe might come looking for her after France had been liberated, so she had delayed her visit.

When she arrived home and explained everything to Martin, he was anxious and concerned by her revelation that Christophe had requested whether he could contact her.

'Our life now is devoted to each other and Lucie. Nothing will prevent that, I promise you,' she assured him, and he took her into his arms and caressed her.

A few days later, Marie-Claire opened a letter from her mother. She was eager to find out her mother's reaction to the letter she had sent her.

4th June 1945

Dear Marie-Claire,

Thank you for your letter which we were so relieved to receive. We are thrilled to discover that we are grandparents and long to meet our dear little granddaughter. Can you send a photo of Lucie as soon as you can, please? We long to come and visit the three of you some time in the future.

Papa and I would like to tell you how proud we are of you and Martin. However, Papa remembers you having received a letter, telling you that you had passed your first course as a FANY. He remembers asking you whether there was more to the training, and you replied that you couldn't say anything. That was when he guessed that you were preparing for some kind of covert work, probably in France, and that being employed as a FANY was just a cover. And when we last saw you, you told us that you were going to be away for some time and that you would send us a postcard from time to time. We thought that rather strange. We did receive these occasionally, showing different places in Britain.

After you finally left, Papa was certain you were going to France, but he said nothing to me at first. But when he eventually told me his suspicions, I was terrified and couldn't sleep properly for a long time. You cannot imagine how relieved we were when we finally received your letter. Postcards in between said little, but at least proved that you were still alive.

Marie-Claire smiled to herself, remembering how Miss Atkins had asked her to write several pre-dated postcards to her parents.

What we couldn't understand was that the postcards stopped for several months and then we started to receive them again and we felt so relieved.

The news about André's disappearance shook us. He must have joined a Maquis, knowing he might give his life for his country. It is dreadful, though, that no one has been able to corroborate that or tell Marguerite where he is laid to rest. Maybe you can tell us more when we meet.

We look forward to your reply.

With love from Maman and Papa—bisous

Marie-Claire put the letter down onto the coffee table, happy to learn of her parents' delight about becoming grandparents. Hopefully, in some measure, Lucie compensated for all the misery and uncertainty that her parents had been through because of her long absence. Thank goodness her mother hadn't asked any direct questions about André, but she realised that when her mother did visit them in France, she would pursue the subject relentlessly.

A few months later, just before Christmas 1945, Marie-Claire, Martin, Mamy and Lucie were waiting for the arrival of her parents when a car drew up outside their house in St Jean-le-Blanc, not far from Mamy's home which was also an old, terraced house.

Marie-Claire's heart quickened as she hurried to open the front door. Josette stood before her and threw her arms round her daughter, crying, 'Oh my darling Marie-Claire. At long last.'

'Yes. It's wonderful to see you, Maman,' replied Marie-Claire, feeling how much thinner her mother had become as she hugged her. She then leapt into her father's open arms and kissed him. 'You're just as cuddly and podgy as ever,' she told him in English, laughing.

'Less of the podgy, Marie-Claire,' he answered, grinning all over his face.

Mamy embraced Josette and Charles, saying, 'Thank goodness you managed this trip.'

Martin came to join them with Lucie in his arms and welcomed them.

'Oh, what a darling,' exclaimed Josette as soon as she saw Lucie. 'I can't wait to cuddle her.'

'All in good time, Maman. She needs to get used to you,' said Marie-Claire, caressing Lucie's cheeks. 'Lucie, this is your second Mamy I've been talking to you about and this is Papy,' she said, putting her arm onto her father's shoulder.

'Papy,' said Lucie. 'Papy, Papy,' she repeated, looking at him, clearly puzzled.

'And what gorgeous fair hair, she's got, hasn't she? I can't wait to run my fingers through it,' said Josette. 'And it looks so silky.'

'That's why we've let it grow long,' said Marie-Claire.

'Lucie's got Marie-Claire's lovely blue eyes,' remarked Josette, 'but, Martin, does she take after someone in your family with her beautiful fair hair?'

'No. Most of my family have auburn or dark hair,' he replied.

Trust Maman to pick up on that, thought Marie-Claire, and she noticed Mamy look away from Josette. After an awkward pause, she replied, 'Remember, Maman, some of Dad's family, on his father's side, have fair hair.'

'Fair hair. Yes. But not fair and silky like Lucie's,' replied Josette.

Dad cleared his throat and suggested, 'Why not let's get to know Lucie, Josette, and play with her?'

Good old Dad. He always knows how to break any tension, thought Marie-Claire.

'A good idea,' added Martin. He put Lucie down and led her to a box of toys. 'Choose something to show your new Mamy,' he told her. She selected a worn teddy bear and ran back to her mother who persuaded her to go and play with Josette.

'Meanwhile, let's all have some aperitifs and celebrate,' said Martin and went away to prepare some.

After clinking their glasses with each other and saying, 'A la tienne,' to each person, Martin asked about their journey to Orléans.

'We came by train and ferry,' replied Charles in French. 'We were given a huge reduction on the train to Dover by the rail manager for whom I used to work.'

'How generous of him,' said Mamy.

'How much bombing took place in London?' asked Martin.

'Lots of bombs were dropped on London and elsewhere throughout the war. And after the Allies landed in Normandy at the beginning of June1944, the Nazis took their revenge by firing doodlebugs and rockets on London and elsewhere in England. You might have read about all this in your newspapers,' said Charles.

'Yes. But it's moving to hear about it all from you,' said Martin.

'Cities like Portsmouth in the south and Coventry in the Midlands, were almost destroyed. Thousands of people were killed. They launched the doodlebugs from Le Touquet and other places along the northern coast of France, as well as from Holland,' explained Charles.

'Doodlebugs? queried Mamy.

'Doodlebugs were pilotless planes. They did a lot of damage,' replied Charles. 'They made a sound like a lorry engine going fast. When the noise stopped, you realised they'd run out of fuel and would explode onto the ground below. It was carnage. Awful. Thousands of people were killed.'

'How dreadful,' said Mamy.

'Martin, how did you meet Marie-Claire?' asked Josette.

'I was in a Maquis close to Tours,' he said. 'We worked in tandem with a Resistance circuit, led by a British army officer.'

Marie-Claire intervened. 'And only a small proportion of citizens went into the Resistance. Lots of people reported their friends, neighbours, and sometimes even family, to the Gestapo.'

'Oh! No!' said Josette. 'It's unbelievable.'

'I can assure you that it's true, Maman. Gisèle works in the town hall, and we were all shocked when she told us that immediately after the Occupation ended in Orléans in the summer of 1944, the council employees found mountains of letters from citizens denouncing others.'

'All the more reason why we should admire people like you and Martin,' said Charles.

'Have you heard any more about André?' asked Josette.

'No,' replied Marie-Claire.

'I can't understand it at all. How is Marguerite? She must be in a dreadful state.'

'She's improving slowly, thanks again to the local priest who helped her enormously when she lost Philippe. She's now gone back to live in her own home and she's making progress, but it's slow. She has good days and bad ones, so we'll have to see how she is.'

'It must be worse for her this time, not knowing anything at all about André,' said Josette.

'There are lots of people who just disappeared, Josette, whose families know nothing about them,' said Mamy. 'Do you remember Jean Zay?'

'Yes. Of course, I do. I remember you telling us about him when we returned for our annual holidays here. Wasn't he the Minister of Education who modernised schools and institutions, as well as introducing summer holiday camps for children? But what has that got to do with what we're talking about now?' asked Josette.

'He disappeared in June 1944, and no one's seen him since. Rumour has it that he was taken out of prison by the Milice and killed,' replied Mamy.

'Oh no! Surely not?'

'He was partly Jewish, and he was also a Freemason. Things that both the Boches and Vichy hated. They arrested him in Bordeaux in 1940 for desertion when he tried to join the rest of the legitimate government on a ship going to North Africa. You have a lot to learn, Josette, about what it was really like for us under Pétain and the Boches. They imprisoned Jean Zay in 1940,' said Mamy.

'Pétain's influence will remain a stain on the honour of France for a long time,' said Marie-Claire, noticing her mother visibly shaken. 'But now let's talk about more cheerful things,'

'At the weekend we're all going to Olivet. Gisèle and Maurice have invited us all to lunch,' announced Martin.

'Oh, that's marvellous. We look forward to that,' said Josette.

'I'm going to serve lunch for us here now,' Marie-Claire told them.

Gradually, Lucie started to enjoy playing with Josette and soon Charles joined in.

Towards the early evening, there was a knock on the door and to Marie-Claire's delight it was Nicholas and Xavier. After introducing them to her parents, Lucie rushed up to Xavier and gave him one of her toys which made him laugh. 'She's like the little sister I never had,' he told Josette and continued to play with her while the others talked.

Marie-Claire took in a deep breath. Deceiving Xavier weighed deeply on her every time he came. If only she could have Martin's child, then Xavier would have a blood cousin of his own, but so far, they hadn't succeeded.

'Marie-Claire explained to us how you, and your late sister, took Marie-Claire in because she had to leave Tours for security reasons and that you've kept in touch with her throughout all these months while Martin was still fighting in the Maquis. Charles and I can't thank you enough,' Josette told Nicholas.

'It's normal to help family and we knew Martin intended to marry Marie-Claire,' replied Nicholas.

'We understood why they couldn't get married straight away because Marie-Claire's paperwork was in England.'

After offering Nicholas an aperitif and talking further, Nicholas told Xavier that it was time to return home, much to the young boy's disappointment. He clung to Marie-Claire, making her realise that she represented a kind of mother to him. He often came to Orléans with Nicholas to see her and her family.

Uncle Georges arrived at the weekend to join Josette and Charles. Marie-Claire always enjoyed his visits; he was relaxed and had a warm and generous personality.

'Will Marguerite be coming?' Josette asked Marie-Claire. 'We would very much like to see her.'

'At the moment, Marguerite is not too good, I'm afraid,' explained Marie-Claire.

Charles looked across at Josette and she remained silent.

Towards the end of the family meal, Uncle Georges asked Josette if she and Charles were contemplating returning to France.'

Josette hesitated which prompted Charles to reply. 'For the time being, we'll be staying in England. We have my family there and friends as well. I also have my pension to consider.'

Marie-Claire looked over at her father. He'd explained to her earlier that Josette was deeply upset to learn about what had gone on in Occupied France and how so many people had reported others to the Gestapo. 'It's not the country I knew, Charles,' she had told him.

Before their departure, Josette gave Lucie a small parcel to open. When she'd torn it apart, she shrieked with joy on discovering a white bunny with large brown glass eyes.

Marie-Claire prompted Lucie to say 'Thank you, Mamy' in English much to her parents' delight.

'Next time we see her, maybe she'll know more English words,' said Charles.

'And next time we see you, it will be in England. I promise you,' added Martin.

CHAPTER THIRTY-TWO
LUCIE'S DESTINY IN 1961

Martin's health was deteriorating fast in January 1961 due to a terminal illness. He was poring over a photograph album, frayed at the edges, which contained snapshots of his life with Marie-Claire and Lucie.

'What a wide variety of guests we had at our wedding,' he said, pointing to several maquisards and Resistance people. He looked at the clock and said, 'Lucie will soon be here. We must tell her the truth about Christophe, Marie-Claire. I keep asking you. We should have done it long ago.'

Lucie could be heard opening the front door. She had come home from the lycée where she was studying for her final school exams.

'Salut,' she said, embracing them. 'Sorry I'm late but I had an extra lesson on my own with Mademoiselle Lanvin.' She picked up the album that was lying on the coffee table, sat down and began to look through it. 'I haven't seen this for years,' she told them. 'What's prompted you to pull this out, Maman?' She pointed to a photograph of Marie-Claire standing in woodland and holding a Sten. 'Who took this?'

'Papa. He shouldn't have taken that photo because it was a breach of security,' said Marie-Claire, grinning at Martin. 'He took others as well and a friend in the Resistance developed them and left them with his mother. I never knew that she lived in Tours at the time. He had many secrets and probably still has,' she said with a laugh.

'Maman, would you work in the Resistance again if you had the choice?'

'In some ways, definitely, but not in others.'

'What do you mean?'

'It was thrilling to take part in operations to oppose the Boches. For instance, destroying railway lines and blowing up trains carrying Nazi armaments and other supplies. The most exciting one we ever carried out was blowing up transformers in the electricity power station in Tours. It led to cutting the electricity supply to the factory where the Boches were making parts for their fighter planes.'

'How exciting, but what sort of things upset you?'

After a few moments, Marie-Claire replied, 'Denouncements and reprisals. Friends, neighbours and occasionally those close to you, denounced others to the Nazis. They did this to settle old scores or even because they supported Pétain and the Occupiers. It was shocking. And the reprisals that followed were awful, but I'd rather not talk about any more of this, Lucie.'

'Some things are best left unsaid,' said Martin.

Lucie looked across at her mother who said, 'Your father's right, Lucie. Please believe me.'

Lucie shrugged her shoulders and continued looking at the album until she showed her mother a photograph taken of hundreds of people surrounding the statue of Joan of Arc on her horse in the Martroi Square in Orléans.

'The crowds were celebrating the freedom of Orléans and General de Gaulle was the guest of honour. Papa and I were both there,' said Marie-Claire.

'Oh yes! I remember you telling me now. Here's Papa. He's lining the square with other Resistance fighters and they're all holding rifles. But don't they look shabby in their makeshift clothes?'

'Smart uniforms weren't dropped from the sky by the Brits for the occasion, Lucie,' said Martin with a chuckle. 'Most of us had just come from a war zone.

The Maquis had little money and we were living at that time in the forest outside Orléans.'

'I loved browsing through this album when I was younger,' she replied and continued to look at the rest of the photographs. There was a long silence and Marie-Claire could see Lucie looked intently at a photograph of André with his elder brother, Philippe. 'These are the two eldest sons of Marguerite, aren't they?'

'Yes,' replied Martin.

'Tell me more about them. When I asked about them long ago, you just clammed up. Why was that?'

Marie-Claire sighed. *She is as determined and persistent as I am at times.*

'I'll tell you some of it, Lucie,' replied Martin. 'As your mother already said, she tries to put some events behind her.'

Marie-Claire cleared the coffee cups from the table and went into the kitchen from where she could still hear the conversation continuing.

As he revealed André's execution, and briefly the reasons for it, Martin kept reference to Christophe at a minimum.

'What an appalling thing to happen. I can now understand why Marguerite always seemed so withdrawn and didn't join in any of the conversation.'

'It was a harrowing time for her, Lucie, and she still hasn't fully recovered from the shock of it all, even after all these years.'

Lucie continued looking at the album. One photograph caught her eye. 'Who are these two women?' she asked, as her mother returned to the room.

'Jeanne and Patricia. Jeanne was married to a doctor called Arnaud, one of our circuit members. He died in Buchenwald Concentration Camp. Our wireless operator, a vet, and another circuit member called Jacques, were sent there too. All of them died except Jacques. All of them were denounced.'

'By whom?' asked Lucie.

'André's denouncement of Arnaud led to the others being betrayed.'

Lucie remained silent for a few moments and then closed the album, as her mother walked back in. 'How awful. We're told little in school about all this kind of thing. Why do you think that is, Papa?'

'It is a period of French history that is still a difficult and delicate subject to talk about,' he replied.

After a pause, Lucie asked, 'Why did you bring out this album today?'

'Because I have something important to tell you,' Marie-Claire replied softly.

'You're going to tell me something that will shock me, aren't you? I can sense it.'

Marie-Claire looked at Martin who wiped his brow.

'Go on. Tell her, please,' he told Marie-Claire.

She began to explain what she had avoided telling her daughter for many years. 'It's about Christophe, whom Martin mentioned to you. We trained together in England for our work in France. After that, we were sent to France to carry out sabotage and to encourage French people to resist and train them. First, I worked for a man called Marcel and then Christophe replaced him. We worked together in June, July and part of August 1943 in the Tours area and ran a Resistance circuit.'

'That was a short period together. What happened after that?' asked Lucie.

Marie-Claire looked again at Martin and then at Lucie. 'I fell pregnant with you, my darling, and at that time Martin and I knew each other only as friends.'

Lucie stared at her in disbelief. 'You aren't trying to tell me that Christophe is my father. You can't be. You can't be,' she replied, her voice increasing in volume.

'Yes,' whispered Marie-Claire. 'Christophe is your blood father. Martin is your father who has always loved and cared for you. He loves you as his own child.'

Lucie stood up, contorted with anger. 'Why did you never tell me? Why? Why? It's not right, Maman and Papa, not to have told me long ago!'

'I never had the courage to explain everything. I knew we had to tell you some time, but I kept putting it off. Also, I couldn't tell you without the rest of the family getting to know about it. (I didn't even tell Mamy that you weren't Martin's child).'

'I can't believe what I'm hearing,' cried Lucie.

'Lucie, I couldn't tell you at a young age why I abandoned your father. It would have been too traumatic for you.' She clenched her hands, looking across at Martin. 'Papa and I could never agree with each other as to when we should tell you such devastating news.'

'Papa, when would you have told me?'

'When you were about nine or ten years old, but Maman begged me not to.'

'How could I possibly have told both families that I had deceived them?' asked Marie-Claire, noticing the anger in her daughter's eyes. She had seen the same glint in Christophe's eyes when she had confronted him in the barn outside Montrichard.

'You were only thinking of yourselves.'

'Lucie, please don't say things like that,' said Martin. 'Times were quite different in 1943. Your mother is French, and as a Frenchman, I felt responsible for her in her difficult circumstances when she had discovered that she was pregnant. When your mother left Christophe, he came and hid in the Maquis camp for a few days and left, meaning your mother had no way of contacting him, I had already fallen in love with her, but at that point I didn't know where she was either. When we finally met later, I found out everything. I gave her the chance to escape possible arrest by the Gestapo. We never told you this before, but she killed a German officer and was on the run. She was in grave danger and had to leave the area as soon as possible.'

Lucie sat down. There was a long silence, but Marie-Claire could see the distress in her eyes. Tears were beginning to trickle down her face. 'It's a shock for me to hear all that. Surely you can both appreciate how I feel?'

There was a long silence before Lucie continued. 'Maybe Christophe realised that Benoît wasn't going to give in and that he had no time in which to find another Maquis who would join the fight against the Boches,' said Lucie. 'Did he survive the war?'

'Yes. A British army officer in Paris had to interview me because of my disappearance and he told me Christophe was alive.'

'Was Christophe his real name?'

'No. Christophe was the name he used while working in the Resistance. It was used for security reasons. All I know is that his real name is Paul. His father forced him to attend the army academy in Sandhurst in England and he became an army officer. His hometown was in Surrey in the south of England. We weren't supposed to know our real names. Our war was a clandestine one. Secrecy and security were the most important things to remember. Each day our lives depended upon these factors.'

'What did he look like?' asked Lucie.

'He was tall with fair hair like yours.'

'He was honourable,' said Martin, 'and we could trust him with Resistance work. He was good company too and mixed well with the maquisards, but he didn't exert enough influence on Benoît over the business with André. And as I told you already, he wouldn't listen to your mother's pleas.'

'Do the grandparents and the rest of the family know about all this?'

'No,' replied Martin quietly. 'And I think it would be kinder not to tell them. They think that André died a hero's death. But getting back to our situation, as far as the family was concerned, your mother was expecting my child. Your great-grandmother from St Jean-le-Blanc was ahead of her time. She made sure that your mother's family in Orléans didn't know that she was unmarried by buying your mother a wedding ring. My family did know, and they understood Marie-Claire had false identity papers and couldn't get married.'

'Do you mind if I try to find Christophe? I think he should know that I exist. I realise now why you didn't tell me years ago. I love you both. I've had a wonderful life with you both and I'm grateful for everything you've done for me.' She paused for several moments. 'Just give me a time to absorb it all. I can understand Papa's reasons for wanting to protect you, Maman,' she said and left the room.

'Martin, darling, you handled everything so well just now,' Marie-Claire whispered. 'Once Lucie has absorbed everything and thought about it, she won't want to put our families into turmoil.'

Martin squeezed her hand and said, 'We know our daughter. She's a caring person. It will all work out in the end.'

Marie-Claire looked into his warm eyes. He was always there for her and supported her whenever she was in difficulty, and he'd loved Lucie as his own child. Without him and the help of his family, she might never have survived the war. It had been her greatest regret that she had been unable to have Martin's children.

During the final months of Martin's life, Lucie spent as much time together with her parents as she could. Marie-Claire talked to her daughter more about her time in the Resistance.

'Tell me that story about when you and Papa were locked in each other's arms when the farmer's daughter went past you in Tours.'

Marie recounted the story and emphasised that it was then that she realised Martin had fallen in love with her. And at that point she was still passionately in love with Christophe. 'Always remember that, please, Lucie.'

'And what about Papa later?'

'I grew to love him deeply, but not quite in the same way as Christophe. I must be frank with you.'

'Christophe was your first true passionate love.'

'Yes,' replied Marie-Claire. 'Sometimes, in retrospect, I think that I was wrong to have denied him his right to know you. But we were living under German occupation. At that point I had no idea where he was. He was on the run and may have been killed. How would you and I have coped during those first few months of my pregnancy without help? At first, I was reluctant to reveal that I was pregnant to my own family. Martin's brother and sister were marvellous in taking me in.' She caressed Lucie's hand. 'Martin told me once that he had felt guilty in pursing me and denying you the right to grow up with your own father.'

'I can see now that it was an impossible situation and Papa realised this and came to your rescue.'

Marie-Claire nodded but did not reply.

Towards the end of March 1961, although heavily sedated, Martin found an inner strength to call out for Marie-Claire and Lucie. He whispered with difficulty, 'I love you both. Lucie, go and find Christophe and I hope all will be well.' He motioned them to hold his hands. Marie-Claire saw his eyes lose focus, his breathing started to rattle, then his chest sank, and he departed.

'Rest in peace, Papa,' said Lucie, caressing Martin's forehead while it was still warm, fighting back her tears. 'I will find Christophe as you asked.'

Many people attended Martin's funeral, including several maquisards, and members of the Libé-Nord Resistance movement. During the Catholic service Lucie noticed two women who were visibly distressed and whom she had never met before. Later during the wake, she remembered having seen photographs of them in her mother's album and she remembered they were called Jeanne and Patricia. As she circulated round the hotel room, where the wake was being held, one of the women approached her.

'My name is Jeanne, and your mother and I worked together in a Resistance circuit along with Patricia who's standing with your mother. Marie-Claire knew all my family—my husband, Arnaud, our two daughters and Arnaud's mother.' She caught her breath. 'My husband died in Buchenwald.'

'Jeanne, it's all coming back to me. My parents told me about Arnaud. I was sorry and appalled about what happened to your husband,' she said. Jeanne smiled at her and thanked her. 'Maman told me that she met you and Patricia after the Occupation and that you both came to the wedding in the autumn of 1945 and that you still meet occasionally.' Her eyes met Jeanne's. 'Did you see much of Christophe after Maman fled?'

'Only for a short time. He was a good man, but somehow it all went wrong towards the end. Your mother should have stayed to support him. He should have stopped working with Benoît and found another Maquis group.'

'My parents talked about Christophe before Martin died,' replied Lucie.

Jeanne remained silent for a few moments before replying. 'After Marie-Claire disappeared, we all wondered what on earth had happened, but she contacted us after the Occupation finally ended.'

Soon they were joined by Patricia who continued talking about Marie-Claire and the circuit. Jeanne intervened. 'Why don't you come to the annual commemoration of those résistants who were deported? It's held annually in Tours in April. Patricia and I attend every year. We remember Arnaud, Luc the vet, and Emile, our wireless operator who lost their lives in Buchenwald. We also remember those who died in the Great War. In fact, the next commemoration is in three weeks' time.

Sometimes people from your mother's organisation attend.'

'Yes. I'd like to come,' replied Lucie.

'You can stay with me,' suggested Jeanne. 'Come for a week and get to know the area where your mother worked with Christophe.'

Later, after the wake, Lucie pulled out Jeanne's card that she had given her and was surprised by its details: *Jeanne, Comtesse de Montillac, Château Nivronne. Bléré, Val du Cher*. Maman had never mentioned anything about Jeanne being a countess living in a château.

CHAPTER THIRTY-THREE

CEREMONY IN TOURS DURING APRIL 1961

When the train arrived in Tours, Jeanne was waiting for Lucie on the platform. 'I'm so pleased to see you again,' she said, embracing her. 'I know Arnaud would be thrilled if he could see us together. He knew Martin well. When Marcel was badly shot in the leg, Martin and Arnaud looked after him.'

'Jeanne, I have something to tell you about Papa and Christophe.'

As they walked towards the car, Jeanne said. 'Marie-Claire warned me that you wanted to talk about something important. I can guess what it is. In fact, I've often thought about it, but I've never raised it with your mother.'

They climbed into the car, but before Jeanne started up the engine, Lucie said, 'Martin was not my father. Christophe is and his real name is Paul. And the reason my mother turned against him is because of that business to do with André and the arrests.'

Jeanne put her hand on Lucie's and patted it gently. 'As I told you at the funeral, your mother came to see us in Tours after the Occupation ended. She told us what had happened between Christophe and her and why she turned her back on him. But she has never divulged your true parentage. I guessed it because I knew she and Christophe were having an affair and the timing of your birth made it obvious that he was your father. You've got Christophe's fair hair and his stature. Patricia also came to the same conclusion. Despite that, we never challenged your mother. She would have explained everything if she had wanted to.'

'My parents only told me a short time before Papa died, but he wanted to tell me when I was much younger.'

Jeanne gasped. 'Families do have their problems, but that is really sad. I think that she should have stayed with Christophe, given she was expecting his child. The impact of war can be felt long afterwards. My eldest daughter, Angéline, is thirty-eight years old and is happily married with two delightful children. She's a doctor, like her father, but my younger daughter, Stéphanie, is single and has few friends. She saw her father being dragged away by the Gestapo when she was only seven years old, and it has affected her badly. She works for her sister as a receptionist at the surgery; she couldn't work in any other environment.'

Once Jeanne had left Tours and started to drive through the villages and small towns in the Cher Valley, some bordering the River Cher, Lucie recognised some of the names her mother had mentioned when she had talked about her activities in the area.

'I'd love to visit Véretz and Azay-sur-Cher,' said Lucie. 'Maman told me that she used to meet Emile, her wireless operator, in this area and that the priest in Azay hid him in the attic of his presbytery some of the time before he himself was arrested, denounced by a young female parishioner.'

'Would you like to visit the presbytery in Azay if I can arrange a visit with the resident priest? He knew Father Dominique Lemars, the priest who helped your mother and Emile. As you probably know, both Emile and the priest were arrested and later Luc and Jacques, both circuit members, were arrested too. All of them perished, except Jacques, in Buchenwald Concentration Camp.'

The next day, Lucie cycled into Azay-sur-Cher and walked along the riverbank. She sat down on a seat that was flaking and cracked in places. Maybe this was where Maman used to sit when she was waiting for Emile.

She walked into the little town and made her way to the presbytery, attached to the church, where she was welcomed by Father Laurent, an elderly priest with thick white hair and warm dark eyes.

'It's good of you to receive me,' said Lucie.

'On the contrary, it's an immense pleasure for me to meet Valérie's daughter, although I understand her real name is Marie-Claire.'

As the priest talked to her about the Resistance movement, Lucie became overwhelmed by his graphic account of the arrest of Véretz's parish priest by the Gestapo in 1944. The priest had been dragged out of his church at the end of having said Sunday Mass, in front of all his parishioners.

His description of what took place on the day of liberation in Tours made Lucie understand even more why her mother had become disillusioned and bitter about the huge support for Pétain and about events in France during and after the invasion. 'I was among the crowd in Jean-Jaurès Square in Tours on the night of the thirty-first of August 1944. However, the atmosphere inside that crowd and elsewhere in the city became ominous. At times it developed almost into a civil war,' said the priest, wiping his brow.

'Suddenly a group of people started to strip some women, who had previously had intimate relationships with German soldiers, and shave their hair. The new mayor, Jean Meunier, the Resistance leader, was standing on the balcony of the magnificent town hall with other dignitaries and took the microphone and told the crowd that a bomb attack was imminent, despite freedom having been won in Tours. The crowd dispersed, and thanks to the mayor, the police took charge of the women and led them away to safety.' The priest smoothed back his thick white hair off his forehead and as he did so, Lucie saw tears in his eyes. 'The mayor, a brave and honest man, had saved people from a dangerous uprising. The following morning when the mayor and others appeared again on the town hall balcony, someone in the crowd aimed a shot at them. The bullet brushed past the mayor's eyebrow. It was awful, especially so soon after the previous incident.' He stumbled over his next few words. 'There are forever dark and ugly shadows in the minds of many Tourangeaux who witnessed these dreadful events. And to think we were supposed to be celebrating our freedom from the Nazis.'

After a long silence, Lucie looked up at the priest and said, 'Thank you, Father, for your hospitality. What you have told me is devastating and shameful.

How could any French citizens act in such a heinous way?'

As she approached Véretz, Lucie admired the château overlooking the River Cher with its slate towers glistening in the afternoon sun. Once she had reached the village, she went into Notre Dame, a sixteenth-century church next to the château, where she lit two candles, one for Papa and the other for Christophe. She thought about what the priest in Azay had told her. Also, she recalled her mother's words about the dangerous life she had led in these little villages and further afield. Also, the risks she had taken by cycling during through the night to deliver messages. Christophe had considerable responsibilities because he was head of the circuit and he too had taken huge risks.

On her return to Château Nivronne, Jeanne told her that they were going to visit Patricia in Larçay. On arrival they were warmly received.

'Your mother landed in a tiny plane, called a Lysander, in a field at St Martin-le-Beau at around two thirty in the morning. It's not far from here,' Patricia told her.

'You mean she arrived there alone?'

'No. She was with another agent. They were met by a man who had guided the plane onto the field and his assistant. He gave her a bicycle and she set off on her own. She hid in a wood until curfew ended and then made her way here. Then Jacques, another résistant, brought her to us at the château.'

'Jeanne told me that when my mother came to see you in Tours after the Occupation, had ended, both of you guessed that Christophe was my father. Do you think my mother was too harsh on him in the way she dismissed him from her life?'

'Yes, I don't like to admit this, but I think she was unkind in not telling Christophe about you after the war ended. She knew from London that he had survived the war. I do understand why she left him because of what happened to André. Jeanne and I disagree about the latter point.'

Jeanne intervened, 'The fact is that if you do find Christophe still alive, you must ask yourself whether it would be too much of a shock for him now to meet you and be told that Marie-Claire and he are your parents. Would it bring all the misery of losing her back to him? You don't know his present circumstances. He's probably married and has children. Just imagine what effect it would have on his wife if he'd never told her about your mother. He might not accept you because he was in a desolate state after she vanished.'

Lucie could see that Patricia was beginning to become upset. 'Let me explain. I went to the Maquis in the Amboise Forest and saw Christophe there. He explained that he had hoped that a friend in Vierzon would help him return to London, but he found out that he had been arrested so he came to the Maquis camp to hide. He was worried where Marie-Claire had gone, terrified that she had been arrested by the Gestapo after killing the German officer. Apparently, he only stayed at the camp for a short time.'

Lucie cleared her throat. 'It's so upsetting to hear how devastated he was about my mother.'

Patricia replied, 'I can understand your distress. The fate of those who were arrested broke Christophe. I found that he had lost enthusiasm for fighting the Boches. In fact, he seemed to have fallen into a deep state of depression. Soon after that he returned to England. So, think carefully before you go ahead looking for him.'

Lucie remained silent for a while. 'I will do that, but even so I genuinely want to trace him and see if we can get to know each other. Christophe and I could become close friends. Who knows?'

The next day they prepared for the ceremony at Tours which was to take place at the town hall situated in the large Jaurès Square. As Jeanne drove through the villages that Lucie had already visited, Lucie wondered if any British people, who had been involved in the Resistance in the Centre region of France, would attend the ceremony.

When they arrived inside the town hall, there were already several dignitaries in dark suits, accompanied by their wives, standing in front of a large urn.

'That is the urn I told you about, Lucie,' whispered Jeanne. 'It contains ashes of the résistants who were killed or died in the concentration camps. Over there to the left is a memorial to those who had perished in World War One.'

A middle-aged man, wearing a tricoleur sash, walked over to the three women.

'It's Monsieur Trudeau, the present mayor of Tours,' whispered Jeanne to Lucie.

'You do us a great honour, Jeanne and Patricia, by attending the commemoration every year,' he told them.

'Monsieur le Maire, I'd like to present Lucie Sautereau to you. Her mother was an SOE courier in Tours in 1943.'

'Enchanté,' said the mayor. 'Tell me more.'

Jeanne spoke briefly about Marie-Claire and Christophe.

'Do you know if there are British people due to attend the ceremony this year who fought in this area during the Occupation?' Lucie asked him.

The mayor replied, 'We often have visitors from England who were involved in the Resistance in this country, as well as French résistants. A Frenchman, called Daniel, often mixes with them. This year there is no one from England, which is unfortunate. Now, if you will please excuse me, I must go and give my speech.'

A little later everyone stood to attention as the mayor addressed them.

'Today we honour those who fought in the Resistance movement and who were deported. Some returned. Others didn't.' He gave a long pause. 'We must also remember those British and other foreign nationals in the SOE and other Allied intelligence services who were caught and deported, many of whom also never returned. Pray silence for two minutes while we think of these courageous people whose sacrifice led to France's liberation.'

After the pause, a group of former résistants laid sprays of flowers in front of the urn, containing ashes of deportees and the memorial devoted to those who had given their lives in the Great War. The veterans lowered their banners and flags with gold lettering on them, representing their regiments or combat associations. The 'Marseillaise' was then sung. Then the flags were raised again.

Afterwards, people started to circulate. The mayor walked towards Lucie, followed by a handsome man in his late fifties.

'Mademoiselle, allow me to introduce you to Monsieur Daniel Durand who trained with the British and fought in France and now lives outside Tours. Please excuse me while I'll leave you together, as I must circulate.'

'Bonjour, Mademoiselle. As the mayor said, I trained in England like lots of French nationals.'

Lucie's heart raced. 'I'm looking for anyone who trained in the SOE who might have known my parents. My mother was a courier in Tours and the surrounding area, and my father was her organiser and trained with her.' She took out a photo from her bag and showed it to Daniel.

'My goodness! That's Valérie. We trained together on the same SOE courses. She would have known me as Didier because we all had code names. I'd love to meet her and what is her real name and where does she live?'

'In Olivet, south of Orléans, and she's called Marie-Claire. You'd be welcome to visit her.' She scribbled her mother's details, as well as her own, on a piece of paper and gave it to him. 'I'm due back in Orléans the day after tomorrow.'

He pulled out a card from his wallet and gave it to her. 'Here are my contact details. I'll phone your mother after you have returned to her.'

'She'll be absolutely delighted, I'm sure. As I said earlier, I'm trying to trace my father who was also on your course. My mother didn't stay with my father, but I can't go into any details here. All I know is that his real name was Paul and that he came from Surrey. His field name was Christophe. Tall and fair-haired. Apparently, I look very much like him.'

'My goodness! I trained with Christophe and your mother. In fact, you do look like him.' He paused and looked at her closely. 'Of course, you have your mother's wonderful blue eyes. We all had a marvellous time together. We were young and on the brink of challenging and dangerous missions. Occasionally we slipped out to a local pub. The three of us succeeded in going on to the next course at Beaulieu which was all about covert warfare. Your mother was a brilliant student and outshone most of the others.' Lucie nodded and smiled at him. 'After the course finished, I never saw either of your parents again. The men were supposed to have gone on a course in Scotland before Beaulieu, but we were urgently needed in France and in any case, we were already trained soldiers.' He looked closely at her with concern. 'I don't want to pry, but I'm sorry they didn't stay together. Also, I'm afraid that he might not have survived the war. You should prepare yourself for that.'

'Would the British War Office in London help me find him?' she asked him.

'No. Not from my experience. I fell in love with an English girl called Florence on the SOE course. After the war, I had a devil of a job trying to locate her and the people at the War Office weren't at all keen to help me find her. Eventually I did, and we married soon afterwards in true French style I might add,' he said with a laugh. 'Then we settled down in a village outside Tours. Do you have any other details about your father?'

'Paul used to be a teacher in a boys' school in Surrey before going into the British Army is all I know.'

'I never saw Christophe after I left for France, but I do know someone who met a man called Paul here on a few occasions after the war and struck up a friendship with him. Paul took part in the Normandy Landings and won several medals. My friend, Thomas, usually comes to this ceremony, but he's not here today. I'll phone him tomorrow and see if he knows where Paul comes from. Thomas lives in Surrey too. I'll let you know what I find out.'

She explained how Martin had brought her up as his own daughter, even knowing that she had no blood tie to him and explained that he had died.

'That takes a lot of courage and love to do a thing like that,' said Daniel.

'What sort of a person was my father?'

'Very sociable and the typical English gentleman. He was in love with your mother before they were sent to France, but I think he was already engaged to someone else. He was a popular recruit.'

Daniel outlined the training that he and her parents undertook in Wanborough and Beaulieu. 'Your mother was brilliant when she went on the surveillance exercise and outwitted people who followed her. I reckon she gained the highest marks for that test out of all the students.'

Lucie in turn told Daniel what she knew about her parents' clandestine activities and asked Daniel where he had been sent.

'Dijon. It was a hotbed of collaborators, and we lost a lot of people in our circuit as a result. Even young women grassed on some of our people.'

'How did you land in France during the Occupation? My mother flew in a tiny plane called a Lysander and was dropped outside Tours.'

'I arrived in France by Lysander too. Dijon to be exact. None of us would have been able to carry out our operations were it not for those brave pilots who flew those little planes—Lizzies they called them.' He wiped his eyes. 'I knew one of them; his Lysander crashed as he was trying to land at Tangmere, and he was burnt to death.'

Lucie's face stiffened. She could see how distressed Didier had become. His eyes had darkened and the troubled look that swept his face tore through her. She recalled her mother had looked across at her pilot as he was listening to a soulful male singer on a record at Tangmere, before he flew her and another agent to France. Her mother had often talked to her about this. Lucie had often thought of that pilot. Did he make it back to Tangmere?

After a pause, Daniel checked his watch and said, 'As I said, I'll phone your mother after you have returned. It will be marvellous to talk to her and of course, I'll talk to you again.' He paused, 'I'll wait until I see Marie-Claire, but I have some sad news for her: her closest friend, also an agent and known as Francine, died in dreadful circumstances near Blois, but don't say anything to her yet.'

'Of course not.' She waited a few moments, remembering her mother having talked a lot about her friend Francine. 'We must meet each other again at next year's reunion here in Tours. Maybe Paul will be with me,' she replied, smiling at him.

'Oh, but Florence and I will meet you and Marie-Claire long before then. That's for sure. Now I must be off.'

She felt a tap on her shoulder and turned around to find Jeanne and Patricia wanting to know the outcome of her long conversation with the stranger.

After she had told them everything, Jeanne told her, 'You've struck gold and I'm sure you'll soon be with Christophe. Or I should say Paul?'

CHAPTER THIRTY-FOUR

GODALMING IN AUGUST 1961

It was already 7 p.m. Paul never seemed to have enough time to finish all his paperwork for his bookshop and he had been less able than usual to concentrate for the last couple of days.

He had been strangely unsettled since the last meeting of the French society he had formed and run in Godalming.

Who was the young girl he'd seen at the meeting who reminded him of Marie-Claire? Surely, she must be one of her relatives? Why had she come to the society and why had she surveyed him closely throughout the speaker's talk and then walked after it had ended?

Two taps on the shop door disturbed his thoughts. He stood up and walked towards the glass-paned entrance door where he stopped in his tracks, astonished by the person he saw standing outside. It was none other than the young woman who had unsettled him. On opening the door, he told her that the shop was closed.

She gave him a smile that made his heart lurch. 'I'm sorry I have disturbed you, Major Ferguson, but I haven't come here to buy any books,' she said in a French accent.

'Then how can I be of assistance?' was all he could manage to reply.

'It's a long and delicate story,' she said, having suddenly transferred to her native tongue. 'I need to talk to you.'

Feeling unaccountably shaken, he invited her in. 'Come and sit down in the back of my shop and tell me why you've come here,' he answered in French.

For a moment they sat opposite each other in awkward silence at the table covered in papers, until Paul asked her again, 'Why have you come to Godalming? Why did you keep staring at me two nights ago at the talk about Vichy France?' He saw that the young woman looked upset and unsure of herself and realised he should have been less direct.

'I don't know where to begin, Major Ferguson. I'm afraid what I must tell you will come as an enormous shock,' she told him. After a few silent moments she said, 'You're sitting opposite your own daughter. My name is Lucie.' She stopped to regain her thoughts.

'Marie-Claire gave birth to me seven months after she left you in the Tours area.'

Paul looked into her eyes, unable to find his words for a moment. 'I-I can't believe it,' he found himself stammering. 'Y-you do look like her with the same beautiful blue eyes, but you have the fair hair that I had when I was young and you're tall like me. However, did you find me?'

'You have a friend called Thomas and he knows someone called Daniel who trained with you under the name of Didier.'

'Good gracious me!' exclaimed Paul.

'Marie-Claire, my mother, was your SOE courier and she and you argued about my mother's cousin André and his execution. I take no sides in this, believe me. I wasn't alive at the time, nor can I possibly criticise either of you.'

The way in which Lucie was explaining her appearance was both kind and thoughtful, thought Paul, feeling confused and overwhelmed by her revelations. He had no doubt that she was his own child, a daughter from his love for his dearest Marie-Claire. Determined to remain at least outwardly calm, he told her, 'As I already said, you have those same sea-blue beautiful eyes as Marie-Claire's. And I've never seen anyone else with eyes like that. In Heaven's name, why did she never tell me about you?'

'The same reason she never told me that I had an English father until a few months ago.'

He felt himself go cold and struggled to find his words. 'What happened to Marie-Claire after she left me?'

When Lucie described how Martin Sautereau had arranged for Marie-Claire to take refuge with his family, as she was on the run, had married her and had brought her up as his own, Paul felt a wave of anger sweep through him.

'Married Marie-Claire and brought you up as his own daughter?' he repeated. 'I fled to Benoît's Maquis in the Sologne, after Marie-Claire turned her back on me, despite my having looked for her everywhere in the Tours area and I had been taking risks in doing that. Martin was still in that Maquis. He must have known something about Marie-Claire's whereabouts.'

'Martin didn't know where Marie-Claire was immediately after she left you. It's true my mother should have tried to contact you through the organisation after the war and given you the chance to know me, but none of this is my fault. I think I will go now.'

Collecting himself, Paul urged her to sit down again. 'Please, please don't go. I'm in a state of shock, as you must have been when you found out your true parentage. Of course I want to get to know you. Please believe me, Lucie.' He paused. 'I always wanted some children but now I have the honour—yes, I do consider it an honour, to have a daughter of my very own and whose mother I adored and still do.'

Lucie wiped her eyes. 'Are you married?'

'I'm a widower and I have a stepson, Michael, whom I consider my son.'

'Did you ever tell your wife about my mother?'

'No. Time passed by. I kept meaning to tell her. Finally, I decided to put the past behind me. It worked sometimes, but I was tempted to revisit my box of memories where I have photographs of Marie-Claire and other items. Every time I looked at her, I felt magnetised towards her. Then I put the box away for several months, then years. If I had told my wife, she would have sensed that I still loved your mother.'

'Martin died three months ago. It was a long illness.'

Paul took his time to reply, wondering if Marie-Claire would agree to meet him. 'Does Marie-Claire know you've come to find me?'

'Of course.'

Lucie explained that Marie-Claire had introduced her to circuit members Jeanne and Patricia. She'd gone to a ceremony with them in Tours when she had met Daniel. When she'd told him she was looking for her English father called Paul and that her mother had been in the SOE, Daniel had asked her to describe her mother. She'd shown him her picture and he recognised her instantly. He told her that his field name was Didier. Through one of his English friends called Thomas, she'd finally found him.

'My goodness! Didier trained with me and your mother. And yes, I met Thomas in Tours just after the war and we still meet regularly. He lives not far from here.' After gathering his thoughts, he continued. 'Have you any photos of your mother with you?'

Lucie smiled at Paul in the same direct way her mother used to look at him. She pulled out some photos of Marie-Claire with Lucie when she was a lot younger and a recent one of Lucie and Marie-Claire.

Paul took his time to look at the photographs, fighting back his tears. He looked up at his daughter and said, 'I was happily married to my wife, who was a war widow, but Marie-Claire has always been the love of my life.' He cleared his throat. 'I should have forced André to leave the Maquis right from the beginning and if Benoît hadn't agreed, Marie-Claire and I should have formed another circuit and sought other maquisards to help us.'

His conversation was interrupted by tapping on the entrance door. He went and opened it. A young man came in and he immediately looked at Lucie. When Paul failed to introduce her, he said to the young man, 'Michael, I thought we were going out for a meal tonight?'

Take the plunge, thought Paul. He beamed at Lucie and said, 'This is Michael.' He took a deep breath and continued, 'Michael, this will come as a complete surprise to you, just as much as it has to me during the past hour. This young French lady is Lucie and she is my daughter. I knew nothing about her. Her mother was my courier in the SOE in France during the French Occupation.' Michael stared wordlessly from one to the other of them and Paul continued, 'I don't quite know how to handle the rest of the evening.'

Michael paused for a moment. 'There's going to be three of us going out for dinner, Paul. I'm delighted you've found your daughter, especially after you and Mum couldn't have any children. And it's a pleasure to welcome you, Lucie.'

Paul put his arms round Lucie and kissed her cheek. He looked into her eyes, identical to those eyes that had bewitched him all those years ago. 'Will your mother ever agree to meet me?'

She smiled at him. 'Give her time,' she replied, 'but the fact she helped me to find you, tells me that she soon will.'

Acknowledgements

I wish to thank my daughter, Laura, for her help both IT wise and in so many other areas. Equally I would like to thank Ray-Anne Lutener, author and editor for all her work formatting the novel and getting it onto Amazon and Immi Howson, copy editor, for transforming the novel into a much better read.

Grateful thanks also go to Colonel (Retd) Nick Fox, MBE for all his help with SOE training and other SOE matters. Thanks also go to Christine Hammacott, Graphic Artist for her excellent cover. I cannot thank Julie Roberts, published author and leader of the RNA Reading Chapter, enough for all her huge help support and endless encouragement. Also, thanks to Liz Harris, published and self-published author, who has given me so much help and so much of her time.

Grateful thanks to Alison Burke, RNA and self-published author, as well as Ian Titman-Reade, Lysander expert, who have both given me so much help and so much of their time. Not forgetting Janet Glover, RNA organiser for the RNA Writers' Scheme who has given me much encouragement and help.

Also, all the writers at the Reading RNA for their encouragement and support. Without the support and help of the above marvellous people, the novel would never have seen daylight.

About the Author

My fascination with languages led me to Germany and France when I was in my teens. I worked as a language assistant in Bavaria for six months and I worked in Paris, as an au pair, for one year.

Whilst studying at the Alliance Française, in Paris, a teacher's story captured my curiosity when she explained to our class that she had lost her husband during the Occupation and that she was bringing up their children on her own. I sensed that he had been in the Resistance.

The subject of citizens denouncing others to the Gestapo shook me, even more so when I learned that of one of my French friends had been denounced in this way, at a very young age. He had been sent to Buchenwald during this time and fortunately survived.

My presentation in French, about my SOE novel, about five years ago at the Institut France-Grande Bretagne in Orleans was well received, particularly by a daughter of a prominent political resistant murdered by the French Milice (rough paramilitaries appointed by the French Head of State, who was controlled by the Nazis).

I frequently travel to France and meet with French friends. One friend's father, a prominent SOE leader, was denounced and sent to a concentration camp. When he returned after the Occupation, his eyes were emotionless for a long time.

These discoveries, amongst others, throughout my years, have inspired me to write 'Beyond the Horizon'.

If this period of history interests you, I set out below five books which I value highly. Of course, I read many more books on the subject of France under the Occupation.

I carried out a lot of research with the help of Lise Schnel, archivist at Tours Archives. And I had considerable help from the relatives of people I have mentioned in the article above. Added to this, I have, of course, visited all the places mentioned in the novel.

-Mireille Meunier-Saint Cricq: Jean Meunier: Une Vie de Combat (CLD éditions 2008)

-Francis J. Suttill: Shadows in the Fog (The History Press 2014)

-Elizabeth Nicholas: Death Be Not Proud (The Crescent Press 1958)

-Pearl Cornioley: Pauline: (Editions par exemple 1995)

-Robert O. Paxton: Vichy France: Barrie & Jenkins (1972).

Printed in Great Britain
by Amazon